THE BLAFT ANTHOLOGY OF
TAMIL PULP FICTION

THE BLAFT ANTHOLOGY OF
TAMIL PULP FICTION

selected and translated by

PRITHAM K. CHAKRAVARTHY

edited by

RAKESH KHANNA

PUBLICATIONS
PRIVATE LIMITED

Chennai

First published in India in 2008 by
Blaft Publications Pvt. Ltd.

First printing May 2008
Second printing August 2008

ISBN 978 81 906056 0 1

Translations and all editorial material
copyright © 2008 Blaft Publications Pvt. Ltd.

Blaft Publications Pvt. Ltd.
#27 Lingam Complex
Dhandeeswaram Main Road
Velachery
Chennai 600042
email: blaft@blaft.com

Printed at
Sudarsan Graphics, Chennai

dedicated to
the many great Tamil pulp authors
we didn't have space for

CONTENTS

TRANSLATOR'S NOTE

This book is an attempt to claim the status of "literature" for a huge body of writing that has rarely if ever made it into an academic library, despite having been produced for nearly a century. While a good deal of Tamil fiction has been rendered in English, it has primarily been members of the literati who have enjoyed this distinction. Even the recent translations of more popular authors such as Sivasankari and Sujatha seem to be selections of their most serious, "meaningful" work.

As a schoolgirl in mid-sixties Chennai, I grew up on a steady diet of *Anandha Vikatan, Kumudham, Dhinamani Kadhir, Thuglaq, Kalaimagal* and *Kalkandu*. These magazines were shared and read by practically all the women at home. Then there were other publications, less welcome in a traditional household, with more glamorous pictures and lustier stories. These we would regularly purloin from the driver of our school bus, Natraj, who kept a stack of them hidden under the back seat. I doubt if he knew what an active readership he was sponsoring on those long bus rides.

So, from the days when our English reading consisted of Enid Blyton, Nancy Drew and the Hardy Boys up until we grew out of Earl Stanley Gardner, Arthur Hailey, and Hadley Chase, we also had a parallel world of Ra. Ki. Rangarajan, Rajendra Kumar, Sivasankari, Vaasanthi, Lakshmi, Anuthama... and especially Sujatha, who rocked us back in the seventies with his laundry-woman jokes. As school kids, though we did not understand what they actually meant, we were definitely aware of the unsaid adult content in them. His detective duo Ganesh and Vasanth were suddenly speaking a kind of Tamil that was much closer to our Anglicised language than anything we had seen before on paper. We were completely seduced by the brevity of his writing.

Households would meticulously collect the stories serialized in these weeklies and have them hard-bound to serve as reading material during the long, hot summer vacations. We offer an excerpt from one of these serials in this collection: *En Peyar Kamala*, by Pushpa Thangadurai, with sketches by Jayaraj. I remember when this story was being serialized in the mid-seventies. The journal was kept hidden in my mother's cupboard. The subject matter was deemed too dangerous for us young girls. Since I was not allowed to read it at home, naturally, I read it on the schoolbus. Thanks to Natraj.

Then came college days, my political awakening and my increasing involvement with theatre activism, during which I consciously distanced myself from reading pulp fiction and moved to more "serious stuff". Two and a half decades of marriage, two daughters, many cigarettes and a lot of rum later, I got called upon to return to it. When Rakesh—a California-born, non-Tamil-speaking Chennai transplant who had developed a burning curiosity about the cheap novels on the rack at his neighborhood tea stand—approached me with the idea of doing this book, it was fun to discover that the child in me is still alive and kicking. I used to think of this as *my* literature. I still do. I just took a little vacation from it.

Of course, time had passed, and things had changed. The latest pulp novels were thin, glossy, ten-rupee jobs with bizarrely photoshopped covers. Actually, they weren't new; they had been around for three decades—I just hadn't read one yet! It took some time to catch up; I spent a year searching through library records for the most popular books, going on wild travels to strange book houses and the far-flung homes of the many different authors, artists and publishers, taking many crazy bus journeys and visiting many coffee houses, and doing a kind of pleasure reading I realized I had been badly missing for the past thirty years.

The corpus of pulp literature that has been produced for Tamil readers is vast, and there is no hope of providing a representative sample in a single volume. We decided on a selection of stories from the late 1960s to the present; a few notes on the earlier history of the genre follow.

The Tamil people take great pride in speaking a living classical language, a language which had written texts even as early as the 6th century B.C. Two things were necessary prerequisites for the reading habit to be spread throughout the general population. The first was printing technology, which until the early 19th century was available only for government agencies and for the printing of the Gospels. The second was education. In ancient society, education was privileged cultural capital, available to only a few caste groups. For fiction to move from the sole preserve of the "patrons of literature" into the hands of the masses took three centuries from the time when the European colonists first stepped on this soil.

Yes, the colonists brought us "literacy". But even after the British democratized it, it took a whole century to grow into the larger public. Four decades after printing technology became available to more than just the state government and the missionaries, novels became a hit among the middle classes—though this new form of fiction still encountered some opposition.

The first books for popular readership, besides translations of the British literary canon, were typified by *Prathaba Mudhaliar Sarithiram* (1879), an ultra-moralistic Christian novel about the dangers of a hedonistic lifestyle. This and other early Tamil novels were usually serialized in monthly periodicals. In the early 20th century, the literary journal *Manikkodi* was at the forefront of a Tamil renaissance driven by leftist, humanist writers such as Pudumaipittan, Illango, and Ramaiyya. At the same time, in a wholly separate sector of the readership, the British "penny dreadful" (and after World War I, the American dime novel) inspired another crop of Tamil authors, including Vaduvoor Doraisami Iyengar. His Brahmin detective hero, Digambara Samiar, held a law degree and a superior, casteist morality which set him apart from the gritty underworld in which his investigations took place. The criminal activity in Iyengar's plots reflects the major issues of the era: the smuggling of foreign goods and subversive anti-British activities.

By the 1930s, popular fiction was in full swing. Here are some guidelines laid out by Sudhandhira Sangu in a 1933 article called "The Secret of Commercial Novel Writing"*:

1. The title of the book should carry a woman's name—and it should be a sexy one, like 'Miss Leela Mohini' or 'Mosdhar Vallibai'.

2. Don't worry about the storyline. All you have to do is creatively adapt the stories of [British penny dreadful author G.W.M.] Reynolds and the rest. Yet your story absolutely must include a minimum of half a dozen lovers and prostitutes, preferably ten dozen murders, and a few sundry thieves and detectives.

3. The story should begin with a murder. Sprinkle in a few thefts. Some arson will also help. These are the necessary ingredients of a modern novel.

4. You can make money only if you are able to titillate. If you try to bring in any social message, like Madhaviah's *The Story of Padhmavathi* or Rajam Iyer's *The Story of Kamalabal*, forget it. Beware! You are not going to lure your women readers.

From the 1940s onwards, besides the preoccupations of World War II and India's independence, printing became even more widely available and magazine subscriptions skyrocketed. The material for these magazines was provided by Gandhian, reformist writers such as Kalki and Savi. Around the same time, the Dravidian movement got going, with a concomitant interest in stories about the Tamil empires of ages past and in reclaiming a history pre-dating Sanskrit culture and the Vedas.

One of the most famous writers of this era was Chandilyan, whose historical adventure/romance novels are still widely read. We agonized about whether to include an excerpt of one of these, finally giving up because of the density of the flowery, epic prose, the complexity of his-

---

* *Novallum Vasippum* (The Novel & Readership), A. R. Venkatachalapathi; pg. 22, Kalachuvadu Pathipagam, 2002

torical and cultural references, and doubts about whether his work could really be considered "pulp".

The understanding of pulp fiction in a Western context is based on the cheap paper that was used for detective, romance, and science fiction stories in the mid-20ᵗʰ century. Tamil Nadu in the 1960s had its own pulp literature, printed on recycled *sani* paper and priced at 50 paise a copy. In the 1980s, with the advent of desktop publishing, printing in large volumes became more economical, and thin pulp novels began to appear in tea stalls and bus stations. There are a number of popular writers—Balakumaran, Anuradha Ramanan, Devibala, and many more—who we left out of this anthology because their work, though often printed on sani paper, seemed to aim to do more than simply entertain; we felt they did not quite fit most people's idea of "pulp fiction". Some older authors like P. T. Sami and Chiranjeevi were seriously considered but decided against for reasons of space. Perhaps they will find a place in a future sequel! Also missing here are two authors who, sadly, passed away in early 2008: Stella Bruce, who wrote family-centred dramas, and Sujatha, whose work straddles the popular fiction and high-literature genres. Unlike our pulp writers, Sujatha's books can be found on the shelves of more upmarket bookstores, and some of his books were translated into English by the author himself.

The oldest writing in this collection is the story by Tamilvanan. His detective character Shankarlal, with his impeccable morality and uncontrollable cowlick, was a Dravidian echo of Iyengar's Digambara Samiar—but a well-traveled one, who brought back tales of exotic foreign locales. Then there is *En Peyar Kamala*, Pushpa Thangadorai's report from the sordid underworld of North Indian brothels. There is Ramanichandran, who actually tops the popularity list of all the busy writers in Tamil with her tightly crafted romance stories. There is Vidya Subramaniam, with her tales of urban women navigating a world full of demands and constraints. Finally there is the madly prolific crop of writers who currently dominate the racks in the tea shops and bus stations—Rajesh Kumar, Subha, Pattukkottai Prabakar, Indra Soundar Rajan—and the writers whose short stories fill out the publications of the big names. These writers churn out literally hundreds pages of fiction every month. The speed of production has the effect of making the plots somewhat dreamlike, with investigations wandering far afield, characters appearing and disappearing without warning, and resolutions surprising us from out of the blue.

Yet, for all their escapism, these works in no way leave behind the times they were created in; they contain reactions to, reflections on, and negations of what was going on. Our selection by no means exhausts the ocean. But hopefully the bouquet we finally managed to put together can give the reader some sense of the madness and diversity of this flourishing literary scene.

Rakesh and I would like to thank the following people for helping to put this book together: the authors and artists and their families; Gowri Govender, who opened her library for me to freely borrow from; Dilip Kumar, who put me on to authors popular before my time; Candace Khanna, Sheila Moore, and Kaveri Lalchand for their valuable feedback; Rashmi, for all her support and suggestions; and Chaks, who brought Tamilvanan into our text and also patiently waited for the many hours we spent in the nights to finish.

—*Pritham K. Chakravarthy*

Title page from the February 1992 issue of Subha's *Super Novel*.
The letter from the authors at left reads: "Hello, thank you for bringing it to our notice that although K.V. Anand's cover picture for the
last issue featured a character in handcuffs, no such scene occurred in
the story. This is proof that our readers pay great attention to every
detail in *Super Novel!* We had to change the climax at the last moment,
and did not have time to change the cover. Sorry."

SUBHA

Subha is the *nom de plume* of not one but two authors: Suresh and Balakrishnan. This extraordinary writing partnership began when the two friends were schoolmates and continues to the present day. Since 1983, they have co-authored around 550 short novels, 50 longer novels serialized in magazines, more than 400 short stories, and a number of screenplays and dialogues for Tamil cinema and television. Most of their stories feature the spunky young couple Narendran and Vaijayanthi of Eagle Eye Detective Agency, along with their co-worker John Sundar. The two authors now run their own publishing company, which in addition to their three monthly novels also brings out non-fiction titles and the occasional special "team-up" story in which Naren and Vaij collaborate on a case with Pattukkottai Prabakar's detective couple, Bharat and Susheela.

Suresh and Balakrishnan live with their families in adjacent apartments in Adyar, Chennai.

HURRICANE VAIJ

ஒரு சின்ன புயல் (1993)

✂ 1 ✂

THE AUTOMATIC DOORS closed behind Narendran as he entered the airport lounge. With his hands in his pant pockets, he chose an empty seat next to a granite pillar, sat down, and crossed his legs. His eyes scanned the lounge, trying to figure out who the anonymous phone caller could have been.

Was it the man in the blue shirt, at the water cooler? Or the guy in the green shirt, browsing through a heavy book in the bookshop? What about the one in the gray safari suit, rubbing his lips after burning them on a tasteless airport espresso? Or the one with the traveler's bag, talking to the policeman?

"Naren! Very, very urgent. Can you meet me at the domestic terminal at the airport? I have arranged for someone to meet you there. I am unable to come and see you directly at the Eagle Eye office. Please, please, please!"

Narendran could easily have ignored the phone call. But since Vaijayanthi had taken her mother to the homeopathic doctor, he had no company at the office. There was no good reason *not* to make a trip to the airport. And so, here he was.

But after five minutes of waiting, Narendran was already losing patience. The television monitor was displaying a list of planes that were indefinitely delayed. The words "Check In" flashed in red, next to the number of a flight that would probably not take off for another several hours. Some bratty kid was pointing at the ceiling, screaming like an air raid siren for his mommy to get the chandelier down for him so he could play with it.

He felt something nudge his elbow. He turned. It was the arm of the person sitting next to him.

"Car number TN-O9-7611 is waiting for you outside. They've got your information," the man said, hardly moving his lips.

"And who are you?"

"You don't need to know."

"I don't make a habit of jumping into the cars of people I don't need to know."

"Listen, I could tell you my name, but it wouldn't be of any use to you. I'm here at the airport on a different errand. I was asked to give you this information. That's all!"

Narendran got up, irritated.

In the car park, he found a green Fiat with the matching number plate. He opened the rear door and got in. Despite what he'd told the guy, this was the third case he'd been on where someone had arranged to meet him this way. So he sat and waited. After a moment, the driver

2

showed up, climbed in, and started the car. Narendran tapped him on the shoulder.

"I don't have any answers for you," said the driver.

"I don't have any questions. I just want a match, pal," said Narendran, a cigarette between his lips. The driver handed him a matchbox with his left hand. The car sped away from the airport.

Dragging deep on the cigarette, Narendran looked at the driver in the rear-view mirror. A square face, thick moustache, brutal brow, small scar next to the left eye—and a *rudraksh* tied around his neck, just visible above his top shirt button.

"Look, I'll limit myself to really easy questions. Where are we headed?"

"To my employer's house."

"And do you know your employer's name?"

"You're going to see him soon. Can't you be patient till then?"

"Why don't I try to guess who your employer is?"

"Think you can?"

"If I can't figure out something that simple, what have I been doing working at Eagle Eye all this time?"

"Fine. Go ahead and guess."

"Your employer is Surya Shekar, the opposition leader."

"How did you know?"

"Well, you have a tattoo of the three doves, the party symbol, on your left wrist."

"Any party cadre member might have the same tattoo. He could be employed elsewhere, you know."

"Fair enough. But you also have a ring with the same design. I read in *Dhinathanthi* that Surya Shekar presented rings like that to twenty of his employees. Third page, second paragraph. Didn't you read it?"

"You're good."

"I'm good, eh? Think I'm as good as your boss? Or better?"

The driver didn't answer that.

"What's going on, anyway?"

"No idea, sir. I was told to wait at the airport for you and to bring you to the guesthouse. That's all I know."

The car turned off at Nanganallur and took two left turns and three rights before heading through an empty field towards a bungalow. A watchman opened the gates.

There was a long cement driveway, with potted plants on either side. The car stopped and Narendran got out. The roof of the bungalow was tiled in the Kerala fashion, with red Mangalore tiles. A string of brass lamps hung above the doorstep. The heavy teak door opened onto a huge, square front hall. And there he sat, slumped on one of the sofas: Surya Shekar.

◢ 2 ◣

He was a dark man, with white hair and white teeth. A thick moustache covered his dark lips. His chin had a deep cleft. He wore a silk shirt, a polyester *veshti*, and a thick gold chain with a leopard claw pendant around his neck. He smelled strongly of perfume.

"Come in, Naren!"

Narendran sat down in front of him. He had seen him often on television, and once in person, at the beach. The strength and pride that had seemed evident then was absent now. He looked scared and miserable.

"Do you know why I brought you here?"

"I imagine it's a very big secret."

"My son has been missing since yesterday morning, Naren..."

"Arthreyan?" Narendran asked, surprised. "Arthreyan is a V.I.P. How can you be so casual about him going missing?"

"There are a few complicated issues, Naren. That's why I wanted to see you in private."

A heavily mustached man brought two cups of filter coffee on a tray.

"Naren, what do you think of my son?"

"You want me to be honest? Or should I be careful, since I'm talking to the leader of a political party, and commenting about a son to a father?"

"You can be honest. Anyway, I know you don't have any party affiliations."

"All right then. Arthreyan is a good-looking man. Still in his twenties. He has a young wife—it was a love marriage—and she's pregnant now. He wanted to start his own business after finishing his engineering degree, but you pushed him into politics. He participates in party functions reluctantly. Still, the other senior members of your party are not too thrilled to see him join you."

"Not bad! You describe it like you were there watching."

"You're having a rough time right now, because your party's not in power. Otherwise, Arthreyan would have been able to gain even more popularity. Your party is striving to change the popular view that there are no educated people in politics. You were grooming Arthreyan to become your second-in-command. In the general executive committee meeting next week, you were hoping to get him elected to an important post. The media has already started talking about him as a potent political force. That's why, when you tell me he's gone missing, I'm surprised."

"I'm dying here, Naren. But even this, I have to hide from the public..."

"Why?"

"Why indeed?" Surya Shekar asked.

He rose from his seat and began pacing across the room. Narendran noticed for the first time how tall he was.

"Tell me, what's my party's main agenda?"

"Well, all the parties claim to have different agendas, depending on who they're talking to. So I'm not sure what you mean."

Surya Shekar laughed aloud.

"Secularism; rationality; humanitarianism; atheism; never to trust a god-man. We make public pronouncements that the astrologers should be hacked to death..."

"Yes, I've heard them."

"But it's not easy to be a disbeliever twenty-four hours a day, Naren."

Narendran kept silent.

5

"When I was in power, it was easy not to believe in any god. But since I've been chased out, I'm unable to place all my trust solely in other men. I am being honest with you, Naren. In today's world, all anyone thinks about is how to outfox the other fellow. Politics is all about defeating your enemies. I've come to understand that man needs God to save him from himself.

"But I can't say this publicly. I rip God to pieces on stage, and then apologize to Him in private at home. My daughter-in-law is even worse; she is a total believer, praying twice a day, fasting once a week. My son is a strong believer too. I had organized a special puja, to bless Arthreyan with a bright future. It took place in the ashram of Swami Dhayal, and lasted for three days. It was kept a complete secret. Nobody except my family knew about this. Yesterday my son left for the conclusion of the puja, at dawn. We gave the story that he was visiting a distant relative.

"At eight in the morning, while returning from the puja, his car met with an accident near Chengalpettu. The driver swerved to pass a stationary lorry on the road. He lost control and the car skidded into a nearby field and caught fire. A crowd gathered, and the police arrived. Only one person was admitted to the hospital, listed as injured: the driver. Not my son. Even when the driver regained consciousness in the hospital, he carefully avoided any mention of my son."

"Why?"

"Because Arthreyan was not alone in the car. A disciple of Swami Dhayal was accompanying him. If this fact becomes public knowledge, our political enemies will seize it and use it to tear us apart!"

"So you can't make it public that Arthreyan is missing."

"Correct. But I *must* have my son back within two days, or else the executive committee elections will go on without him."

"Are you suspicious of anyone specific?"

"Yes! The ruling party! They could have engineered this so that Arthreyan would be absent for the party election. Most of my party members were formerly members of that party, and their loyalty can be easily bought back. But with my son in power, they won't be bought off so easily. That's why the ruling party is so scared about him taking over."

"Are you sure it's the ruling party?"

"We can't discount the possibility."

"What? Now you're confusing me."

"Sorry. I spoke like a politician, didn't I? I do suspect the ruling party. But I have no proof. If I go public, and then turn out to be wrong, it could turn against me."

"So you need my help to find Arthreyan?"

"And to be secretive about it," added Surya Shekar. "You name your price, and I will provide whatever other assistance you need."

"How much do the police know?"

"The car skidded while trying to avoid the lorry. The driver was hurt. Those are the only facts the police have on record."

"I'll need to speak to the driver, and go to the site of the accident."

"Naren, if the ruling party is involved, then I can get political mileage out of this. But I cannot risk letting it slip that I am a believer."

"Who knew that Arthreyan was visiting the Swami?"

"My family, the driver, and my assistant."

"And within your family?"

"My wife, my daughter-in-law, and myself."

"I suppose I shouldn't waste my time questioning any of them?"

"Of course not; there's no way any of them would plot against Arthreyan."

"How do I reach you in case of an emergency?"

"I'll give you my personal number. In case anyone else answers, though, don't say you are from Eagle Eye. Give a fake name—Adalarasu."

The telephone rang. He picked up the receiver.

"What...? Keep it safe. Don't speak to anyone about it. Wait there for me." He cut the phone call, and turned again to Narendran. "A new problem," he said.

"Blackmail?"

"No, no... A letter has just arrived. They don't know who dropped it in the mailbox. A strange and intriguing letter—it says Arthreyan will soon be the ruler of the nation! It says he needs time to be trained for the job, so we are not to search for him; he will return soon."

"Is it signed?"

"No. But the person who wrote it must know where Arthreyan is."

"Ask them to put that letter in a polythene cover, and to be careful not to smudge any fingerprints on it."

"And send it where?"

"To the Eagle Eye office."

"Naren... I'm worried. I sometimes think maybe I should go to the police about this."

"That's entirely up to you."

Surya Shekar hesitated for a moment. "No, I trust Eagle Eye completely. My car will drop you off back at the airport."

"See you." Narendran got up to leave. The car was waiting.

⋈ 3 ⋈

The hospital was in Alwarpet—a large compound, surrounded by palm trees which cast long shadows on the marble walls. Narendran found a safe place to park his Bullet. Vaijayanthi got off the pillion and checked her makeup in the rear-view mirror.

"You must be the only woman in the world who checks her makeup before going in to see a patient," said Narendran.

"We should look our best when we visit sick patients, Naren. Our appearance should cheer them up. If we look sloppy, it might rub off on them, no?"

"Very true," remarked Narendran with mock seriousness. They entered the clinic. An old nurse wished them "Happy New Year," and guided them to the room where the driver, Samson, was recovering. Walking quickly over the white glazed granite floor, and deftly avoiding a speeding stretcher, they entered Samson's room. Laid out flat on his back, Samson turned his head to see them. There was a line of stitches on his jaw.

"How are you, Samson?" asked Narendran, sitting down at his bedside.

Samson looked at him and Vaijayanthi cautiously. His eyes rested longer on Vaijayanthi. "Who are you? How do you know my name?"

"We were sent by your employer. I wanted to check if your left hand was tattooed, but it's bandaged."

"It was fractured. Are you Naren?"

"Narendran, yes."

"My boss told me to answer whatever questions you asked."

"Tell me exactly what happened yesterday."

"We left Mallithoppu at dawn..."

"Swami Dhayal's ashram is in Mallithoppu?"

"Yes. We were coming down Chengalpettu Main Road. I was doing eighty kilometres an hour. There was a truck parked in the left lane. Just as I was overtaking it, another lorry came in from the opposite direction. I swerved to avoid it and the car skidded off the road."

"Who was in the car then, along with you?"

"I was in front, driving. The young master and another man from the ashram were in the back seat."

"They were in the car when it overturned?"

"Yes. But when the car caught fire and people from the nearby villages came to pull me out, they said I was alone."

"Did the lorry stop? The one that ran you off the road?"

"No. It sped away. The lorry that had been parked on the left had also gone. They must have had a plan to kidnap the young master."

"Where exactly did the accident take place?"

"There is a small roadside temple, to a god called Mukarundhasami, on Chengalpettu High Road. The accident happened just past that temple."

"Did the police come to make inquiries?"

"They did the inquiry here. But I insisted I was alone in the car. They asked me if I remembered the lorry numbers, and I told them I didn't. But I do remember one of them."

"Very good," said Narendran. "Which one do you remember, the parked one or the one that was going to crash into you?"

"The one that was parked. I noticed the number from a distance. TN-09-A-4510. I memorized it, just like that. But I don't know the other one…"

"No, that's good. Do you suspect anyone in particular?"

"Yes. The ruling party MLA, Sundaragopal Ananthanarayanasami!"

"Hell of a name! Why do you suspect him?"

"He's the one most threatened by Arthreyan's rise. They were classmates in school. He knew, even then, that Arthreyan was brilliant…"

"Who told you all this?"

"Arthreyan himself told me."

"Samson, do you really think it would have been possible for Arthreyan to have been kidnapped in such a short time?"

"Why not, sir? There was a gap of at least three minutes before the villagers gathered, and I was unconscious. The kidnapping could easily have happened during that time."

"Thank you. We'll meet again later."

"Please come before seven in the night, sir."

"Why?"

"I haven't been able to sleep properly. I'd like to go to bed early tonight."

"Fine."

Narendran returned to the car park with Vaijayanthi.

"That's one great advantage to working in a hospital, Vaij…"

"What?"

"You get to learn which medicine will make which part grow bigger."

"I don't get it…"

"Check out that nurse, you'll understand."

A 38-26-38 figure in a tight uniform was marching into the hospital. Narendran drummed his fingers softly in time with her steps: *dha-dhum-dha-dhum-dha-dhum*. The uniform bounced in rhythm. Vaijayanthi shot

Narendran a hard look, her eyes like burning lasers.

"Do you want me to ask her what the medicine is, Vaij? Maybe you could take the same dose."

"Ask her slipper size while you're at it," snapped Vaijayanthi.

◢ 4 ◣

The inspector looked up with a smile. "Yes?"

Narendran returned the smile. "I'm Narendran. From Eagle Eye Detective Agency."

"Please, have a seat. What can I do for you?"

"There was a road accident in Chengalpettu division yesterday morning. A car ran off the road and caught fire."

"Yes?"

"The insurance company asked us to investigate the accident."

"What do you want to know?"

"I would like to see the spot. Have you found anything? Any interesting tidbits of information?"

"Tidbits? You mean like jam, mango pickle, *chakrapongal...*?"

Narendran laughed, a little more than necessary. "Good joke!"

"Nothing interesting so far," the inspector continued amiably. "The driver says there were two lorries, but he doesn't remember anything about them. How do we find out?"

"Hmm. Difficult."

"How have you come, Mr. Narendran?"

"In my Maruti car..."

"Then you can reach the spot in ten minutes. Ask for Mukarundhasami temple."

"Thanks, Inspector."

Narendran shook his hand, and came outside.

"So what does he say?" asked Vaijayanthi from the car, eating ice cream.

"You were able to find ice cream here, in this village?"

"I bought it in Madras and brought it along in an icebox."

11

"Clever girl!" teased Narendran, getting into the car. A few minutes down the road, they stopped to make inquiries at a tender coconut stall.

"What would you like, sir? Can I get you a coconut with lots of water?"

"Please. And I'd like to ask you one other favor, my friend."

"What?"

"Yesterday there was an accident here…"

"Oh, yes, sir! The car overturned. I was the first one to run to it. I sleep right here every night, even if it's raining or very cold," said the coconut vendor, pointing to an old ruin behind the stall.

"How many people were in the car?"

"Just one man, the driver. His head was hurt… he got a bad cut on the cheek, and his left arm was broken. The car caught fire, and then the villagers came running."

"He was the only one in the car?"

"Just him."

"No one else? Maybe somebody was thrown out by the crash?"

"No chance, all four doors were locked. We dragged the driver out through the window. How could there have been anyone else?"

"Fine. You saw the car first. Did you also see the two lorries that knocked it off the road?"

"There was only one lorry. It was going past that banyan tree over yonder."

"That must be two kilometres from here!"

"Farther than that. But that car wasn't near any lorry. My guess is the driver was drunk and had fallen asleep. He's blaming the accident on a made-up lorry to save face."

"Are you sure?"

"Why would I have any doubt? When the car toppled over there was no lorry around. Here, take your tender coconut. They're as sweet as sugar, taste it and see. Do you want a straw?'

"Yes. Give madam one of the big coconuts."

"Coming up!"

"Tell me, is that temple I see over there the Mukarundhasami temple?

"Yes, sir."

"How does it come to have that name?"

"They say that when Lord Raman was going to the forest, Surpanaka saw him. When she came to ogle at him, Raman's younger brother stopped her here and chopped off her nose. That's the legend, anyway."

"But Raman never came to this part of the country!" Narendran objected.

"What do I know about it, sir? Am I Raman, or Ravanan? I'm just telling you the story my mother told me. Here, madam, take this. Careful not to spill it on your sari."

After paying for the coconuts, Narendran drove down to the site of the accident. Pieces of shattered glass were scattered all over the ground. The plants nearby were charred. There were dark tire marks in the earth. Even the chalk lines that the police had drawn were undisturbed. There was nothing else of interest.

While Narendran and Vaijayanthi were on their knees examining the scene, a shadow fell on the ground.

"Who are you? What are you looking for?"

It was someone from the village nearby. Narendran questioned him.

"We came running even as the car was rolling over. There was just the driver, no one else..."

Narendran and Vaijayanthi shared a meaningful look.

"I have one doubt," said Vaijayanthi.

"Please ask, madam."

"Where does this name Mukarundhasami come from?"

"Oh, that. They say that the *Mahabharatham* was written using Ganesh's trunk as a pencil."

"Wait, that's not right—it wasn't the trunk, it was the tusk..."

"Who knows, but that's how the temple gets its name."

"So it's Ganesh in there?"

"That's right."

"But we were told it was a Surpanaka temple."

"Who cares what the name is? Light your camphor, make your wish—and watch it come true."

"What fabulous faith!" exclaimed Narendran.

"Naren, I think the driver is lying," said Vaijayanthi, back in the car. "It doesn't look as though any lorry ran him off the road after all."

"So what's he covering up? Maybe he staged the accident?"

"Naren, Samson must know where Arthreyan is."

"Yeah. Let's get back to the hospital right away."

Narendran put the car into gear.

Chennai.

John Sundar stood at the door of Eagle Eye.

"What's up, Naren?"

"I came to get my revolver," said Narendran, panting after his dash up the stairs.

"Why? Expecting trouble?"

"The driver is lying. Maybe my gun will get the truth out of him. I gave you the lorry number...?"

"It was a false lead. That plate number belongs to a moped. Want to guess who that moped's first owner was? Samson!"

"Rascal! So he just gave me a fake number that he knew by heart."

"If you confront him with that, it should be enough to get him to start telling the truth. I don't think you need the revolver," said Vaijayanthi.

"No harm in carrying some extra protection."

Narendran tossed the car key onto his desk and rushed out on his Bullet.

At the hospital, just as Narendran was parking his bike, the power went out. The entire place was plunged into darkness. Scattered emergency lights went on and footsteps raced all over the place. Narendran walked in with the help of his torch. He ran up the stairs; several nurses had started lighting candles. He tried Samson's door. It was locked from the inside. He knew hospitals didn't encourage that. In fact most hospi-

14

tal room doors didn't even have a bolt on the inside. Was this clinic an exception? Even if it was, why would Samson lock himself in?

He pounded on the door. "Samson, open up!"

The nurse in the corridor was shocked. "Who are you?" she demanded.

Narendran lost his patience. Every second was precious now. He banged hard on the door with his shoulder and the latch gave way. The door swung open. He sprang in, holding his torch. There was a shadow near the window. Samson! He had a foot over the window sill, ready to jump out.

"Stop right there, Samson! I've got a gun," threatened Narendran. He pointed the torch at his face. Samson hesitated.

"Samson, hurry!" whispered a voice from outside.

In two steps, Narendran was at the window. He peered out. The man below was caught in the beam of light from Narendran's torch, and momentarily stunned.

"Samson, who's that?" he whispered.

Samson grabbed hold of the back of Naren's neck with a vise-like grip. In his hurry to catch a glimpse of the man outside, Narendran had put his head through the window like a ringmaster sticking his head into a lion's gaping maw. Samson tightened his hold. But Narendran was no fool, and he still had both hands free to defend himself. He gave Samson's chin a hard knock with his torch and cracked his pistol down on the fractured arm.

Something suddenly whizzed past him. Samson was thrown across the room. When Narendran swung the torchlight on his face, he saw a red patch growing on his forehead. His eyes were emptying fast. His lips seemed to be moving. Narendran leaned in closer.

"Control... tower..." Samson gasped.

Narendran dropped him and ran back to the window. There was nothing but darkness below. A nurse came rushing in to investigate the sound of the gunshot; she caught sight of Narendran holding the gun, turned to see the body on the floor, and collapsed in a faint.

"You nosey bum, I was wondering where you were all these days. Come in," said Paulraj, the police inspector, ruffling Narendran's hair.

"It was him! This is the man who shot Samson!" the nurse screeched.

"Did you *see* him kill him?"

"The gun was in his hand, and Samson was dead on the floor. What else could that mean?" cried the nurse.

"It means that not everything you see is true," replied Paulraj. "Look at this innocent face. Does he look as if he could shoot a man? Think!"

The nurse looked at Paulraj in widening alarm, and quickly left the room.

"Why have you come here, Naren? How did you happen to have a gun and a torch? Who killed Samson?"

"I don't have the answer to that last question. I came here investigating an insurance case, to question Samson. When I got here, he was trying to escape through the window. I was trying to stop him when someone from below shot him. I only got a quick look at the killer—there wasn't much light."

Just then, the current came back on. Not wanting to disturb the other patients, Paulraj had the body laid out on a stretcher and quietly taken away.

"Are you going to do the post-mortem here?"

"No. It's better to have it done at the government hospital. Who is this Samson?" asked Paulraj, getting an FIR from Narendran.

"A car driver," replied Narendran evasively. "His car was involved in an accident. I was investigating the insurance claim."

"As usual, you are very cleverly avoiding having to give me any useful information."

"Sorry Paulraj. Goes with the job."

"But I have discovered one thing. Tell me if I am correct."

"What?"

"I know that you're working for Surya Shekar."

"Who's Surya Shekar?"

"Come on man... you didn't see me while you were waiting in the airport. I was there arranging the security for the Prime Minister's visit. I saw you speak to a man and then go off in a car. Of course, you'd have no way of knowing that Fiat was registered in the name of Surya Shekar's wife!"

"Impressive work."

"I realize you have to be secretive about this. But please ask me if you need anything."

'Thanks, Paulraj. I'd better get going, though—right after I go down to the morgue to check Samson's pockets."

But, disappointingly, the pockets were empty.

Vaijayanthi was sitting on the table, swinging one foot.

"Tell me again, what were Samson's last words?"

" 'Control towers.' "

"Maybe he'd been to Moonlight Agency, to meet Bharat."

"What makes you say that?"

"Sounds like a slogan from one of Susheela's T-shirts."

"Vaij, be serious. Please don't distract me. Now I'll start thinking of all the other slogans on her T-shirts. Last time I met Susheela..."

"Stop!" ordered Vaijayanthi. She got off the table. "Sorry to have distracted you. Let's put our brains together and think."

"Vaij, I forgot something," said Narendran, jumping up.

"What?"

"I told Surya Shekar to send that letter he received to the office."

"I didn't forget it. The letter came by courier. I checked it... not much to go on, though."

"Where is it?"

"Top drawer."

Narendran opened the drawer and took out a plastic bag with the letter in it. Someone had ripped opened the envelope. Inside it was a piece of pink paper neatly folded. Ordinary paper, the kind any stationery store would carry. The letters had been typed on a typewriter with a well-used ribbon.

"'Arthreyan will one day become the ruler of this nation. He must be trained to serve his country well. Do not look for him. He will return when the time is right,'" Narendran read aloud. "What do you think of this, Vaij?"

"Confusing. Maybe it's just meant to show that Arthreyan's kidnappers don't plan to hurt him?"

"Then why did they shoot Samson down so mercilessly?"

"There's no stamp on the envelope. Someone dropped the letter directly in the mailbox. We could have it checked for fingerprints—but this can't go to the police. Paulraj wouldn't be able to keep it a secret."

"Why don't we tear the cover in two, and give Paulraj the part without Surya Shekar's name on it?"

Carefully, Narendran cut the cover in two with a penknife, and put one piece back in the plastic cover.

"Vaij, do you think there is a connection between this letter and the control tower?"

"The letter is sort of a command—commands come from control towers...?"

"The airport has a control *room*, but no control tower..."

"Naren, what do you call the tower in a fort, where soldiers stand guard?"

"That's a watchtower. Big prisons have them, too."

"Maybe Samson was confused, and meant that?"

"So then what?"

"First, we need to find that tower. Then figure out the connection between the tower and Samson."

"There's another area I have to check."

"What's that?"

"The red light area..."

"Naren!"

"You've got a one-track mind. Don't you see a connection—red light, danger, devotion?"

"How does devotion come in to this?"

"What color is *kumkum*? Red, right?"

"Fine. Tell me what your 'red light area' is."

"I think we need to visit Swami Dhayal's ashram. That was the last place Arthreyan was seen. Of course, we'll need to inform Surya Shekar."

"Shall we start now..."

"Now? If we go now, at midnight, Swami Dhayal will throw us out."

"Don't be hasty. Let me complete the thought. I meant, let's call Surya Shekar now and let him know our intentions. Then we can set off early tomorrow."

"Good plan," replied Narendran, reaching for the phone.

⚜ 6 ⚜

It was red in the east. The sun rose like a red flower, with orange clouds surrounding it like petals. There was a misty breeze; dew drops hung from the tips of the blades of grass. The air smelled fresh and green.

Narendran was driving the Maruti. It was chilly.

"Naren, look at this scenery. So beautiful!"

"Why do films always have song duets performed in parks or on snowy mountaintops? It'll be a good change to sing in a car, no?"

"Shall I sing, then?"

She began humming softly. Narendran stopped the car to let some cattle cross the road. An old woman was walking past with the calves.

"Paati, how do I get to Mallithoppu?"

"Are you going to see the Swami?"

"Yes, paati."

"Seems like all the fancy cars are headed there only. Go, go—he'll give you flowers and blessings too, I'm sure. See that thatched roof over there? The ashram is just a little further on."

The last stretch of the drive was on a dusty dirt path. Beyond that was the bamboo fence of the ashram. He parked the car out on the road. They removed their footwear next to a board that asked politely, "Please do not step on the ashram floor with your dusty shoes."

The wet grass tickled their bare feet. The air was brisk. The ashram was in the centre of the compound. A looped recording of a chant, "Om Namo Narayanaya," droned in the distance. The water pump at the well burbled along with it. A disciple, bathing in the cold well-water, stopped at the sight of the two detectives.

"Who are you?"

"My name is Narendran. I've come to see the Swami."

"The elder Swami?"

Unsure of who that was supposed to be, Narendran replied simply, "Dhayal Swami."

"He's doing his prayers. He meets people only after seven. Please have a seat here," he said, pointing to a cement bench.

"It's so peaceful here. Almost makes me want to become a *sanyasi* myself," said Vaijayanthi, sitting down.

"Uh-oh. Maybe it was a mistake to bring you here. Next thing I know you'll change into saffron robes, and run off."

Two lovebirds were chirping. A cow mooed somewhere. The loud chants emerging from inside the ashram were charging the atmosphere. A disciple came up to them. "He wants you to come in."

The entrance was low. It seemed as if it were done on purpose, to humble the devotees. A man seated on a tiger-skin rug looked up at them. He opened his wet eyes wide, and raised his eyebrows. He spoke in a whisper so hushed it was difficult to catch his words initially.

"God has sent you here. What have you come for, my son?"

"I'm investigating the disappearance of a man named Arthreyan, who was last seen here."

"What do you want to know? He was a devoted student. My disciple who left with him has not returned, either. Did you know that?"

"I've been engaged to find both of them."

"If God wills it, then they will be found. Here, take this," he said, offering them crystallized sugar and kumkum.

"One small request, Swami..."

"What?"

"Just before he died, Samson, the driver who picked up Arthreyan and your disciple, said the words 'control tower'. I can't make any sense of that. I was wondering if Arthreyan had said anything to you, Swami, which might explain..."

"Arthreyan came here to pray and to meditate. He accompanied me in my prayers. Our relationship did not extend any further."

"Did Arthreyan mention any particular person from whom he might be facing danger?"

"He wanted my help to win over his enemies, not to be saved from them. Now, my son, it is time I returned to my prayers."

He was making it very clear that he wanted them to leave. Narendran touched Vaijayanthi lightly. She got up.

One of the disciples came to the gate to see them off. Narendran asked him, "The man in the car with Arthreyan—what was his name?"

"Jeevakan."

"How old is he?"

"Once we come here, into the service of God, we disregard age..."

"Well, how about this, then... How many years ago did Jeevakan descend to this world to serve God?" asked Vaijayanthi.

"Twenty-four years ago, madam."

"Thank you."

The sun had turned from yellow to hot white. They got into the car.

"So what do you think, Naren?"

"The swami seems to be a true sanyasi. I don't see anything too shady about him. He may invoke the name of God to make false promises to people, make them wait for miracles that won't happen. But I don't think he's involved in the kidnapping."

"So, what does 'control tower' mean?"

"We have to check everything in the city that could possibly be called a control tower. You mentioned the fort; we should look at Fort St. George. And check the lighthouse, and Central Prison..."

The noon sun glared down. Narendran stopped the bike under a tree on Beach Road. "No clues about Arthreyan," he sighed. "All we've got is this oppressive heat."

"Nothing in the fort or the lighthouse. We still have to check the prison!" said Vaijayanthi.

"I've asked Paulraj to fix it up for us. We already know the jailer, so it shouldn't be too hard. Let's have an ice cream and then head over to the prison."

"Sounds good."

Narendran parked his bike in front of the tall prison gates just as the last bit of Vaijayanthi's ice cream cone disappeared. They entered the prison. The jailer came forward with a smile to shake their hands.

"We would like to know about your control tower, sir."

"Watchtower, you mean? We have three of them. Each one is thirty feet tall and has someone on watch duty throughout the day. After dark, powerful searchlights switch on automatically and scan the grounds throughout the night. Each tower is equipped with a wireless telephone. The watchtower guards can use it to communicate with the ground office, or amongst themselves."

"Can I see one of them?"

"Seenu, take them up one of the towers. Seenu here is in charge of the East Tower."

Seenu had a huge paunch, broad shoulders, and held himself ramrod-straight. They went up the steps at the end of the corridor. The tower room was circular. A rifle stood ready on its stand.

"You can aim all the way up to the corner there. I once shot an escapee myself, at that distance," said Seenu with pride, pointing to the compound wall.

"Is that right?" replied Narendran.

"Yes sir! My photo came in the papers, too. I have the clipping downstairs. I'll show it to you afterwards."

Narendran checked out the tower. Was there anything here that could be remotely connected to Arthreyan's kidnapping? The rifle? The bright lights? Maybe the wireless? No—there was nothing here of interest, just as there had been nothing in the ashram, nothing in any of the other towers they had visited. It was useless—they had exhausted all their leads.

They came back down from the tower.

"See, here's my photo." Seenu was holding up an old newspaper clipping. Narendran took it politely, and gave it a quick look.

PRISONER'S ESCAPE BID FOILED! POLICEMAN REWARDED, read the headline. Underneath were two photographs: one of a slightly younger and slimmer Seenu, and the other... Narendran had seen that face somewhere! Where?

Then he had a sudden memory flash. This was the man who had been urging Samson to jump out of the hospital window, the same man who had later shot him in the head.

"Who's this here?"

"His name is Adhisayaraj. He was in for smuggling. Like an idiot, he beat up a guard, and then tried to jump over the compound wall. I saw him and shot him in the ankle. He had to do another three years here for that. He was just recently released, sir."

"I need all the information you can give me about him, Seenu. The name of his visitors, his address, every single detail..."

"Rasiklal Seth is sure to know his address."

"Who is this Rasiklal Seth?"

"He's a pawnbroker, who had loaned him some money. He came here once, to the prison, to scream at him. I remember that."

"Can I have Rasiklal's address?"

"Of course. The jailer will be able to help you with that."

⚡ 7 ⚡

Rasiklal Seth's tiny pawnshop, not more than seven feet from one end to the other, was on Triplicane Main Road. Seth was sitting relaxed on a round cushion. Jewels and silver vessels lined the glass shelves around him. As soon as Narendran stepped in, Seth called out, "I don't trade in vehicles. That looks like a police bike. What did you do, steal it? Get lost, I don't need the trouble."

Narendran laughed. "Sethji, I don't want money from you. I'm here to *give* you some money."

"You're going to give me money? How much?"

"I want an address. Give me that, and I'll reward you."

"An address?"

"Yes, Sethji. You once lent money to a man called Adhisiyaraj. You visited him in prison. I need his address."

Seth took his time answering.

"I don't think he has a permanent address, other than the prison. Actually, you can ask in Nandhini Wines. They'll be able to tell you."

The entrance of Nandhini Wines was crowded with stacks of empty cardboard boxes. Half-naked women pasted onto the pillars advertised a variety of different liquors. Business was brisk. Narendran hesitated near the counter. The bearded owner gave him a nod, and Narendran went up to him. "I need to meet Adhisiyaraj," he said quietly.

The owner pointed him to the back of the wine shop. An arrow-shaped sign on the wall pointed the way to "The Bar". Narendran entered and sat on a chair. The tiny, filthy space was filled with cigarette smoke and the smell of beer. After a few minutes, the owner walked in and asked, "Who are you?"

"You don't need to know me. Just tell him the boss sent me."

"Which boss is this?"

"Driver Samson's boss."

"Right. Adhisiyaraj will be here in ten minutes."

"Fine. I'll be waiting in a Maruti at the end of the road. Ask him to meet me there." Narendran told him the license number and went back to his car. He had dropped his bike at the Eagle Eye office and picked up John Sundar, who was waiting in the shadows.

He sat in the back seat. After a few minutes, a figure approached, cautiously. Adhisiyaraj opened the car door and got in. He held a small pistol in his hand.

"I couldn't figure out who you were. That's why I brought this…"

Narendran switched on the car light. Adhisiyaraj's reaction was sharp.

"You? The one from Samson's room, that night…!"

"I'm Narendran."

"Why did you come for me? You've walked straight into a death trap…"

"You think so? With this bullet aimed at your throat?" asked John Sundar, appearing from nowhere and pointing his gun through the car window. Adhisiyaraj went motionless. Narendran lost no time in snatching the pistol from his hand. "Get in, John, and start driving," he said, pointing the pistol at Adhisiyaraj. They rolled up the dark tinted windows to keep the events inside the car a secret from the street outside.

"Let's give him a little welcome gift, Naren," John said, as he cracked Adhisiyaraj's temple with the butt of his gun. Adhisiyaraj collapsed on Narendran's lap.

When Adhisiyaraj opened his eyes he found himself bound to a chair in the Eagle Eye office. Narendran sat opposite to him.

"Good, you're awake. Take a look at this."

Adhisiyaraj looked groggily at the two electric wires in Narendran's hands.

"These pack a four hundred volt punch. According to modern scientific theory, that's enough to electrocute a man. Even a tiny touch will give your blood a good charging up. Want a taste?"

Adhisiyaraj's face paled, and he squirmed with impotent rage.

"What do you want?"

"The truth."

"What truth?"

"Why did you kill Samson?"

"It's a lie. I didn't kill him."

"Time for a taste, perhaps?"

Narendran touched Adhisiyaraj's hand with the wires. Both Adhisiyaraj and the chair jumped an inch off the ground. He was obviously surprised to find that Narendran was not bluffing.

"Aagh! What is this?"

"I told you already, four hundred volts."

"What do you want to know?"

"Why did you kill Samson?"

"It was nothing personal. My job was to get him out of the hospital. If there was any danger of him being caught, I had orders to kill him. They had shown me your photograph. So when you showed up, I shot him."

"Who dropped the letter in Surya Shekar's mailbox?"

"That was me."

"Now for an easy question. Who are you working for?"

"If I refuse to answer, you electrocute me. If I answer you, they'll finish me off. What's the difference?"

"'They will finish you off' is in future tense. But 'I electrocute you' is in present tense, and there's no escaping it if you keep quiet. Which one do you prefer?"

"I don't know their real names. I just heard them calling the boss 'Vanilarasu'."

"Strange name."

"I think it means *one who rules the heavens*."

"Did I ask if you were a dictionary? Where do I find him?"

"He has a huge bungalow in Perambur."

"Address?"

"There's a signboard that says 'Amarabharati Advertising'. But there's no advertising agency there. He's involved in some sort of secret project."

"What project?"

"I don't know the details. There's a secret room, no other employees. Some funny business."

"Have you heard of Arthreyan?"

"I've heard the name, but I've never met him. Who is he?"

"Never mind. John! Let me go check if this joker's giving us fact or fiction. Keep him under electric watch until I get back."

John nodded eagerly as Narendran handed him the wires.

8

Perambur. A dark street, empty except for a single lazy buffalo. The tube light had been stolen from the lamppost. The Amarabharati Advertising signboard was in a sorry state of repair.

"Naren!" whispered Vaijayanthi. "This place stinks. I can't stand it."

"Vaij, this is the only spot where I can get a clear view of the bungalow."

"How long are we going to stand here?"

"Just a little longer. Until the kid John arranged for shows up."

"John? Kid? What?"

"Here's the plan. A young kid is supposed to come in a little while and knock on the door. He'll hand them a letter that says, 'Danger from Eagle Eye approaching fast. Meet me at the street corner. Adhisiyaraj.' As soon as Vanilarasu comes out to search, I'm going into the bungalow. If I'm not back out within an hour, then you do what you need to do. Are you worried about being here left alone? There are a lot of stray dogs."

"I have my karate. That'll protect me from any dog... or any tiger, for that matter."

"The kid's here," said Narendran.

The boy, hanging on to his torn shorts with one hand, was banging on the doors of the bungalow. The entrance light switched on, and the door opened halfway. A head peered out.

Was this Vanilarasu?

He had large eyes. A long beak of a nose, hooked slightly to the right. Spectacles. A mouth full of crooked teeth, a wild mop of hair, a creased brow. He took the letter from the boy and shut the door. The kid didn't wait around.

Vaijayanthi looked at Narendran, who signaled her to be patient.

After a few minutes, the door opened again. The man came out in kurta and pajama, carrying a large electric torch. He shut the door, locked it with a heavy padlock, and headed to the end of the street.

Narendran winked at Vaijayanthi and took out a large bunch of keys. Together they moved to the locked door. The sixth skeleton key clicked, and he went in. Vaijayanthi relocked the door and returned to her hiding place.

He waited to let his eyes adjust to the darkness. Then he started to move. The room opened on one side into a small balcony. An electric mosquito repellant device shed a dim blue glow. Bamboo chairs lined the wall. In the centre of the room was a table, and on it a calendar with the Amarabharati Advertising logo. Next was a smaller room. On the left was a dimly lit kitchen, redolent with the aroma of coffee. There was a pressure cooker on the counter; Narendran opened it. Inside was a dish with rice. The dry grains on the sides of the cooker showed that a large quantity of rice had been prepared. Why would a single man need so much rice? Narendran shut the cooker. He checked the drawers on the counter. While he was opening the second drawer, he heard the front lock being opened.

Quickly, he shut the drawer and moved into the darkness. Footsteps neared and passed the kitchen. Narendran swiveled on his feet and peered out. He saw a dark figure turn to the right and approach the staircase. It bent down and moved something, then lifted a square board. White light filled the square—a secret passage! The figure went down the passage and shut the trap door. Narendran put his right ear to the door and listened. He heard footsteps receding down a staircase. When the sound faded, Narendran silently opened the trap door and entered the passage. On tiptoes, he walked down narrow wooden steps towards the light. To his left was a seven-foot glass wall. The bottom of the staircase was lit by the light from behind the glass. Narendran worried that if someone was behind the wall they might see his shadow. So he got down on all fours and moved forward along the floor.

"What is this stupidity, creeping about like a stealthy mouse? Get up and come here!"

The voice brought Narendran's head up with a start.

"Hello. I am Vanilarasu." He came out from behind another glass door that Narendran had not noticed. He looked even more bizarre up close.

Narendran stood up.

"If you have any weapons, you may as well hand them over now. That pretty little bimbo you brought along is already here inside…"

"What?"

"As soon as you left Vaijayanthi, my men picked her up and brought her in. Apparently, she demonstrated a few karate kicks. When they threatened her with your life, she quieted down. So, are you wondering how I found you out? I've been keeping close watch over the employees of Eagle Eye."

Narendran pushed Vanilarasu aside and went into the room. Vaijayanthi was flanked by two gun-toting thugs. She looked upset with her failure.

"You must be wondering how she was brought in. That's a different doorway, over there. This secret room has twenty entrances."

Narendran held out his pistol. One of the goons took it from him, then patted him down and found the knife hidden in his sock.

"Who did you come looking for, Narendran? Was it Arthreyan? He's not here. Once you'd found out about this place, it couldn't have been long before the police knew about it as well. So I moved him. He's been relocated, to my laboratory. Are you interested in seeing it?"

"If I say I'm not, will you let us free?"

"Naren, Naren! I'm not abducting you. I just want you to understand the nature of my experiment. Then I want to give you a chance to let me proceed willingly. You musn't interfere with my plans." Vanilarasu spoke to him in the patient tones of a teacher coaching a student. Vaijayanthi looked at Narendran. He signaled her to stay calm.

"Shall we proceed, Naren?"

"Yes, I suppose so," said Narendran.

"I have a small favor to ask of you. My men will blindfold both you and Vaijayanthi, and bring you there in separate cars. That will keep both of you quiet."

Narendran and Vaijayanthi were blindfolded and led back up the wooden steps. He could hear the sound of the shutters being pulled down and car doors opening. From the feel of the seat, he guessed that the car was an Ambassador. He heard the second car start.

"I'm here beside you, Naren," said Vanilarasu. Narendran shut his eyes, tried to make himself comfortable, and began gathering his strength.

⋈ 9 ⋈

Sodium-vapor lamps bathed the yard in a yellow glow. Vanilarasu got out of the car and helped Narendran out. He walked him down a dewy path and knocked on a door. The door opened, and they stepped up half a foot onto a platform. The coolness of the open air gave way to an indoor warmth.

Vanilarasu took off Narendran's blindfold. He shook his head to clear his vision. He was walking down a narrow corridor, lit by lamps along both sides. The door at the end of the corridor was open, and fumes of sandalwood incense poured out. Past the door was a very small room. Inside was an electric frame with blinking red and yellow lights. Pictures of the deities Ganesh, Lakshmi and Saraswathi filled the frame. The incense sticks burned in front of them. Vanilarasu piously touched the floor, rose, and beckoned him on. "Come, Naren!"

It was all exceedingly strange.

"I am a person humble enough to accept that in spite of the rapid growth of scientific knowledge, not even a drop of sand can move in this world without divine grace," said Vanilarasu with a smile.

"Where is Vaijayanthi?"

"Who do you want to see first, Arthreyan or Vaijayanthi?"

Narendran stayed quiet. They passed through more rooms, and finally entered a huge hall. Vanilarasu signaled Narendran to keep silent, and made him sit on a chair. He then pressed a button on the wall, and the lights in the room switched off. A square pane of glass became visible, lit from behind.

Behind the glass window, Narendran could see a drowsy Arthreyan seated on a dentist's chair. A metal ribbon was tied to his forehead. Several electric wires connected the ribbon to a huge apparatus, something like a refrigerator. Circular monitors on the machine showed digital pulses.

Opposite Arthreyan's chair was a television, on which was playing an old newsreel of Jawaharlal Nehru standing on a platform giving a speech. Several other political leaders occupied the stage along with Nehru.

Arthreyan's eyes were fixed on the TV screen. His tortured expressions seemed to be reacting to Nehru's oratory.

Vanilarasu switched the lights back on. The room became bright again, and Arthreyan disappeared.

"What are you doing to him?" demanded Narendran, agitated.

"I am developing him," replied Vanilarasu, lighting a cigarette.

"It looks like you're scrambling his brains."

"Don't be silly. I am involved in a sacred mission. Do you have any idea how much this laboratory cost me? Three and a half lakhs! My entire savings. I am spending over twenty-five thousand a month on this experiment. There is not a single selfish thought in this endeavor. My only aim is to develop this country into a superpower!"

The strange light in his eyes was terrifying.

"Naren…" Vaijayanthi's voice made him turn around.

The two thugs who had brought her in stepped aside. She ran across to him, hugged him, and then collapsed unconscious in his arms.

"What is this?" snapped Narendran.

"What's what? She's fainted. Nothing to worry about! We've given her some chemical gas. She will be fine soon."

"If anything happens to her…" Narendran did not finish the threat. Instead he took Vanilarasu by his shirt and thrust him against the wall. The cigarette fell to the ground. The two goons came over in a hurry and tore Narendran off.

"Naren, I thought you were a reasonable person. Instead, you are acting foolish. You must realize that I had to knock Vaijayanthi out. This is a secret place, the headquarters of my great experiment. If you and she join forces, you could spoil my entire mission. You could escape with Arthreyan. But I need him for three more days to complete my project. I cannot allow you to disturb him now. That's why I gave her a dose of gas, to keep her out of the action. Her life is not threatened."

"If she's even slightly hurt, I'll dismember you," snarled Narendran.

"You will understand my noble intentions when you learn more about the experiment. I suppose I'll have to bear your anger and frustration until then." Taking Narendran's hand, he said, "Let's go."

"Wait," said Narendran. He bent down, lifted Vaijayanthi in his arms, and followed him out. The thugs tried to snatch her back, but Vanilarasu stopped them with a smirk. "Oh, no! Please, do not separate the royal couple."

He went into a different room, this one with a huge waterbed. Sitting on it, he pointed to a sofa and said, "Sit, Naren."

Narendran laid Vaijayanthi on the sofa and sat next to her. Then, to his surprise, he felt her silently drawing lines on his back with her fingernails. *She's been faking all along!* But he kept his face expressionless, and stared stonily at Vanilarasu.

"Did you know, Naren, that I am a trained doctor?"

"Yeah? I never saw you featured in *World This Week*. Why should I care about what you are? You could have introduced yourself as a temple beggar, and I would have believed you."

"What audacity! Your temerity has not been diminished at all, I see."

Narendran had more interesting things to occupy his thoughts than Vanilarasu's lecture. A situation had presented itself. Vaij was pretending to be unconscious. She couldn't suddenly spring to action in front of Vanilarasu. Slowly, Narendran eased back into a comfortable position, so that he was pressed against her youthful breasts. He tucked her hand between his thighs, and slowly caressed her cheek. His little finger traced her soft lips.

A thrill ran through her body. Naren could feel it—but she could not reveal anything. Smiling inwardly, he continued to look at Vanilarasu with a worried expression.

⚘ 10 ⚘

Vanilarasu stood at the window, staring into the darkness, as he spoke.

"My father was a neurologist, an extremely intelligent man. He stood first in all his classes in medical college. But when he was about to take over as the head of the hospital, there was political interference. A second-rate doctor with strong political connections was chosen for that prestigious position, and my father was ignored. This affected him deeply. He made me take up medicine too, and taught me everything he knew. He had discovered a cure for epilepsy. If he had been nominated, he would have won a Nobel Prize and become world-famous. But the government did nothing to support him. They even tried to submit his work under a different doctor's name, but my father refused to reveal his research. He saw that he had no future in India, and decided to move to America. There, a leading hospital honored him. The American Medical Council lent him its full support for his research. He taught me everything he discovered during those years. But the fact that he was unable to use his genius to help India hurt him deeply. He worried that because of the political corruption in India, brilliant minds like his would forever be lost to other nations.

"This weakened his heart. 'Vanilarasu, the blood in my body is Indian blood,' he told me. 'It flows only for India. The country must be rescued from ruin! Indian politicians are propagating communalism, racism and sectarianism. They are disrupting the unity of the nation and exploiting the divisions in society for their own enrichment. All this must change! India needs a young mind, one that is honest and free from corruption, which will lead her onto the right path. It is your duty to develop such a mind. All that I have taught you should be used for this goal alone.' This was his speech to me before he died."

Vanilarasu was choked with emotion. His eyes were wet with thoughts of his beloved father.

"I returned to India with this single purpose. I had been selected to carry out this noble mission, to develop the young mind that would become the future leader of India. I enlisted the help of science. I have done extensive research on the human brain: I know where thoughts originate, and where they are translated into action. There are a hundred billion cells in the brain. Their action and interaction creates waves. It is

33

these waves that activate the movements of the body. It is like the unified music of a philharmonic orchestra. If even one instrument is out of tune, the music loses its harmony. This effect can be seen in the mentally ill. And even if the music is harmonized—we prefer certain songs to others, don't we? Similarly, some brains are merely good, while others are extraordinary."

Narendran yawned.

"You might find all this boring, but it is, without doubt, extremely powerful knowledge. A mind that is musically inclined can be trained in the musical arts. It can then create wonders with that training. Similarly, if a mind is inclined towards politics, it can be trained to sharpen the qualities of leadership. Do you agree?"

Narendran gave a nod, and Vanilarasu's voice gathered more strength.

"That's exactly what I am doing! The leader of any nation has to face thousands of hurdles. A leader might make a good decision once, then follow it with a stupid one. This is the fault of the neurons in his brain. If only there were a leader who could make the right decision *always*—then all the problems in that nation could be solved. The country would see nothing but progress, progress, and more progress!

"And so, we come to Arthreyan. My computers are training his mind. They are teaching him about the historical decisions made by great Indian leaders, about all the problems that they have had to face. All this is being recorded in his memory. It is crucial that the process not be interrupted. I have rigged the machine with an alarm; if his head were to be removed from the headband, within two seconds, the alarm would sound, and alert the whole building."

"How can a computer train a human mind? Especially here, in some tiny hidden laboratory?" asked Narendran. His hand was slowly creeping into Vaijayanthi's cleavage when two sharp fingernails pinched him in the back.

"Ow!" Narendran yelled.

"Why are you shouting?" asked Vanilarasu.

34

"I didn't mean to. The hundred billion cells in my brain made me do it."

"You are mocking me, and my experiment. Long ago, the world mocked Socrates and Newton. Your mockery does not hurt me. You asked me how a computer can teach. Have you heard of laser beams? They can be made thinner that a strand of hair. They can be made small and precise enough to aim at each individual neuron in the brain. My research has proved that information—*any* information—can be permanently implanted into the brain cells using such lasers. I am attempting to implant new information in Arthreyan's brain without damaging the memories that he had already accumulated. I have code-named this experiment of mine 'Control Tower', since the brain is indeed where all control lies."

"Is Arthreyan your first guinea pig?"

"No. I have already experimented on two other individuals."

"And were those experiments successful?"

"Not entirely. My candidates were not… politically matured enough," he replied, avoiding Narendran's eyes.

"Can I see them?"

"I was going to show you myself. Leave your friend here, and come with me."

Narendran rose reluctantly and followed him. Vanilarasu opened a door and switched on the lights. A man who had been sleeping on a bed jumped up in terror and hid under the bed whispering, "Please! Don't shoot me!"

"He was greatly affected by the Mahatma's assassination," explained Vanilarasu. "He believes that someone will come to shoot him with a concealed pistol. Very unfortunately, he failed to learn anything else from his lessons on the Mahatma."

Vanilarasu shut the first door, and opened a second one. No sooner had they stepped inside than a man who had been hiding behind the door grabbed hold of Narendran, dragged him to the centre of the room, and pushed him to the floor. He tore at his clothes and was about to hit him with his shoes, when Narendran finally managed to throw him off.

Quickly, Vanilarasu pulled Narendran out of the room and relocked the door.

"That one... he was affected by the scenes he saw of the Assembly sessions."

Narendran gave Vanilarasu a hard look. "When both your earlier experiments have been such complete failures, how is it fair to subject Arthreyan to the same treatment?"

"No experiment is a success from the word 'go'. Were airplanes invented in a single day? Or penicillin, for that matter? No scientist can claim to be absolutely perfect, to have had every single study turn out a success. Arthreyan is a man of strong character. He has earned a good name with the public. He is next in line for power. He is capable of extending his power beyond this state, to govern the whole country. But his father is a crook and a thief, a man who uses politics only for personal gain. I was compelled to free Arthreyan from Surya Shekar's clutches, and develop him into a better human being. Now do you understand my intentions? Can you understand why my experiment must be allowed to proceed to completion? I have assembled an entire security team around me, to ensure there is no threat to the project from the military or the police.

"You are my guests tonight; you will sleep in separate rooms. Tomorrow, Narendran, you'll be released. You will visit Surya Shekar and tell him his son is undergoing an excellent training program. The experiment will last only three more days. To avoid any disturbances during this crucial time, I will continue to hold Vaijayanthi as an insurance against further meddling by Eagle Eye. My men will take good care of her. They won't do her any harm, I give you my word."

I'd like to see them try it, Narendran thought to himself. *She'll break their hip bones.*

⁄ 11 ⁄

Narendran sat on the bed, looking around him. It could have been a room in any cheap lodging house. It was 11:45 at night. The door was locked on the outside. Which part of the city was this? Was it a suburb, or were they within the city limits? Which room was Vaijayanthi locked in? As Narendran sat puzzling and cracking his knuckles, he heard faint footsteps outside the door. Becoming alert, he lay back down on the bed, and shut his eyes. The lock turned silently, and the door opened slowly.

Beneath his blanket, Narendran steeled himself. Even as he got ready to pounce on the person, he heard a whisper. "Naren…"

"Vaij! How did you…"

"Shhhh! When they gave me the gas, I didn't inhale it. I only pretended to faint. You took advantage of that, didn't you? Rascal!"

"Vaij, there's no time to fight about that now…"

"Fine, I'll spare you… till later. I flirted a bit with the man who carried me to my room. I know Vanilarasu assured you they wouldn't try anything, but that guy wasn't going to pass up the opportunity. All men are alike."

"Hey!"

"It only took two kicks to bring him down. I tied him up, stuffed a rag into his mouth, took his keys and came here."

"Where's Vanilarasu?"

"Sleeping in the front hall. He gets up pretty frequently to check on Arthreyan. We would need to open two doors to get to him—only one door to get to Arthreyan."

"But if Vanilarasu keeps on getting up to check, he'll notice if Arthreyan is missing. Vaij, come closer; I have an idea…"

"No, please tell me your idea from a safe distance. If I bring my ear closer, you'll aim your lips at my cheek."

"Can't you pick on a better time to fight with me?"

"Okay, tell me your idea."

Narendran told her.

"*Dhool*, that's great!" cried Vaijayanthi.

Narendran and Vaijayanthi tiptoed to the rooms where the two other patients were locked. They opened the first one, and tapped the man on the bed. He woke up with a start, but before he could scream, "Don't shoot," Narendran gave him a chop on the neck and the man fell faint in his arms.

"Sorry, brother! I'm only using you because you're already insane. It's nothing personal," he whispered, dragging him along the floor. He noticed that the man was young, in his early twenties, and had long hair. "I wonder if you're Jeevakan, the swami's disciple?"

They heard footsteps approaching. Narendran and Vaijayanthi pressed themselves against the dark wall as a security guard came down the passage, whistling. He swung his torchlight beam carelessly over the opposite wall, and then disappeared into the next room.

They dragged the man to the laboratory. They came to the chair in which Arthreyan was sitting, surrounded by beeping computers. Narendran stood puzzling over which wires to disconnect before removing the headband. Finally, with a muttered incantation—"Jai Hanuman!"—he simply lifted the band. To his surprise, it came off smoothly. Moving fast, he freed Arthreyan's hands and feet from their clamps, and laid him on the floor. Arthreyan was lost in some invisible world, his eyes wide open and glazed. Immediately, Narendran placed the unconscious man on the seat, and connected him to the headband. The whole operation was completed in less than two seconds. They dragged Arthreyan towards the main entrance, but as they reached it, the lights came on. Narendran crouched down.

Vanilarasu had come in to check on Arthreyan. Did he look closely enough to notice that it was a different body in the chair? The lights went off again, and Narendran hoped they had gotten away with it. But it was disturbing, and they could not afford to lose time.

"Quick!" he ordered, and they rushed to the door with Arthreyan. Suddenly Vaijayanthi grabbed his hand—and pointed to a man who had entered the room silently, and now stood staring down the barrel of his gun at them.

"And where do you think you're going?" he asked.

Narendran had just a second to plan his strategy. He threw Arthreyan at the man and simultaneously swung himself out of the way. The man wasn't expecting to be attacked with a human body. He fell flat on the floor and dropped his gun on the ground. Vaijayanthi picked it up in a flash. But at the commotion, someone had turned the lights back on. Even as Narendran stood wondering if all their plans had been foiled, Vaijayanthi pressed the trigger. *Phut! Phut! Phut!* One by one, she shot out the light bulbs, and there was darkness again.

Narendran and Vaijayanthi lifted Arthreyan and raced out of the laboratory. Another guard's torchlight followed them down the corridor. Vaijayanthi turned and fired another shot, this time hitting the guard in the leg. His torch flew from his hand and clicked off. Narendran opened a door; they were outside the building. He turned and bolted the door.

There was a bright moon out. By its light they located a garage and rushed towards it. Narendran opened the lock on the corrugated metal garage door with one of his skeleton keys. Inside, by a great stroke of luck, was an unlocked car with the keys still in the ignition. "Vaij, get in," he ordered. But when he turned the key, the engine sputtered and failed to start.

The door he had bolted was being pounded on hard from within. With a last jolt it flew open, and Vanilarasu and two others rushed out. Vaijayanthi, leaning out of the passenger door, squeezed off a shot which hit the ground near their feet.

The car came to life. Narendran put it into gear and peeled out of the garage. In the rearview mirror, he saw them rushing to another car. He guessed that Vanilarasu had stopped his henchmen from using their guns for fear of hitting Arthreyan.

Both cars flew down the road.

✗ 12 ✗

He had no idea where he was. This was all unfamiliar territory to Narendran. He didn't know which way to turn; he could have been going in circles, for all he knew. There were too many bends in the road for him to reach a good speed. The other car was gaining on them.

The road ended abruptly at a sugarcane field. Vanilarasu must have chosen this bungalow because of the huge fields surrounding it. There was no one around to be disturbed, even by the sound of the guns.

Without warning, Arthreyan sat up in the back seat and intoned in a loud voice, "*Jai Jawan, Jai Kissan!*"

They turned back and found a paved road. Narendran gathered some speed. He was doing sixty, then seventy, then eighty kilometres when Vaijayanthi yelled, "Naren!"

He saw immediately why she had screamed. In front of him the road was coming to an end right at the edge of a steep precipice! He pumped the brakes, but they were going too fast.

"Vaij, roll Arthreyan out of the car! You jump out too!"

"What about you, Naren?"

"Just do it!"

Vaijayanthi and Arthreyan tumbled out as the car neared the ridge. At the very last moment Narendran jumped out too. But he banged against the swinging car door, and as the car flew into the ravine, Naren bounced down the steep slope until he caught hold of a bush.

"Naren!" Vaijayanthi screamed, racing to the edge. Just behind her the second car drew up to a halt, and Vanilarasu ran up to them with two other men.

"Where's Arthreyan?" he demanded.

Arthreyan had rolled behind a boulder; Vaijayanthi realized that they had not seen him. "He went down with the car," she lied.

She threw her dupatta for Narendran to catch hold of, but Vanilarasu snatched it away. He approached Narendran and began kicking at his hands.

Narendran's knuckles were bleeding; if he lost his grip he would drop a hundred feet. The bush was slippery with dew and his grip was not strong enough. Vanilarasu's foot didn't help any.

Vaijayanthi saw that in their haste, the goons had forgotten their weapons. But first, Narendran had to be rescued.

As Vanilarasu lifted his foot for another kick, Narendran summoned all his courage, released the branches, and caught his right ankle with a firm grip. Vanilarasu lost his balance and fell. Struggling against Narendran's weight, he too began to fall over the edge. So Vaijayanthi grabbed at Vanilarasu's hand and pulled.

The goons also rushed to help. With their combined strength, both Vanilarasu and Narendran were pulled to safety. Once both were standing, Narendran gave Vanilarasu a mighty slap. He punched him solidly in the chest, grabbed his arms, and wrenched them behind his back.

"Now tell your men. If they make any trouble, you go over the cliff."

"You idiots, step back!" Vanilarasu screamed.

Using Vanilarasu as a shield, Narendran pushed the thugs over to the car. "Vaij, open the boot."

He crammed the two henchmen into it and slammed the door.

"Naren, don't, they might suffocate."

"No great loss. You start driving. I'll keep Vanilarasu down here."

It took just one karate chop for Vanilarasu to fall like a log. Narendran bound his hands and feet with a length of rope, threw him into the back of the car, and rolled him onto the floor. Then he sat Arthreyan down on the back seat. "Mr. Vanilarasu, would you be kind enough to guide me to the nearest police station?" asked Narendran from the front.

"Naren!" A beaming Surya Shekar grabbed hold of Narendran's hands. "If it weren't for you, I would have lost my son forever."

"What did the doctor have to say?" Narendran inquired, politely.

"If the experiment had continued for two more days, Arthreyan's brain would have been permanently turned to mush. He's undergoing treatment as we speak. Thank God we were able to save him in time. What about your reward?"

"Your driver, Samson, betrayed you without compunction. Why was that? Only because today's politicians freely and fearlessly betray all the trust the citizens place in them. This situation must change. All I ask is that you allow Arthreyan to grow up into a good and honest leader. That will be more than enough reward."

"Criminal cases have been filed against Vanilarasu and his men, Naren. I am worried my son's name will be dragged into this mess."

"Won't that be good publicity? Why should you object to the free advertising?"

"You know, you're right. The entire staff of Eagle Eye has helped me. I am so grateful—to all of you."

"Now it's your turn to help the nation!" Narendran said, shaking his hand.

Vaijayanthi's mother opened the door.

"Come in, Naren, she's getting ready for a party. Sit down, I'll get you some coffee."

As soon as she left, Narendran tiptoed to Vaijayanthi's room. He opened the door slowly and whistled.

"Which idiot's opening the door while I'm dressing?" snapped Vaijayanthi.

He stopped the whistle midway and whispered, "It's me—Naren!"

This back cover of a Subha novel in *Ullaasa Oonjal* invites the reader to come up with a story to fit the picture, and mail it in for possible publication.

அன்பான வாசகர்களுக்கு!

இந்த இதழ் தீபாவளி சிறப்பு மலராய் மலர்ந்துள்ளது... உங்களது அபிமான எழுத்தாளர் ராஜேஷ்குமாரின் முழு நாவல் இடம் பெற்றுள்ளது.

அத்துடன் தீபாவளி போனஸாக குறு நாவல் ஒன்றும் வெளியாகி உள்ளது...

தீபாவளியை குதூகலமாகக் கொண்டாட இப்போதே தயாராகிட்டீங்கன்னு நினைக் கிறேன்.

கொண்டாடுங்கள்... சந்தோஷ வெள ளத்தில் நீந்துங்கள்... இந்த சந்தோஷம் வாழ்நாள் முழுவதும் நீடிக்க எங்களது மனப்பூர்வமான நல்வாழ்த்துக்கள்.

மீண்டும் சந்திப்போம்!

அன்புடன்,
ஆர்.எம்.குமரவேல்,
ஆசிரியர்.

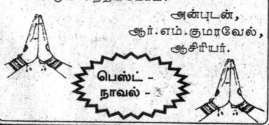

பெஸ்ட் - நாவல் -

LETTER FROM THE EDITOR

in the Deepavali 2007 issue of *Best Novel*

Dear Reader!

This issue is offered to you as a special flower garland for Deepavali. It carries a full-length novel by your favorite author, Rajesh Kumar, and some short stories as an added Deepavali gift.

I'm sure you are busy with preparations for Deepavali. Celebrate... Swim in the ocean of happiness... We wish for that happiness to last throughout your lifetime.

Until we will meet again!

With love,

R. M. Kumaravel

Editor, *Best Novel*

RAJESH KUMAR

Rajesh Kumar may well be the world's most prolific living writer of fiction. Having begun his writing career in 1968 with the publication of the story "Seventh Test Tube" in *Kalkandu* magazine, he has written and published more than 1,250 novels and over 2,000 short stories. The selection at virtually any newsstand in the state of Tamil Nadu will include several of his books; the back covers typically feature a ghostly, haloed image of the author's head, complete with a trademark asymmetrical hairstyle and oversize sunglasses. His shorter stories are frequently found in weekly magazines like *Kumudham* and *Anantha Vikatan*. In the mid-nineties, the boom years of Tamil pulp publishing, annual sales of his novels were in the millions of copies.

Commonly bad-mouthed by readers of more serious Tamil literature, not least because of the liberal use of English words and slang in his prose, his stories are nevertheless good fun, highly imaginative, and cover an astonishingly wide range of genres. Here, we have selected a sample of his more recent tales.

Rajesh Kumar lives in Coimbatore with his wife.

IDHAYA 2020

இதயா 2020 (2007)

SEVERAL BALDING SCIENTISTS reclined on fibreglass chairs facing a digital screen. Pictured on the screen was a very unusual sort of robot. Ten metallic hands with long, hooked fingers protruded from its body. Pranesh, the designer of the robot, was addressing the scientists in perfect English.

"You are looking at one of the assembler robots that I have created. This one is for industrial use, and can be employed in construction and assembly. It has two hundred arms. Suppose fifty sundry parts have to be assembled; this robot can complete the task in a few short minutes. It has been engineered totally electronically, and has no hydraulics or neutrolics in its design."

"Can we please see a demonstration?" asked one of the scientists.

"Sure," replied Pranesh, and led the ten scientists to the demo room. In the centre of the room stood the assembler robot, as majestic as a Roman soldier. The scientists gathered around it. Pranesh stood in their midst, and continued: "I have completely dismantled a car, just for this demo. The robot will begin to function when I give a command. It will reassemble the car in a mere fifteen minutes." He took a remote control out of his pocket, and, with a press of a button, brought the robot to life. It lifted an arm and its eyes turned green. Pranesh then pressed the start button and ordered, "Assemble it!"

The robot turned to the car parts. The cylinder plug, cylinder head, carburetor, fuel pump, and air-conditioner found their respective places, and the car became whole again in just fifteen minutes. "Would one of you kindly start the car? This room is large enough for you to have a test drive!"

A young scientist got into the car and drove it around the room, while the audience applauded loudly.

"Fantastic, Mr. Pranesh!"

"Thank you."

"How high have you priced it?"

"This is the most significant invention of the year 2020," said a foreign scientist. "We must have this for our country!" Another interrupted him hastily: "No, *my* nation should have it first!"

Pranesh laughed. "Please wait! You must see my other creation, Idhaya 2020. I will name my price for both of them later. Whichever nation agrees to my price will get both the robots."

"What is Idhaya 2020?" asked one of the scientists.

"It is a female robot."

"What? How can there be a gender difference among robots?"

"I'm sorry, you must understand that my Idhaya is different. She is not a mere machine, as you imagine."

"Then?"

"Come, meet her!" Pranesh led them to a new room, and showed them another robot, made from silicon.

"She is my Idhaya 2020, a 100% humanized robot. She can think for herself. Because of the bio-memory chip I have implanted in her, she can differentiate between good and bad, and make decisions. She can gossip with my wife, and has learned from her how to play the *veena*, how to draw *kolams*, and how to do beautiful embroidery. When my wife is busy in the kitchen, the robot helps her. And...."

"And?"

"She can provide good protection, as well."

"How is that?"

"She can shoot down a burglar. She can be a good friend and body-guard to an independent woman. She has strong human values. I began designing her in 2015 and completed her in 2020; this is my lifetime achievement."

"Can it really differentiate between good and bad?" inquired a scientist.

Pranesh laughed. "That is the specialty of my Idhaya 2020. Why don't you pose a few questions to her, and see for yourself?"

"Can it talk too?"

"Of course! It will speak like a woman."

One of the scientists stood in front of Idhaya. "Which is better for health, whisky or brandy?"

Idhaya opened her metallic mouth and spoke in a melodious female voice, enunciating every syllable. "Both are dangerous to health."

"Can AIDS be cured?"

"No."

"What about telling lies?"

"That is wrong."

"And stealing?"

"That is also immoral."

"Which is the crime that can never be forgiven?"

"Betrayal!"

The scientist who had been questioning her applauded. "Excellent, Idhaya! Can you give us a poem please?"

"Of course I can."

"Go on then!"

"Even with its death impending at dusk,
it sheds no tears at dawn.
Flower!
From its smile, learn about life,
oh Man!"

The scientist rushed to shake Pranesh's hand. "Superb, Mr. Pranesh! It is truly amazing what your bio-memory has achieved in Idhaya's silicon body. So how have you priced her?"

Pranesh smiled. "Please wait. You should witness yet another demonstration of Idhaya's abilities. I will quote the price after that."

"What is that?"

"There is a pistol hidden in Idhaya's body. She can shoot down any assailant."

"Is there a chance of her missing her target?"

"Never. I have hung a rubber ball in this room—there, a hundred feet away. When I command her to, she will shoot it."

"Please!" urged the scientists.

"Idhaya!" Pranesh said. "Shoot that rubber ball hanging from the string!"

"Your wish is my command," replied Idhaya, removing a pistol from her waist. Her arm rose slowly and took aim—but not at the rubber ball!

Even as the shocked scientists watched, the trigger was pulled and Pranesh went down in a pool of blood.

Idhaya turned to the scientists and calmly explained, "Pranesh taught me that I should shoot down anyone with evil thoughts. This man may have been a famous professor, a genius at creating excellent robots, a man of great intellect—but he had no human values! He had no idea of how

49

to treat a woman. His wife Vatsalya was a beautiful and intelligent lady. She was my friend since the day I was born. She taught me to play the veena, to draw kolams, and to do embroidery.

"Today, the beautiful Vatsalya is no more. She committed suicide last month. Pranesh drove her to it. He was a sadist! How can any man be jealous simply because his wife is beautiful? Well, he was. Vatsalya was abused every day. He insisted that she sleep naked in an air-conditioned room. She was of a fairer complexion than he. So, do you know what he did? He poured a can of red paint on her head.

"I could go on forever listing the forms of his abuse. Vatsalya could not take it anymore—and so she killed herself. I am not a human; I cannot shed tears for her death. Men like Pranesh may be geniuses, but they have no hearts, and so they should not be left alive in this world. I decided some time ago that I would kill him, but I wanted to do so with people like you as witnesses. Today, I was able to accomplish that. It is an embarrassment that *he* is the one who created me. I am ashamed, and so I would like to destroy myself, as well."

Having made this speech, Idhaya turned the pistol in slow motion towards her own temple, and pulled the trigger.

The scientists watched in shock as the silicon head shattered into tiny cells.

MATCHSTICK NUMBER ONE

முதல் தீக்குச்சி (2007)

by RAJESH KUMAR

⚡ 1 ⚡

"Good morning, Daddy!"

Saravana Perumal, the High Court judge, woke up to the sound of a gentle voice near his ear. He opened his eyes to see his daughter, Ajantha, standing by his bed smiling. He patted her cheek gently and replied, "Good morning." He looked at the window, and saw that it wasn't fully light outside yet. "What time is it?"

"Half past five."

"Is your mother awake?"

"She woke up at five."

"And your brother? Where's Kishore?"

"He woke up at four to go jogging. What time did you get to bed, Appa? Did you finish writing the judgment?" she asked, folding up her father's bedsheet.

"Oh... around one in the morning. And yes, I finished."

"So what *is* the judgment, Appa?"

Saravana Perumal laughed. "You'll come to know by eleven o'clock."

"Oh Appa, *please* tell me, I promise I won't tell anyone. I have to know! The girl who was murdered was a student at my college."

"So, you have an opinion on the case, do you?"

Even before Ajantha could reply, Amirtham, Saravana Perumal's wife, came in with his coffee—and *her* opinion. "Even a child could guess the verdict in this case. Three rich boys kidnap an innocent girl of eighteen, sexually abuse her, kill her and then dump her body in the Coovam River. Of course, those boys should be hanged to death! That's what you've written, isn't it?"

Saravana Perumal merely smiled and said, "Sorry, you'll have to put up with some suspense. You'll know only at eleven. I'm not allowed to reveal it before then, not even to you."

"Please don't feel sorry for those sinners just because they're young, and let them off with a life sentence. They should all be hanged!"

Saravana Perumal finished his coffee and rose. "Have you switched on the heater, Amirtham?"

"Yes, dear."

"I'll have a shower, and then take the judgment to Kapaleeswarar temple to be blessed."

"I'll come to the temple with you," said Amirtham.

"What? And leave Ajantha here alone?"

"Kishore will be back from his jog by the time you finish your shower."

"What if he goes to play tennis after his jog?"

"He won't. I asked him to come straight home."

"You have so much faith that your son will obey you? Don't be so sure, he's a useless fellow!"

"Don't scold my son so early in the morning, please."

"Why shouldn't I? I told him to continue his studies, and to go for a Master's of Computer Applications as soon as he finished his Bachelor's. Instead, he goes and starts some 'computer training centre' with his friend, and spends all his time playing tennis and cricket..."

"Enough! Come on, go have your shower...."

Saravana Perumal went off to the bathroom, Amirtham back to the kitchen, and Ajantha to the front gate to pick up the newspaper. She opened the first page, which read:

JUDGMENT TODAY

CHENNAI, June 27th—Last year, a college student named Damayanthi, 18, was allegedly abducted by Suresh, 24, Kamalakumar, 23, and Alphonse, 24. The girl was raped, murdered, and thrown into the river. The judgment on this case will be announced today. The case rocked the entire state of Tamil Nadu when it was first tried at the session court, and has now appeared in the High Court. Furthermore...

The telephone rang. Ajantha threw the paper down and picked up the receiver.

"Hello?"

"Is this Ajantha?" asked a male voice.

"Yes..."

"Ajantha, have you forgotten my voice? This is your uncle, Ananthakrishnan..."

"Oh! Good morning, Uncle!"

"Good morning. Is your father awake?"

"Yes, Uncle—he's in the shower."

"Is your mother around?"

"Yes..."

"Call her to the phone."

Ajantha put her hand over the mouthpiece and called to her mother. "Amma, Ananthakrishnan Uncle is on the line. He wants to speak to you!"

Amirtham came out wiping her wet hands.

"Namaskaram! This is Amirtham. He is in the bathroom..."

"That's okay, I'll pass on the information to you. I just met the marriage broker while I was on my morning walk. He told me that that boy, the one who owns the estate in Kunoor, is arriving from Germany today. He'll be staying in Chennai for a couple of days. Shall I arrange it with him to come meet Ajantha while he's in town?"

"Wonderful! Why don't you ask him to come over tomorrow, at ten in the morning. Who else will be coming with him?"

"Just his parents. The visit will be a mere formality. He already approved Ajantha, as soon as he saw her photo."

"You should come tomorrow, as well. It will make the evening more pleasant."

"Of course I will. I'm retired, after all. No use in sitting around the house."

Amirtham put down the phone and turned to Ajantha. "It must have been an auspicious moment when I opened my eyes this morning. Take a day off from college tomorrow. That Kunoor estate boy is coming to see you!"

Ajantha's eyes were brimming with dreams. She visualized the boy from the photograph that the marriage broker had shown her. *He was so handsome—like a film hero! I fell for him, just seeing his photo—what will happen when I see him in person? Should I dress in a silk sari tomorrow or stay casual?*

The doorbell interrupted her thoughts. Ajantha looked at the clock: 6:05. *Must be the maid.*

She opened the door to find a man of about 40, wearing a kurta and pajama, carrying a briefcase, a cloud of strong perfume hanging over him.

"Yes?" asked Ajantha.

"I need to see the judge."

"And you are?"

"My name is Pandarinathan. Your father knows me well."

"Is it important?"

"Yes. There's a matter I can discuss only with him."

"Please come in, have a seat. He's having his shower."

Pandarinathan walked into the hall as though he owned it, and made himself comfortable on the sofa. His eyes scanned the room.

Disturbed, Ajantha ran into the kitchen, where Amirtham was making idlis. "Amma..."

"Is that the maid? Ask her to sweep the compound first."

"No, it's not the maid. Someone called Pandarinathan is here to see Appa."

"Pandarinathan? I don't know any friend of your father's with a name like that. Where is he?"

"Sitting in the hall..."

Amirtham peeked through the kitchen curtain. She turned to Ajantha, confused. "I don't recognize him."

"I don't like his face."

"Is your Appa still in the shower?"

Even as she said this, Saravana Perumal emerged from the bathroom, looking fresh, with a towel around his waist.

⋇ 2 ⋇

The signboard read SANDAL OIL FACTORY: A GOVERNMENT UNDERTAKING. An old watchman stood at the gate. A young man of about thirty drew up on a bike.

"Is the chairman inside? I have to see him."

"Yes. You are from...?"

"The Central Excise Department."

"Please go in, sir," said the watchman, saluting, and the young man entered the compound.

The air was redolent with the scent of sandal. The workers had left for the evening, and the compound was empty and silent.

The young man handed a card to the peon in front of the chairman's room. After a moment, he waved him in. The air conditioning made the office as cold as a hill station.

"Good evening, sir," the young man greeted Krishnakant, the chairman. "I'm Navaneeth, from New Delhi—Scrutiny Officer for the Central Excise Department," he said, reaching out to shake the chairman's hand.

"Have a seat, Mr. Navaneeth. I wasn't expecting you—your department usually informs us before they send anyone."

Navaneeth smiled. "Quite correct sir. But I'm from the Scrutinizing Department. It's our job to make surprise visits."

The chairman leaned forward, his arms on the glass tabletop. "So, what's the purpose of this visit?" he asked.

"I'm following up on a letter I received."

"What letter?"

"See for yourself." Navaneeth took out an inland letter from his briefcase and handed it over to the chairman.

The letter read:

Dear Sir,

Greetings! This to bring to your attention some major looting going on at the Sathyamangalam sandal oil factory. This factory produces about a thousand litres of oil a day. Of this, about five hundred litres is top grade oil, which is kept separately in a godown about a kilometre away. Everything is fine until this oil reaches the godown. The looting happens there. I shall list the irregularities for you.

Irregularity No. 1: The actual stock of oil is never properly recorded in the ledger.

Irregularity No. 2: The top grade oil is smuggled out of the factory, and the rest is mixed with essence.

Irregularity No. 3: The chairman, Krishnakant, is exporting the top grade oil under false names to several foreign countries.

Irregularity No. 4: The chairman's nephew is also marketing some of this oil to local merchants in smaller bottles, and making millions in the process.

I am writing to you about these irregularities because it is the duty of an Indian citizen to expose them. I have done my duty. It is up to you to take action.

Sincerely,
A Heartbroken Soul

The chairman rolled his eyes. "Some jealous person writes a letter, and you come here treating that as evidence?"

"The department never ignores any information it receives. We have to verify the truth."

"So... what do you want me to do now?"

"What do you have to say in reply to these allegations?"

"It's rubbish, that's what I have to say!"

"I'll need to confirm that for myself, sir. Can I check the godown?"

"Can't you come back and do the checking tomorrow?"

"Sorry. I need to do it now."

Krishnakant thought for a moment, and then picked up the phone and dialed a number. "Hello, Magudapathy? Please come to my room at once."

He then turned back to Navaneeth. "I've been the chairman of this factory for the past eleven years. There has never been a single inquiry about me until now. People in the business even call me 'Mr. Clean'."

"I'm aware of that, sir. But, as I've said, it's our duty in the Scrutinizing Department to inquire into any allegation that comes to us..."

Magudapathy came into the room, a slim, gray-haired, bespectacled man of about forty. Pointing to Navaneeth, Krishnakant said, "He is from the Central Excise Scrutinizing Department. He wants to check the sandal oil in our godown. Take him there in the jeep and show him everything."

"Yes, sir."

"Mr. Navaneeth, you can ask Magudapathy for any details."

Navaneeth stood up. "Thank you very much for your kind cooperation, sir," and left with Magudapathy.

⚡ 3 ⚡

Ajantha ran up to Saravana Perumal as he came out of the bathroom.

"There's someone here to see you, Appa."

"Who is it?"

"His name is Pandarinathan. I don't like the look of him!"

"Ajantha, why didn't you tell me as soon as he came?" Saravana Perumal dressed hurriedly, and went into the hall.

"Welcome, Pandarinathan!"

"I'm sorry to trouble you so early in the morning, Judge sir."

"No trouble at all! Come; let's go to my office." With that he led the man up the stairs to his room on the first floor.

In the kitchen, Amirtham and Ajantha looked at each other, puzzled.

"What's going on, Amma? Appa seems so happy to see that Pandarinathan."

"Yes... and he almost never invites anyone up to his office."

"Amma, shall I go up and spy on what's happening?"

"I was just about to suggest it myself!"

As silently as she could, Ajantha crept up the stairs to the closed door. She knelt on the floor and peered through the keyhole. Inside, her father and Pandarinathan were laughing about something.

"So, how is S.G.?" asked Saravana Perumal.

Pandarinathan shrugged. "What about him? He's fine. He's got two cabinet ministers in his pocket, so every venture he makes is a success. It's only the issue of his son that's troubling him now."

"Well, he doesn't have to worry about that anymore."

"S.G. will only believe it when he sees a copy of the judgment."

"Here, I'll give you one. Show it to him. I've acquitted all three on the grounds that the crime has not been substantiated with sufficient evidence."

"Will the public accept this judgment?"

"Who cares? They'll argue that it's unfair for a couple of days, sure, but then they'll move on to another issue."

"S.G. will be grateful to you for the rest of his life."

Saravana Perumal chuckled. "Is that all I get? His thanks?"

Pandarinathan jumped. "Oh! I'm sorry, sir, I almost forgot." And with that, he opened the briefcase, which was packed full of bundles of currency notes.

"How much is here?"

"Five for now. The other five after you've read out the judgment."

"You have a copy of the judgment right there in your hands!"

"Still, that's not the same as you announcing it from your chair in front of a crowd of hundreds gathered in the court."

"Fine. Ask S.G. to come the court at eleven sharp; he can listen to it himself."

"Of course, he'll be there. I'll come along too."

Saravana Perumal took the currency bundles and hugged them to his heart.

"So, may I leave?"

"Yes, you may go. Be careful that the copy of the judgment does not leak out to the media."

"Certainly, sir."

Ajantha heard Pandarinathan approach the door, and took to her heels, hurrying silently down the stairs. She ran into the kitchen, breathless, and called, "Amma!"

"What? Why are you running like this? What happened? You're sweating and shivering..."

"Amma, let that man go first. Then I'll tell you what I heard."

Pandarinathan was now on his way down the stairs, and Amirtham peered out to look. She turned back to Ajantha. "You're right, Ajantha. He does have a look about him—as though he's capable of just about anything. Your Appa never encourages friends like this. Why now?"

"It's all because of money, Amma! He took a bribe from that man!"

"Don't worry. I'll take it from here."

Amirtham waited until Pandarinathan was past the front gate, then hurried up the stairs.

⚲ 4 ⚲

The godown was a kilometre away from the main road, tucked amidst thick portia trees. It was an old building, slightly done up and fenced in. Magudapathy stopped the jeep in front of a rusted gate. A head popped out of a square opening in the gate and swiftly pulled back to open it. The gates swung in with a loud screech. The jeep entered the compound and parked under a tree. Navaneeth got down from the jeep and looked around. There was no one else except the watchman shutting the gates.

"Mr. Magudapathy, why aren't there any workers around?"

"There are seventeen laborers working in this godown. But their shift finishes at half past five. It's past six now. The supervisor normally stays later, but he's on leave today, sir."

"I find it hard to believe that a place like this, storing crores worth of sandal oil, doesn't even have basic security."

"There's really no need for extra protection, sir. We have no reason to be afraid of theft in this area. Our neighbors are all farmers who mind their own business."

They entered the godown. A room on the right, the main office, was lit with a dim 40-watt bulb. Magudapathy extended a ring full of keys to the watchman.

"Kalimuthu, please open the office."

The watchman grabbed at the keys like a dog pouncing at a biscuit, and ran to the door.

"Are all your records up to date?" asked Navaneeth.

"Yes sir, they're in perfect order."

Kalimuthu opened the office door and switched on the tube lights. Magudapathy and Navaneeth entered the room. Magudapathy opened a drawer and pulled out a ledger, which he handed to Navaneeth. "This is the stock register."

"I don't have time to go through each page. How much oil is in stock at the moment?"

"Twenty-five thousand litres, sir."

"Can I check the stock?"

"Oh course, sir. Kalimuthu!"

The watchman went with the keys to open the storeroom, and Magudapathy and Navaneeth followed him. By now, it was completely dark outside.

"Sir, it's surprising that you would go through all this trouble just because of an anonymous letter."

Navaneeth laughed. "Whatever it may be, an anonymous letter or a complaint signed by a committee, it's the duty of our department to verify the truth in it."

"Well, you can go ahead and check, sir. There's no shortage in the stock."

"I'll be very happy if you're right. In that case, I'll record that everything is in order, leave to Coimbatore and take my flight back to Delhi."

The godown shutters were raised to reveal a room full of long shelves, lined with yellow plastic barrels of oil. Navaneeth looked at the shelves, pointed to a barrel at random, and said, "Open this!"

Magudapathy looked at Kalimuthu, who opened the barrel. Navaneeth took out a measuring ladle full of oil, and sniffed it. He then produced a quality testing instrument from his bag, and dropped a tiny drop of oil on the instrument's surface. It emitted a beeping noise, and a red light flashed.

Magudapathy's face darkened. Navaneeth smiled at him and asked, "What do you to have say about this?"

Magudapathy stayed silent.

"That's right, you can't give me any excuses. The quality tester doesn't lie. I need to know how much of the twenty-five thousand litres of sandal oil here is adulterated."

"I'll be happy to answer that, Navaneeth," came a voice from behind them. Navaneeth spun around. The chairman Krishnakant stood there smiling, one hand in his bulging coat pocket.

⚄ 5 ⚄

Amirtham and Ajantha stormed into Saravana Perumal's room. "Who is this Pandarinathan?" Amirtham demanded, her voice loud and challenging.

"Why are you raising your voice at me?"

"It's my duty to speak up when you're behaving strangely."

"What do you mean?"

"Appa," Ajantha cut in, "you always said that justice and the law were your two eyes. So tell us, how come you're suddenly ready to sell your own eyes?"

"What are you talking about?"

"Don't try to hide it from me Appa. I saw everything. You accepted money from Pandarinathan and gave him a copy of the judgment."

Saravana Perumal glared at his daughter angrily. "And where were you? How did you see that?"

"Through the keyhole."

"So, you've started spying on me now, have you?"

"Spying on someone is nothing compared to what you've done! How long has this sort of thing been going on?"

"It's not what you think. I'm not selling anything. I'm only making a small adjustment."

"And the price for that 'small adjustment' is five lakhs! Am I correct?"

Saravana Perumal sighed and said, "Now listen to me carefully. I am going to retire in another two years. I wanted to make some money by then."

"And for that you will change your judgment?"

"This judgment is fair!"

"You call this fair? You've acquitted three criminals who raped and murdered an eighteen-year-old girl. That's fair? How can you live with yourself?"

Saravana Perumal snorted. "A judge cannot make his judgment based on sensationalized media reports. It's my duty to study the facts."

Amirtham cut him short. "And you found out that those scoundrels did not rape or murder the girl?"

"I found out that there were no eyewitnesses. Not while the girl was kidnapped, raped or murdered. Isn't there a real chance those three could be innocent?"

"Then who killed the girl?"

"I have said in my statement that the police should make efforts to find the real culprit."

"If you really believe this judgment is correct, why accept money for it?"

"Ajantha, this is none of your business. You're too young to understand. Now get out of here and let me speak to your mother."

She opened her mouth to speak, but Saravana Perumal pointed forcefully at the door. Ajantha left, and Amirtham turned to her husband with tears in her eyes.

"What is all this?"

"An easy way to make a lot of money. I need to marry my daughter and son off; we wanted to buy that bungalow in Adyar..."

"Please, stop! I am content with what we have. You're in a respectable, prestigious position now. Imagine how terrible it would be, if it came out that you accepted a bribe!"

"Nothing will come out. Amirtham, there is corruption everywhere you look these days. It's no longer considered a crime to give or accept a bribe. Every person names his price, depending on his status. So don't trouble yourself too much about this, and try to make Ajantha also understand. Please don't say anything more. I'm hungry. Go get my breakfast ready."

Realizing that further talk would only infuriate him, Amirtham quietly went downstairs.

✎ 6 ✎

Navaneeth smiled at the chairman.

"Welcome, sir. Nice of you to make things easy for me by coming here yourself. So tell me: how much of your stock is adulterated?"

"Right now, about 70%."

Navaneeth whistled. "You're a very bold man."

"The water's way over my head already. What does it matter now if I'm a few inches or a whole foot under?"

"Since you're being so frank, I think it's time I stopped this 'inspector' routine and came to the point."

Krishnakant raised his eyebrows. "What do you mean?"

"I am not really from the Central Excise Department."

"What? Then… who are you?"

"Do you know Harikumar, the Minister of Human Resources Development?"

"Yes."

"I'm his *benami*. He keeps his money under my name."

"And that anonymous letter?"

"I wrote it myself. But Harikumar is the one who found you out and planned this whole thing. He could easily have exposed you to the police. Instead he thought he could take a cut of the loot."

Krishnakant thought for moment and then asked, "How can I trust that you're really Harikumar's man?"

Navaneeth chuckled, and took a mobile phone from his pocket. "I'll call up the minister's private number. Do you want to speak to him yourself?"

Krishnakant reached for the phone. First he dialed the Delhi STD code and then the number that Navaneeth called out. The call was received almost on the first ring.

Krishnakant asked in English, "Is this the Ministry of Human Resources Development?"

"Yes."

"Can I please speak to the Minister? This is the chairman of the Tamil Nadu Sandal Oil Board speaking."

A moment later, the Minister came on the line, speaking in English with a strong Hindi accent. "Mr. Krishnakant! I suppose my trusted friend Navaneeth has told you about everything already. I hope you find our arrangement agreeable?"

"Yes, sir."

"Good. From now on, please consult with Navaneeth for all your planning. You must be very careful that nothing is ever traced back to you. There is one more thing we need from you, and it will have to be done tonight; Navaneeth will tell you the rest. I'll be coming to Chennai next week. I'll be there for five days. We'll meet then."

The minister disconnected the call and Krishnakant returned the mobile to Navaneeth.

"What do you want me to do next?"

Navaneeth replied with a smile. "Officers from the Central Excise Department are coming to investigate your godown. There is a good chance you'll be exposed."

"Why should I worry when I have the minister by my side?"

"The minister's not going to save you this time."

"Then who will?"

"Agnidevan!"

"Who?"

"The Lord of Fire. This godown must be destroyed in an 'accidental' fire before the investigation takes place. Crores worth of sandal oil, lost in a fire caused by electrical error."

Krishnakant looked at Navaneeth, shocked. "Is there no other way for me to escape?"

"No. The investigative officer is an example of that rare type whose loyalty can actually be bought by a government salary! He won't be corrupted, either by money or threat."

"When do you expect them to come?"

"They could come any moment. So you better get ready for the fire right away."

Krishnakant rubbed his brow anxiously and then turned to Magudapathy. "Can you manage it tonight?"

"Of course, sir."

"Hide the unadulterated stock first."

Magudapathy answered with a smile, "You don't have to tell me that, sir."

�ം 7 ✎

It was half past ten in the morning. Saravana Perumal was getting ready to leave for the court. As he was locking the copy of the judgment in his briefcase he saw a shadow at the door and looked up. It was his son, Kishore, six feet tall, with a strong body. Today his face was hard.

"Appa, are you leaving for court?"

"Mm-hmm."

"And you're going to read out a sentence for which you've taken a bribe?"

"So, your mother told you."

"Appa… When did you change?"

"Kishore, the law is an artifact of man. It's not the unbreakable word of God. Since I was a student at Law College, I've been studying the nuances of the law. I know whose slave it can be, and whose master; whom it fears, and whom it will threaten."

Kishore looked at him disgustedly. "Appa, each word you utter feels like acid to my ears. If a judge like you can subvert justice, it bodes ill for the future of the nation."

"Kishore, your fears for the future are baseless. It's been sixty years since our country became independent. In those sixty years, has even one politician or minister been imprisoned for corruption? Never! Why? Because the law is afraid to lay even a finger on them. All over India you have politicians who take bribes, possess wealth beyond their official income, employ goons to knock off their enemies, shift party allegiances to retain power, and ignore the electorate that has given them their mandate. Not one of them has ever been apprehended by the law. Because the law is just a pet dog for them."

"Appa, let the politicians and ministers be corrupt. Why do you have to join them?"

"I have not joined that list. I have different objectives."

"If you acquit those three butchers, won't that encourage more such crimes?"

"Watch and see how it ends up."

"Appa!"

Saravana Perumal looked at his wrist watch. "I don't have the time to chit-chat with you. I have to be in the court by eleven." He strode out of the room, past Amirtham and Ajantha, who stood watching him silently, and went out through the portico to his car. Krishnan, the driver, opened the door and Saravana Perumal got in.

Kishore raged into the hall where Amirtham and Ajantha were standing.

"What did Appa say?"

"He gave me a long lecture trying to justify what he's done."

"How could he have changed so much?"

"Money, of course. When he saw those lakhs of rupees stacked up in that case, his mind fell into the gutter."

"How can we bring our father back?" asked a worried Ajantha.

"We have to, somehow. Or else he will no longer be a father to us; he'll just be a demon."

"But *Anna*, we cannot do anything that will sully Appa's name."

"No. We'll have to be very secretive. No one will know about it."

"What's your plan?"

Kishore began to explain. "The first step is..."

⚡ 8 ⚡

Magudapathy brought the Matador van to a halt in front of the gates of the sandal oil godown, and called out, "Kalimuthu!"

The watchman came running. "Sir?"

"Is anyone there in the godown?"

"No sir."

"There are four cans of petrol in the van. Take them in."

The watchman nodded, opened the side door of the van, and removed the four cans one by one. Magudapathy got out, took a mobile from his chest pocket, switched it alive, and dialed.

"Hello?" said Krishnakant's voice.

"Sir, Magudapathy, I've got the petrol."

"How many litres?"

"Forty."

"Will that be enough?"

"Of course, sir. This is an oil godown. We just have to sprinkle the petrol all over and the whole place will be burnt to ashes by dawn. We have to make sure no one reports it to the fire department too early."

"Who'll be awake to watch the fireworks, so late at night? Is the watchman there?"

"Of course. He'll be facing the investigation as the first witness."

"Please make sure he's got his story straight for the police tomorrow."

"I'm on it, sir."

"Be careful, Magudapathy. If we're caught, we'll all end up in the cooler."

"Don't worry, sir. When I'm up to mischief, my mind works extra sharp."

"Good. Call me once you're done."

Magudapathy switched off his mobile and entered the compound. The watchman was standing besides the petrol cans. "All set, Kalimuthu? You know your lines?"

"Yes, sir. After I set the fire, I walk a kilometre down the road to the next sandal oil factory and ask for help. If they ask me why I didn't call from here, I say the telephone was out of order. My story for the police is that the main electrical switchboard suddenly exploded, and the sparks set the place ablaze. I didn't have time to get to the fire extinguisher. I tried calling the fire service but the phone was out."

Magudapathy smiled. "Perfect!" he said. "Don't change a word."

"Don't worry, sir. I'll repeat it like a parrot."

"Good. Now get to work."

Kalimuthu sprinkled can after can of petrol all through the godown. Within fifteen minutes the stench of petrol fumes had overpowered the perfume of sandal.

"Kalimuthu, I'm off. Throw the match as soon as I'm gone."

"Yes, sir."

Kalimuthu waited for the tail lights of the van to disappear before striking the match and flinging it onto a stack of petrol-soaked burlap sacks.

9

The crowd around the courthouse was larger than usual. Political party cadres, news media reporters, the general public...

At eleven sharp, Saravana Perumal took his seat. He waited a moment for the murmuring of the audience to subside before he began reading out the judgment.

"Suresh, aged 24, Kamalakumar, aged 23, and Alphonse, aged 24, are accused of raping and murdering Damayanthi, a college student. Though the prosecution did bring forth their witnesses, their statements are not sufficient proof that the accused are guilty. Furthermore, there was not a single eyewitness. The medical report does not conclusively prove sexual molestation."

There was a pin-drop silence in the court. Saravana Perumal continued.

"There is insufficient evidence to back up the claim of the police department that the accused are guilty. This court will hereby acquit the accused of the said crime."

As Saravana Perumal bent to sign the statement, the political cadres gave a loud cheer, and a few ran over to hug the three boys and celebrate. The young men were garlanded and lifted high in air.

"Long live the judge!"

"Long live justice!"

Saravana Perumal had retired to his chambers, when his phone rang. It was Pandarinathan on line.

"Thank you very much, sir!"

Saravana Perumal laughed. "You don't need to thank me. Those youngsters still have their whole lives ahead of them. The prosecution failed to come up with sufficient proof. The judgment would have been the same even if this case had come under some other judge's jurisdiction."

"S.G. sends his personal thanks, too. I shall come over to your house this evening."

"No, let's not meet at my house. There's a small marital dispute in progress."

"Do you want to come over to S.G.'s place?"

"Sure, I don't mind. When should I come?"

"After seven in the evening. You can take the Nasik coupons with you when you go back."

"What if I'm seen?"

"Come on, nobody's going to see you."

"No, Pandarinathan. If some investigative journalists from *Nakeeran* or *Junior Vikatan* happen to see me there, they'll ruin my name. Don't you remember what happened to Judge Sambamurthy two years back?"

"Of course."

"So?"

"Alright. Early tomorrow morning, S.G. will come and meet you while you're on your walk."

"Where?"

"New Boag Road."

"Okay." Saravana Perumal had just finished the call when his driver entered the chamber.

"Aiya!"

"What is it, Krishnan?"

"I found this envelope on the front seat of the car."

Saravana Perumal opened the envelope, took out a letter, and began to read.

Dear Judge S.P.,

My pen refuses to write your name in full. Where else but in India would Lady Justice be made to prostitute herself for money? I do not like your judgment. Therefore I think you do not deserve to live. Get a big photo of yours ready to be garlanded.

Desperately seeking to abolish injustice,
Matchstick Number One

"Sergeant!" called Saravana Perumal, sounding worried.

The sergeant on guard ran in with his bayonet. "Yes, aiya?"

"Do not allow anyone to enter my room."

"Yes, aiya."

He turned to the driver. "Krishnan, wait in the car. I'll come in half an hour."

Saravana Perumal rang up the police commissioner. "I've been threatened with murder by someone displeased with a judgment I gave this morning. You have to take action."

"How did the threat come?"

"By letter."

"Where are you now?"

"In my chambers."

"Stay right there. I'll be there in ten minutes."

⚡ 10 ⚡

The fire at the sandal oil godown blazed till dawn. A crowd of villagers had gathered near the burnt-out building. Two fire engines were busy spraying water on the smoking embers. The chairman, the police inspector, and the district collector stood huddled to one side in hushed conversation.

"The watchman says there was an explosion in the main electrical board," said the collector.

"Yes, sir," nodded Krishnakant.

"Sandal oil is expensive stuff. The stock here was worth crores of rupees. Krishnakant, you should have had the wiring of the godown checked."

"I have a routine monthly check done."

"Then, how did this happen?"

"Accidents can occur at any time, no matter what precautions I take. I have no control over unfortunate events like this."

"The watchman was alone here during the accident, wasn't he?"

"Yes, sir."

"How many years has he been working here?"

"More than eleven years, sir."

"Could he have been bought over by subversive elements?"

"Never! He's a loyal man."

"Mr. Krishnakant, you must be aware that sandal oil does not burn like other oils. I suspect arson."

Krishnakant wore a shocked expression.

"If we can take the watchman into custody and question him, I am sure we can find out the truth," said the police official.

At a nod from the collector, the policeman walked off towards the watchman, while Krishnakant looked on anxiously.

"How much oil did you have in stock?" the collector continued.

"Twenty-five thousand litres."

"And you couldn't save a single barrel?"

"In spite of their best efforts, the fire service couldn't recover anything."

By now the media had arrived on the scene and began bombarding them with questions.

"Is this the work of a foreign hand?"

"It's too early to say."

"But the rumor is..."

"Please. You have to wait for the investigations to be completed!"

Krishnakant felt someone tap his shoulder. He turned around to see a smartly-dressed young man of around thirty with neat, cropped hair and a mustache. Krishnakant raised his eyebrows.

"I need to speak with you in private, please," said the man in a low voice.

"What is it?"

"Not here. Could we walk over there, please?"

Krishnakant could hear the quiet command in the tone and went along.

Once they had put some distance between themselves and the crowd, the man said, "My name is Sundarapandian. I saw your employee, Magudapathy, buying four cans of petrol at a bunk on Banari High Road. This morning your godown is burnt to the ground. There must be some connection, sir!"

Krishnakant could only stare.

Saravana Perumal came home for lunch. Kishore was in his room and Ajantha and Amirtham were in the hall. A thick silence hung over the house. As Saravana Perumal settled into the sofa, Amirtham asked him, "I heard you got a threatening letter. Who was it from?"

"Someone calling himself 'Matchstick Number One.' Let him keep writing letters. Who cares? Just some dud firecracker, a dog chasing a car and barking."

"All these years, you've never had a black mark on your record."

"Look here, Amirtham. When we make bold moves, they are bound to get some reactions. But there's no need to take those too seriously."

"We are not able to take this so casually, Appa," said Ajantha.

"Will you two cut it out? I came home for my lunch, not to hear your preaching," he snapped, going to the dining table. "If I hear one more word, I'm leaving!"

"Amma, why are you starving Appa?" said Kishore, walking in. "He's tired after a long day of judging. Serve him his lunch."

Saravana Perumal glared at him. Kishore smiled and went on: "Why are you looking at me like that, Appa? We've got a special menu for you today. Currency *kootu*, currency *poriyal*, currency *avial*, currency *sambar*. I'm sure you'll love it!"

"Joker, eh? Very funny! Nothing can be achieved without currency in this *Kali Yuga*. Today you're idealistic, but one day you'll realize the importance of money."

Amirtham began serving the food, but Kishore butted in again. "Wait, Amma. We should tell Appa what we did. Then he can finish lecturing us and eat in peace."

Saravana Perumal looked up. "What is it you've done?"

"Oh, nothing much. We just took the five lakhs that Pandarinathan gave you this morning out of your cupboard with the spare key. We distributed one lakh to Kapaleeswarar Temple, one lakh to Ashtalakshmi Temple, one lakh to Vadapalani Temple and gave the rest to Udhavum Karangal Orphanage. Now that dirty money has been purified!"

"*Deyyyyy!*" shouted Saravana Perumal, and lunged for Kishore's throat. Ajantha jumped between them.

"Appa, there's no point getting angry with us. You earned the money unethically, so we tried spending it ethically. And if you ever bring tainted money into this house again, we'll do the same thing."

Saravana Perumal now turned to Amirtham. "Did you put them up to this?"

"Oh no! I don't want to take exclusive credit for it. All three of us had a role to play."

"How did you have the heart to waste five lakhs on temples and orphanages?"

"What a question, Appa! If you'd earned that five lakhs through hard work, maybe we would have thought twice about it. But after all, it was easy money!"

Saravana Perumal, speechless with rage, shoved his way past them and went up to his office.

⚔ 12 ⚔

"How do you know Magudapathy?" Krishnakant asked, worried.

"He lives one street over from mine," said Sundarapandian.

"Why were you at the petrol bunk last night?"

"I wasn't at the bunk, sir. I had gone to visit a relative who lives near the bunk. That was when I saw him."

"He could have been buying petrol for some other reason."

"At midnight?" asked Sundarapandian.

"You've got it all wrong. There's no connection between the fire at the godown and his buying petrol."

"Then let's tell the police, and see if *they* think there's a link."

"Are you trying to blackmail me?"

"I don't know anything about blackmail; or whitemail either, for that matter. I just wanted to inform you about what I saw. If you're calling this is blackmail, then maybe I *should* go straight to the police!"

Krishnakant grabbed Sundarapandian's hand. "Please, wait..."

"What?"

"We need to talk. Later."

"Later? When?"

"Come to my house."

"I don't know where you live."

"17, Durga Nagar..."

"Okay. I'll come."

"Please don't leak your story about the petrol."

"Whether the petrol story leaks or doesn't leak will depend on how you treat me. But where is Magudapathy?"

"At home."

"I suppose he'll show up a little later, pretending he knows nothing. Smart chap." With that, Sundarapandian left.

Krishnakant went back to the collector, who was talking to a forensic officer.

"It'll be easy to tell if it was arson or not," the forensic officer was saying. "The ash can be chemically tested for the presence of petrol or kerosene. That would push the carbon level up about three times higher. If it was really an accidental fire, the carbon level will be very low."

Krishnakant's thoughts were racing. He hadn't known such tests existed. Now he had to find a way to shut Sundarapandian up, or else Magudapathy would be in deep trouble.

✗ 13 ✗

The telephone woke Saravana Perumal up from his siesta.

"Yes? Saravana Perumal here..."

It was the police commissioner. "Sir, there's been an unexpected development. The three men you acquitted this morning have been kidnapped."

"What?"

"In all three houses, a hand-lettered poster was left on the walls."

"What did the poster say?"

"'Lady Justice has lost her voice. We'd like to bring her to the intensive care ward for treatment. For that, we need the blood of Suresh, Kamalakumar and Alphonse. So we're taking them. Signed, Matchstick Number One.'"

"That threatening letter I got had the same signature, sir."

"Perhaps it's the name of a new subversive group. They must be angry with you, too. You should be careful, both at home and in the courtroom."

"This isn't the first time I've been in a situation like this. I'm not too worried. I'm sure you can put an end to this group. Deploy one of your special squads."

"We've already done that. We're determined to find the three young men within the next twelve hours."

"Yes, you must. Or else it will look like a high court judgment has no power."

As Saravana Perumal put down the receiver, Ajantha called from the portico, "Appa, come quick!"

He rushed to the portico. On the opposite wall were five posters, hand-lettered in red ink.

SARAVANA PERUMAL! WHO DID YOU SELL YOUR SOUL TO?
HOW COULD YOU DISHONOR LADY JUSTICE JUST FOR NASIK PAPER?
YOU HAVE A WIFE AND A YOUNG DAUGHTER.
GO LEARN FROM THEM WHAT HONOR REALLY IS.
JUDGE, YOU HAVE TO CLEAN UP YOUR ACT...
OR YOU'LL SUFFER MARUKAAL MARUKAI!

Saravana Perumal's face darkened. But he hid his worry behind a smile and said, "This is just the work of some jobless imbeciles. We should learn to ignore the barking of stray dogs."

"Appa, a dog only barks at someone who has done something wrong," said Ajantha. "Your wrongdoing has been exposed. People today are not silent goats. They are aware of what goes on around them."

Saravana Perumal beckoned the security guard. "Did you see who put up those posters? Why didn't you stop them? You've been here this whole time!"

"Sir, I've had an upset stomach since morning. The posters must have been put up while I was in the toilet."

"Pull them down!"

"Yes, sir."

Ajantha turned to her father. "Go ahead, Appa, tear down the posters. But when will you clean up your heart?"

Saravana Perumal smiled at her and said patiently, "You go and help your mother in the kitchen. This isn't your business. Go dream about the man from Germany who is coming tomorrow at ten in the morning to meet you. Don't worry yourself about anything else."

"Appa..."

"What?"

"I don't want to get married now."

"Why not?"

"There's an uneasiness in my heart."

"All that will only last a couple of days. You'll be fine soon."

Amirtham came in, asking, "How will she be fine? How can she marry in peace when she's in so much torment?"

Saravana Perumal raised his left forefinger at her, "Everything in this house should be as per my wish. If you keep going around with long faces, I will soon lose my temper. Even my temper has a limit, you know?" He looked at them long and hard, "This is your last chance. Or I will walk out of this room forever!"

The wife and daughter were frozen with shock. They stood, still as statues, watching Saravana Perumal walk back into the house as if nothing had happened.

⚡ 14 ⚡

Durga Nagar.

Sundarapandian had located the bungalow and was at the gates at five in evening. The gate was unlocked. He gently pushed it open. It swung back noiselessly. He peered in and saw Krishnakant seated on the lawn, signaling him to come in. As Sundarapandian entered the compound, the Doberman tied to the portico pillar began barking. Aside from that, the bungalow was completely silent. He stood in front of Krishnakant, who pointed to a plastic chair in front of him. He sat down. After looking at him for a few moments, Krishnakant said, "I'll come straight to the point. How much do you want?"

"What?"

"Money!"

"For what?"

"So that you won't leak the story about Magudapathy and the petrol."

"As if you don't know the going rate!" laughed Sundarapandian.

"I'll give you a lakh of rupees. Take it and leave town."

"Nope, too little! A lakh today is what a thousand was a few years ago."

"Okay, you name your price."

"I'm not sure you'll like it."

"Ask!"

"Fifty lakhs."

Krishnakant, shocked, took off his spectacles. "This is daylight robbery!"

"I'm just asking for a cut of what you've already robbed."

"It's not like you think! The most I can offer is two lakhs."

"That's forty-eight lakhs short. Not enough. Try another deal." Just as Sundarapandian finished saying this, he heard footsteps behind him. He turned around to see Magudapathy and Navaneeth coming towards them. Sundarapandian rose hesitantly.

"Sit down, young man!" Krishnakant ordered. "They're here to help us."

Magudapathy and Navaneeth stood on either side of him and pressed him back to the chair.

"So what was that rate you wanted? Fifty lakhs? Why not make it a crore? We spent years looting that amount. You think you're entitled to that much just because you happened to witness a petrol purchase? Does that really seem fair to you?" asked Navaneeth.

Sundarapandian gathered his courage and asked, "So how much are you willing to give me?"

"We're not giving you anything, Sundarapandian."

"But he agreed to give me two lakhs!"

"That offer has expired."

"I'll go to the police!"

"You'll have to be alive to get there."

Magudapathy produced an ugly knife from his pocket, and Navaneeth brought out a pistol from his.

⁄ 15 ⁄

The minister was yelling at the police officials in broken English and coarse Tamil.

"I'm ashamed to call myself a minister. It's been ten days since those young men were kidnapped, and you've got no leads. What kind of police work is this?"

The Deputy General of Police spoke hesitantly. "Sir, we've tried everything. We have no clue about who kidnapped them, or how."

"So will you drop the case?"

"No, sir."

"Then?"

The police officials stood silent. The minister stood up, hitched up his *veshti*, and began pacing. "Nair, I have a thought."

"Tell me, sir."

"Some subversive group has kidnapped those three as a protest against the judgment. So they must have been present in court when the judgment was read out."

"Could be, sir."

"The court proceedings that day were videotaped by all the news channels. Why don't you check those tapes frame by frame for a clue?"

"Good idea, sir. I hadn't thought of it."

"Nair, it's not enough just to dress up in your khaki uniform and pin your medals on your chest. You must also learn to think."

"Sorry, sir..."

"What good is your 'Sorry'? Remember that these three are no ordinary young men. They are the sons of the industrialists who are the pillars of the ruling party... *my* party. If anything were to happen to them, the government would be toppled."

"Don't you worry, sir. We will take care of everything from here."

"Go study every video made that day."

Once the police officials left, the minister took out his mobile and dialed a number. "Pandarinathan? I don't want to depend solely on the police. I want you to send our men out on the hunt for a clue, as well. Make sure the police don't come to know of our efforts."

"Yes sir. I'll come back with some good news in twenty-four hours time."

⁄ 16 ⁄

Saravana Perumal welcomed the groom's party at the portico and took them in. The groom's parents entered, hand in hand, and the shy, handsome groom followed in his sky-blue suit.

"We wanted to be here at ten sharp. But there was a heavy traffic jam on Mount Road and we had to move inch by inch. We're sorry we're half an hour late."

"No matter. The auspicious time today extends until noon," said Saravana Perumal. Drawing Kishore close, he continued, "This is my son, Kishore. He runs a computer coaching centre."

Saravana Perumal seated everyone in the hall, excused himself, and went to Ajantha's room. Amirtham and Ajantha were sitting on the bed surrounded by jewel boxes.

"What's the problem?" he asked.

"Your daughter is refusing to wear any jewels."

"Why?"

"Ask her yourself."

"Ajantha, why won't you wear any jewels? They have come to see you!"

"Have they come to see me or my jewels?" asked Ajantha.

"You are taking your anger at me out on the groom."

"I'm doing no such thing. I want to look simple, not decked out in gold."

"Fine. Do as you please," he grumbled, and returned to the hall where the groom's party was discussing modern computers with Kishore.

The groom's mother asked Saravana Perumal, "Is my daughter-in-law ready to see us? Tell her there's no need for very heavy make-up and all that. Ask her to remain casual."

"That's exactly what she's insisting on to her mother in there."

The telephone rang in the next room.

Kishore rose up. "I'll take the call."

He hurried to answer the persistent phone.

"Hello?"

"Is this Judge Saravana Perumal?"

"No, this is his son."

"Ask that jerk to come to the phone."

"Hey! You're disrespecting my father!"

"I don't waste my respect on people who sell their consciences for money."

"*Dey!*"

"Oh, so you're getting angry? Fine, I'll tell you what I had to tell him. Go in and tell the groom that this wedding will not take place."

"Why not?"

"We don't want the daughter of a man who frees rapists to be happily married."

"Who cares what you want?"

"We are the Warriors of Justice. Anyone who crosses us deserves to die!"

Kishore stood speechless. Saravana Perumal touched his shoulder. "Who is it?" he asked, taking the receiver. But the line had been cut.

"Who was that?" he asked again.

"Not now Appa. I will tell you later."

"Was it a threatening call?"

"Yes."

"Did he say I would be killed?"

"No Appa."

"Then?"

"He said Ajantha's wedding should be called off."

"And if it's not?"

"None of us will be spared."

Saravana Perumal laughed. "Oh, that. I got a call just like that last night."

"So what do you think? Should we go ahead with the wedding?"

"Kishore, we cannot live in fear of every threat. Anyway, Ajantha's wedding is three months away. By then the police will have apprehended these subversives."

◢ 17 ◢

Suresh, Kamalakumar and Alphonse heard the door creak open, and they sat up—with some difficulty, for their hands and feet were bound in iron chains. They could see a man silhouetted in the torch light.

"Get up!" he ordered. They struggled to their feet.

"Come with me."

Their iron chains grated on the floor as they followed him out. The place looked like an old ruined bungalow. Bats flew around in the semi-darkness.

"Hurry up!" barked the man with the electric torch, herding them into the open.

Dark openness. There was no light except for the stars and a slim moon. The cool breeze made the captives shiver. Suddenly the man turned around and said, "Sit down!"

Suresh, Kamalakumar and Alphonse looked at each other apprehensively, and sat. When their eyes became accustomed to the darkness, they could make out several men standing around them.

Who were they?

The man with the torch began to speak.

"Suresh, Kamalakumar and Alphonse, this is a court. An open-air court! A judge bound by law and ethics will now try your case. His conscience will be his only guide. When the judge comes and takes his seat on that mound of earth, your trial will begin."

The torch was switched off. The three young men were left staring at the mound in trepidation. Five minutes passed. Then a figure emerged from the crowd and sat on the mound.

"Let the trial begin!" he said.

One man stepped up to the mound and said, "Your honor! The three young men in front of you, Suresh, Kamalakumar and Alphonse, are the heirs of the three biggest business tycoons in the state. Though they claim to be students, they have never stepped into a college to learn— only to abuse women. They indulge in every imaginable vice. Last year, they kidnapped Damayanthi, a student of Sahayamary College in their car, raped and murdered her, and then threw her body into the river. The police initially refused to file a case against them. It was only after all the college students in the state went on strike that the police finally agreed to meet their demands. But when the case came to court, the judge was bribed, and they were acquitted. On the day of their release, the party cadres celebrated with firecrackers, as though it were Deepavali. A regular court can be corrupted. But it is the duty of this open-air court to punish them. They must be put to death!"

The judge asked, "Suresh, Kamalakumar and Alphonse, what do you have to say for yourselves?"

"We are innocent."

"So you did not commit the said crime?"

"No."

"Then who was the culprit?"

"We do not know."

"Was the judge paid a bribe of five lakh rupees?"

"No. His judgment was honest."

The judge roared with laughter. "Perhaps the judge was threatened by your fathers?"

"Our fathers would never do anything like that."

"But he *was* threatened. I know it for a fact. Do you want to know how?"

The judge rose and walked up to the three young men and said, "Deva, bring the torch light here. Let them see me."

The man with the torch light came and switched it on.

The face of Saravana Perumal grinned down at them.

⊀ 18 ⊀

The grin widened.

"Are the three of you shocked? I am, indeed, the same Saravana Perumal who sold his conscience, then dressed in black robes and freed the three of you. Do you know what your fathers threatened me with? They said they would murder my entire family if I dared to be honest in my judgment. I thought hard. Your families, with the ruling party's support, could do whatever they wished to me. I had no power to defy them. So I pretended to sell my honesty and named a price. They agreed happily. I acquitted you in the High Court. But here, in the Open-Air Court, they have no authority. Here, under the Indian Penal Code, Section 302, I sentence the three of you to be hanged by your necks until you are dead, for the kidnap, rape and murder of Damayanthi."

The three young men froze in terror.

Two men from the group lifted the boys to their feet.

Saravana Perumal continued. "There are forty-one of us here, members of a movement that began a year ago. Most of us have been affected by those immoral forces that impede the law. We are honest, retired police officers and judges."

The three were led into a forest. After a ten-minute trek, they arrived at a huge banyan tree. They stopped under it. Three thick ropes were hanging from one of its branches, with nooses already tied. Underneath them was a long bench, on which the three young men were made to stand. They cried and begged for mercy.

Saravana Perumal laughed. "I'll bet that girl Damayanthi cried the same way."

Black hoods were pulled down over their faces.

"The three of you took that one girl's life together," Saravana Perumal intoned. "Now, you must die together."

Even as the young men begged, the ropes tightened around their throats and the bench under them was kicked away. The three bodies convulsed for half a second, and then went still, swinging gently in the breeze.

"Pugazhenthi!" called Saravana Perumal.

"Sir!" said a young man, stepping forward.

"Is there a trial tomorrow?"

"Yes, sir. You have to try the three men accused of torching the sandal oil godown. Sundarapandian's case."

"Where is Sundarapandian?"

"Here, sir," he said, coming forward.

"Shall I give the judgment tomorrow night?"

"Please, sir."

"Fine. Court will be convened tomorrow night at eleven."

"Aiya... these three bodies?"

"Dump them in the elephant pit," commanded Saravana Perumal as he walked away.

⚡ 19 ⚡

The police officers were standing at attention in a row, and D.G.P. Nair was yelling at them. "Krishnakant, the chairman of the Sandal Oil Board, his employee Magudapathy, and Navaneeth, a friend of a central minister, have disappeared, just like Suresh, Kamalakumar and Alphonse did. We still don't have a clue about where they may have been taken. The Chief Minister keeps railing at me, with his fourth-class language and stale whisky breath."

"Sir?"

"What?"

"It's about Krishnakant. On the morning after the fire, it seems, he was approached by a strange man, who told him something that seemed to make him very anxious."

"Who told you this?"

"One of the constables at the scene. Marudhachalam, from Sathyamangalam. He says he could point out that stranger if he were to see him again."

"Good. Have it checked out thoroughly. I want results in twenty-four hours!" Just then his mobile phone rang in his pocket. He answered it.

"Yes…"

"Sir, Q Branch has just reported in. Apparently there's a hunter who claims he saw some men disposing of three bodies in an elephant pit."

"Who is this hunter, and which part of the forest is this?"

"The hunter's name is Jalapathy, a retired army officer who was on a deer hunt. The forest is in Ponneri."

"See that the media doesn't find out about it. I'll start immediately."

The D.G.P. got up to leave.

⚡ 20 ⚡

Early morning, three o'clock. The car pulled into the driveway. Saravana Perumal noticed that the hall lights were still on. He came inside to find Amirtham, Ajantha and Kishore seated on the sofa.

"What happened? Why are the three of you still awake?" he asked.

Amirtham replied, "You went out at ten last night. Where have you been all this time?"

"I told you, I went to the City Club."

"For what?"

"To play cards. As usual."

"We called the club. They told us you had not come in at all."

"I must have been inside. Maybe the person at the desk didn't see me."

Kishore rose up, furious. "Appa, how many more lies are you going to tell?"

"What lies?"

"We know you didn't go to the club."

"Then where was I?"

"Selling off the rest of your conscience! You must have gone to collect more of that filthy money."

"Kishore, I'm not the demon you imagine me to be. I need to sleep now. I am very tired. Can we postpone our argument till the morning? Good night!" He walked to his bedroom, leaving them dumbstruck.

✗ 21 ✗

The minister, followed by two police officers, walked down the corridor of the General Hospital to the morgue. He wiped the sweat from his temples and entered the room with a strained face.

The bodies of Suresh, Kamalakumar, and Alphonse lay on slabs of ice on a long steel table, enveloped by the smell of formalin. The minister looked at them for a few minutes, and then asked, "What happened?"

"They were hanged."

"All three?"

"Yes, sir. Hanged, and then dumped into the elephant pit. That's when the hunter saw them."

Nair brought in the sixty-year old hunter.

"Were you able to see the faces of the men who did this? Could you recognize any of them?"

"I wouldn't know them, or even how many there were. It was very dark. There must have been about four or five men. I was at least fifty feet away."

"Nair, what steps have been taken to apprehend these criminals?"

"We are thoroughly combing the entire forest for them."

"They must be caught alive, Nair. No one is to be shot. We need to know who the ringmaster is. And fast, so that we don't lose Krishnakant and those other two the same way."

"Yes, sir. Please stop worrying, sir. I'll find them within the hour," said the D.G.P., giving a smart salute.

✄ 22 ✄

Seven o'clock in the morning.

The phone jingled. Saravana Perumal sat up in the bed and answered.

"Yes?"

"Sir, it's me, Sundarapandian."

"What's the matter?"

"The police have discovered the bodies of Suresh, Kamalakumar, and Alphonse."

"How did they find out?"

"A hunter saw us while we were disposing of the corpses."

"Are the police already combing the forest?"

"Yes, sir. But most of us escaped."

"Have you brought Krishnakant and the other two along?"

"No, sir. There was no time to wait for your go-ahead. So we hung them in the same tree and left their bodies there."

Saravana Perumal laughed. "You didn't need my permission! That corrupt gang had been looting the nation of its natural treasures. They were traitors. They deserved to die. I am very proud of what you've done."

"Sir, we've put up another poster on your wall, so that the police will not suspect you."

"What does the poster say?"

"'The judgment you gave yesterday was wrong. The judgment we have given now is the correct one. These judgments will continue. If you still refuse to change, then this judgment will be for you too. Signed, Matchstick Number One.'"

"Excellent! Who composed it?"

"I did, sir."

"You're sure the watchmen didn't see you putting up the posters?"

"I'm sure, sir."

"We'll lie low for some time and then resume our operations. Let the rest of the group know."

"Yes, sir."

Saravana Perumal switched the phone off. There was a knock on the door. Amirtham entered with his coffee and a smile.

"Are you still angry with me?" she asked.

"What's this, Amirtham?"

"I was very wrong about you. I jumped to the conclusion that you were selling your conscience. I'm sorry; please forgive me," she said.

"Me too, Appa!" said Ajantha and Kishore, coming into the room.

Kishore continued, "Appa, I overheard your conversation on the cordless phone! I was shocked at first... and then thrilled! I'm so happy you have taken this route to see that justice is upheld. I told Ajantha and Amma everything."

Saravana Perumal smiled at them fondly. "I was worried that you might not approve of this method of enforcing the justice. That is why I hid it from you. I know what we've done is not completely legal. Ideally, no individual should have to take the law into his own hands. But in this political climate, it is becoming increasingly difficult to avoid. Whichever party comes to power tries to bring the law and the courts under its complete control. If a judge dares to defy them, he must be ready to sacrifice his life. He must even put his family at risk. That was why I decided to pretend to go along with their wishes, and then secretly become the matchstick that burns down injustice! Those three poisonous scorpions, Suresh, Kamalakumar, and Alphonse—they live no more!"

His voice was loud and passionate. Just then the door bell rang.

✗ 23 ✗

Kishore opened the door. D.G.P. Nair took a look at him, and asked, "Are you Saravana Perumal's son?"

"Yes, sir."

"Is he in?"

"Yes, sir."

"I need to see him."

"Please come in."

The D.G.P. entered, with a battalion of officers.

Saravana Perumal came into the hall smiling. "Good morning!"

"I'm sorry, Mr. Saravana Perumal, but I am here to arrest you."

"Why?"

"We have caught your accomplice, Sundarapandian."

Saravana Perumal's expression did not change.

"Do you want to know how we caught him? A constable noticed him speaking to Krishnakant at the site of the fire. The constable identified him from a photograph. We found out that he was staying in a lodge in Madras. The crime branch caught him there while he was calling you from a telephone booth outside the lodge."

"How do you know that he was calling me? Did you listen to the conversation?"

"No, we saw your phone number written on his palm. We learned from your watchman that you were out till three in the morning last night. You are a prime suspect in the murders. We have to take you into custody for further questioning."

Saravana Perumal smiled. "I was expecting this to happen sooner or later—though I had hoped it might not come for another few years! Still, I have no regrets. I used myself as the first matchstick to reinstate justice. Even though this matchstick is burnt out, there are many more left in the box. They will continue to strike to burn down corruption and injustice!"

He turned to the D.G.P. "Come along, Mr. Nair—let's go."

As Saravana Perumal left with the police, Kishore's eyes followed his father with pride and determination.

Matchstick Number Two was all ready to strike!

முதல்
தீக்குச்சி

ராஜேஷ்குமார்

"குட்மார்னிங்
டாடி...!"

வலது காதுக்குப் பக்கத்தில் வெல்வெட் மிருதுவோடு குரல் கேட்டு கண் விழித்தார் சரவணப் பெருமாள் - ஹைகோர்ட் நீதிபதி.

மகள் அஜந்தாவின் புன்னகை முகம் பார்வைக்குக் கிடைத்தது. மகளின் கன்னத்தை

1   பெஸ்ட் நாவல் - 1

First page of the first edition of
Matchstick Number One

91

SILICON HEARTS

சிலிக்கான் இதயங்கள் (2007)

by RAJESH KUMAR

A CROWD OF media reporters thronged around scientist Roger Stewart outside the control room at NASA, asking a flood of questions. The flashes from their cameras bathed him in light. A bald-headed senior journalist asked, "What is the floor area of this *Sky House* you plan to launch in the next couple of hours?"

"A hundred and fifty square feet. The *Sky House* room is about ten by fifteen."

"Are the astronauts Flora and Johnson really married to each other? Or did NASA just bring them together for the purposes of this experiment?"

"Oh no, they really are husband and wife! They got married last year. Flora and Johnson are both qualified astronauts. We are taking advantage of their enthusiasm to participate in this experiment."

"What is the purpose of this experiment?"

"I thought I had made it clear. Flora and Johnson are being sent up in the *Sky House*. The spaceship will be stationed outside the gravitational pull of the Earth. Flora and Johnson will resume their lives as a married couple in a zero-gravity environment. The first part of the experiment will be to determine if Flora can conceive under such conditions. If she conceives, the next phase will be to study the fetus, and to ascertain whether its development is normal or if there are any marked differences due to the absence of gravity."

A reporter interrupted, "It would appear that Flora and Johnson will be onboard this spaceship for quite a long time."

"True, but if Flora conceives immediately, then they can deliver the child and return to Earth within a year. It all depends on how long it takes for Flora to get pregnant."

"Is it possible to become pregnant when there is no gravity?"

"This experiment is designed to answer precisely that question."

"Can we meet Flora and Johnson?"

"Unfortunately you won't be able to meet them in person. But you can interview them via video conference, using this digital screen," the chief scientist said, tapping a keyboard. The screen came to life, showing Flora and Johnson in their spacesuits. The reporters waved and greeted them with a "Hi!", and then began their questions.

"How do you feel at this moment?"

"Wonderful," replied Flora.

"Do you believe it's possible to have a child in space?"

"Do you think we would embark on this journey if we didn't? I am going to experience something that no other woman in the world has ever been able to experience."

"You'll be living for over a year in a single room, in each other's constant company, eating food that tastes like paste. Don't you think you'll get tired of it?"

Johnson laughed. "When we're furthering scientific progress, how can we worry about getting tired? We have been trained to be able to live in that enforced solitude. Our aim now is to go into space, copulate, and return with our child to Earth."

"So, the two of you will go up—but three of you will come back?"

"Yes, that's right!"

"All the best! We're all very eager to see your child."

"Thank you! We shall meet again!" The smiling images of Flora and Johnson disappeared from the screen, and the reporters turned back to Roger Stewart.

"Will the launch be punctual?"

"As of now, there is no change in the time of the launch. The count-down begins in an hour. You have just enough time to go down to the refreshment room, eat well, and then get to the visitor's tower!"

The reporters left in a hurry.

An hour passed. Roger entered the control room, where a number of other scientists were seated at their computers in front of a large window with a view of the launch pad. "Are Flora and Johnson in position inside the spaceship?"

"Yes, sir."

"Can we start the countdown?"

All the scientists nodded in unison—except one. Roger turned to him. "Is there a problem, Mr. Henderson?"

"I believe there's a small error."

"What?"

"There is a possibility of a leak in the cryogenic cylinder."

"Is that right? Where is the report?"

Henderson took a printout of the report. Roger read it, and looked up angrily at Henderson. "Mr. Henderson, please read the last line of this report."

"'Proceed: no risk factors.'"

"What's the problem then?"

"Sir, kindly note the cryogenic cylinder's active position success rate. Ninety-nine point nine percent."

Roger's face changed slightly.

Henderson went on. "At present, it's only a point-one percent risk. It's true that the spaceship is in no immediate danger—but there is a chance the percentage could increase during the journey, and that definitely gives us reason to worry."

"Yes. What you're saying is correct. Can you rectify this immediately?"

"We'll need a few hours to set it right. It will mean a delay in today's launch..."

"How much time do you need?"

"We'll have to begin our check from the fuel tank. So it will take at least six hours."

"Get it done!" Roger ordered. Sweat dripped from his brow as he left the air-conditioned control room. Again, the reporters surrounded him at once.

"Have you begun the countdown?"

"Not yet."

"Why not?"

"There is a small technical snag. The scientists are setting it right. It's expected to take at least six hours."

"So when is the new launch time?"

"We hope to begin at six in the evening. Report to the visitor's gallery by five."

Flora and Johnson, now out of their spacesuits, were on their way to their quarters to rest until the launch. Johnson drove. "I wasn't expecting a delay at the last moment."

"Thank God they found out about the problem in time."

"Do you think they'll be able to set it right by six this evening?"

"Of course. But there will be other snags, like in the pathfinder, for instance, or in the body shield..."

"What are you saying, Flora?"

"The truth!"

"What?"

"*Sky House* will never take off. From now on, every hour, a new series of snags will be found."

"Why do you say that?"

"Because there's a virus in the master computer that nobody knows about."

Johnson brought the car to a sudden halt.

"What? How do you know there's a virus?"

Flora, staring into the distance, replied in a tight voice, "Because I'm the one who uploaded it."

"F-l-o-r-a! Why would you do such a stupid thing? You've committed a serious mistake."

"It's not a mistake, Johnson. I want to have my baby here on Earth. I do not want my child to be born like some guinea pig in a laboratory, in the middle of space, without my family around me. My child should be able to breathe this natural air. That is all I want. I tried to make you see it my way, but you wouldn't listen. If I had argued with you back then, it would have led to separation, maybe even divorce. I couldn't bear to lose you, Johnson. I want you—and I want my baby to be born here, on our home planet. I pretended to be keen on the trip into space and chose the right moment to corrupt the computer program.

"Now the ship is unfit to be launched. The NASA crew will need another three years to scrap this machine and build another spacecraft. By then, I will already have borne you two children. You might accuse me of ruining a spaceship worth millions of dollars. But being a mother is more precious to me than those dollars! Which do you think is more important, Johnson: motherhood or money?"

Johnson stayed silent for a few moments. Then he hugged Flora, saying, "I accept. Our baby will be born here, on this Earth. Shall we begin the exercise right away?" And he leaned over to kiss her red lips.

THE RAINBOW

வானவில் (2007)

by RAJESH KUMAR

"You're SURE TO WIN the first prize this time. Come on, take a ticket!"

Suppaiyan, the lottery agent, was set up at the temple entrance, with an array of lottery tickets laid out on a mat. On seeing Kanniappan, he threw out his usual sales pitch.

Kanniappan, the guide, was hooked immediately. "I've already purchased tickets for nearly every state lottery. Do you have any new ones for me?"

"There's a new one from Uttar Pradesh. Do you want one?"

"Yes. Give me one where the numbers add up to five."

Suppaiyan laughed. "Of course! I'll give you one just the way you want."

"But I won't be able to pay you until evening."

"I know that already."

Kanniappan put the ticket into his well-worn purse and rushed into the temple. He was half an hour behind schedule today.

The reason he was late was that he had been caught by a storm early that morning. He had been fast asleep, wrapped in a woolen blanket, when the storm had arrived in the form of his wife, Soundram, shaking him awake. The storm had subsided only half an hour before he left home.

The reason for her anger was straightforward. The four children born of their five-year-old marriage were crying their eyes out in hunger. Soundram had pounced on Kanniappan in a fury. "What the hell did you do with your earnings yesterday?" she yelled in her throaty voice.

Kanniappan replied casually, "Some earnings! I was only able to make ten rupees all day."

Soundram stood arms akimbo. "I would like to know where those ten rupees are," she demanded.

"I spent it."

"On what?"

"Do I have to tell you?"

"Yes! You married me, didn't you? You made me bear four children, didn't you? Then yes, you have to tell me!"

Kanniappan looked at her for a few moments and then said, "Look here. I didn't waste it all. Of that ten, I drank three rupees worth of toddy, as usual. Another three, I spent on a meal at Iyer's hotel. With the balance, I bought a lottery ticket."

Soundram roared with laughter. "It's fine that you had your toddy and your meals. But you could have given me the rest. I would have at least fed my children with rice congee. Why do you have to play the lottery? You keep on buying them, all the colors, every month. What do you have to show for it?"

Kanniappan got up patiently and replied, "Soundram, you don't understand. Why do I spend money on the lottery? Is it just for my pleasure? No! It is for you, and for my children. Pandi, the man with the fortune-telling parrot, tells me every time he reads my future: 'Brother, you will win a huge sum of money before the end of the year. Don't get frustrated; keep playing!' I am hoping a lottery win will wipe our poverty away forever."

Soundram interrupted him. "Ay! If you were truly lucky, you would have hit a jackpot in the first lottery you played. Why do you have to spend so much on it? One ticket a month, maybe I can accept."

"You shut up! Don't try to advise me. I'll slap you silly, just watch."

"That's all you *can* do: slap your wife around. You can't feed her, you can't take her advice, but you can beat her. If you had put all the money you spent on the lottery so far in the bank, you would have saved at least ten thousand by now. With that money, you could have gotten your sister Sivabagyam married last month, to that teacher. I should curse your mother; I don't know how she could have trusted you to be a good son!"

"Shut your trap!" he roared. But Soundram had not finished.

"If I keep my mouth shut, then your eyes will also remain shut. You cannot think for yourself, nor can you listen to reason."

Enraged, Kanniappan grabbed at her hair.

"*Anna!*"

He turned on hearing the feeble call. His timid sister stood at the doorstep. His hold loosened, and Soundram began again.

"Bagyam, your brother may be incapable of earning millions. But he's strong enough to beat up his wife. I'm only asking him to feed his children, but instead he's dreaming of becoming a *crorepati* with his lottery tickets. You have a job, you go to earn money in the button factory. But your brother?"

She could not continue. With her four children as her audience, she collapsed against the wall in tears.

"She is no woman!" grumbled Kanniappan, as he left for work. "She is a demon. Look what words come from that mouth. As if I am purposely delaying my sister's marriage! Wait until just one state lottery makes me a winner. Then she'll know my real worth. Pandi's predictions have always come true for others. How can he be wrong about me alone? Once I win, then there will be a long queue of men waiting to marry my sister."

"Hey Kanniappan! What are you daydreaming about? Can't you see who is in front of you?"

Kanniappan looked up, startled. Sivasailam, the trustee of the temple, stood there in a silk *veshti* with a dark red border, like a true devotee of Shiva. Kanniappan saluted him. "I'm sorry sir; I didn't notice you. There was a small skirmish at home… I was thinking about that."

"Did Soundram say something harsh, Kanniappan?"

"Yes sir, she did. You are our senior; can you please advise her?"

Sivasailam laughed out loud. "But Kanniappan, she is right! It was wrong for you to have gotten married before getting your sister married. At least, you could have delayed having children. But you didn't. Now that you have four little ones, shouldn't you try to be a responsible father? Even if you earn only a rupee or two, shouldn't you start trying to save something? Tell me, is it true that you spend a lot of money on the lottery?"

"Yes sir, it's true. I'm hoping that one jackpot will wipe away my misery."

Sivasailam could not control his mirth. "When luck wants to come to you, Kanniappan, it will knock right at your door. Until then, you stay smart."

Kanniappan had no reply.

"Fine. Now hurry, there are some college students waiting at the temple *mandap* who want to look at the sculptures. They need a guide. I told them I would send you. Be quick, maybe you can make some good money today."

He saluted the trustee and ran towards the temple.

There was a group of students waiting there. Kanniappan approached them and saluted. One of the students asked, "Who are you?"

"I am the guide."

"Did the trustee send you here?"

"Yes, sir."

"What's the charge for your service?"

"Nothing stipulated, sir. I will accept whatever you give."

"Fine. Let's start."

By evening, Kanniappan had made around twenty rupees. He was sailing home joyously when the lottery agent Suppaiyan called him.

"Kanniappan, aren't you going to pay for the lottery you bought this morning?"

Kanniappan arrogantly handed him a ten-rupee note.

"Wow! So you struck gold today, did you?"

"Yes I did."

"I'll give you a bargain; twelve lottery tickets for nine rupees. Do you want them?"

Kanniappan's face shone with expectation. "Really? Won't it be a loss of three rupees for you?"

"Of course, it will be a small loss. But this is my special offer just for you. Do you want them?"

"Yes. I'll take them. This is luck beckoning me."

So instead of his change, Kanniappan took twelve colorful tickets (forgetting to check that the drawing dates printed on them were still in the future). Puffing away on a beedi, he strode into the toddy shop with his remaining ten rupees in his pocket. He drank five rupees worth of toddy, then headed to the food stall nearby, and added pepper-fried fish and chicken chops to his treat. The food stall owner put Kanniappan's thirty paisa change into his pocket, and helped him to stagger out of the shop. Kanniappan returned home, tired.

"Amma! Appa is back!"

Hearing the cries of her children, Soundram came out of the house. "How much did you make today? Please give me the money, the children are starving."

Kanniappan laughed. "Oh, I made a pile. I earned twenty rupees."

"Wow!" Soundram could not believe her luck for a moment, but a closer look at her husband had her wondering. She ran her fingers through his pockets, and found only three ten-paisa coins. She could no longer control her anger. "What did you do with that money?"

"Oh, have I actually managed to spend twenty rupees that fast?" he asked in a silly humor. Soundram, of course, was not in a laughing mood.

"Chee! You are not a man at all. Why should you want a wife and children? Ay, Rajappa, come here." Her eldest son came, dressed only in a pair of torn trousers. "Take this thirty paisa, and get some cassava from

Kupputhai. Share it with your brothers. Drink water at the street-tap when you return, and then get to bed."

Kanniappan was already taking the last puffs from his beedi and looking for a place to lie down. He flicked the butt into the gutter, and sat down outside the house. Soundram stood close to him, and inquired very softly, "Are you in any shape to understand what I am about to tell you?"

"What do you have to tell me?" slurred Kanniappan.

"The family of that teacher, the one who came to see your sister six months back, came again this afternoon."

"Really?" Even in his inebriated state, he was excited.

"Yes, and he does seem to like your sister. They are ready to go ahead with the marriage. They are not demanding any dowry. They said if we can give them five thousand rupees, they will cover the rest of the wedding expense themselves. Your sister also likes that fellow. She's been refusing marriage till now. But this one, she has accepted immediately."

Kanniappan managed to ask, "What did you tell them?"

"What could I say? I said I'd consult with you once you returned from the temple, and get back to them."

Kanniappan shrank against the wall. "What do we do now?"

"Why, get her married, of course!"

"Are you crazy? That thirty paisa I just gave you is all the money I had in the world. I am completely broke. How will we have a wedding?"

"You'll have to borrow. You cannot postpone the marriage indefinitely," snapped Soundram.

"Who will lend me that kind of money?" wailed Kanniappan helplessly.

"Then your sister is never going to be married."

Kanniappan sprang up. "Why don't we tell the groom straight out, we can't afford a single paisa. So if he wants the girl, he has to get married at his expense."

"Chee! Has the liquor dried up the last drop of honor in you? They are being so generous to us. They want no dowry, just five thousand rupees as our share of the wedding expense. You don't want to give even that? Get out and make arrangements to borrow that money. Go!"

"I cannot manage even one pie."

"Then your sister's marriage?"

"Let her wait."

"For how long?"

"Till we can find her a groom who won't make us spend anything."

"She's already twenty-five."

"So let her wait till she's thirty. What's the hurry now?"

With her heart on fire, Soundram glared at him. Kanniappan was beyond care. He was snoring.

The next morning at ten, Kanniappan sat in the mandap waiting for someone who wanted to hire a guide. The sun was scorching hot, but the cold stone of the floor provided some relief.

"Anna!"

Kanniappan turned around, and then leapt to his feet, surprised to see Sivabagyam. She should have been at work at the factory. What was she doing in the temple mandap?

"What, Bagyam? Why aren't you at work?"

"I took the day off," she replied softly, not looking up at him.

"Why?"

"I had to talk to you."

"For that, you took a day off? Why couldn't you talk to me at home?"

"I didn't want to shame my brother in front of his wife and children. So I couldn't talk at home."

"What do you mean?"

"About my marriage…"

"Oh!" He grinned sarcastically. "So you're mature enough to demand a talk about your marriage, are you?"

"I matured 12 years ago."

Kanniappan's face went red with embarrassment. "So what do you want to tell me?"

"Anna, I have no parents, no other relations I can discuss this openly with. Only you. But if you're not keen on discussing it..."

Kanniappan interrupted, "I want to discuss it. I just don't have any money right now."

"When did you ever? And I don't believe you ever will. You can't even manage to feed your children; how can you get me married?"

"Hey Bagyam, watch what you say!"

"Anna, save your threats for your wife, not me. I was listening to both of you last night. When you were twenty-five, you wanted a wife, and so you got one. Now that I am twenty-five, you casually say I should wait till I'm thirty to find a husband. If you had controlled your expenses a little, you could have got me married long ago. But now you're in debt to everyone in town. You seem to have forgotten that there is something else you owe; there is a virgin girl in your home, and you owe her a husband. Anyway, I have decided to settle this debt myself. From my earnings, besides giving you a share, I've managed to save five thousand. I've left it with Sivasailam sir. I'll get it for you now. You don't have to mention this to anyone. Let the world believe that you are getting me married at your own expense. That's important for your prestige." Sivabagyam was left breathless after pouring out this speech.

Kanniappan was choked with tears. "Bagyam..."

"Anna, I'm a woman; I have to be sold off someday. I'll manage, one way or another. But there are five lives dependant on you. If you go on the way you're acting, very soon your whole family will be out on the streets."

He could find no way to comfort his weeping sister.

Kanniappan, the guide, had finally been guided onto the right path.

THE F.L.R.

புது பிரம்மா (2007)

by RAJESH KUMAR

PROFESSOR VINAYAK LOOKED UP from the internet to refresh himself with a Revital pill. As he reached out for his mineral water bottle, his secretary Udhaya peeked in and called out hesitantly, "Sir...?"

Vinayak lowered the bottle. "Yes?"

"Tiwari, the industrialist, is here to see you. His son Sanjay has come with him."

The professor looked at his digital wristwatch. It was already nine in the night. "Fine, ask them to come in. You may leave, if you're done."

Udhaya nodded, and shut the door behind her as she left. The professor switched off the computer and sat back to wait. The fifty-five-year-old Tiwari entered, along with his twenty-five-year-old son. They had the full, pink faces of people who were used to counting profits in crores.

Tiwari greeted him. "Sorry to disturb you at this hour, Professor."

"No problem. Please come in, have a seat. I've seen several advertisements about Tiwari Enterprises in the media. Tell me, what can I do for you?"

Before Tiwari could reply, the cell phone in the professor's pocket rang. He answered the call. It was from Doctor Chandramouli.

"Yes, tell me, Doctor."

"The surgery was successful. Ramamirtham has survived. It's a miracle; I still can't believe it!"

Vinayak laughed, "I told you so, Doctor. My F.L.R. is infallible. You wouldn't believe me; you swore that there was only a twenty percent success rate for this sort of surgery, that it was unlikely that Ramamirtham would survive. I had to force you to go ahead with the operation. You mark my words, Doctor; Ramamirtham will live for another twenty-two years."

Vinayak disconnected the phone and looked at the duo in front of him.

"Sorry about that. Please tell me what you came for."

Tiwari began hesitantly. "Actually, we wanted to discuss exactly the same matter that you were just talking about on the phone."

"I don't understand...?"

"We heard that you have invented a machine that can read a person's fate."

"Who told you that?"

"A colleague of yours."

"What do you want to know about it?"

"If such a machine really exists, we're interested in marketing it globally."

"Sorry, Mr. Tiwari. It's not for sale. I invented the F.L.R. for my personal research."

Sanjay, who had been silent until then, asked, "What is this F.L.R.?"

"A Fate Language Reporter."

"Can we see it?"

Vinayak hesitated a second, then got up. "Please come," he said, and led them to the next room.

Inside the air-conditioned room was a state-of-the-art computer attached to a complicated-looking apparatus made of fibreglass.

"This is the F.L.R.," said Professor Vinayak.

As both Tiwari and Sanjay stared at it skeptically, the professor switched on the computer. He produced a rectangular printout and gave it to Tiwari.

"Please have a look at this, Mr. Tiwari."

The sheet was filled with strange graphs.

"What do you see?"

"Just a bunch of hen scratches!"

Vinayak laughed. "Would you believe me if I told you that this is a map of a man's fate?"

"What? This is what fate looks like?"

"Yes! This is the fate of a dear friend of mine, Ramamirtham—the same Ramamirtham you heard me discuss with the doctor just now, on the phone. He's a heart patient. I told the doctor that according to his fate report, Ramamirtham should live for another twenty-two years. And he has not only survived the surgery; he is also improving rapidly."

Tiwari cut in. "There are many who would claim that there is no such thing as preordained fate, that it's all just a superstition."

"Superstition? None of the things mentioned in our mythologies are superstition, Mr. Tiwari. Even as science advances by leaps and bounds, all the latest discoveries are closely related to what our mythologies have always claimed was possible. The ancient texts told us of *pushpaka vimanam*, the flying vehicles of the gods; we used to think it was just a story. But today we fly across the world in airplanes. In the *Mahabharatham*, the charioteer Sanjayan related the events of the Kurukshetra war to the blind Dhritarashtran, even as those events were unfolding, despite the fact that Sanjayan sat hundreds of miles away. Today, with live telecasts on our telelvisions, such a feat has actually become possible. Our forefathers claimed that there was life in the heavens; today there is evidence from the Pathfinder mission that the planet Mars may support life.

"Our forefathers had logical explanations for all the fantastic feats they wrote about. It takes us time to rediscover that logic, but eventually we do—and then we have a scientific basis for accepting that the events in the epics are actually possible. Until then, though, we go on dismissing them as superstition. The same thing applies to fate."

"It's all a bit difficult to believe."

"But you must believe it, Mr. Tiwari; it is the truth. Every man's fate is written when he is born."

"Where exactly is it written?" asked Sanjay, somewhat sarcastically. "Inside the skull, or on the outside?"

"Neither."

"Then?"

"In fact, fate is recorded in a human brain as electronic waves. My F.L.R. will translate those waves into a graphic language."

"Professor, with these graphics… can you predict all the events in the life of a person?"

"That is what my analysis is all about. But so far, I have specialized in one area alone."

"What is that?"

"With my analysis I can predict the lifespan of a person, but I cannot say *how* he will encounter death. It could be natural, accidental, maybe even a suicide."

"Why, then, are you reluctant to make the F.L.R. public knowledge?"

"Sorry, but I'm not interested in becoming an astrologer. Also, my experiment is not yet complete. As of now, I can only predict when a person will die, not any other details. To be able to report the entire fate of a subject… that will take a very long time."

Tiwari thought silently for a minute, and then asked, "Would you be able to use the F.L.R. to find out how long my son and I will live?"

"Of course. But…"

"But what?"

"A person's ability to lead a joyful, exciting life depends upon his ignorance of when the time will come for him to die. That knowledge has the potential to consume one's happiness. In fact, I have never used the F.L.R. to read my own fate, for that very reason."

Tiwari smiled. "Professor, in a way, I agree with you. But my son and I would still like to know our fated lifespan. We won't be devastated if the F.L.R. says our lives will be short. It's just that, if we know how long we are going to be alive, then we can plan the progress of our business accordingly. We are not afraid to die."

The professor shrugged and replied, "Okay. It wouldn't be kind of me to refuse, when you seem so clear about it. Please come, have a seat on the fibreglass chair next to the F.L.R. It will take just two minutes to report your fate and then predict your lifespan."

Tiwari thanked him, and sat on the chair. Vinayak opened a cabinet attached to the F.L.R. and removed a purple helmet, which he fixed onto Tiwari's head. He then pressed a feather touch membrane button. The computer screen read:

`Receiving Electronic Signals...`

When precisely two minutes had passed, the screen flashed

`Fate Language Report Generated`

and a sheet covered with complicated-looking graphs emerged from the printer. Vinayak took the page of graphics and looked it over for a few minutes before turning to Tiwari.

"How old are you now?"

"Fifty-five."

"Then you have thirty more years to live. That is, you will die at the age of eighty-five."

Tiwari visibly bloomed. "Thirty years! There is a lot I can achieve with so much time!" he crowed.

Next, Sanjay sat on the chair, and had his fate read.

Professor turned to him and asked, "And how old are you, Sanjay?"

"Twenty-five, sir."

"You will live for another seventy years. That is, you will die at the age of ninety-five."

Sanjay's face shone as if dusted with a fresh layer of rouge.

Fifteen days passed. The professor was relaxing in his home when his cell phone rang.

"Yes?"

"Vinayak? This is Tiwari..."

The professor laughed. "I've been waiting to hear from you for two weeks now. So, how is Sanjay?"

"Wonderful! He's very happy, eating regularly, coming to the office, chatting with his friends. For the past six months, he's been obsessed with the fear of death. But he's completely forgotten that now!"

"Tiwari, try to make sure that your son doesn't go to any more quack astrologers. Those fellows are all the same. When they're asked to make predictions for rich boys like Sanjay, they will deliberately invent some grave misfortunes in his future and then demand money for elaborate pujas to appease the planets. And it's not only his money he'll lose, but his peace of mind as well."

Tiwari laughed. "Well, I don't think he'll ever go to another astrologer now. He has complete faith in your F.L.R."

"I was nervous right up till the end. I was worried that Sanjay wouldn't be fooled—that we wouldn't be able to pass off that ordinary graphics printer as a 'Fate Language Reporter'."

"Vinayak, you are a true genius at computer graphics. There's no way that Sanjay was going to think that you were conning him. Anyway, thank you so much for your help!"

"No need to thank me. Just be careful never to let Sanjay find out that we've been friends since childhood!"

Q & A
கேள்வி பதில்கள்

with R AJESH K UMAR

RK: I AM OFTEN asked why it is that most of my novels are about crime. When I started out as a writer, there were many stalwarts already in the field, like Parthasarathy, Jayakanthan, and Lakshmi. Their novels were primarily "socials". I knew I could never compete with them and earn a name for myself. So I decided to take up a genre that they never tried: crime.

Every man is capable of crime. Lying, hurting someone's feelings, wanting another man's wife—these are also crimes. Outwardly, everyone shows only the face that they choose; in private, there is a different self. The level of criminality may differ from person to person, but no one is completely free of it.

I have been writing for thirty years. I am yet to become tired, or experience writer's block, or run out of ideas. That's because words breathe into me constantly. I must write at least ten pages a day, or else I become restless.

I am sometimes accused of plagiarizing English novels. Let me tell you something: I never even *read* English novels. In the time I would have to take to read a thick English novel, I can write two novels myself. I do read books in English, but they are reference books relevant to my stories. Most are general knowledge and science books. If any of my readers still doubt me, they are welcome to come and search for English novels in my house.

Some people don't think crime novels count as literature. My answer to them is that the first crime novel in this world is the *Mahabharatham*—which has every imaginable sort of intrigue—and the next is the *Ramayanam*. The great epics themselves depend on rape, molestation, abduction, and murder for their plots. It makes me laugh when I am accused of spoiling society with my crime novels. I don't just dream up my plots from out of nowhere. There are enough murders, rapes, and political dramas in the daily newspaper to keep me busy for another full lifetime.

What is the message I have in my crime stories? "He who sows evil will reap his punishment." We are creating awareness among the public here. I seriously think we should be awarded the Gnanapeet and Sahitya Academy Awards.

Do you write the story to fit a title, or the title to match a story?

—*K.R. Thangavelu, Kannampalaam*

RK: I've done both. Sometimes I think of a smart title and then weave a story around it.

The Indian cricket team seems to be taking a bad beating recently, no?

—*V. Balaji, Chennai*

RK: The other teams are developing new methods of batting and bowling, but we have stuck to our time-tested methods. Tendulkar is just as capable as Jayasurya of Sri Lanka, who hit 80 runs in only 17 balls. But we don't make the effort. Our cricket team is too busy advertising soft drinks, having affairs with film actresses and abandoning their families. Where is the time for practice? If the string of losses continues, the cricket board should disband the team and look for a new one. Of course winning and losing is part of any game. But we have seem to have made a habit of losing!

What is the difference between sexy and vulgar?

    —*Ilankadhiravan, Kovai*

RK: Exposing a navel is sexy. Spinning a top on it is vulgar.

Do we need the caste system anymore?

    —*G. Prem, Theni*

RK: Yes. Like we need a spoon of pickle on a plate of feast.

Heh, heh... To which caste do you belong?

    —*V. Balaraman, Trichy*

RK: In Tamil Nadu I am a Tamil; in India I am an Indian; to the world I am a human... Will that suffice, Balaraman?

Can you name any place that is entirely free of corruption?

    —*Jasmine, Karumathampatti*

RK: The cemetery.

I am suffering from hair loss due to stress. Do you worry about such things?

    —*Anonymous, Madurai*

RK: Why should I worry about you losing your hair?

Cover of a Rajesh Kumar novel,
from *Dhigil Novel*

Cover of the Deepavali 2005 special Rajesh Kumar issue of
Great Novel

VIDYA SUBRAMANIAM

Vidya Subramaniam works in the Directorate of Social Welfare in Chennai; she has been writing short stories and novels for twenty years. Of the authors in this anthology, she is the only one to have been previously translated into English. Her protagonists, generally middle-class urban women, are more independent and self-reliant than many in Tamil popular fiction, and her stories often have a glimmer of a feminist edge.

ME

நான் (1987)

"STOP RIGHT THERE!"

Just as I was going to step inside the house, I heard Amma's command and froze. I looked up at her.

"Why do you want me to stop here? Can we discuss this *inside* the house, please?"

I had been expecting Amma to blow up like this for a week. She turned wordlessly back inside, and I followed her. I left my handbag on the table, went to wash up, came back, sat on the floor, leaned against the wall, and prepared to listen to a long tirade.

"Tell me, then," I said.

"What do you want me to say? You have to tell *me* what's going on."

"What?"

"Every day for the past week, some guy comes home, you dress up and go out with him. I need to know what it all means."

I stared at Amma. Was she really my mother? Sometimes I didn't believe it.

"I'm hungry," I said. "Please give me my food."

"I can't even show my face outside this house."

"Is there any food for me here, or do I have to go out for that, too?"

"Oh, the questions I have to face! I want to die!"

"Is that right? You want to die *now*? Then how come you didn't want to die of shame when people asked you why your eldest daughter was yet to be married?"

"Who will marry you now?"

"I did get some proposals, remember? You were the one who refused."

She lapsed into a stony silence. It only caused my anger to build up even more, and finally it all spilled out, like a volcanic eruption.

"You were scared. You had three daughters after me, and they all had to be married. The government granted me the job I'm working at now on compassionate basis after Appa's death. You decided that meant I should be responsible for the house Appa left behind. After that, every marriage proposal I got, you would find some novel method to ward it off. I worked like a dog, did overtime—and I earned money. I gave it all to you. Even to buy my underwear, I had to beg from you. Have I ever demanded anything for myself? If my bra was worn out, I would cover myself with my sari, rather than ask for a new bra. I had only six saris to wear in rotation.

"And for whose benefit? Just when I could glimpse hope on the horizon, who was there to blindfold me and lead me back into the darkness? It was you! Do you remember? I even asked you up front: 'Amma, why are you refusing to get me married to a widower? I have no problem with that. I'm over thirty-five; I can't be too choosy.' And what did you say? 'Someone will come. Wait. Be patient. Don't be hasty. After all, you have a mother; it's my responsibility to get you a husband, isn't it?'

"I can't understand why you are still holding me back. I've paid for my sisters' education, and gotten them married off, just as you wanted me to. What else is left to stop me?"

Amma cried, "Listen, there's a problem for me here, too! If you get married and go away, what will become of me? I don't have a son to look after me!"

"So? Just because you don't have a son, I'm expected to sacrifice all sexual pleasure?"

"Don't be crude!"

"You're forcing me to be crude."

"I am looking for a man who will marry you and agree to live here, in this house."

"And if you don't find one?"

"I *will* find one."

"I'm not your only daughter. You have four of us. You can divide your time between the four."

"No, that would look bad. If you were my son, then it would have been your duty to keep me."

"And if my future husband doesn't agree to your condition?"

"You won't marry any man, unless he does agree."

"What if he initially agrees, but changes his mind after we're married?"

"I will write down the condition on revenue stamp paper, and get him to sign it before the wedding. If he changes his mind I'll then go to court and demand justice."

"Tell me honestly, did you actually give birth to me, or did you find me in a dustbin?"

"Oh dear Goddess, Angala Parameshwari! Do I really have to listen to this from my first-born daughter?" She shed crocodile tears for a while. Then she demanded again, "Who is he? Have you got married in secret? Tell me!"

"Not yet. But I have slept with him a few times."

"Oh, Goddess Mahamayi!"

"Even if *She* had been born as your eldest daughter, She would have done the same thing. You chased away every man who wanted to marry me. For the sake of your future, you made *my* future a bed of nails. Why should you be able to eat three meals a day, have three new saris a year, while I stay a frozen virgin?"

"Wench, do you think that pleasure is the only important thing in life?"

"If I did think like that, I would have left you and run off with him the very first time we went to bed. What could you have done? Weddings and *thalis* are just for the outside world. These things are simply a license to have sex. If our hearts are united, we have no need for social licenses. In case you die, I need someone for myself! You want to know who he is, do you? He is the man I chose to have sex with, and he will be that special someone for my future."

"What arrogance is this? It's completely unacceptable! How can a good woman be so shameless?"

"What is acceptable or unacceptable in our society was not written by God. Every human child is naked when it is born. Adam and Eve did not wait to exchange wedding rings before going to bed. All that is, today, has evolved over time. A thousand years ago, in this same nation, a woman was able to select her mate from thousands during her *swayamwaram*. A few hundred years back, the custom changed to shaving widow's heads or throwing them onto the funeral pyres of their husbands in the name of *sati*. Sorry, but I'm not about to shave my head, or immolate myself. If you don't like our relationship, tell me; I'll leave here, and move in with him. You won't be allowed to visit. You can, of course, move in with one of your other daughters. If you want me to have a marriage, then this is your only option. You can't have your cake and eat it too. You have annihilated even my smallest desires with your greed. I'm an ordinary woman. This is my fair and just demand! I don't care what this society thinks of me. If you want to stay with me, then stop interfering in my sex life. Bless me, as you should, that I have finally found some pleasure."

I went to bed.

RIPPLES

சலனம் (1987)

by VIDYA SUBRMANIAM

MANONMANI HAD JUST sat down for her dinner when she noticed the state of the house. There were cobwebs covering the ceiling; most of the shelves were coated with a layer of dust. It had been well over a month since the house had gotten a thorough cleaning. At least one full day a month had to be set aside for this work, or else the place started to look grimy.

She couldn't just announce that she would take a day off from work to clean, or Ravi would get upset. He would insist that they do it together on a Sunday. But that was no good—it was impossible to clean on a weekend, when the children were under your feet.

So Manonmani decided to take the next day off. Of course, she didn't tell Ravi.

"What Mano, aren't you late?" he asked her the next morning.

"I called in and got permission to take an extra hour," she lied. She saw him and the children off, and then began her systematic cleaning. She removed all the unnecessary paper waste from the shelves and threw it away. Then she got rid of all the out-of-date medicine canisters and empty tonic bottles from the medicine shelf. Before clearing away the cobwebs, it made sense to move the beds out of the way, up to the terrace.

So she took off the old pillow covers and began rolling up the mattress. That was when she saw the twice-folded paper that had been tucked away under the bed. Without a second thought, Manonmani pulled it out and read it.

The letter began, "My dearest Ravi…"

Shocked, she sat on the cot to continue reading.

… I have already written you five letters. Why this silence still, Ravi? Is there a rule somewhere that says that a single woman can fall in love only with another single man? Is it a crime to fall in love with a married man? If so, then whose crime is it? The woman who fell in love, or the man who made her fall in love? Maybe this is why they say love is blind.

What can I do, Ravi? I've tried my best to reclaim the heart that I've lost to you. But I have failed. I promise you that my love will in no way harm your family life. Won't you just give me a chance to speak with you? At the very least, I expect a smile in response to this letter.

Loving you always,
Sowmya

Manonmani sat, motionless as a stone, remembering.

"Mano, there's a woman who seems to like me a bit too much. What should I do?"

"Oh, I'm sure there's long queue of women out there, dying to fall in love with you! I'm the one who went crazy for a moment, and married you."

"Hey, this isn't some bluff. I'm telling you the truth."

"Okay, fine, who is it then?"

"I keep running into her at the poetry readings on the beach."

"Oh, so now I know why you're always going to those readings!"

"Come on! I'm just being frank with you. Do you think I would share this with you if I had even a single guilty thought?"

"Okay, okay! So you've got some other woman in love with you. What are you going to do about it?"

"I'm ready to do whatever you command."

"I would kill you myself!"

"So you'd rather I didn't go ahead with it?"

"If I insist that you don't, you'll only get more interested. Do whatever *you* think is right."

"What kind of answer is that?"

"That's all I can say."

"Suppose I returned her affection?"

"I would say 'Off with you, you prick!' and leave you forever."

"That's only if you came to know I was having an affair. What would you do if I never revealed it to you?"

That conversation had taken place almost five months back. The letter under the bed read as if he was yet to respond to her advances. Thank God for small mercies!

But back then, he had been open about it. Now he had hidden this letter. Why? Had he begun to have secrets of his own? Did it mean that he had fallen in love with Sowmya? Manonmani nearly burst into tears.

No Mano! Don't become emotional! Suspicion can kill. Be patient!

But... how can I keep quiet about this? That scoundrel, was there anything I didn't do for him? Why would he hide this from me?

No...Maybe he just forgot! Of course he will tell me about it... maybe even tonight. Manonmani tried to feel confident.

When the children returned home from school, she served them hot tea. She remained patient until seven in the evening, when he should have come home. But he didn't; she was still waiting at nine. Had he gone to meet *her*? She tried reassuring herself: *He'll tell you—if he's still the same old Ravi. Of course he'll tell you.*

He returned at a quarter past nine. While serving him dinner she began a casual chat.

"The house was filthy. So I took a day off to clean it. Even then I didn't have enough time to change the bedcovers or wash the pillowcases."

There! She had given him a hint that she might have found what was hidden under the bed. This was his cue to be honest.

But Ravi's response was just, "This is so like you. Why won't you listen to me? Couldn't it have waited until Sunday, when I could have helped? Why waste a day of your leave for this?"

After dinner, he lay in bed, lost in a Sidney Sheldon novel.

She snatched the book from his hand. Sitting next to him, hugging him, she asked, "Do you have to read as soon as you come home?"

"Don't interrupt me... I'm right at the good part of the story!"

"You used to talk to me more often. Please, let's talk..."

"So what should I talk about?"

"I didn't used to have to tell you what to talk about!"

"I don't have anything to say now. If you have something to say, tell me, and I'll listen."

There! He *was* hiding something! Forcing back tears, she continued, "So, why were you late this evening?"

"I went to a poetry reading."

"At the beach?"

"No, a different place today."

"Take me with you, sometime. I want to see what goes on at these things. What poem did you read today?"

"I didn't read today."

"Why?"

"What kind of a question is that? I didn't read, that's all," he snapped, and turned his back to her.

Oh God! He's hiding the truth. I'm losing him already...

She was unable to sleep. Once he starting snoring softly, she got up and checked all the pockets in his shirt and pants. Then she took out his purse. There was a sheet of paper tucked between the banknotes. She opened it.

A rigid heart,
a heart of iron, has become a bent cane.
What pride it held!

All is now crushed,
the iron is gone.
Two magnetic eyes
caught in a magnetic web.
You, iron flower,
When will you be free?

The same handwriting! She got up to search the purse methodically until she found another paper.

There are no handcuffs here;
the feet are still free.
Why, then, such distress?
It is the heart that is captured.
Let me go, let me go,
the heart wails softly.
Who is the captor?
What is binding it?
The pool was still and clear;
who caused the ripples?
Let's beckon that cupid
here, and give
one smarting slap
shall we?

This was *his* handwriting. Had he lost the courage to give her the poem?

The poem mentioned *ripples*...

She went to the toilet to have a good cry. Then she washed her face, came back to bed, and started to think.

What are you going to do now, Mano? Man's temptation is nothing new. Are you really going to call him a prick and walk off? It's easy to make that threat—not so easy to put it into action. You're getting riled up over a faceless woman. You have no idea how this all started. In these modern times, men

*and women work side-by-side outside their homes. Temptation is common to
both. Who doesn't have secrets? Don't you have any?*

Manonmani was shaken. She looked back into her heart and
memories.

"Come in Mano, please have a seat."

"Did you call me, sir?"

"Yes. You took leave yesterday, on short notice?"

"Sorry, sir. I had to go to a family function. I was delayed there."

"That's alright," he smiled.

"Anything important, sir?"

"Nothing much, but I was bored yesterday. The office looked
empty."

Manonmani looked at him, startled.

"Please don't take any more leave, Mano. Without you here, I find
this place unbearable."

"Sir!"

"Are you shocked by what I said? But it's the truth!"

"Why, sir?"

"I don't know."

Those words echoed in her mind the whole day. The next day, she
dressed up a little more than usual.

"Wow! You look beautiful! That sari matches your complexion."

The words would have charmed any woman. Mano softened a bit.
She returned the compliment: "And that striped shirt suits you well,
sir."

"Thank you. Today's my birthday, Mano."

"Is that so? Happy birthday!"

"Is that all I get? Why don't you come out with me for coffee this
evening?"

"Where to?"

"Wherever you want to go. Shall we go to Buhari's, by the beach?
They have a beautiful terrace."

She agreed. Not with any immoral intent; it was just exciting that a man still found her attractive enough to spend his extra time with her.

They sat opposite each other at Buhari's, and ordered cutlets. Their order took a long time to arrive.

"Why do they take so long?"

"No one comes here to finish business deals, Mano. They come for a peaceful meal. Or they come as couples... so they don't mind if it's slow."

She looked around them. At every single table, a couple was seated, engrossed in romantic conversation. Except them, of course!

"How do you feel, Mano? Do you like the atmosphere? I come here a lot. Have you ever come here with your husband?"

"Tch! He has no time for all this. Tell him there's a poetry reading, and he will jump up and run out. The only other place he goes is to his office. God knows which client he's meeting with now."

"Forget him! Do you like this place?"

"I do. It makes me feel very relaxed."

"Of all the things I like about you, Mano, I like your smile the best. Such a lovely smile! It's not only your lips, but your eyes. Your face lights up like a 1000 watt bulb. That's why I keep calling you to my room, just to look at that smile."

After that night, she stood frequently in front of the mirror, smiling, to check if his comment was true. She even asked Ravi.

"My friend told me I look beautiful when I smile. What do you think?"

"Who said that? You look like a demon!"

He was joking, of course. Still, she was hurt.

After that, she said yes whenever *he* invited her out in the evenings. She didn't think she was doing anything wrong. She liked being asked. It was a good friendship. It pleased her that *he* observed her so keenly. She felt good when *he* complimented her. "Why doesn't my husband notice any of these things about me?" she wondered. She never sat back to wonder what was drawing *him* to her.

So when *he* asked her one evening, "What are we doing, seeing each other like this, Mano?" she replied, "It's just friendship."

He laughed and said, "Bah humbug! I like this nearness. I'm really happy when I'm with you. What do you feel, Mano?"

"Nothing!"

"That's a lie."

"No… it's true."

"Are you saying you're not as attracted to me as I am to you? Then why do you come out with me every time I ask you?"

It was a good point. Why *was* she saying yes? Why was she doing this, with no thought for her children or her husband? For the first time, she felt a shiver in her body. She was struck by the sudden fear that maybe she was going down the wrong path.

"I think we are in love with each other, Mano!"

She was truly scandalized by this announcement. "Sundar, I'm married! I'm the mother of two children!"

"So am I Mano—married and a father. My son is ten years old. But that can't stop my feelings, can it?"

"Sundar… this is very wrong. Isn't it possible for a man and a woman to have a platonic relationship? *I* think so."

"What silliness. You're just scared of damaging your own self-esteem, if you agree."

"No!" she nearly screamed. "No, Sundar. Please, let's not meet outside the office, or go out for coffee or to the beach anymore."

"Why? Because you're afraid you'll be tempted to do more? Then you've contradicted yourself; you *do* want this to go further."

"Whatever it may be, Sundar, we have to live with certain moral codes and ethics. Those rules can't be broken so carelessly. Never mind if they are right or wrong."

"So it's true; you *are* attracted to me. You're only scared of our society, and our culture. If not for all these cultural codes, then you would sleep with me—is that right? Fine, Mano. I shall, for your sake, respect the ethics and culture you hold so dear. It's really not your body I care for; it's the soul inside that I love. That's why I've never made an attempt to touch you. A piece of your spirit belongs to me, anyway; I will think of you wherever I am. I doubt you'll forget me, either. It's not quite so easy as you think."

She had never gone out with him again. She had even asked for a transfer to a different office. Still, even Ahalya had taken pride in the fact that Indran was attracted to her. Mano was no different. Even now, after all this time, the memory of his words still excited her. It was a thrilling feeling that somewhere out there was a soul that truly loved her.

Every woman wants to be loved. A married woman is no exception. Her honor might prevent her from acting on it; she might remain virtuous because of social pressures. But it was a rare woman indeed who was entirely spared from the effect of these ripples.

Temptation, for either man or woman, is not a modern phenomenon. There is a private space in each one that cannot be shared even with the most loving, trusting spouse. She had private secrets herself, so how could she begrudge Ravi his? Just because he was a man, was he more likely to cross the limits? No, he wasn't like that. Even on nights when she refused his advances because she was tired, he had been understanding. "Forget it Mano; there's always tomorrow." Today, a new love had crossed his path. But he would not forget his home, his wife and children. He would defeat the temptation the same way she had. His new love would, in the same way as hers, eventually become buried in his heart as pleasant memories. And she would not begrudge him this. If she did, it could destroy their marriage.

Mano was at peace. At last, her head clear, she rolled over to go to sleep.

Maya Maan, by Vidya Subramaniam; cover art by Ubaldu

Cover of an Indra Soundar Rajan novel,
Naan Irukkiren, published in *Crime Story*

INDRA SOUNDAR RAJAN

Indra Soundar Rajan is something of an expert on Hindu traditions and mythological lore. Most of his novels deal with cases of supernatural occurrence and divine intervention, often based on or inspired by true stories reported from various locales around South India. Another extremely prolific writer, he has penned more than 500 short novels, and has also written scripts for many popular and long-running television serials.

He lives in the ancient temple city of Madurai with his family.

THE REBIRTH OF JEEVA

ஜீவா, என் ஜீவா (1993)

∦ 1 ∦

The laws of Karma require the death and rebirth of man. It is folly to suppose that a soul, merely through the act of dying, could free itself completely from the effects of the actions of its living days. Unconsciously, these effects are embedded in a person's brain cells, and even after the body dies, they remain embedded in the soul. Thus the thoughts are carried forth as currents into a newly fertilized uterus, and become part of a new body, to be activated whenever necessary.

—Upanishad

UMA WAS HAPPY. She had an angelic look about her as she packed a *salwar kameez* into her suitcase.

Her mother, Visalam, looked up from folding the clothes. "So, how long is this tour?" she asked.

"A week, Amma. The college has done a really good job of arranging everything. Instead of making the standard trip to Kodaikanal or Ooty, we thought we'd make it educational this time. The history students are going to Mahabalipuram, Belur and Chithannavaasal. The botany students are touring the Kolli and Javadu Hills. Every class is going somewhere that relates to their subject." Rolling up a *churidhar*, Uma turned to her mother with an excited look. "And the best part is…"

She was interrupted by Avinash, her elder brother, who appeared in the doorway. "What's the big deal, anyway? You act like you're planning to skip the train and bus, and trek the whole way on foot!" he teased.

"Stop teasing, *Anna*. Do you have any idea how much planning has gone into this? But, you know, we *are* going to have a hiking tour to one place."

"Really? And which place is that?" he asked, changing into his *lungi*.

"Velamangalam," Uma replied.

Avinash's face paled. "Velamangalam?"

"Yes, Anna. There's a very ancient Shenbaga Devi temple there," she continued, and then suddenly noticed that all the color had drained from his face. "What? Why are you looking so troubled?" she demanded.

"It's just that the Velamangalam Shenbaga Devi temple is a total ruin now. Our magazine has published reports of a lot of illicit liquor brewing and prostitution going on in the area. Also, the route up to the temple is supposed to be dangerous. The mountain path is so badly damaged that hardly anyone goes there anymore. And it's said that the few women who *do* go up never return alive. There have been quite a few reports about cases like this. So, forgive me if I'm a little worried!"

Avinash was the sub-editor of a popular magazine, and very worldly-wise; she couldn't simply dismiss his concerns. Although his words made her feel anxious, she rushed to defend the trip. "Anna, it's not like I'll be traveling alone," she said. "There's going to be a big gang of students along with me. Half of them are boys."

But Visalam could not be so quickly reassured. "And just what are you supposed to be learning by wandering all over the countryside? College tours, hmph! I'm not sure I'm going to allow you to travel anywhere at all. What's the need for a virginal young girl to go traveling to such a dangerous place? Your uncle's son Raghav will be arriving soon from Delhi. Before long he'll marry you, and after that the two of you can go off on all the adventures you want. Not now!" she exclaimed.

Uma's face hardened. The joy that had illuminated her face fizzled like a sparkler in the rain. "Anna, why do you have tell such horror stories in front of Amma? Now look, she's started making excuses to stop me from going. It's just a college trip, and we chose Velamangalam for a bit of adventure. We'll be very careful and safe. You don't have to worry, it's not like we're babies." She slammed her suitcase shut.

Visalam gave Avinash a silent, pleading look. Avinash rubbed his jaw thoughtfully. "Okay, Uma... I don't want to dampen your spirits. But please, be careful. If you climb that hill, you should start only after ten in the morning, and be sure to be back by sundown. If anyone gives you any trouble, don't let them provoke you. Velamangalam is an important enough agricultural town that our magazine has a correspondent there. If necessary, you can call on him for help. His name is Ganesan. Here, I have his card; you keep it," he said, handing over a visiting card.

Visalam watched Uma tuck the card in her handbag. "I brought you up too much like a boy. Now you're too fearless," she said, screwing up her mouth.

Uma grinned, and looked at her watch. It was almost time for the van to arrive.

"So, what time do you leave?" asked Avinash.

"Soon. We'll be traveling in a Maruti van. They should be picking me up any minute," said Uma.

"But what do I tell Raghav?"

"Tell him I've gone on a college trip."

"He'll feel bad that you've gone on a vacation just when he's visiting us."

"What else am I supposed to do? Who told him to visit now, anyway? Why can't he come later?"

"Uma, this is your future husband you're talking about! Don't insult him!"

"As of now, he's just my cousin. I'm not thinking about future husbands yet. So I'll refer to him however I wish."

Surprised at Uma's bluntness, Visalam shot a concerned look at Avinash, hoping for his support. But he just grinned.

"Why are you grinning? You, at least, could show some more responsibility," Visalam nagged at her son. "Raghav has an important job, and earns well. How can you let your sister speak so flippantly about him? If she goes on like this after her wedding, what will my brother and his wife think of me as a mother?"

Uma ignored them both, and finally Avinash got impatient as well.

"Amma! You are making a scene about nothing. You have to learn to be more lenient with girls today. It's not like how it was with women in your time. They won't just nod and agree to everything, like those fortune-telling bulls that bob their heads to the beat of a drum."

From outside came the loud honk of a car horn, followed by excited shouts.

"Anna, the van's here," Uma called out, picking up her suitcase. Visalam peered out the window.

The van was bright purple, with several heavy pieces of luggage tied to the top. Seven or eight young men and women were crammed inside. A boy wearing dark sunglasses craned his neck out of the window and yelled, "Uma!"

"Coming, Dinesh!" Uma called out as she hurried out the door.

"Aren't you going to say your prayers before you leave?" Visalam shouted from inside.

"You say them on my behalf," Uma replied, her bangles jingling as she waved. Avinash waved back, a slightly troubled expression on his face as he watched the van disappear over the horizon.

The van sped down the highway like an arrow. To pass the time, the crowd inside started a loud game of *anthakshari*. Uma, though, was looking out the window, lost amongst the passing tamarind trees and the green fields beyond. As the day wore on, the sing-along eventually petered out, and after that no one spoke for a long time.

Suddenly, the vehicle shuddered to a halt.

"Hey Raj, why'd you stop?" the passengers called out to the driver.

Four men had surrounded the van. One of them carried a large moneybox. "Sir, we're collecting contributions for the guardian deity of the road, Veera Muniyan…"

"Chee!" exclaimed a student named Bhaskar. Another, Dhayal, started haranguing the driver. "You stopped for this nonsense? What are you, jobless?" Turning back to the students, he said, "Alright, somebody give me some change."

The man holding the moneybox was scanning the crowd inside the van. When his gaze settled on Uma, his eyes bulged. A look of great surprise spread over his face.

"Oh, *Thayee!* My salutations to you!" he cried. "Don't you remember me? I am Vanamalai."

Uma blinked at him, perplexed. "Vanamalai? Who? I'm sure I've never met you before."

"You don't you recognize me? You came with Karunakaran, decorated with garlands, to this very same Muniyan temple. Have you forgotten?" Vanamalai asked, flashing a set of betel juice-stained teeth.

"Uma, he must be confusing you with someone else. Let's get going," called a zoology student named Shankaranarayanan.

"Oh no, sir! I am speaking to the right person. I still remember the words she spoke, exactly eighteen years back…"

Uma arched an eyebrow at Vanamalai.

"What are you talking about? I don't understand this Tamil you're speaking," Shankaranarayanan said. "Eighteen years back? She was hardly even born yet! Raj, come on, start the engine. If we sit here listening to these people, they'll start weaving garlands around our ears."

Raj started the van, and they accelerated away. But Uma, watching out the window, could not take her eyes off Vanamalai. She was starting to get the strangest feeling that perhaps she *had* seen him before.

"Hey, Uma, don't get freaked out! He was just blabbering some bullshit. No need to dwell on it. You've never been to this district before, have you?" asked Bhaskar.

"This is *my* first visit," Shankaranarayan interrupted.

Uma gazed out of the car window. "This is my first visit too, Bhaskar. But I'm having an intense feeling of déjà vu. Somehow, I feel I know this road. Along here somewhere there should be a lone palm tree, with a yogi's tombstone under it."

No sooner were the words out of her mouth than the van rounded a bend, and a lone palm tree appeared ahead, with a weathered grave marker just below it.

"Hey! There it is, just like you said, the tree and the tombstone!" yelled her classmate Vaijayanthi. "What is this, a practical joke? You must be having us on. You've been here before after all."

"No, I swear, I'm not lying!" snapped Uma, as shocked as the others that her prediction had come true. "I've never been here before!"

A few cows that had been grazing in a field had decided to sunbathe in the middle of the road, and the van was forced to slow to a halt. Raj honked impatiently. At the sound of the horn, an old cowherd got up from napping in the field to shoo his cows off the road.

"Can't you keep better control of your animals?" Raj scolded him.

The cowherd look up at Raj. "Very sorry, aiya," he said. Then his eyes fell on Uma, and flew wide open.

"Jeeva! You have returned, just as you promised!" he cried excitedly. "O Thayee, I cannot believe my eyes! This is the divine grace of Shenbaga Devi!"

The crowd in the van stared at him in stunned silence.

⊁ 2 ⊁

A man's sins and good deeds are not the only things that follow him into his next lives. His education, the knowledge he has acquired, the music he has enjoyed—all these things and many others follow him as well. The sage Valluvar has claimed that the knowledge gained by a man in one life is retained through his next seven lives.

—*Chandilya, from his commentary on the scriptures*

Uma's friends were utterly flabbergasted at the cowherd's delighted reaction. "Uma, did you hear that? Does any of this make sense to you? These people actually think you are the reincarnation of someone called Jeeva! Or else we're all going nuts."

Bhaskar yelled out to the cowherd. "Who are you anyway? What is all this nonsense?" The cowherd did not respond; he continued to stare at Uma's face, as though he were in a trance. "Hey! Can you hear me?" Bhaskar demanded again.

The cowherd slowly opened his dark lips. "It is not easy for me to believe, myself. But I cannot dismiss this as a coincidence. There are many things in the world that are beyond human understanding. Jeeva's story promises to be one such miracle."

"Which Jeeva story are you talking about?"

"The very same Jeeva who is sitting beside you in the van."

"She's not Jeeva, man! Her name is Uma."

"She might be Uma to you. But to Velamangalam and the eight surrounding villages of these hills, she is Jeeva."

"*Aiyyo!* Please talk sense!"

"Never mind about me; who are you young people? Where are you headed?"

"We're college students; this is a class trip. We're going for a tour of the Shenbaga Devi temple."

"To that accursed place?"

"Accursed? What's the curse there?"

"You will find out soon enough. But Jeeva, you have arrived at the perfect moment. I was beginning to think that the Goddess had lost Her power. I realize now that I was mistaken. Go on, my lady! You must find a way to end your daughter's suffering, and help your husband recover from his mental collapse. Go!"

Having finished this puzzling speech, the cowherd bent over in a respectful bow. The old man waved his cattle onward, a cheap black Kumarapalayam blanket draped over his shoulders, a few blades of grass clinging to his hair. The students stared after him as though they'd just been presented with a exam paper where they couldn't understand any of the questions. Uma, however, simply stared into the distance, deep in thought. A gray crow watched her from its perch on a tree branch; it seemed to be waiting for a reaction.

From this point in the road, the Velamangalam hilltop was visible in the distance. It was so covered with lush green vegetation that, from this far away, it was difficult to make out the location of the temple. The far side of the hill ended in a sheer stone cliff. It was this huge rock that now drew Uma's attention. As she focused on it, a vivid image swept into her mind; she was being thrown from the top, hurling through the air towards the boulders below...

She screamed. Her friends whipped around to face her. Everybody began to speak at once.

"Uma! What happened?"

"She was looking at that huge rock... what the hell is going on here?"

"Come on, Uma, talk to us. Why did you scream?"

"Hey!" someone yelled at the cowherd. "See what you've done with your crazy stories, you've completely freaked her out! Get lost!"

"Come on Raj, let's get moving..."

The van gathered speed again. Uma continued to stare out the window. Large pearls of sweat had formed on her forehead. A new image came to her; now she was holding a newborn baby in her arms. She could hear the child's sobs. Two little arms reached out; there was spittle around the lips; its eyes were wet with tears. It gave a high-pitched, choking scream. What was she seeing?

Her eyes filled with tears. Her lips quietly mouthed the words, "My child! My dear child!"

Her friends looked at her with concern.

"Uma!" called Sharkaranarayanan. "What's happened to you?"

She was unable to reply; she could not avert her eyes from the horizon. She felt as though the fabric of time had been ripped, and the moments of the present were spilling away into the past, like flour from a torn bag.

The van sped down the highway. They were nearing the foothills of Velamangalam. The village was nestled in a valley on the leeward side of the hill. Television antennas poked upwards from many tiled roofs. Green, fertile fields surrounded the buildings. A number of white cranes, standing on one leg, hunted for crabs in the streams. The scenery took their breath away.

"What should we do first? Visit the village or climb up the hill?"

"Why waste time in the village? We're here to see the temple on the hill."

"Fine—Vaijayanthi, you take the camera. Sharada, you take the tape recorder. Bhaskar, you take notes."

"Hey, wait a second—what about Uma? She's still sitting there all silent. She's just had a very strange experience—we can't just ignore that."

"What experience? We were accosted by two village simpletons talking some nonsense about 'Jeeva' and some goddess. Exactly how is that a big deal?"

"It's nothing. Forget about it."

"Yeah, come on, let's try to be rational, please. We're supposed to be educated, urban people."

As their argument continued, a bullock cart appeared a short distance away, and came to a stop at the foot of the hill. Four men got down from the back of the cart and ran up a path, quickly disappearing among the thorny bushes. The driver of the cart did not go with them. He sat at the front of the cart, smoking a beedi and surveying the area. Catching sight of the van full of students, he arched a curious eyebrow at them, and took another drag of his beedi. As his mouth filled with smoke, his eyes came to rest on Uma. Immediately, his attitude changed; he became anxious, and started to tremble. Uma saw him as well, and her eyes widened with strange recognition. The man jumped off the cart, and then he too scrambled up the path into the bushes.

⚡ 3 ⚡

There are said to be just seven material wonders of the world, but the non-material wonders of the universe are uncountably many. One of these is the miracle of past lives. It is knowledge of his past lives that can lead a man towards enlightenment, and relieve him from his sins. Many strange, complicated, wondrous processes occur after a person's death; it is these processes that determine whether a soul is reborn as a lowly goat or as a divine cow.

—Upanishad

The footpath snaked up the hill through a tangle of branches and shrubbery. The cart driver ran purposefully, pushing the growth aside. Further down the path was a clearing where a fire had been burning. A few men sat around a patch of ground covered with glowing embers. One of them noticed the cart driver's approach. "Hey look, here comes Mamundi," he said in a hushed voice. The crowd turned to look at him as he rushed up.

"What is it, Mamundi? Why are you in such a hurry?"

"Where is Thyagu *Aiya?*"

"He hasn't come."

"Then he must still be at home. I'll go there at once."

"He's busy with the wedding preparations. Why do you need to see him now?"

"I have my reasons—there's no time to explain fully. There's a tourist group on their way to the hill. There is a girl among them… if you laid eyes on her, you would be amazed. We may have locked up the temple and stopped worshipping Her, but the power of the Goddess is limitless; I'm sure of that now. I must be off!"

Mamundi turned, and ran back down the hill with the same speed he had come up. The crowd was left standing bemused around the huge pots of illicit liquor brewing on the low fire.

On the other side of Velamangalam, a stream of tears flowed from a girl's eyes. She was eighteen, but looked far younger. A heavy silk sari hung unnaturally around her small frame. Dark circles around her eyes spoke of a life filled with much more sorrow than laughter. Small burn marks dotted the skin over the whole of her body. Indeed, she looked to be one of the most violated women in the world. Everyone felt sorry for Shenbagam when they saw her, but they knew if they tried to do anything about it, they would be made to share her misery. It was Thyagu, the demon, who was responsible for her plight; Thyagu, that amalgamation of all the most traitorous, murderous, devilish instincts a man could possess; Thyagu, the self-styled monarch of Velamangalam. He was a tyrannical ruler, but one with no wealth of his own. And it was for the acquisition of wealth that the fifty-year-old Thyagu was torturing this girl, who was younger than his own daughter, into marrying him.

Everyone in the village knew the story of how Thyagu had tried—unsuccessfully—to wed Jeeva. Now, he sought to wed her daughter Shenbagam, so he could finally lay claim to the great fortune left by the late chief, Patta Naicker. Thyagu would have to tie the *thali* around Shenbagam's neck by force; but once it was done, no one could deny the marriage. Still, they all knew that no good would come of it. The villagers were sure that God would not stand still in the face of these transgressions, but would somehow come to the aid of this long-suffering, motherless girl, and her mentally imbalanced father.

Ah, Shenbagam's poor father! There he was, beside the garbage bin on the other side of town—that derelict picking through the rubbish and mumbling incoherently to himself. How had he fallen to such a state?

"He might have been a king; he might have ridden through the streets atop an elephant. But just see what fate has done to him; now he crawls through the gutters, completely out of his head. If only Jeeva were still alive, things would have been different." This was how the villagers spoke of him, but they did no more than shed impotent tears; they did nothing to help the poor man. No one dared to defy Thyagu.

At that moment, Thyagu was standing proud like a young groom, decorated in silk and jewellery, clouds of perfume filling the air around him. His lips, however, stank of cheap liquor.

"So what does she have to say? Is she going to wed me and be happy, or does she choose to suffer?"

"Forget about whether she agrees or not," replied one of Thyagu's henchmen. "You want her; that's it. Why ask unnecessary questions? At dawn, you will wed Shenbagam at the temple on the hill. By tomorrow, you will be the inheritor of Patta Naicker's estate."

Just then, Mamundi came running in.

"Aiya, Aiya!"

"What's your problem, Mamundi? Have the police taken the hooch?" said Thyagu, sounding bored. "No matter how much we bribe them, they have to pick on us once in a while to fill their quotas."

"No Aiya, it's Jeeva, who died eighteen years ago... I saw her just now, alive..."

Thyagu was unnerved. "What do you mean?"

"I'm telling you, I saw Jeeva!"

"How can you *see* a dead person?"

"Maybe it's her reincarnation!"

"You expect me to believe that?"

"Aiya, I'm not lying. You can see her for yourself. The girl has come as a tourist, to visit the Shenbaga Amman temple."

"A woman who resembles Jeeva?"

"This is no mere resemblance. It is Jeeva herself! Have you forgotten what she swore as she died?"

No, Thyagu had not forgotten. Even now, her voice still rang in his ears—the words she had sworn with her final, heaving breaths, as her body lay broken among the aloe bushes at the base of the cliff: "You can kill me, you can separate me from my husband and my newborn child. But I shall return! I swear on the power of Shenbaga Amman, I shall return! If Her power is true, I shall be reborn, and then I shall not let you escape. I will make you pay with interest for all your torture! Patta Naicker's wealth was earned through hard work; there is no share in it for a stray dog like you. It will never be yours!" As hard as he had tried, Thyagu had never been able to erase Jeeva's dying speech from his memory.

But now a rational voice in his head raised an objection. *This is the real world, not a movie plot. Why should you be afraid to take a look?* He took a step forward, but was immediately stopped by an old man with a stern expression. It was Rudraiyya, Thyagu's sixty-year-old, bald-headed, conniving uncle, carrying his thick staff in his hand. This man was Thyagu's trusted mentor. No one was sure where he had been born, who he was related to, or who his forefathers had been. All they knew was that Thyagu had never been known to disobey Rudraiyya's command.

"Where are you off to, Thyagu? You want to have a look at that woman?"

"Yes, Rudraiyya. I want to see this so-called reincarnation."

"You don't believe such a thing is possible?"

"Come on, this is the twentieth century. These modern electric crematoriums leave nothing but ashes behind—not even the bones."

"If you truly believe that, then why are you so eager to see her? Better to just ignore this tourist woman. You are to wed Shenbagam at dawn. You should not step on that hill except as a groom."

"Of course, Rudraiyya. Still, why can't I just have a look at this chick? I've heard every person has seven look-alikes somewhere in the world."

"Who knows, it could be true. Nevertheless, you should stay put!"

Rudraiyya's forceful command was obeyed. Still, a doubt lingered on in Thyagu's mind: was it possible that Jeeva had truly been reborn?

⚊ 4 ⚊

Some children are able to learn certain lessons quickly at a very young age. Some are able to sing beautifully, some can dance, some are skilled only in sleeping.... These are traits that develop when the child is still in the mother's womb; the fundamental reason for this is the effect of the child's past lives.

—*Dr. Wilson*

As they approached the Shenbaga Devi temple on the hilltop, the incredible scenic beauty of the area melted their hearts. There were a few young boys tending to a herd of cattle.

"Hey you!" called Dinesh, one of the students. "Come here—what is the name of the goddess of this temple?"

"Shenbaga Devi."

"Can you tell us anything more about it?"

"Well, there's supposed to be an underground passage beneath it."

"Really?"

"Really! The passage leads to the house of Patta Naicker."

"Where is that? And who is this Patta Naicker?"

"Who knows? That's what they say in the village, though."

The sun was setting fast. While the rest of the students were strolling along, Uma walked purposefully towards the *dwajasthambam*, the column connecting heaven, earth, and the netherworld. Tied to the side of the column, a saffron flag flapped in the wind; a mountain eagle was perched on the top. Uma felt that she knew this column well, that she had been here at least a hundred times. Bhaskar approached her. "What's wrong, Uma?" he asked. "Why are you staring at the dwajasthambam like that?"

"I have a feeling I've seen it before."

"Oh no, don't start that again! That story those villagers fed you has still got you hallucinating. We came here for a picnic; this is supposed to be fun, as well as educational. Have you forgotten that completely? What is all this nonsense?"

"It's not nonsense Bhaskar. I have a strong feeling."

"Ok, fine. You have a feeling. Can you please forget about it now?"

They passed the dwajasthambam and came to the *mandap*, with its sixteen pillars. The place was in ruins; bats and rodents had taken over, and an overpowering stench filled the air. The sun had now set, and darkness was thickening. While the other students were using their torches to explore the rest of the temple grounds, Uma walked steadily through the darkness, up the sixteen steps, to the closed door of the *garbhagraham*—the inner chamber of the temple that housed the idol. She pushed the door; it opened with a loud creak.

"Bhaskar!" she called out. Bhaskar came running with a torch.

"What are you doing here, Uma? It's getting dark. We should be leaving soon."

"Just shut up and come along with me."

Some instinct told her to shut the door of the garbhagraham behind them. She and Bhaskar stood facing the idol. On their left, set in the wall, was a series of small niches, each housing a brass *diya*, caked with dirt. Uma reached out towards one of the oil lamps and gave it a twist. As she did so, the idol and the pedestal on which it sat began to move.

Bhaskar's eyes nearly popped out of his head. "Uma, how did you know about this?"

"Later. Help me turn this lamp fully. Please!" Bhaskar stepped up to help her. As he turned with all his strength, the pedestal started to move faster, to reveal the entrance to a tunnel.

"Follow me," Uma beckoned him.

"Hey Uma, what is this? This is like something straight out of one of those cheap Telugu mythological films dubbed in Tamil. Where can this tunnel lead? I'm scared, Uma."

"Don't be. This tunnel leads to my house."

"To your *house*? You want me to believe this tunnel is over a hundred miles long?"

"Will you please just shut up and come along?" she said, starting down the steps.

"Uma, the gang will be worried about us."

"Let them worry. I'm worried about my daughter, and that's more important."

"You're hallucinating again. Oh god, I thought this trip was going to be fun! I wasn't expecting it to turn into a Vitalacharya movie!"

Uma, ignoring Bhaskar's chatter, forged ahead deep into the tunnel. He followed behind her. At the end of the steps they came into a huge hall, with large portraits hung up and down the walls. The faces of the portraits were hidden under a mass of cobwebs. Two doors stood at opposite ends of the room. One was marked with the words "The Foothills", and the other with the words "House of Patta Naicker".

Uma pointed at one of the portraits. "Bhaskar, dust that one off, please." Reluctantly, he obeyed. Slowly, the portrait became visible—and then Bhaskar stopped, dumbfounded.

"Uma, this is a picture of you!"

"Yes, it's me. Next to that one is my father, Singa Naicker, and my mother, Manonmani. My grandfather, Patta Naicker, is over there."

She swung Bhaskar's torchlight over to another portrait. As they wiped away the grime, a picture emerged of a majestic-looking old man in a silk turban and silk *sherwani*. He wore a huge gold chain with a Lakshmi pendant around his neck, and sandal *pottu* on his forehead. He had the unmistakable look of royalty.

Bhaskar was weak with disbelief. Beside him, Uma burst into loud sobs.

"Why are you crying, Uma?"

"I don't know! Bhas, there's a huge sadness weighing on my heart. I don't have any control over my thoughts anymore. I keep hearing someone—my daughter—praying: 'Amma, please save me!'"

"My god, what are you saying? This is all so unbelievable!" Bhaskar cried out. "Those people we met on the road, who called you Jeeva—they must have really known something! There must really be something supernatural going on! Otherwise how could you identify these portraits? This is totally thrilling! What an experience! Uma, what are you going to do now? Why did you come here? First, tell me that!"

"One minute." Uma was scanning the floor with her torchlight. Soon she found what she was searching for; a wooden chest. She opened it to reveal a diamond-studded crown. Excited, she heard Jeeva's last words echo through her mind: *Patta Naicker's fortune was earned through hard work—there is no share in it for a stray dog like you. It will never be yours!*

The will was still there, beneath the crown. The document was old and slightly damaged, but it was safe. They marveled at these plans, laid down so long ago, to safeguard Patta Naicker's estate here in this secret temple chamber.

"Bhaskar, let's go back outside now. But you have to promise not to tell anyone what you saw here."

Bhaskar laughed out loud. "Even if I did, do you think anyone would believe me?"

"I have been guided here for an important purpose, and fate has chosen you as my companion. Come with me now. This door will lead to the bottom of the hill."

Bhaskar looked back up at the stairway down which they had come. The pedestal had swung shut behind them; there was no other way but forward. They opened the door of the passage to the foothills, and immediately a large bat flew in, as though it had been waiting for them. Startled, Uma gave a yelp, and fell back onto Bhaskar.

Whatever the time or circumstances, when a young woman and man touch each other, some chemical reaction is bound to take place. Bhaskar now felt the full effect of that chemistry. Beautiful Uma, a healthy eighteen years old—when a voluptuous breast brushes against a man's broad chest, what need is there for special reactors to produce nuclear energy?

Bhaskar felt a surge of lust speed through his nerves. There was a moment of uneasy silence. Somehow, they both managed to compose themselves. Slowly Uma backed away from his chest, saying, "Sorry, Bhas."

"The pleasure was mine," he teased. But Uma was no longer in the mood for jokes.

The door had opened onto a steep rocky passage. The tunnel was cramped and suffocating, and they had no way of knowing how long it was. But Uma was holding tightly onto Bhaskar's hand, and he hoped the trek would never end.

Eventually, they emerged from the tunnel into a tangle of bushes on the leeward side of the mountain. There was no one around. Bhaskar raised his arms to stretch—and then suddenly froze. Perched on a rocky ledge, just an arm's length away, were dozens of cobras, standing erect with their hoods outstretched. Their eyes glinted in the torchlight.

The sound of faint sobs could be heard from far away. Quietly, trying not to disturb the serpents, Uma and Bhaskar moved towards the noise. The cobras relaxed back onto the ledge, as though bathing in the light of the full moon.

The sobs grew louder. As the two approached the sound, they realized the source was a tiny hut, illuminated only by a small lantern. Bhaskar tiptoed up and peeked into the hut. Inside was a very old woman, weeping aloud. Who was this woman, crying so pathetically while the rest of the world slept?

Bhaskar silently beckoned Uma to come and have a look. Peering into the hut, Uma recognized the woman as Azhagammai Paati—a woman who had witnessed the births of four generations. Uma gasped aloud, "Paati! You're still alive?"

The old woman looked up, startled. In a tremulous voice, she asked, "Who's there?"

"It's me, Jeeva," Uma announced, not even conscious of using the other name. The old woman's eyes twinkled with joy.

"Jeeva? The granddaughter of my brother, Patta Naicker? Is it really you?" She hobbled up to Uma. "Oh, dear Goddess, Mother Shenbagam! Once again, You have proved Your divine grace. So, Jeeva, you have truly been reborn! I was crying just now, thinking about you, my blood boiling because the entire lineage of Patta Naicker is going to the dogs. Early tomorrow morning, your daughter Shenbagam is going to be married to that demon Thyagu. Once that happens, no one will be able to recover Patta Naicker's fortune. You have arrived just in time, my child!"

"So you expected me here, paati?"

"I had to have faith, my child."

"But is it really possible for a dead person to come back to life?"

"It must be possible, because you have done it!"

"No... My name is Uma!"

"It's true, in this birth, you are Uma. But in the previous one, you were Jeeva."

"How can we expect anyone in the world to believe that?"

"But this town will believe it. Anyone who sees you will be convinced that you are Jeeva's reincarnation."

"I've been having some disturbing thoughts about that other life. But it's all so confusing. What if this is all just a bad dream?"

"Of course it's not a dream; this is real. The soul of an honorable woman who has been unjustly killed will never be able to rest in peace. Especially not one who has been blessed by the Goddess Shenbaga Devi! It may have been your fate to die unjustly. But you have returned to avenge that death. You are a true daughter of the Goddess. Ever since you were killed, She has refused to be worshipped. Now at last, things will be set right. Tomorrow morning, you must put a stop to the marriage, and save your child!"

"What marriage, paati?"

"Thyagu, who was responsible for your death and disgrace, plans to wed your child to lay claim to Patta Naicker's estate. He raised your daughter as his prisoner, and tomorrow he is going to wed her. He already has a daughter of his own who is older than the girl he's going to marry—it's despicable! But no one has had the guts to challenge him."

The old woman's words were making Bhaskar's head spin. "Uma, I'm willing to accept that in a previous birth, your name was Jeeva. But all this is too much. Who is this Thyagu? And what is this wedding?"

But the old woman had no patience for him. "You! If you only knew the whole story, it would kill you!"

"I'm dying already here, what's the need to bring the past into it?"

"Paati, please," begged Uma, "Tell us everything that has happened, so that not only I, but my other friends too, can understand what's going on."

"Where are your other friends?"

"We got separated. We'll have to go look for them."

"Uma, you stay here," said Bhaskar. "I'll go find them."

"No, we'll come along with you. I'll explain everything," said the old woman, taking her stick.

"But paati, the path is full of snakes!"

149

"They are my guardians, Jeeva. They are the reason why no one comes up this path. Thyagu has allowed me to live only because he thinks I am too old to be bothered with—and because he is afraid of those snakes."

They walked back to the foot of the hill, where the rest of the students were waiting. It was well past eleven o' clock. The group looked at the old woman in surprise.

"Where did you two disappear to? And who is this old hag?"

The old woman simply walked to the van and sat down inside it, and prepared to answer their questions. Slowly, she traveled in time, back to 1975.

The group remained unaware of the two pairs of eyes watching their every move from behind a nearby tree.

↗ 5 ↗

Think good thoughts. Avoid negative thinking. Once the mind has fallen into the gutter, even if it later manages to pull itself out, the negative effects remain throughout the lifetime of the soul. Of all God's creations, a man's mind is the most precious. It should be handled like valuable glassware. Otherwise, the reverberations will be felt through the next seven rebirths.

—*Dr. Wilson*

"Patta Naicker's name was revered throughout the district," Azhagammai began. "Singa Naicker, my nephew and his son, was an equally good man. Singa Naicker's wife, Manonmani, was the quiet daughter of Thudiyalur Zamin. Manonmani's brother, Thyagu, on the other hand—oh God!

"The Indian government had passed the Land Ceiling Act, which abolished the feudal *zamindari* system. Even after that, these two families remained very wealthy. But Thyagu lost all his father's money gambling on horses. Anyone would have thought it impossible to completely squander such a huge fortune, but Thyagu managed to do it. His father died shortly thereafter, of despair. Having lost both his father and his money, Thyagu came and settled here. That was the moment when all the bad luck arrived in this town."

The old woman began to cry again. Uma was amazed to find that she could actually clearly picture all the characters of the old woman's story. The memories came flooding in. Incredibly, each remembered image of her previous life was still stored somewhere in the cells of her brain.

"Singa Naicker and Manonmani had only one daughter, Jeeva," the old woman continued. "She was beautiful; it was as if Shenbaga Devi Herself had been born on Earth. That beauty, burnt to ashes on the funeral pyre, has now been reborn! Imagine how many other mysteries there must be in this world, far beyond our ability to comprehend!"

The students sat listening in awed silence. Only Bhaskar had the presence of mind to switch on the tape recorder and record the tale.

"Jeeva's grandfather loved her very much. He used to ride with her around the town in his chariot, the girl dressed in silk, decked out in gold and diamonds. While the rest of the town watched them in awed respect, there was one man who completely ignored them. That man's name was Karunakaran. When a woman accustomed to admiration notices someone ignoring her, it is natural for her to become curious and interested. So it was that when Karunakaran came on a full moon night to the Shenbaga Devi temple to worship, Jeeva saw him, and fell in love. Here was a man who could not be won over by material wealth. He didn't spare a glance at Jeeva; he was deep in meditation. His devotion captivated her, and she was determined to have him for her husband. But Karunakaran was from a lower caste. His family worked as stable keepers in the *zamin*. Even so, he had managed to complete a college degree. He was a proud man.

"Although Jeeva loved Karunakaran, Manonmani wanted her to marry her brother, Thyagu. Thyagu, of course, wanted the same thing. But Patta Naicker could not stand Thyagu. Why should he allow a drunkard and philanderer to marry his granddaughter? Jeeva hated her uncle as well. Thyagu came to realize the strength of this opposition, and understood that he would never be able to marry Jeeva... unless the situation could be changed.

"During this period, Patta Naicker and Singa Naicker, father and son, went to the Kolathur forest together to hunt. God knows what happened there, but no one ever saw them alive again—it was their corpses that returned from that place. We were told that they were killed by a tiger. Manonmani knew her brother was behind these deaths somehow, but she could not get him to confess. After some time, Thyagu renewed his attempts for Jeeva's hand. He had taken over the reins of the family. With the two lions out of the picture, the jackal took command!

"Jeeva's love for Karunakaran was strong, and though he had been reluctant at first, by now Karunakaran had come to love her strongly as well. When Thyagu learned of their affair, he lost his temper completely; he beat Jeeva badly and locked her inside her room. But this was a mistake, for Jeeva knew about the secret underground passage to the Shenbaga Devi temple. She escaped through the tunnel and married Karunakaran at the temple in secret. When they returned home as a wedded couple, Thyagu was forced to accept it. He pretended to bless them. He had to, because in his will, Patta Naicker had bequeathed his entire fortune to his granddaughter Jeeva, her husband, and—for some strange reason—*Jeeva's daughter.* How did Patta Naicker know that Jeeva would have only one daughter? Perhaps it was because of what the temple astrologer at Vaidheeswaran had predicted, so many years ago!" At this, Azhagammai produced an old, tattered notebook, and handed it to the students.

Uma and her friends looked in wonder at the strange notebook with its yellowed pages. The front cover bore a picture of Gajamuka Vinayagar. On the first page was a short prayer; on the next, a horoscope chart; and on each of the following pages, a four line stanza in Tamil—predictions for the future. Although they could read the words, they were not able to completely comprehend the meaning of the cryptic poetry. Helpfully, the astrologer had also provided the meanings of the verses in prose. Vaijayanthi, peering over Uma's shoulder, fixed on one passage, and began reading it aloud.

"'You, Patta Naicker, will suffer an untimely death. After your demise, your family will fall into a period of ruin. Your own son will be murdered. Not one member of your family will be allowed to die a natural death. But, by the grace of the Goddess Shenbaga Devi, after your great-granddaughter is born, your family will regain their luck. Jeeva, your granddaughter, who will die young and tragically, will be reborn as Uma, and save your family name. Until then, leave your material wealth in the care of Shenbaga Devi, the Goddess of your family line. From the beginning of this period of trouble, Shenbaga Devi will accept no worship. Two score years afterwards, the fire will be relit at Her feet, and honor will be restored to your descendents.'"

As Vaijayanthi finished reading the prediction, the crowd fell into shocked silence, their mouths hanging open.

"Now do you understand how we knew when we saw her that Uma was Jeeva come again? My child, this is the handiwork of fate!" declared Azhagammai.

"Paati, paati… please continue your story. You stopped at a crucial moment. Thyagu was pretending to be a good person and to have accepted the marraige. What happened next? How did Jeeva die?" demanded Bhaskar eagerly.

"Yes, yes, I shall tell you! Thyagu, of course, would stop at nothing to get Jeeva. He manipulated Karunakaran, fooling him into thinking he had changed for the good, gaining his trust, and then slowly and methodically corrupting him. Around this time, Jeeva became pregnant. Her mother, Manonmani, had already died from a snake bite. So Jeeva had no one left but Karunakaran—and by now, he was in Thyagu's clutches. Thyagu had turned him into a hard drug addict. He was perpetually doped up and unable to think straight. Thyagu was again in power, and began taking control of Patta Naicker's holdings. Jeeva was aware of her uncle's treachery, but was powerless to do anything but pray. She knew Thyagu was hunting for Patta Naicker's will and the jewels. Among these, the diamond-studded crown was the most precious. Even in the days before Independence, it was said to be worth a crore of rupees. Today, it must be worth many times that. Thyagu hoped that even if he failed to get the will changed, he might at least manage to get his hands on the diamonds.

"I was Jeeva's only remaining friend and support. Every day, she would lie on my lap and weep about the plight of her husband and her uncle's evil plans. It still hurts to think of that time. She placed all her hope and trust in the Goddess of this temple on the hill. Every day, she went there to worship. She would enter the garbhagraham, shut the door, and pray. I would stand guard outside. She refused to allow even me inside. When I asked her why, she claimed she was doing a special puja that had to be performed naked.

"Soon, she gave birth to a girl, as beautiful as the mother.

"By now, Thyagu had hatched a new plan. He had a quack doctor brought in from somewhere, who examined Karunakaran and certified that he was impotent. At first, Karunakaran did not believe it, and went to a different doctor for a second opinion. Thyagu coerced that doctor, as well, to confirm the diagnosis. Karunakaran became suspicious about Jeeva's virtuosity. He refused even to see his newborn baby. When the time came for the child to be named, Jeeva wanted to perform the ceremony in the Shenbaga Devi temple. There, the diamond-studded crown was placed on the child's head.

"I can still see the scene in my mind. Jeeva was waiting for her husband to come so she could go on with the ritual. When Karunakaran finally arrived, pumped full of drugs, he demanded to know who the child's father was. Jeeva was shaken. She fell at his feet and swore the child was his. The whole village, gathered there for the ceremony, stood watching this public spectacle in disbelief. It was then that one of Thyagu's henchmen, Parasu, stepped up. 'Tell him, Jeeva!' he said, 'Tell him it is our child!' Both Jeeva and I went wild with rage; I tried to catch hold of him and make him stop. But he didn't. Turning to the crowd, Parasu announced, 'When Jeeva came to know that her husband was impotent, she became despondent. She begged me to father a child for her. I didn't want to, but she was adamant—without an heir, her family's fortune would revert to the possession of the temple. She forced me to oblige... In a way, Jeeva is also my wife.'

"And that was how the naming ceremony was ruined. It became a name-spoiling ceremony. I can still remember Jeeva's tears."

As the old woman's story concluded, a hushed silence hung in the van. It was finally broken by Uma. "Yes paati, I too remember that day. I still remember that bastard who dared to slander my virtue in front of the entire town. I will not allow that bastard to survive! Paati, *I must kill!*" she screamed at the top of her voice. At her side, Bhaskar tried unsuccessfully to calm her down.

At the tree outside, one of the two men who had been hiding there listening to the entire tale had gone pale with fear. Unable to control the volume of his voice, he blurted out: "It's true then, that Jeeva is reborn. And she remembers my face, Pandi! Oh God, I fear for my life…"

The group in the van clearly heard his words. Shankaranarayanan and Bhaskar jumped out, and the two men ran for it—and but one of them stumbled, and was caught. "Hey! Who are you?" the students demanded. Someone switched the headlights on, and Uma got a look at the man's face. Then she, too, jumped out of the van. "Parasu! Bastard!" she shouted. "You ruined my life that day. Did you really think you would get away with it?"

Parasu broke free of Bhaskar's hold and dashed away, with Uma chasing at his heels. Soon, though, he came to a sudden halt. Just ahead of him was a deep gorge, filled with old termite mounds, the abodes of snakes.

Uma was still advancing menacingly towards him. Silently, the students followed in a crowd, carrying their bright torches. Someone whispered, "Uma! He's trapped, leave him there!" The old woman, however, remained watching from the van. She looked calm, as though she already knew what was about to happen.

Parasu, of course, was a hardened criminal. He could easily have torn Uma apart. But now, as he saw the spirit of Jeeva in her, his courage evaporated away into fear. His terror made his legs weak, and he kept moving, helplessly, towards the edge.

Finally, his body slid down, and he crashed into the termite mounds, smashing them apart. Snakes reared out, reflexively attacking the intruder. He was dead by the time he reached the ground. His dying cries echoed all across Velamangalam.

Uma simply stood above, watching Parasu. She felt one of the great burdens lift from her heart. Her friends gathered around her and trained their torch beams on the site of the accident. Parasu's body lay there, unmoving, with froth foaming at his mouth.

"Please, do not feel pity for him," said Azhagammai, approaching slowly. "He deserved a death a hundred times worse than the one the snakes have given him. When a man plays games with a woman's honor, he should be prepared to meet such an end."

Uma began to weep. "Oh Bhaskar, what's going on? I have no control over my actions anymore. It's as if I am possessed by someone else. I want to see my brother, Avinash. I need to talk to him. Please take me to my brother," she wept.

Azhagammai hugged her and said, "Jeeva, you have avenged yourself on one of the villains. There is one more you have to finish off, in order to save your daughter. Now is not the time to spare thoughts for Avinash, whoever he may be." The friends looked at her in alarm.

"Paati, this was supposed to be an educational field trip for us. We never dreamt of getting involved in anything like this," said Shankaranarayanan. "Up until now, we've simply watched as the events have unfolded. But now, here, in the dead of the night, a man has lost his life because of Uma. We cannot take this casually. We have to leave this town, and at once!"

There was a murmur of agreement from the others. "Yes paati—that was a riveting tale you told, but no one will believe us if we repeat it," said Vaijayanthi. "No one believes in ghosts and reincarnations anymore. And even if it is all true... we're scared!"

The old woman realized that witnessing Parasu's death had shaken the students badly. "Fine," she said. "Do as you please. Leave, if you must."

They started to breathe a sigh of relief, but she was not done. "Still, I doubt it will be so easy. Shenbaga Devi has brought you this far, at this time, for a reason. She may not let you run off so soon. Anyway, I have complete trust in Her."

Still reeling from what they'd witnessed, the students returned to the van to find yet another surprise waiting for them there. It was Uma's brother Avinash, and Ganesan, his reporter friend.

"Anna! What are you doing here?" Uma asked, hugging him tightly.

"After you left, I couldn't stop worrying. I called Ganesan to inform him that you were here. He asked me come immediately. He had heard a rumour that a girl who had died eighteen years ago had been reborn with identical looks, and he guessed that it might be my sister. I was shocked. But he had seen you, and he had also seen the dead Jeeva. So he told me about all the recent happenings in the village. He thought it was best for me to come down in case there was any trouble," explained Avinash.

"Anna, this old woman has told us the entire story of Jeeva," said Uma. "I know the story is true. I can remember everything, this village, the temple on the mountain top—I even remember your friend Ganesan here. He has a scar on his back, which he got when he slipped on the temple steps as a child."

"Avinash, it's true!" Ganesh marveled. "I do have a scar on my back. Uma is Jeeva come again."

The students now turned to Azhagammai. "But paati, you still haven't quite finished. How did Jeeva die?"

The old woman resumed her tale. "Karunakaran, his brains already addled by his drug addiction, lost his mind completely when Parasu came forward with his slanderous allegations. He tore at his clothes and ran down the hill like a madman. A few of the villagers ran after him, but the rest remained to witness what followed.

"Now Thyagu began to speak. 'Because Karunakaran has gone mad, and because the child is Jeeva's and Parasu's, Jeeva should now become Parasu's wife. Patta Naicker's estate will be handed down to Parasu and his child. Jeeva must now forget Karunakaran, and begin her life afresh, with Parasu as her husband.'

"At this, Jeeva took her child and ran into the garbhagraham and locked the door. She didn't come out for a long time. All of us stood there, waiting. Thyagu demanded to know what was happening inside, and threatened to break down the door. Finally, he did. Inside, Jeeva and her child had fainted at the foot of the idol. The diamond crown was missing. Thyagu dragged her out, and then Parasu, pulling her by the hand, demanded that she come to live with him. She threw them both off, screaming, 'I am pure and innocent. What they claim is a lie!'

"She ran with the child. Thyagu chased her. The town stood by as silent witnesses; they knew what would happen if they dared to interfere. The child slipped out of Jeeva's hands and fell between the rocks. She started to howl, but Jeeva did not look back at her. I ran and took the child and pacified her. Jeeva climbed up to the top of the cliff and cried out, 'You have accused me unjustly. I am a pure woman. I will make you pay for your lies.'

"Thyagu approached her, demanding to know where she had hidden the diamond crown. She sprang on him like a wild beast and began biting him. But he pushed her off the cliff, and then threw a huge rock down at her. The stone smashed her head; she howled in pain. The crowd couldn't see whether Jeeva had jumped off the cliff on her own accord or if Thyagu had thrown her off—but I saw. From the bottom of the hill, with her last breath, she threw her final challenge to Thyagu.

"No one in this town has ever forgotten that curse she swore. From that day forward, the garbhagraham has remained closed. Jeeva had gone in with the diamond crown, but it had disappeared completely. Thyagu is still searching for it—that, and the will. The whole town knows what Patta Naicker's last will and testament says—that in order for the fortune to come to him, Thyagu would have to marry Jeeva's daughter. Now there is no one left to challenge him. Everyone knows that even if they dared to go to the police or the courts, Thyagu would manage to bribe them off." And with that, Azhagammai finally finished her story.

"Paati, what happened to the mad husband?" asked Bhaskar.

"He sleeps outside my house," said Ganesan. "You can find him at the garbage heap, or else at the Muniyappan temple, or else under a tree."

"Didn't anyone try to take him to a mental asylum for treatment?"

"They did, but it didn't do any good, and eventually Karunakaran's family abandoned him. Thank god that Thyagu has at least permitted the villagers to feed him with their leftover scraps."

"But why has that rogue allowed him to survive for so long?"

"He leaves Karunakaran there to remind the villagers what happens to those who challenge him. He must feel that Karunakaran doesn't pose any threat."

"Hasn't Thyagu found any clue about the will and diamond jewels?"

"No. That's why he is going through so much effort to marry Jeeva's daughter. The poor child is now like a wilting garland in that evil man's clutches."

"Is the girl willing to marry him?"

"What young girl would willingly marry a fifty-year-old man? But there's nothing she can do. Even the local police have given their blessings for the union."

"So this is the first matter we must attend to. We can settle everything else later."

"Let's not leave this mountain temple quite yet," said Bhaskar. "We'll wait for dawn. But how will we be able to manage Thyagu's gang?"

"We need to get the police involved—not the local police, they'll be no use. Avinash and I will go to see the district superintendent," said Ganesh. "We'll leave immediately." He and Avinash climbed into the van, and sped off.

The moon watched everything from up above. The students waited under a tree for dawn.

⋇ 6 ⋇

Not everyone can understand the mysteries of the universe. Those who do understand, do not talk about it. Those who have seen do not reveal, and those who reveal, have not seen. That is why we argue about these mysteries with no true comprehension. Let us stop our argument for a moment and reflect. Only from this reflection will there be true enlightenment, and that will follow us through each birth.

—*Upanishad Saram*

Dawn came, the sun appearing as an orange ball in the east. It spread its fingertips through the window pane in Patta Naicker's bungalow. Thyagu looked up at the rays of light with bloodshot eyes. These were not the clear eyes of a man freshly awoken at dawn after a good night's rest; they were the eyes of one who has spent a long, sleepless night tossing and turning in fear.

His entourage gathered around him, with Rudraiyya chief among them.

"Is all this distress because of the oncoming wedding, or because your spy Parasu was captured by the group in the van?" asked Rudraiyya. Thyagu remained silent.

A man came running in.

"Aiya! We found Parasu dead at the bottom of the hill, in the snake pit, his body turning blue. But the group that came along with Jeeva has still not left. They are still camped there," he said.

Thyagu began to tremble. Dark patches of sweat began to appear on his silk *dhoti* and *jibha*. His heart, which had not shrunk from any demonic deed in the last fifty years, felt fear for the first time. He was struck dumb, unable to think.

Rudraiyya took that moment to tease him.

"Thyagu, stop worrying yourself sick about the dead. Concentrate on marrying Shenbagam."

"That's right, aiya," agreed another henchman. "The auspicious time is between half past nine and ten. It is now a quarter past six. There are many rituals to be completed before the actual wedding takes place. You must leave immediately for the hilltop."

"Have you invited everyone in the town?"

"We haven't missed a single person. Already, the priest must be preparing the garbhagraham..."

Indeed, a Brahmin priest was at that moment readying the temple. As he washed the floor, he kept looking up at the Shenbaga Devi idol with tears in his eyes. "There are so many purifying rituals that should be performed, when a temple that has been under lock and key is re-opened after so long," he mumbled. "But 'Go and do the pujas,' he says, 'nothing will happen. If the Goddess does get angry, I'll deal with the conse-quences.' Sinners! Murderous thieves! Forcing me to be an accomplice to their wicked deeds!

"Oh, Thayee! You have been deprived of Your regular worship. That man is a sinner, but he has been living a royal life all these years. How is it that You, who are the Mother of All Goodness, can suffer these trans-gressions in silence? Have You lost all Your divine wrath and power? If so, then how will Your worshippers ever find their strength?" he wondered, as he dressed the idol in a new sari. He searched for the sacred lamp, but could not find it. He noticed one of the small diyas in a niche in the wall. It seemed to beckon him. It was dark with years of disuse. He tried to remove it, but found to his surprise that it was fixed inside...

The crowd assembled on the hill that morning was spectacular. Thyagu's henchmen stood at the bottom of the hill welcoming the villagers. Some of them came just to watch the proceedings; others came dreading what was about to happen, but powerless to stop it.

At about eight o'clock, as the crowd was walking up the path, the van full of students drove up and stopped at the foot of the hill. The students jumped out. Last of them all came Uma—along with another man. A collective gasp went up from the crowd. It was Karunakaran!

He was dressed in clean clothes, and his mad expressions and insane twitches seemed to have fallen away. The people could not take their eyes off him. The news traveled quickly up the hill. The crowd turned, and began running down the steps. "What a surprise! Jeeva, you really have come," cried an old woman. "Oh Mother Shenbaga Devi, we were wrong to doubt Your power!" She fell on the steps, crying in devotion.

Uma ignored the crowd and began helping Karunakaran up the steps. The henchmen stationed at the foothill were too surprised to try to stop him.

"How come that madman has become so quiet all of a sudden?"

"If Thyagu sees him, he'll kill him."

"Hey!" one of the henchmen shouted to the youths. "Who are you?"

"We're college students," said Shankaranarayanan.

161

"What do you think you're doing here?"

"What's the problem? Anyone can visit a temple," said Vaijayanthi.

"This is a private temple. The owner is getting married here today."

"Oh, that can't be right: the real owner is right here with us!"

"Where did you find this lunatic?"

"Next to the garbage bin."

"Just you wait, you are all going to become mad like him!"

"Listen mister, I'd rather go mad than turn into a heartless goon like you."

Their argument was becoming louder and more animated. The crowd stood around watching, unable to believe what was happening. The news reached Thyagu, who was getting ready in the stone mandap at the right of the temple. He was so worried, he forgot the cigarette between his lips, until it burned him. He sprang up as if stung by a snake. Rudraiyya pressed him back into his seat. Thyagu threw away the butt and immediately lit another cigarette.

"You are supposed to be brave," said Rudraiyya. "But this Jeeva issue seems to have weakened you! What do you think she can do? The local police inspector is our chief guest for the wedding. What are you so worried about?"

"Has the inspector arrived?"

"He's on his way."

"Then what are my men doing? Do they think I pay them to get drunk and play cards? Why don't they beat those students up and send them back where they came from?"

"Thyagu, we can't have violence here. This is a wedding! Let them come. What can they do? We can give them some confetti to throw, too, if you want. Let them join in the celebration. It's just a college group that has come on a field trip. Why do you get so worked up just because one of them resembles Jeeva? If your guilty conscience is disturbing you, just stop listening to it."

Rudraiyya's advice had its usual calming effect on Thyagu.

The crowd had already reached the newly decorated garbhagraham of the Shenbaga Devi temple. But where was Shenbagam?

⚡ 7 ⚡

In every century, the fact of reincarnation is proven anew. It is our Rishis who know the real secrets of our past lives. Look carefully and you will find it for yourself; Prahaladam reborn as Raghavendra, Adhiseshan reborn as Lakshmanan.

—*Keeran, Poet*

Behind the temple on the hilltop, Shenbagam was suffering in the hands of the wives of Thyagu's henchmen, all in the name of being readied for the ceremony.

"Come dear, please, be a good girl. If you are accommodating with Thyagu Aiya, he'll decorate you with gold and jewels. If you protest and make things difficult, you risk being killed! Your father has lost his mind, your mother is long dead. You're very lucky to get such a groom. Now stop weeping and smile!"

Shenbagam did not have the strength to utter a single word. She was terrified.

This is the man who raised me from my childhood, she thought, sobbing to herself. *Today, he says he will become my husband! How can his relationship to me change from that of a father to that of a husband overnight? Oh, in this age of Kali Yuga, any injustice is possible!*

One of the wives tried consoling her, but it was no use.

In the garbhagraham, the idol of the Goddess stood freshly oiled and gleaming black, decorated for the first time after years of neglect. But the lamps inside refused to stay lit; a strange breeze, that seemed to come from no direction at all, kept blowing them out. The priest considered this a terrible omen. A great sin was about to be committed here, and his heart bled with the knowledge that he was an accomplice to it.

Outside, the drummers began their rhythm. The wedding hall was being decked for the celebration. The people gathered to sit on the blanketed floor.

Shenbagam was brought to the platform. "If you start crying again, I'll pluck your eyes out!" threatened one of the wives in her ears. Shenbagam's body was trembling, her legs weak.

The priest chanted the prayers tonelessly. The local police inspector had arrived, dressed in full uniform. Thyagu welcomed him in person, and served him a cold Lehar Pepsi. The inspector took his seat at the side of the stage.

The thali was taken on a platter around the audience to be blessed. Before it had gone very far, a woman snatched the sacred thread from the plate and stood up. Thyagu rose in anger, and a buzz ran through the crowd, as the woman asked in a loud, calm voice, "Tell me, is this bride old enough to be married?"

"Who is this wench?" shouted Thyagu. "How dare she ask such a question?"

"Cool down, mister. Or you might find yourself behind bars," called out a commanding voice. The crowd turned their heads around to see Savarimuthu, superintendent of police, standing at the back of the assembly along with Avinash and Ganesan.

The local police inspector, shocked to see his superior there, lost his nerve completely, and hurriedly stood up to give a salute. He realized that the woman who had grabbed the thali was also a plainclothes policewoman.

Thyagu's face turned blood red.

"We received a complaint informing us that this was a forced wedding," said Savarimuthu, approaching the platform. "Thyagu, you are over fifty years old. You want this eighteen-year-old girl for your bride, is that right?" He walked up to Shenbagam, and asked her in a soft voice, "Tell me truly, do you want this wedding to take place?"

Shenbagam looked up at him in tears.

"Then get up! Arrest Thyagu!"

The superintendent's eyes swung over to the local inspector. "So, you are presiding over this ceremony, are you? Of course, such a blatantly illegal wedding would require a policeman to be the chief guest! What are you thinking? Does the police department exist to act as yes-men for rich criminals?"

The local inspector hung his head in shame. The crowd watched, speechless. None among them had ever dared to raise a finger against

Thyagu. Today, an unknown group of students had managed to get him arrested!

"Sir," Thyagu roared indignantly at the superintendent, "this is no forced wedding. The bride has expressed her willingness to marry me, we are proceeding in accordance with the wishes of the late Patta Naicker, and I am fulfilling the promise I gave to my sister, Manonmani, before her death. It was planned before that I should marry my sister's daughter Jeeva. Unfortunately, that was not to be. Karunakaran—that madman there—ruined our hopes for marriage, and he ruined Jeeva's life as well. That's why she had an affair with Parasu. This girl, Shenbagam, is the daughter of Jeeva and Parasu, my good friend. It was Parasu's hope that his daughter would marry into the family of Patta Naicker. There is no other male in that lineage, apart from myself. I have proof, in writing, of his desire that I should marry his daughter Shenbagam."

The superintendent of police was completely flummoxed. Uma, who had been sitting silently until then, rose to her feet with a furious expression on her face. "You bastard," she screamed at Thyagu, "are you really going to try and present the same performance that you staged eighteen years back?"

Thyagu, seeing Uma for the first time, stared at her in disbelief. *That face... those eyes... the exact same beauty!*

"You think just because you threw me off a rock and smashed my head in, you can win everything? It wasn't enough to kill me, now you want to ruin my daughter's life as well. Well, it won't be so easy, Thyagu. Yes, it's true: I died then. And it's also true that I've been reborn now. What was that you said? That I had an affair with Parasu? You know what happened to him, don't you? He became a midnight snack for a horde of snakes and scorpions. You're next, Thyagu! Get ready!"

Throughout all this commotion, Shenbagam remained sitting on the platform, shivering like a hatchling dove, not knowing what was going to happen. The crowd kept looking back and forth at her and Uma.

The superintendent was equally mystified. He walked up to Avinash, who was staring at his sister in disbelief, and whispered, "Mr. Avinash,

I don't know what to believe here. I came along with you because you claimed this was a forced wedding. What exactly is going on now?"

Uma turned to Shenbagam.

"Shenbagam, I am your mother speaking. This man loves nothing in the world but money. This is all a part of his plot to steal the fortune which is rightfully yours! Do not let him deceive you. He falsely accused me, and took my life."

Shenbagam spoke in a trembling voice. "You're... my mother?"

"Yes, the same mother who was pushed off that cliff by Thyagu. My body was destroyed, but the truth still survives. I have come now to save you."

At this, the police superintendent laughed out loud. "Avinash, what is all this? Has your sister gone mad, claiming to be this girl's mother? This is the twentieth century, you know. We've just launched a space rocket from Sriharikota."

"No, sir! She speaks the truth! Ask any of the villagers!"

"This is, indeed, the same Jeeva who died so many years ago," said an old woman, walking up to the superintendent. "There is no doubt in my mind."

"What nonsense is this? I'm not interested in all these wild stories and beliefs. The wedding can take place only if the bride is willing; that's all I care about. You, woman! Stop crying and tell me—do you agree to this marriage?"

Shenbagam was too terrified to speak. She imagined all the unspeakable things that Thyagu might do to her if she were to say no.

"Can you hear me? Answer!" commanded the superintendent.

It was too much for Shenbagam. She fainted.

Another man stood up from the crowd. "Superintendent Aiya, this woman standing here is Jeeva, as she claims to be. We are all sure that this is a forced wedding. We refuse to be mere spectators any longer. This miracle has shown the power of the Goddess! We have nothing more to fear! I, too, have a daughter. If I don't speak out against this sin, her life might also be in danger of ruin."

Now one of students stepped forward. "Mr. Superintendent, sir, we were as confused as you at first. We couldn't believe it either. But we have come to realize that Uma is indeed Jeeva's reincarnation. Please believe us."

"Sir, there was a similar case in Rajasthan, do you remember?" asked Vaijayanthi. "Maybe you read about it in the newspaper? A young Rajasthani girl in the fifth standard suddenly remembered her previous birth and started speaking in fluent German. That girl is still alive. The world is full of miracles like this."

"Look, suppose you're right. How can I make a legal case? The law doesn't recognize the supernatural."

"Sir, I can give you concrete proof that Uma is Jeeva. If I show you, will you believe us?" asked Bhaskar.

"What's your proof?"

"Jeeva was the only one who knew where Patta Naicker's will was kept. She's also the only one who knew where Naicker's priceless diamond crown was hidden. If Uma can retrieve both of these items, will you accept that as proof?"

Thyagu rushed forward. "Never mind the superintendent! Even *I* will believe her if she can do that. If she can do what she claims, then I will leave Shenbagam and go away from this town forever."

Bhaskar gave Uma a nod.

Uma removed her footwear, bent in prayer to the Goddess, and entered the garbhagraham. Inside, she selected the small oil lamp in the niche in the wall, and turned it. The idol rotated on its dais. The trap door under the idol opened, and Uma went down the steps. Bhaskar and the superintendent of police rushed to the entrance and looked down after her. The people of the village watched in wonder; everyone had known that there was a cavern in the hill, but the location of the entrance had remained a secret. The priest was trembling. Thyagu, alone, remained strangely calm.

After what seemed like hours, Uma's head appeared in the opening of the trap door. She looked completely disappointed.

"Uma, why have you come back empty handed?" asked Bhaskar.

"Bhaskar, there's nothing there! Everything we saw is gone!" she said miserably.

"So, my dear!" Thyagu spat. "You came to know about the tunnel under the temple, and thought you could cheat us? But both the will and the crown are safe with me! If you really were Jeeva, you would not have gone down that passage at all; you would have led us straight to the safe in my house. You and your friends came up here with an elaborate plan to get your hands on Patta Naicker's fortune. When I sent Parasu to warn you off, you got him killed by a snake. It is you and your gang that should be arrested, not me! Not to mention that you've spoiled my wedding! Superintendent sir, what do you have to say to all this?"

"What is this, Uma?" grumbled Avinash. "You claimed you alone knew where the will and jewels were. Now you don't even seem to know what you're talking about! The superintendent is already giving me looks of death."

Uma pleaded silently to the Goddess. *Why? Why did you force me here, and then make a fool of me in front of this entire village?*

"Don't waste any more words," said Rudraiyya, pushing Thyagu forward towards the stage, "Tie the thali."

Thyagu took the thali in his hands and walked up to the still-unconscious Shenbagam.

Finally, the police superintendent found something to which he could object on solid legal grounds. "Thyagu, you cannot tie the thali around the neck of an unconscious person or one who is asleep. That's illegal."

The wives of the henchmen jumped up and tried to shake Shebagam awake, to no avail—she remained out cold. Thyagu wrung his hands. "You've had your way," he said to the superintendent. "I am still unmarried…"

"Relax, Thyagu," said Rudraiyya reassuringly. "You can still wed her tomorrow. You are Shenbagam's fated groom. Why worry? The superintendent was only doing his duty. You shouldn't blame him."

"You!" said the superintendent accusingly to Avinash. "You're supposed to be a responsible magazine editor. How could you waste my time like this? Because of you, this wedding has come to a halt."

"Sir, please don't come to hasty conclusions. Just last night, Uma saw the will and the crown here in the secret chamber. They must have been removed since then."

"Please don't waste any more of my time with your childish *Ambulimama* fairy tales," snapped the superintendent. "Leave this place at once. As for you, Mr. Thyagu, you may go ahead and wed this girl once she regains consciousness. I'm very sorry." He turned to leave.

The crowd watched, motionless. Uma was sobbing openly, as Avinash looked on ashamed. People were splashing cold water on Shenbagam's face, and she slowly awoke. The priest, worried that the auspicious hour had slipped away, consulted with Thyagu.

"From now on, every hour is an auspicious one for us," said Thyagu.

"No, let's wait for the next good time..." bleated the priest.

"If you keep going on like this, I'll bury you. The only reason I'm still being nice is because you told me about the secret passage this morning," Thyagu whispered menacingly into the priest's ears.

Uma and her friends were now surrounded by Thyagu's henchmen. Avinash and Ganesh were taken hostage. The villagers did not even dare to breathe aloud, but simply gaped, like geckos who had lost their tails.

Thyagu's men rushed him onto the platform to tie the thali. On his way to the stage, the local inspector, standing straight again, murmured to him, "So, good times are back again! All these years you've been drilling into the hill, searching for that treasure—how did you finally manage to find it?"

"It was sheer luck. This morning, while trying to pull a lamp out of the wall, the priest discovered the entrance to the tunnel. All this time I'd been digging, the trap door was right here under the idol! After that, it was a simple matter to find the treasure. Thank god we didn't lose face in front of the superintendent," whispered Thyagu triumphantly.

Rudraiyya was beckoning Thyagu to hurry. But he and the inspector, still dizzy with joy, continued. "*Thalaiva*, we don't have to depend on selling hooch or running brothels or rowdyism any longer," crowed Thyagu. "Now Patta Naicker's estate will be mine! With that diamond crown alone, I could bribe off a hundred inspectors like yourself. My only regret is that I've had to wait until I'm on the verge of old age before I take possession of this fortune. If only I'd been able to get hold of it in my youth! Hang on there a moment... let me go tie the thali, and return as a millionaire! Don't forget, there'll be a big party tonight!" Thyagu ran to the stage, where Shenbagam sat like a sacrificial goat, a mere puppet of fate.

Uma glared at the Goddess. The idol stood silently, apparently ready to witness still more atrocities. Looking around wildly for help, she turned to Karunakaran. "Go! Stop him!" Uma screamed. "That's our daughter that will be their victim!"

Then, just as Thyagu held the ends of the thali together at the back of Shenbagam's neck and was about to tie the knot...

A bullet raced out of nowhere and plowed through his shoulder!

Five more bullets followed, and flew straight into his temple. Thyagu collapsed, blood pouring from his wounds.

Superintendent Savarimuthu, who had not yet reached the bottom of the hill, ran back up at the sound of the shots.

Away from the temple, standing on the same rock on which Jeeva had sworn her final curse, stood a woman holding a hunting rifle, her eyes burning with rage. Next to her was a suitcase.

It was Meenakshi—Thyagu's first wife.

Meenakshi calmly put down the rifle and approached Uma with the suitcase. She opened it to reveal the will and the diamond crown.

"Uma, you are indeed Jeeva reborn. I have no doubt about it. My husband knew nothing about the will or the crown until this morning. No woman can tolerate her husband marrying another girl young enough to be his daughter. That man was a demon, beyond all redemption. He had to be annihilated. Because no one dared to challenge him, he was able to rule for twenty years. It was my mistake to have accepted a thali from this man; my life was already cursed. Therefore, the responsibility fell to me to rid this world of him." She spoke fearlessly. "From this moment forth, may the family of Patta Naicker thrive! Make arrangements for Karunakaran's treatment, and get Shenbagam married to a good man. May this story be a lesson to the world that justice will always prevail."

The superintendent stepped up to Meenakshi and arrested her, as the villagers looked on both her and Uma with gratitude.

∕ EPILOGUE ∕

Ganesh wrote an interesting article, which Avinash published in his magazine, along with photographs. The story of Jeeva's rebirth created a buzz throughout the land.

Uma now lives in Velamangalam. The people who live in Patta Naicker's bungalow know her not as Uma but as Jeeva. It may look incongruous when Shenbagam addresses her as "Amma", but it soothes her heart.

Karunakaran's condition is rapidly improving.

Shenbaga Devi temple now holds three services every day. They are very well attended. Because of Uma, the temple has become quite famous. The story has even been taken up by the international media.

Uma's friend Bhaskar has realized, sadly, that his chances of love with her have slipped away. Uma's cousin, Raghav, feels the same sadness.

"So, Uma, what are your future plans?"

"To help my husband recover, and to get my daughter married," she replies calmly, with a smile.

Uma does not even have to say it. She is one of the many fantastic miracles of this universe.

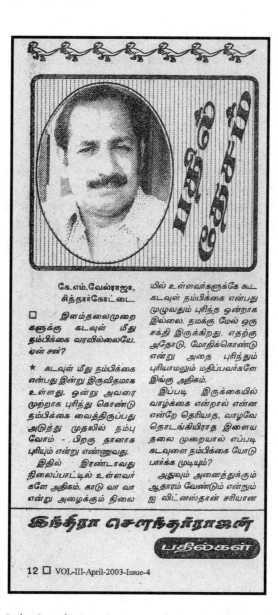

கே.எம்.வேல்ராஜு,
சித்தார்கோட்டை.

□ இளம்தலைமுறை
களுக்கு கடவுள் மீது
நம்பிக்கை வரவில்லையே.
ஏன் சார்?

★ கடவுள் மீது நம்பிக்கை
என்பது இன்று இருவிதமாக
உள்ளது. ஒன்று அவரை
முற்றாக புரிந்து கொண்டு
நம்பிக்கை வைத்திருப்பது
அடுத்து முதலில் நம்பு
வோம் - பிறகு தானாக
புரியும் என்று எண்ணுவது.

இதில் இரண்டாவது
நிலைப்பாட்டில் உள்ளவர்
களே அதிகம். காடு வா வா
என்று அழைக்கும் நிலை

மில் உள்ளவர்களுக்கே கூட
கடவுள் நம்பிக்கை என்பது
முழுவதும் புரிந்த ஒன்றாக
இல்லை. நமக்கு மேல் ஒரு
சக்தி இருக்கிறது. எதற்கு
அதோடு, மோதிக்கொண்டு
என்று அதை புரிந்தும்
புரியாமலும் மதிப்பவர்களே
இங்கு அதிகம்.

இப்படி இருக்கையில்
வாழ்க்கை என்றால் என்ன
என்றே தெரியாத, வாழவே
தொடங்கியிராத இளைய
தலை முறையால் எப்படி
கடவுளை நம்பிக்கை யோடு
பார்க்க முடியும்?

அதுவும் அனைத்துக்கும்
ஆதாரம் வேண்டும் என்றும்
ஐ விட்னஸ்தான் சரியான

இந்திரா சௌந்தர்ராஜன்

பதில்கள்

Indra Soundar Rajan's answer column in *Crime Story*.
Note the dinosaurs.

172

Q & A

கேள்வி பதில்கள்

with INDRA SOUNDAR RAJAN

Is it wrong to check your daily horoscope before you set out somewhere?

—*Minnal Paridha Naseer, Karur*

IS: Yes, in a way. You must be wondering why I say this, given that I believe in astrology. But I have my reasons. I don't think these modern predictions are given using actual, exact calculations of the positions of the stars and planets. I know how long those calculations can take! Your next question will be, "Then are all the magazine predictions just a lot of hot air?" No, it's not that either. It's just that the predictions are very general. The predictions could turn out to be wrong because the planetary positions in a particular person's horoscope may vary.

Therefore, it's not very smart to take your daily horoscope as God's word. You can think of it as a news tidbit, if you wish.

When troubles keep on piling up, one after another, how does one continue to believe in God?

—*P.N. Shanmugam, Thenkasi*

IS: It's a mistake to even entertain such doubts, Shanmugam. God is not the one who sends those troubles to us. That's not His job. Our pains and pleasures are all due to our own fate. Even though we are told over and over again the right path of life, we continue to do wrong. We find our own unique excuses: we either promise to say sorry to God later, or count on Him for forgiveness, or convince ourselves that what we're doing is not a sin. When our mistakes return to us as troubles, then we blame God.

I know you're going to come back with: "I have a friend who has never sinned at all. Do you know what great troubles he has had?"

But there may be sins that he has committed without your knowledge. There are also the leftovers from his previous births to be accounted for. If we make a mess, then it's our responsibility to clean it up. We must pay the debts of our karma ourselves.

There are those who claim that one cannot escape fate, that there is no rem-edy for it. Whatever has to happen will happen. What do you have to say to this?

—Ramasami, Karaikudi

IS: Obviously, whatever happens is because of fate. Everything has to happen because of fate, and it should be so. Not only true knowledge; even science has to follow this rule.

But your course of life does not simply follow its fate of its own ac-cord. First understand that. When such a course is disadvantageous to us, we seek remedies. Of course, some of these remedies are false. The trick is to find the true one...

Saying "sorry" after knocking into someone is also a remedy, one that is found commonly throughout the world. But not every bad deed can be atoned for with a mere apology. Sometimes the punishment may be huge. If you run over someone with a motorcycle, a sorry will not suffice. You will have to face the consequences.

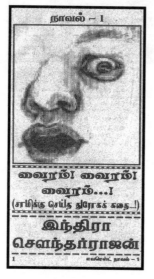

Title pages from Indra Soundar Rajan novels

Left: Cover of an issue of *Aanandha Novel,* featuring the second installment of Indra Soundar Rajan's *Pallavan. Pandian.. Bhaskaran...*

Right: Cover of an issue of *Mangaiyar Novel,* featuring Indra Soundar Rajan's *Kadhal Kutravaali!*

Back-cover advertisement for Indra Soundar Rajan stories in

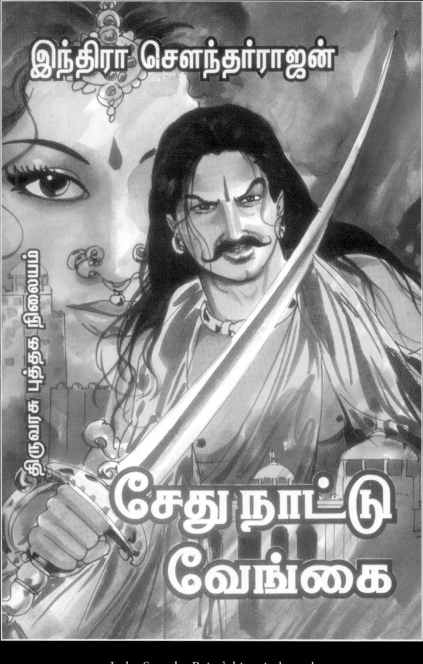

இந்திரா செளந்தர்ராஜன்

திருமகா புத்தக நிலையம்

சேது நாட்டு வேங்கை

Indra Soundar Rajan's historical novel
Sethu Nattu Venkai, cover by Shyam

ஆயிரம் அரிவாள் கோட்டை

இந்திரா சௌந்தர்ராஜன்

Kottaippuratthu Veedu by Indra Soundar Rajan, cover art by Maniam Selvan

Top: *Today Crime News,* featuring serialized installments of Indra Soundar Rajan's lengthier novels. **Bottom:** Indra Soundar Rajan novels in *Crime Story.* Montage artists unknown.

Covers from eighties/early nineties issues of *Ungal Junior* featuring the Pattukkottai Prabakar novels *Miss India Missing* and *Iruvil Arugil Nizhalil.* Photographs by K.V. Anand.

Ungal Junior covers for
the Subha novels *Padhungukuzhi* and
Ragasiyangal Virapathargalla!
Photographs by K.V. Anand.

Indra Soundar Rajan covers from
Pocket Novel, Everest Novel, and *Today Crime News.*

Front and back covers of *Everest Novel*,
with inset photo of Indra Soundar Rajan (**left**),
and *Novel Neram*, with photo of Rajesh Kumar (**right**).

Clockwise from top left: Front cover from *Best Novel* issue featuring Rajesh Kumar's *Matchstick Number One* (Christina Aguilera vampire image apparently originally posted to www.freakingnews.com by "joshmax"); back cover from *Everest Novel* (inset photo is Rajesh Kumar); covers of Rajesh Kumar stories in *Detective Novel*.

Clockwise from top left: Subha novels in *Ungal Junior* and *Super Novel,* with photos by K.V. Anand; cover from a more recent *Subha Novel*; back cover ad for a two-part Indra Soundar Rajan story (part 1 published in *Crime Story*, part 2 in *Ladies' Novel*).

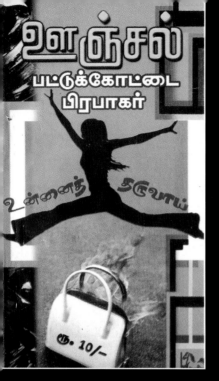

This page: Covers from Pattukkottai Prabakar novels in *Oonjal*.

Opposite page: Covers from *Detective Novel* and *Novel Neram*, featuring stories by Rajesh Kumar and "P.K.P." (Pattukkottai Prabakar). Photoshop artists unknown.

Following Pages: (left) Covers of *Super Novel* and *Ungal Junior*. Photographs by K.V. Anand. **(right)** Back cover of *Ungal Junior* showing Suresh and Balakrishnan, with lobster claw; picture of Pattukkottai Prabakar, from a back cover of *Namathu Great Novel; A Novel Time* cover of the Prabakar romance *Soladhe Sey* ("Don't Talk, Just Do"); *Ullaasa Oonjal* cover of the Prabakar novel *Kutra Sangili*. Artists unknown.

ராஜேஷ்குமார்
டிடெக்டிவ் நாவல்

1205

7/-

பி.கே.பி.
டிடெக்டிவ் நாவல்

6/-

பி.கே.பி.
டிடெக்டிவ் நாவல்

ரூ.
6/-

நாவல்நேரம்
ராஜேஷ்குமார்

விலை
ரூ. 6

திக்... திக்... திக்...
ஸ்பெஷ...

சூப்பர் நாவல்

மனித வேட்டை
(மெகா நாவல்)

சுபா

சூப்பர் நாவல்

சுபா

112 பக்கங்கள்
விலை ரூ.
மட்டுமே

கிருபாவுக்கு முன்
கிருபாவுக்கு பின்

சூப்பர் நாவல்

விலை ரூ. 4/-

ஒற்றன் காதலி

சுபா

உங்கள் ஜூனியர்

விலை ரூ. 4/-

பரத் ராஜ்யம்

பட்டுக்கோட்டை
பிரபாகர்

எ நாவல் டைம்

கே - 1996
ரூ.7/-

சொல்லாதே
செய்

பட்டுக்கோட்டை
பிரபாகர்

உல்லாச
ஊஞ்சல்

மாற்றுச் சங்கிலி

பட்டுக்கோட்டை பிரபாகர்

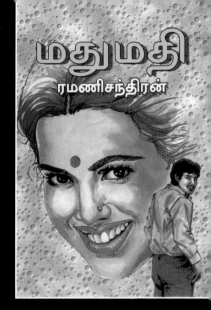

Top: Ramanichandran novels, cover art by Ubaldu.
Bottom: Ramanichandran with her daughter-in-law and grandchildren.

RAMANICHANDRAN

"I'm primarily a housewife," says Ramanichandran, in a voice so quiet it's almost a whisper. "The writing is just a hobby." Her modesty would be laughable, if she didn't seem so completely honest about it. This is the bestselling author in the Tamil language speaking, a woman currently working on her 125th novel, whose stories have been enjoyed by three generations of Tamilian women—and some male reader fans, as well, whom she says come to understand women better through her writing. Ramanichandran has a set of hard-and-fast rules for her subject matter. "No caste conflict, no religious conflict, no terminal illnesses, no characters with serious vices. My stories should make people happy. They're 100% soft romance." If this sounds a little prudish, it's also a major achievement to have produced such a large body of work under such strict constraints, especially considering that nearly all Tamil film and television stories fall back on one or several of these themes.

Ramanichandran lives in Mylapore, Chennai with her husband, son, daughter-in-law and grandchildren.

THE RICH WOMAN
பணக்காரப் பெண் (1973)

"HE'S TOO LUCKY, that guy!"

Tamizh Arasi didn't bother to ask who Pandian meant. It was normal for him to heave a sigh of jealousy whenever he saw anyone riding in a car; these were his usual grumbling complaints every time he waited for a bus. Tamizh Arasi had learned from experience that the best response was silence. Still, it didn't stop his grousing.

"You know who I mean, don't you? There, in that long car, the half-brown, half-white one—the man traveling in that car. See the woman next to him? That's the woman I was supposed to marry. She is very rich.

It was my mother who insisted I marry you instead. That guy got lucky. He got a rich, beautiful woman. And here I am, suffering."

Even as he was ranting, the car passed them. Tamizh Arasi turned to Pandian and started to say something, but then thought better of it, and kept quiet.

"Tsk, what's the point of dwelling on all that now? I should have been more adamant with mother. If I had married a rich woman, I wouldn't have to sit here waiting for the bus."

Tamizh Arasi felt tears welling up in her eyes. She bit her lip to contain herself. She couldn't start weeping openly right here on the road.

Pandian was basically a good man, but every time there were money troubles, his mood would take a turn for the worse. He dreamt of having deep resources of cash, spending well, enjoying himself with his wife and child. But whenever he was forced to control his expenses or forego any small pleasures, ordinary Pandian would become Ugra-Pandian, his ferocious avatar, and at those times he needed someone to vent his frustrations on.

Knowing these tendencies of her son, Pandian's mother had rejected Nalini and selected instead the docile Tamizh Arasi as her daughter-in-law. Infatuated with money even in those days, Pandian had tried to fight against his mother's choice. But she had remained staunch. "That forest fire is beautiful, but only from a distance. If it were to enter a home, it would burn it down. This Tamizh Arasi, on the other hand, is a lamp, a light that will always stand at your side," she had said.

It was true—Tamizh Arasi had been a warm lamplight in his home. Unable to find any fault with her, Pandian would blame his situation on his mother. But Tamizh Arasi always felt that the complaints were meant for *her*, and would shrink away in shame. Sometimes, she had the urge to snap back—but she was not used to using harsh words. How could she speak them all of a sudden? No—she would plaster a smile on her face, and bow her head. That was the best way to keep Pandian calm. In earlier days, she had only had to do this rarely. But now that they had a child, it seemed to happen more and more frequently.

The next day, a letter arrived from Pandian's mother. He became even more irate after reading it. He flung the letter in Tamizh Arasi's face and said angrily, "See what your dear mother-in-law is asking for! A hundred rupees! Where does she think I'm supposed to get it, from the grand dowry your family showered on me? How am I supposed to come up with a hundred rupees?"

"Send her the money we set aside for the insurance. We can pay that next month."

"Then who will suffer next month? I wanted to buy Selvi that frock. I don't want to give that up. I can't be expected to pay the interest for my mother's mistake. She should have realized that such needs might arise, and gotten me married to a rich woman. How can she complain now?"

And so again, he came back to the same grouse.

Arasi felt like crying, but tears would only incense him further. She pasted a smile on over her sorrow, and stood in front of him with a tumbler of cold water from the clay pot.

And it worked; her smile did cool him down, as he took the tumbler from her. "Whatever else you lack, you do have the most pleasant smile," he said, caressing her silky cheek.

"So, about your mother…" she began. This was the best moment to get him to agree.

"All right, all right… I'll give your precious mother-in-law her money," he replied.

She gave a sigh of relief. He kissed her and left.

On his next payday, they left together to buy a frock for Selvi. In the shop, they tried on many frocks. Selvi was a beautiful child, and every frock looked great on her.

"Chee! If I had the money, I'd buy them all. But I've only got twenty rupees to spend. What an unlucky fellow I am."

While he fumed, Arasi took the frock she had selected up to the billing counter.

Just then, a huge car rolled up to the front of the shop. The door opened and Nalini stepped down, decked out in beautiful jewellery, followed by her husband. They entered the shop together. All the shop helpers turned to serve Nalini, leaving nobody to attend to Pandian and Arasi.

Arasi looked at her husband, panicked. The exit was blocked and there was no one available to bill their purchase. "All this attention should rightfully be mine," Pandian griped. "Look at the shopkeepers circling around them! If I'd been born lucky, I wouldn't be standing here now like a lonely orphan."

Arasi watched Nalini browsing through the sleeveless blouses. How could a woman wear such revealing things? Chee!

She pointed it out to Pandian. "Imagine, *Athaan!* And you complain about women who wear their saris low on the hip, to show off their navels..."

"That chap is an impotent one to allow it."

As if he realized they were discussing him, Nalini's husband looked their way, and his eyes rested on Tamizh Arasi and Selvi for a moment. Then he whispered something into the shopkeeper's ears. Immediately, a few of the helpers ran over to attend to them. As Pandian was making the cash payment, Nalini walked up to the shopkeeper and lamented in a high-pitched voice, "None of these are any good. They all look so old-fashioned!" With that, she sashayed out, followed by her husband. He turned around at the gate and gave Pandian and his family a parting look before he got into the car.

Pandian looked at the mass of clothes that were piled up on the counter, and then exchanged a look with his wife. He hated to see people come and browse through all the goods in a shop and then leave without buying anything. "Cheapos," muttered one of the shop employees. Arasi held back a smile, and Pandian looked sheepish.

A few days later, Pandian was waiting for a bus to return home. The buses were few and far between, and the ones that did come were either jam-packed with people or failed to stop at all. His resentment flared higher with each car he watched pass by.

"Lucky jerks! Flying by in their cars—all because they married rich women." He gave another envious sigh.

Just then a car came to a stop in front of him. "Aren't you Tamizh Arasi's husband? Get in. I'll drop you home. I'm Gopal," said the man in the car.

Pandian realized that the man was Nalini's husband. "No, it's alright. I can manage."

"Please, come with me." He got out and nearly dragged Pandian into the car.

Pandian didn't know what to think. He had called him "Tamizh Arasi's husband". Did that mean he knew her?

The car drove up to a huge bungalow.

They sat in an air-conditioned living room. Every inch of the room screamed with luxury. Gopal rang a bell and a servant appeared, served them apple juice, and then hovered nearby looking hesitant.

"What is it?" asked Gopal.

"Madam says she will be back late tonight," he said.

"Fine. You may go."

Pandian couldn't remember ever returning from work without finding Tamizh Arasi there at home waiting for him. He was growing increasingly uncomfortable. To break the silence, he asked, "You called me Tamizh Arasi's husband. Do you know her?"

"I knew her when we were in college. I was two years her senior. Like a divine, fragrant flower of gold, she has both beauty and character. You are a lucky man to have her as your wife, Pandian."

It was all very funny for Pandian. So many times he had envied Gopal's luck. Today, Gopal was calling *him* lucky!

"When I got married, I thought I was the most fortunate man in the world," continued Gopal. "Nalini is extremely rich. My mother, too, was happy that I got a rich wife. But today she regrets ruining her son's life. Now, there is no one unluckier than me. But what's the point of crying about it now?" He lapsed into silence. Pandian did not know how to console him.

Suddenly Gopal asked, "That child you brought along to the shop—she's yours?"

"Yes. My daughter, Selvi."

"Such a lovely child. A beautiful name too. What a blessing, to have a child." There was a deep longing in his voice.

"How many children do you have?" asked Pandian.

"We don't have any children," was the sad reply.

"Have you consulted a doctor?"

"What for? It's not a medical problem—it's because Nalini believes she'll lose her beauty if she has a child! She doesn't understand that motherhood is beauty in itself. Who is she trying so hard to be beautiful for? Pandian, I'm fed up with my life. Maybe a child could make me hang on—but what's the point of hoping for it, when I'm alone in that hope? You need two hands to clap. My mother, too, is longing for a grandchild. Once she asked Nalini straight to her face about children. They had a huge *ragalai*; that day my mother left to my brother's house, and she hasn't returned since. But where can I go? That's the pride of the rich, Pandian. She believes everyone should bend to her will. One word spoken against her, no matter who speaks it—even her husband—and she will blow up in rage. I'm caught in a forest fire, Pandian. I am longing for a child. But she hates the thought."

Pandian was shocked. How could anyone hate the thought of children? He would sacrifice the world for his Selvi. An image appeared in his mind of Arasi and his mother playing with Selvi, and he realized how happy they made him.

"I have learned the hard way," continued Gopal, "that a man should not marry above his status. It will only make his life hell. But I have found an escape route, a path to heaven. Shall I show you my secret method?" he asked—and opened a cupboard to reveal a long row of bottles. Pandian's face fell in distaste.

"Makes you uncomfortable just looking at it, eh? But I need this to keep from going mad. If I had a good wife, I wouldn't need to drown my sorrows with this stuff," he said, unscrewing the top of a bottle.

Pandian could not bear to stay any longer. "May I go now?" he asked, rising. "Arasi will be waiting for me."

"Oh yes, your wife will be waiting for you. How does it feel, Pandian? To be welcomed by your smiling wife when you return home, tired after a long day at work? How wonderful it must be! My wife, too, looks beautiful when she smiles—but I so rarely get to see it happen. As it is, she doesn't find enough time to go out to all the plays and films she wants to see with her friends from the ladies' club. Where would she find the time to spare a smile for her poor lower-class husband?"

Pandian looked at him pityingly.

"Please forgive me—I've bored you with my problems," said Gopal. "Of course, you may go now. But please, do drop in to see me once in a while."

"Arasi!" called Pandian, seeing her there welcoming him, as always, with a plate of *pakodas* and her ever-present smile.

Taking hold of her hands, he said passionately, "Arasi, do you know how very lucky I am? I have to thank my mother for insisting that I marry you—what a wonderful gift she's given me!"

She stared at him, quite taken aback.

"I really am a lucky man," he said. "I'll explain later." And he chomped down on one of the cashew pakodas.

DIM LIGHTS, BLAZING HEARTS

தண்ணீரும் தணல் போல் தெரியும் (1997)

by RAMANICHANDRAN

⚡ 1 ⚡

ARUNA ARRIVED AT THE OFFICE at nine in the morning, as usual, and was surprised to find several of her colleagues already in their seats working. Office hours started at half past nine, but these women generally never reported to work before ten. They always had an excuse handy. Vanaja would blame a broken-down bus; Pavai's standard enemy was the traffic; Sundari's usual excuse was that the isthrikaaran had not shown up.

This wasn't one of those small-fry construction companies that only built homes and godowns. Guna Constructions designed five-star restaurants, high-rise apartment buildings and shopping complexes. The chairman of the company, rather than being a strict disciplinarian, had a subtle way with his employees. He was friendly with everyone, even the lowliest daily wage-earner, and got work done with minimal confrontation. He didn't insist on punctuality, but somehow still made sure that tasks got accomplished on time.

In the rare cases when he did lecture, he would be gentle and tactful. "Look here, if you don't give the details on schedule, the next person can't get the estimate ready in time. Without the estimate, we can't be sure whether it's a profitable deal. To survive among the competition, we need to give quotes that are slightly below those of the other companies. And to get the tender in by the correct date, we need the details from you now. Just a little earlier this morning, and you could have been done already! So, if you wouldn't mind, could you stay until the job is finished?"

Aruna herself had once asked Devanathan, "Why aren't you stricter with them, sir?"

"We don't need to chase profits *that* hard. Even if they're slightly late to work, they can manage to take care of the usual daily chores. But when we take up a new project, they have to be willing to work extra hours to get things accomplished. If I'm going to make such demands on them later, I should be accommodating now, shouldn't I?"

It was a smart method. Aruna's eyes had widened with both surprise and respect, and Devanathan had noticed it. "I want my son Guna to learn these techniques too. That's why I keep him stationed at the construction sites. His mother complains that I'm abandoning him in a desert. But aren't the laborers there also human? If they can work there, why shouldn't he be able to? How will he ever know how to manage them unless he's aware of the conditions at the site? Besides, he has a jeep at his disposal, so he can take off whenever he wants, and a mobile to connect him with the rest of the world."

Whenever he discussed family matters, Aruna would keep quiet and just listen. As far as Aruna could tell, her boss was satisfied with her work—that was enough for her. She had a good job and a good salary. Why bother about her boss's family life? Still, she was pleased that he felt comfortable enough with her to discuss whatever happened in his home.

That morning, she was arranging her stationery on her desk when Devanathan entered and went straight to his office. She soon became absorbed in her work. After about an hour, she left a few letters to be posted with the dispatch clerk, Somasundaram, then sent Krishnan, the clerk, to fetch some reference material, and finally walked towards the typing pool with the letters that needed to be typed.

As she walked down the hallway, she could hear Sundari grumbling loudly, "What is this, *yaar?* We've been waiting since early morning, and the guy isn't even here yet!"

Aruna, wondering why these three habitually late typists had arrived early today, pricked up her ears at their conversation.

"Why? Are you scared all that paint on your face will fall off?" she heard Vanaja's arrogant voice ask. Pavai laughed loudly, as though it was a really good joke.

"What, like I'm the only one who's prettied myself up!" Sundari snapped back. "Are you two going to claim you're not wearing any makeup? I know you both just had facials done at the parlor."

"How did you know that?" they chimed.

"I was coming into the parlor just as you were leaving," Sundari replied, a little sheepishly.

Aruna couldn't help laughing—and also wondering for whose benefit these women had gone through so much trouble.

"Chee, what's the point anyway? Next to Aarthi, that film star girlfriend of his, we'll still look like oil lamps trying to compete with a sun. Why does she have to be so beautiful, anyway?"

"It's true, she's really gorgeous," responded the other two. Aruna had to agree; she had, in fact, just seen Aarthi on her way to work. There had been a traffic jam on account of a film shoot. The bus had been stopped for a long time, but when it finally moved, Aruna and everyone else on board was blessed with a brief glimpse of Aarthi lounging on the bonnet of a white Maruti Esteem. No one could deny that she had stunning looks—without them, of course, she could never have climbed so far up the ladder to fame.

But, Aruna thought, beauty wasn't everything.

As she entered the typing pool, the three typists welcomed her as per their nature. Sundari, who had never liked her, threw a millimetre-wide smile in her direction before turning her entire attention to her machine. When Devanathan's last assistant had resigned due to ill health, and

Renuka, the senior-most woman in the pool at the time, had finally got married at the ripe age of thirty-six, Sundari had hoped she would get the job of personal assistant. But Devanathan had held interviews and selected Aruna for the post instead. Since then, Aruna had become number one on Sundari's list of enemies. Her youthful beauty hadn't done anything to lessen Sundari's indignation. Sundari had hoped Aruna's work wouldn't be up to the mark, but she had been disappointed there, too. Still, she managed to stay civil most of the time.

Vanaja didn't share Sundari's active dislike, but she wasn't especially friendly with Aruna either. She didn't seem to care much what Sundari and Aruna thought of each other. Pavai, on the other hand, liked Aruna quite a bit, and often complimented her on her slim physique and good looks.

Even now, it was Pavai who gave Aruna the biggest and most genuine smile. Handing each of the typists their allotted work, Aruna returned the smile, and asked, "Is there something special going on today, Pavai? You're all looking very festive!"

"*Aiyyo*, Aruna, didn't you know? The chairman's son..." Pavai began.

"Of course Aruna knows that the chairman's son is coming to the office today. Nothing goes on in this office without the chairman's personal assistant knowing *all* about it," Sundari interrupted bitterly.

"It's not like that, Sundari," replied Aruna casually. "I can't help it if he keeps me busy. I wish I had more time to get to know you three better! But anyway, what's this about the chairman's son? Is he getting married or something?"

Surprised, Pavai asked, "Is he? I didn't hear anything about that. I just heard he was coming today."

They were all too embarrassed to admit they had decked themselves out in hopes of catching the eye of the young son of the chairman. Sundari, never subtle, gave the explanation. "Mr. Gunaseelan doesn't appreciate sloppy dressers. So we took a little extra effort. No other hidden agenda."

"Alright, fine. Let's get back to work then. Vanaja, you make three copies of this; Pavai, you make five copies of this statement; and

Sundari, get twenty-five copies of this letter posted today please," Aruna instructed.

As she returned to her seat, she couldn't help but wonder at the effort these women went through for a man. To think of the money and time spent at the parlor, for facials and hairdos and special outfits—all for a man they didn't even know, just because he happened to be the son of the chairman.

Well, his name was Gunaseelan—it meant "epitome of virtues". Who knew what his real character was, whether he was a man of virtues or vices? Probably vices—after all, hadn't they connected him to an actress? Have our women really become so cheap that they'll go to all these lengths to attract such a man? She sat down, disgusted. Taking a tiny mirror out of her bag, she examined herself. Thank God, she hadn't overdressed today. She'd even removed the new earring that her mother had been urging her to wear. No one could accuse her of laying a trap to ensnare a rich man, she thought.

She had no way of knowing that she was about to be accused of exactly that.

⚸ 2 ⚸

Aruna *had* known that the chairman's son was expected in the office that day; she just hadn't thought about it much. She didn't have the time. Devanathan was keeping her very busy that morning. So, after spending a moment regretting her coworkers' cheap behavior, she forgot about the entire episode. After lunch, Devanathan gave her strict instructions that he should not be disturbed. "If anyone calls for me, ask them to call back in an hour. Don't let anyone into my room until I tell you I'm ready," he'd said.

She had another half hour to work in peace. Three phone calls came for the chairman, but they all accepted her explanation without argument and agreed to call back later. When she was about to resume work after the third call, she felt thirsty, and walked over to the water cooler. As she sipped her glass of water, her eyes wandered towards the window.

Initially disinterested, she noticed a white Esteem pulling into the office car park. *Wasn't that the same car I saw Aarthi reclining on this morning?* she thought to herself, and then immediately wondered, *Why should I care whether Aarthi was lying on an Esteem or sitting in a Tata Sumo?* She got back to her seat, and had typed three sentences when a young man walked into the office, and hurried up to her desk.

"Hello, is Appa in there?"

So this was the next generation! Not bad—quite good looking! A pity he's so keen on sowing his wild oats! Aruna also had an uncanny feeling that she'd seen him before somewhere. But that seemed unlikely.

"Yes," she replied. He had already moved to the door. "But please wait, Mr. Gunaseelan! The chairman is presently involved in some important work and has asked not to be disturbed," she called out, hurrying up to block his way to the door.

"Does that apply to me too? Are you sure?" he asked casually.

What an idiot! she thought, irritated. "I'm not sure if he meant to include you or not. But he's my boss, and he didn't tell me he was expecting you, so I can't allow you to enter without his permission."

He gave her a smirk. "This isn't the first time a girl has pulled something like this to try to get my attention. Now listen, I need to go in there and discuss an important deal with my father. So stop this drama and move aside!"

Her face went red with anger. "Who do you think you are? Some Jagadhalaprathaban, with all the women dying for a glance from you?" she demanded. She crossed her arms in front of her chest, and stood firmly, making every inch of her five and a half feet count. "I'm sorry, I can't let you in until your father says I can." She had made a tall announcement; what would she do if he shoved her aside and went ahead? Would she be able to handle his strength?

Gunaseelan was slightly taken aback at her reaction. *I could just give her a tap, and she'd roll over eight times. Where does she get the guts from?* he wondered. Just then the intercom on her desk buzzed. She threw a warning look at him before she moved to take the call. It was Devanathan, needing some information from her. "I'll be there in a minute, sir," she said, and then added softly, "Sir, your son, Mr. Gunaseelan, is here wait-ing to see you."

She hoped Devanathan would say "Ask him to wait." Instead, he said, "Is he? Ask him to come in at once."

She turned back to Gunaseelan, and said in a tiny voice, "Your father wants to see you." He cocked one eyebrow at her, and then entered the room, with her following behind.

She perked up again when Devanathan, without looking up, told his son, "Please wait, Guna, we'll talk in a minute. Aruna, are you ready? I need this statement typed up in half an hour." She couldn't resist flash-ing a victorious grin at Gunaseelan as she sat down to take the dictation. He couldn't do anything but sit there quietly with his arms folded. She finished writing out the statement and, pretending to ignore him, left the room.

When she finally left for home that evening, she noticed that the father and son were still deep in conversation. *It must really be something important after all*, she mused.

In the three months since Aruna had taken up this job, this was the first time Gunaseelan had visited the office. But she couldn't get rid of the feeling that she had seen him before—maybe not on the office premises, but somewhere! After staying away at the site for so long, why was he suddenly getting involved with the business end?

As she waited at the bus stand, she saw the white Esteem pass her, and thought again of Aarthi's pose from that morning. She recalled, also, the gossip in the typing pool that Aarthi had already trapped Gunaseelan. So that was why he thought of himself as a Jagadhalaprathaban! Just because a famous actress was enamored with him, he now assumed that every woman in the world would pine for him. What arrogance!

Suddenly her thoughts were interrupted by a voice. "What happened, why the distressed look? Did you have to fend someone off with your slippers?" It was Sudharsanam, her father. She'd been so preoccupied she hadn't even realized that she had already reached home.

"What, Appa...?"

"Sorry you have to deal with all these stupid chaps. Don't worry, those who sow will have to reap someday. If he misbehaves with a woman today, tomorrow some other man will misbehave with his sister."

Finally understanding her father's line of thought, she said, "No, no, nothing like that, Appa; nobody misbehaved with me. I just had a small problem at the office."

That set off him again. "What problem? If you're having problems in the workplace, why should you continue to work at all? By God's grace, I've earned enough money to get you three kids educated. Why should you have to struggle as well? Why don't you resign from your job tomorrow?"

Sudharsanam was a fairly "modern" man. Still, he didn't approve of his daughter working. What if people thought that he was depending on her income for *his* food, or that she had to work to save money for her marriage? He had only allowed her to go for secretarial training because she had insisted on it. He wasn't enough of an authoritarian to demand that she stay home, but he couldn't resist ranting about her job from time to time.

She hurriedly concocted a believable lie to calm him down. Refusing dinner, she asked for a headache pill, drank a glass of milk, and went to bed early.

But she couldn't sleep. The TV in the other room was turned up high, playing old film songs. Normally, she would have enjoyed the honey-sweet melodies, but tonight they just make her head feel worse. She got up to reduce the volume when she heard the song "*Naan pesu ninapathu ellam, nee pesu vendum...*"

And it was then that she remembered where she had seen Gunaseelan before.

Her former classmates had gathered for an alumnae meeting, and one of them, who happened to be the daughter of the owner of a cinema hall, had invited them for a film.

"It's an old classic—a beautiful film, with wonderful songs. I've booked six tickets. And if you come, I've got another surprise for you there!"

The surprise had been a glimpse of Aarthi. Apparently, she had booked a box exclusively for herself several months back. And it was there, in that box, that Aruna had seen Gunaseelan for the first time—wrapped in Aarthi's tight embrace, necking furiously, not ashamed in the least that they were still visible in the dim light of the theatre!

⚡ 3 ⚡

Aruna's heart started boiling with the memory. How terribly Gunaseelan and Aarthi had behaved that day!

While the house lights were on, they would sit apart like a decent couple. But as soon as the lights dimmed, they would go at it again, apparently oblivious to the fact that the flickering glow from screen made them vaguely visible to everyone in the hall.

The cinema hall owner's daughter, Sanjala, had pointed them out to her friends. She told them that this was a recurring event.

"Why doesn't your father object? How can he allow them to misbehave like this in public, Sanji?" Aruna had asked, disgusted.

Sanjala had just laughed. "You don't understand. Those two aren't the worst of it. Do you know how many couples start hurriedly adjusting their clothes as soon as the lights come on? My father used to book a box for us if we came to watch a film as a family. But because of all these embarrassing scenes, he's stopped."

"But it's your father's theatre! Doesn't he have the right to demand decency here?" Aruna had asked.

"He does, but these box seats are really expensive. Only the super-rich can afford them—people who have plenty of influence. My father can't afford to get in their bad books. They could easily have the theatre shut down, if they wanted. So, he has to put up with this stuff," she had replied.

Aruna had noticed that there was another man in the seat next to Gunaseelan and Aarthi, watching them. Perhaps he was imagining himself in Aarthi's arms?

For days after the trip to the theatre, Aruna had agonized over the lack of decency among modern people. Finally, she had pushed what she had witnessed into a corner of her memory, not often accessed. But today, that memory returned in full detail. To imagine that a man who could behave so shamelessly in public had today accused *her* of making a play for his attention! Hadn't anyone ever taught Gunaseelan that one should first clean one's own home before pointing out the mess in another's?

And he hadn't even had the decency to apologize to her, after she'd been proved right! But, of course, she had left the office before he had.

She recalled now the advice of Sargunam, her tutor in her secretarial course. "Avoid confrontations at all costs. It's all well and good to argue for mutual respect between an employer and an employee. But never expect your boss to admit he's made a mistake. As long as he's the one who's paying your salary, he's always right! Only those who don't fear unemployment should dare to revolt. The rest of us must learn to adjust."

It was good advice, she supposed. Still, what right did Gunaseelan have to speak to her like that?

After all, this was someone who followed a film actress around, carrying her *kuja*. And then he casually strolls in one afternoon claiming he has something important to discuss! What a liar!

After a restless night of confused dreams, she woke up later than usual, rushed to the office, and arrived a few minutes late. Devanathan had already come in. She threw her things onto her desk and immediately went into his office to apologize.

He just smiled at her. "You're four minutes late. That's not a crime! So don't be sorry. But go get your notepad ready. Guna has brought in a very big business deal. We're going to be working really hard for the next few days."

So there *was* something important going on! Of course, she thought, Gunaseelan could be using this as an excuse to spend more time in the city, and get more chances to meet Aarthi.

She looked through the chairman's diary for the day's appointments. When she came to Gunaseelan's name near the bottom of the page, the pen slipped out of her hand. She bent down, irritated with herself, to pick it up, and continued checking the diary. The entry wasn't in her handwriting—he must have written it in after she'd left the day before. The appointment was at three. Why so late? Was he going to serve his goddess till then?

With some effort, she drove all thoughts of Gunaseelan out of her mind, and got to work. There was a lot to do, and she didn't have time for distractions. At lunch, she wolfed down the tomato rice that her mother had packed for her, hardly noticing how tasty it was.

At three, she heard a light tap on her table, and looked up from her work.

"Yes?" she asked.

"I have an appointment with the Chairman at three," said Gunaseelan with mock politeness. "I need your permission to see him, Madam Secretary."

Fuming inside, she replied in a wooden tone, "Since the meeting has been arranged by the Chairman, you may go right in," and returned to her work. But he didn't go in yet; instead, he remained standing in front of her desk. She couldn't continue to ignore him. Angrily, she snapped, "Mr. Gunaseelan, if you truly have to meet the chairman, then please go in. He'll be waiting for you. If not, there are chairs in the lobby for visitors to wait. Please sit there."

But he wasn't paying attention. "I've been wondering since yesterday, Aruna, what you'd look like if you laughed, or even just smiled a bit. I think your face would be very lovely."

She didn't bother to mask her irritation. "I like my face just fine as it is, thank you. You may go now."

"I like it too. I'm only suggesting how you might make it even more beautiful."

"Look, Mr. Gunaseelan, when I decide I want to act in movies, I'll consider your suggestion. At the moment, it's quite unnecessary."

"Is there a rule that says only film actresses can be beautiful? When you have a lovely face, you shouldn't ruin it with a frown," he said.

"Sir," she said exasperatedly, "I have a lot of work to do. I have to deliver this report at your father's desk in half an hour. I don't have time to chat. If you really have an appointment at three, he'll be waiting for you. So, will you please go in?" Again, she turned back to her typing."

He stood looking at her for a moment longer, then went in to meet his father.

His speech had really fired her up. Here he was, probably fresh from hanging around Aarthi's shooting locations and playing his love games, coming here and giving her beauty tips! Did he expect her to be charmed? She'd even tried to drop a hint about the movies, to indicate that she knew what he was up to—and he'd ignored it completely.

She counted to ten several times. Still, her rage did not abate. She drank a glass of water and looked over her work. Again she became angry, this time at herself, for everything she had typed since the conversation was riddled with errors. She tore up the papers and started over.

✗ 4 ✗

The workload over the next few days was huge.

A seven-star hotel and restaurant complex was coming up in Mamallapuram, the project being funded by an NRI investor. It was set to include five hundred air-conditioned rooms, twenty cottages, a swimming pool, shopping arcades, conference rooms, and a gym. The firm was responsible for all aspects of construction. The deal was worth several crores. Since construction material costs had been rising, it took a long time to budget and order material. The foundation work had already started. Gunaseelan was dividing his time between the site and office. He spent the days supervising the construction work, and the evenings doing accounts in the office.

As if this wasn't enough, it came to light that one small patch of the land used for the site had been bought through a crooked agent, who had used his power of attorney to cheat the actual owner. And so poor Gunaseelan had to deal with a legal hassle, on top of everything else.

During these few days, as Aruna worked alongside him, her attitude towards him changed. She began to appreciate his dedication to his work, his sharp intelligence, his keen memory, and his way of relating to his employees. His father, she judged, had indeed trained him well. The way he smiled, nodded, and congratulated people inspired her to work harder in order to earn the same commendations for herself. It was usual at the firm for people to put in long overtime hours during a crunch period. Gunaseelan made sure the employees were paid bonuses for the extra hours they put in. These were well received, and people were willing to put in even more extra hours. Now that Aruna was the secretary for both the father and the son, she went home even later than the others. Devanathan alone would leave promptly at seven in the evening; his doctor had put him on a strict diet.

After he left, Gunaseelan and Aruna would continue to work by themselves for at least another hour. He had stopped teasing her, and she found it very comfortable working with him.

On one such day, when they had worked very late into the night, he offered to drop her home. She declined, explaining that she had already informed her folks, and that either her father or her brother would be coming to the office to escort her back. He cocked one eyebrow at her. Peering out the window and seeing someone waiting at the doorstep, he turned back to her and asked, "Is that your father?"

When she smiled in reply, he asked the watchman to call her father into the lobby to sit. "I should have realized that before," he murmured to himself.

"It's okay," said Aruna. "If family members of the employees are allowed to crowd around in the office, nobody will get any work done."

"Of course, not during office hours—I agree, that shouldn't be encouraged. But in situations like this, we can't make your father wait out on the road! Next time he comes, make sure to let him wait in the lobby," he insisted.

Aruna was pleased. It was never safe for a woman to travel alone at night, so she often asked her father to come if she was staying late. But she also felt guilty for making him go through that trouble at his age. Therefore, she was grateful to Gunaseelan for making things easier for the old man. When she was leaving, he came to the lobby, and introduced himself to her father. "You must forgive us for keeping her so late," he said. "I'm sure Aruna has told you about the current project. She's been very responsible and prompt with her work. She even discovered a calculation error I had made that probably saved us ten lakh rupees." Aruna couldn't help blushing at the compliment. "I think she gets her intelligence from you, sir," he continued, putting a smile on Sudharsanam's face as well.

"What a nice young man. No airs at all," said her father appreciatively, on their way home. She agreed. If only he wasn't involved with Aarthi—but he was, there was no denying it. Even last Sunday, as she was returning from a wedding reception along with her brother, she saw the white Esteem pass her with Gunaseelan and Aarthi in it. The sight of them had been enough to spoil her mood for the rest of the day. The day after that, it had been very difficult to remain casual with him in the office.

The next day Gunaseelan had offered to drop both the father and daughter off at home. Her father had eagerly accepted, before she had a chance to refuse. She hesitated before inviting him into the house, but the rest of her family was excited to entertain Aruna's managing director. Aruna was happy, too, that he seemed to be able to mix naturally with her family—but she also wondered about his motives. Was he just here to get a taste of how common people lived? Why else should he bother with a middle-class family?

That auspicious day arrived when the foundation stone for the hotel was to be laid. A cabinet minister was invited to do the honors. He was a simple man, seemingly unaware of the power of his position, who went through the motions of the function without the pomp and ceremony that was expected of him. Devanathan returned to the office after dropping the minister off.

That evening, the chairman's wife and daughter visited the office. They caused a good deal of excitement. His family had never come to the office until then. The employees had rarely gotten to meet them; indeed, Aruna, relatively new at the firm, had never seen them before. She made tea and served them. The two women complimented her on the taste of the tea, and then, instead of going to sit in the chairman's room, they sat and spent the rest of their visit with Aruna. The chairman finished his tea with them and then left Aruna to entertain them. Aruna was surprised at this.

Kanmani, the daughter, was friendly and unassuming. "How do you manage to maintain your long hair, Aruna? I cut mine, because I was sick of combing out the tangles," she said, indicating her boyish short hair.

Aruna laughed. "My hair never tangles. My mother doesn't allow us to ever cut it, not even the split ends."

"Every mother prefers it if their daughters grow their hair long," said Kalavathi, the chairman's wife. "This girl didn't even consult me before chopping hers off. She has beautiful saris. But when I asked her to wear a sari for my sister-in-law's daughter's wedding, with the sari and that hair—she looked like a man dressed in a sari! It was horrible!"

"Then what did you wear, finally?" asked Aruna with a smile, and at once worried that she was acting over-familiar with her boss's family.

Kanmani didn't seem to take any offense, though. "A *churidhar!*" she said. "That's the universal solution for any hairstyle."

Kalavathi didn't sound very happy with her daughter. "You were happy. No one else was, though. All the girls your age were dressed in 'tissue' saris, all done up beautifully with jewels and flowers in their hair. And there my daughter was in a churidhar! I was so ashamed."

"Sorry Amma, I'll never cut my hair again. I'll keep it at least down to my shoulders, I promise. But don't worry, at least your daughter-in-law will have nice long hair, that you can braid and decorate with flowers...." She stopped in mid-sentence at a glare from her mother.

Daughter-in-law? Oh—so they had fixed on Aarthi, then. It was true, she did have lovely hair. Perhaps the mother didn't approve of her, and that was why she had cut Kanmani's speech off midway. For some reason the thought endeared Gunaseelan's mother to Aruna even more.

That evening, as she was helping Gunaseelan check the accounts, she told him about the visit. He looked up to whisper, "Good, so that's out of the way."

She stared at him, uncomprehending. His response was the usual lift of the eyebrow. He gave her a strange smile that made her blush, and she hurried out of the room.

With the completion of the hotel complex, the atmosphere at work became less tense, and both father and son were visibly more relaxed. The employees went back to their normal work-hours. Devanathan sent Aruna home early as well. But at home, she felt bored. For the past few days she had been working so late that she was rarely ever home—and she had enjoyed it. She was actually glad that things would only be this slow for a few more days. The heavy load would begin again soon.

The next day Devanathan went home at lunchtime. Gunaseelan was going to spend the day at another site. So again she returned home early, to find a surprise waiting for her.

↗ 5 ↗

As soon as she walked in, she noticed that something was different. The house was spotlessly clean. This wasn't the result of the maid's daily sweeping—the whole family must have spent hours prettying the place up. There was a bowl of expensive fruits on the dining table. Had her father got a raise or something?

As Aruna sat down, wondering, her mother brought her a cup of coffee, and kissed her on the forehead. "My dear, I hope no one casts the evil eye on you!"

"Why should anyone do that, Amma?" she asked.

"Listen to what I have to tell you, then you answer that yourself. Guess who came home today! Or perhaps you already know?" her mother asked.

"No, Amma… who?"

Her mother glanced at Sudharsanam, seated on the sofa. "Your chairman, and his wife and daughter," she said.

"What? Really? Why?" asked Aruna, shocked.

"To ask for the hand of our eldest daughter for their only son, Gunaseelan!"

"Stop!" she sprang up. "Don't say that!"

Her father looked at her with a bemused smile. "Why not?"

Aruna's mind raced. It hadn't been by chance that the chairman's wife and daughter had stopped by the office. They had been checking her out! She had thought they were just being friendly to her. Oh, why did they have to waste a trip?

What was she going to tell her parents now? She couldn't come right out and say "I don't want to marry him." That single sentence seemed as heavy as a mountain. Instead she stayed silent, just staring ahead.

"She's just surprised, that's all," Sudharsanam told his wife, who was giving Aruna a worried look. "She scared me a little at first!"

"She scared me a little bit too! I assumed the groom would have told her in the office! It was very decent of him to ask his parents to come here. Such nice folks," said her mother.

Aruna couldn't take it anymore. She had watched this same man necking with a woman in a public cinema hall! Today he wanted to arrange a marriage with her. How could he expect her to agree?

"After the marriage, your father-in-law's going to have to find himself a new secretary!" Aruna's mother prattled on.

"He was sorry about that, too," said her father. "He kept saying he was losing the best secretary he'd ever had, his son was stealing her away from him. Of course he doesn't really mind, since the same girl will become a part of his household!"

Aruna wished her parents would shut up. She finally broke her silence. "Amma, Appa, I need some time to think about this. So please don't build your hopes up too high yet," she said determinedly.

"What? What is there to think about?" asked her parents in dismay.

"I just have to think, Amma. I'll tell you my decision later," she said, and went into her room and shut the door.

Immediately, she dissolved into tears.

It had been thirty days since she had met Gunaseelan. She had been irritated about his relationship with the actress Aarthi, true. But she had also discovered several of his admirable qualities. She had really enjoyed working with him—remaining unaware, the whole time, of the fondness growing in her heart. Had she been conscious of it, she would have talked herself out of it—locking away her feelings if necessary. What a cruel twist of fate, to have the unattainable fruit fall into her hands, and yet have to reject it!

She knew she had to refuse—that much, at least, was clear. Yes, it was a pity, but after all she had never entertained thoughts of marrying him. If she had only *heard* about his dark secret, if Sanjala had just *told* her about Gunaseelan and Aarthi, she might have been swayed, able to convince herself it was just a rumor. But she had seen them with her own eyes, acting even more intimate than the romantic pair on the screen. What reason could he possibly have to want to marry a different woman, and one so far beneath his economic status at that?

Maybe his parents had refused to accept Aarthi as a daughter-in-law. Maybe that was why they were selecting a poorer girl, as an alternative to a movie actress. But was Gunaseelan the kind of man to let his parents make life decisions for him?

No—it must have been Gunaseelan's idea. But why?

Then she began to see an answer. Perhaps Gunaseelan had never intended to marry Aarthi. God knows how many other relationships he'd had with other women besides her—never intending to marry any of them! He wouldn't grant the position of wife to a loose woman like that. On the other hand, he didn't want give up his philandering either. If he married a woman from an equally rich family, he'd have to stop his womanizing; a rich bride wouldn't stand for it. But if he took a poorer woman as his wife, she would have to tolerate whatever he did. She would be too overwhelmed by the sheer wealth of her in-laws to object. Her parents would advise her to bear with his bad habits for the sake of their grandchildren.

A picture formed in her imagination: Gunaseelan lying on a ornate bed, surrounded by liquor bottles and a harem of scantily-clad women. She began trembling. He was capable of it! "Epitome of virtues" indeed!

She waited until her brother and sister had gone to bed after dinner. Then she announced to her parents that she did not want to marry Gunaseelan.

There was only silence for a few minutes. Then Sudharsanam asked, "Have you thought carefully about this? Aruna, marriage is for life. You shouldn't let an opportunity slip through your fingers just because of some minor quarrel or something. So think hard. They are very rich. And if you say no, how will you continue working there?"

She stared at her father for a second and demanded, "Appa, since when are money and riches all you care about?"

"Since I became a father of three children. You'll understand, when you have a family of your own," replied Sudharsanam. After a short pause, he continued, angry now. "Forget about the money. What does that man lack? Looks? Character? Give me one reason why you should say no."

She had a reason—a good strong one. And if the same father who was now praising Gunaseelan to the heavens heard her reason, he would think of Gunaseelan as less than a worm. She couldn't bear to tell him. "Please drop it, Appa," she wept.

"Crying won't solve anything!" Sudharsanam yelled. But her mother whispered softly, "Please, leave her alone. If she doesn't like the match, let's not force her. Now stop it!"

The next day she reluctantly got ready for work. Was this going to be her last day at Guna Constructions? Would she ever be able to find a job as good as this one, with a boss as understanding?

Oh, why hadn't Gunaseelan just stayed out at the construction site? Why couldn't he have left her in peace? What rotten luck!

She entered Devanathan's office carrying a heavy heart and her resignation letter. He read the letter silently, and then looked up at her. "Look here, Aruna. My son is a good man—but you don't want to marry him. Although it saddens me that you don't want to become my daughter-in-law, this is really a private matter between the two of you. You don't need to bring the office into it. Go tear this letter up and throw it away. I might be losing a good daughter-in-law, but I don't need to lose a good secretary too. Go continue your work."

She felt her heart grow lighter. "But sir... your son...?"

He nodded thoughtfully. "Yes, of course, it might be a bit uncomfortable for you for a while. But now that the basic accounts are over, he won't be coming to the office very often. If you do chance to meet him—for the sake of this good old employer of yours, can't you try to adjust?" he asked.

As she went out with the letter, he said, "Wait." She stopped and turned around.

"I don't mean to force you, but... can you tell me why you refused my son?"

There was no way she could tell him that the son he held such a high opinion of was completely immoral. She thought for a moment, and then said, "There is a tale in the *Panchatantram* about a frog and a mouse that were very good friends. They were so close that they decided they never wanted to be separated, and so they bound two of their legs together. Soon, the frog, needing water, started off towards the river. But the mouse, scared of drowning, pulled in the other direction, towards a field. As they struggled there, a vulture swooped down from the sky and flew off with both of them in its beak. I am from a middle-class home. In your home, I would suffocate like the mouse in the river."

Devanathan listened to her carefully, without interrupting, and then let her go.

Aruna was relieved when the time came to go home. She was troubled, though, that Gunaseelan had not come to the office, or even called at all.

But the next day, he did come. He burst through the door quickly, as usual, dragged a chair to her table, and sat down. Staring at her for a moment, he said, "Okay, now can you tell me the reason why you refused me? Please don't tell me fables like the ones you gave my father. I want the truth." His voice was caustic.

She tried to reply, but the words died in her throat.

A full minute went by—sixty seconds of tortured silence. She could not think of a single word that would satisfy this man in front of her.

He thrust his wrist up to her face, pointing out that a minute had passed. "How come you were so eloquent when you spoke to your father and to my father, but you don't have a single word for me? Go on, tell me a story too."

Somehow, she managed to stammer, "I don't like…"

"What don't you like? In all this time you've known me, what have I done to make you dislike me?" he demanded.

His anger sparked hers, too. "Just accept it. I don't like you. That's it," she insisted.

"What is it that you don't like?"

"That's not your business. I don't need to tell you that."

"Don't give me that. I'm the rejected victim here. I have a right to know why I was rejected. Why do you hate me? Come on, answer!" His voice was soft, but menacing.

She stared at him wide-eyed. Wavy thick hair, a regal brow, huge eyes, sculpted lips—and a masculine physique to match this handsome face. How could she hate this man? Aruna's brains were getting addled. What madness was this, to refuse him? She searched her heart and found the answer. The clarity there gave her strength. "I have a solid reason. But this isn't the place to tell it."

"What's wrong with this place?"

"Your father's office is right there. He could walk in on our argument at any moment. He thinks very highly of you, and I wouldn't like to let him down," she replied resolutely.

"Fine, I accept—though I have no secrets from my father, so I can't imagine what you're talking about. I'll take you home in my car this evening. Give me my answer then," said Gunaseelan.

No secrets? How many more lies are you going to act out? she thought, but she said, "Okay, I'll come."

In the evening, as she got into the car, she was deep in thought, wondering how she was going to give him his answer. She was unaware that she was being watched.

The three typists were just leaving the office, carrying their lunch boxes, water bottles and handbags, when they saw her. If Sundari's eyes had the power, she would have burned Aruna down then and there.

Turning to Pavai, she said angrily, "And you claimed Aruna was a good, simple woman. Look for yourself. All that time she claimed to be working overtime, she was spending getting close to the young boss, and now she's finally snared him. I *told* you this was her plan, but you didn't believe me. Now look at her, sitting next to him in his car as though she were his lawfully wedded wife. She's just a regular employee like us. Why does she get this special treatment?"

The other two typists, knowing better than to argue with Sundari, stayed silent. Besides, they were themselves surprised at seeing Aruna get into Gunaseelan's car.

In the car, Aruna was quiet for a very long time. Then she noticed that they were taking a different route, not the one towards her home. Gunaseelan saw her confusion and said, "You're here to give me an explanation, not to get back home. I'm not going to stop the car till I get my answer."

"What if you run out of petrol?" she blurted out, and then bit her tongue in embarrassment.

"I've got a full tank. I can drive for at least ten hours before I have to stop. If you want to spend that whole time with me, I have no objections."

How she would love to! But she said with a sigh, "Aarthi…"

He looked at her surprised and asked, "What about her?" The question seemed a little careless. Maybe he even found it funny.

"I know you have a relationship with her," she said sternly.

"It's no secret that I know her! What does that have to do with our marriage?"

How could a man ask that?

"How dare you?" spat Aruna. Anger made her voice tremble. "You have an immoral relationship with another woman, and you still want me to..."

"Shut up!" He brought the car to a sudden halt. "Aren't you ashamed to speak like that about a woman you don't even know? Aarthi is a friend, my best friend's girlfriend..."

"Oh, such a likely story! What a fertile imagination you have!" Aruna interrupted. "And I'm supposed to believe it was your best friend's girlfriend that you were wrapped all around in the cinema hall?"

"Who told you that?" he asked, not understanding clearly.

"I don't need anyone to tell me. I saw it myself!"

"You saw *what* yourself? What nonsense is this? You saw *someone* in the cinema hall hugging Aarthi—did you see his face? And even if you did, how could you have recognized him in the dark?"

"So is that what gave you the courage, the cover of darkness?"

He glared at her for a second, then looked blankly at the road. "This isn't *my* secret, Aruna—I don't really have the right to tell it. But since this is the issue that's troubling you, it's silly to hide it any more." And he proceeded to give an explanation.

"Aarthi is my friend, and my friend Manohar's girlfriend. She was climbing up the ladder to fame and fortune. But Manohar comes from an ordinary family; Aarthi's parents would never accept him as her husband. So it was difficult for them to meet. They came to me for help. Aarthi's parents didn't mind her going out with men, as long as the men were well-off. So I would pretend I was taking her out, and then bring her to meet Manohar. I did this as a favor to my friends. They only got a chance to meet when I came home from the site. Those opportunities were rare, and they did become over-passionate a few times. And that's when you caught a glimpse of them, I guess."

She listened without interrupting. When he was done, she said, "Very good—nice film plot you've got there. But why did those two have to come to a cinema hall to have fun? Why not go to a hotel room?"

He gave her an odd look. "I thought you would understand it yourself.

If they were totally alone, they might be tempted to cross the line completely. They were afraid of that. It did almost happen once. That's why they prefer a public space now."

Aruna blushed and grew angrier. "Stop lying. I saw you together with her once in the cinema hall, and again riding in your car. Don't lie to me! I even once saw both of you going into Khazana Jewellers together. Do you shop for jewels in semi-darkness, too?'

"No. I went there to buy jewellery for *you*. On the way, I happened to meet Aarthi. I asked her to come with me to help me choose."

She was stunned for a second and then said, "I underestimated you. You are really great, sir." She applauded. "I always wondered how you were so good at your work. It's amazing; you don't even hesitate a second before inventing a new story."

Gunaseelan's face darkened. "What I've said is the truth. If Manohar and Aarthi were here, they could back me up. But she's away shooting for a month, in Europe. Manohar's gone with her as her manager."

"How convenient."

"The shooting won't go on forever. The schedule is only for three months. They've already been there a month now. They'll be back. I'll prove it to you then."

"Even then, why should I believe what they say?"

"Aruna?" He sounded wounded.

"Tell me! Why should I believe her?"

"Why would she lie to you? If she were really my lover, as you imagine, why would she confirm what I've told you?"

"Maybe she wants to continue being your lover, but not your wife. That way she can keep advertising herself to the film world as 'the untouched virgin'—so she won't lose her audience. You will keep her as your lover, but you'll marry a poor woman to stop the world's gossip. That must be it! I'm sure I've got it."

"You're talking crap," he snapped.

"Well, the truth isn't always pleasant to hear."

"Oh God, how stubborn can you be? I don't know how else to make you understand," he said, and before she could move away, he grabbed her in his arms and planted a firm kiss on her lips.

At first, she tried to squirm out of his hold, but she was soon overcome. Time seemed to stand still as they kissed.

They had no idea how much time had passed, when a loud horn from a passing car brought them back to earth. They sprang apart. It took Aruna a moment to regain her composure. She adjusted her clothes. Was this she? Aruna? On a busy public road? What would people think? That car that had honked—had the driver seen them kissing? Oh God… had Gunaseelan been thinking of Aarthi while he kissed her?

It took Gunaseelan even longer to compose himself. He smoothed back his hair, but still sounded breathless as he asked, "Aruna, now you do understand me?"

She looked back at him with fire in her eyes. "Of course I do. I understand how well that actress has trained you. You've become an expert at kissing girls in cars."

Helplessly, he slumped onto the steering wheel, trying to get control over his emotions.

"You're never going to trust me, are you?"

"Never!"

"So now what?"

"So now, please, I beg you, just leave me alone. If I don't have to see you or talk to you anymore, that's probably the greatest favor you can do for me!"

Gunaseelan did not utter a word until he stopped at a corner near Aruna's house. As she opened the car door, he said, "I'm sure you'll be safe walking this distance. I'm sorry, I don't think I can handle meeting your parents. I'll try my best to do the favor you asked." With that, he drove off.

Aruna walked home with a leaden heart.

⚔ 7 ⚔

From the next day onwards, Gunaseelan didn't appear in the office, or even call. There was no news about him. This should have made her happy, but it didn't. She realized that he must have gone out of town, because Devananthan was now supervising both the construction site and the office. Devanathan was looking fatigued and overworked, and it disturbed her. In a way, it was her fault.

But was it right for Gunaseelan to leave town just because a woman didn't want to see him? Wasn't it his duty to take care of his father, to stay around and be responsible for the work at the site? Why didn't he drop in to check on his father's health?

Her head was a jumble of contradictory thoughts. She felt as though she was living in a vacuum. It was difficult to act normal at home, to laugh at her father's jokes and spend time with her brother and sister as though nothing was troubling her.

One day she got a call from Gunaseelan at work. When she answered the phone and recognized his voice, it took her a moment to become professional. He had called her line since he couldn't get through to his father's desk. She put the call through and then waited impatiently. But once the call was done, she did not have the guts to ask his father about it. It was a private matter, she supposed, not for public discussion. She wanted to tell him, "Sir, you're tiring yourself out. Put your son back in charge of the site." But it was not her place.

It was another four days before Gunaseelan called again for his father. This time, she decided not to miss the opportunity. "Sir, please stay on the line after you talk to your father. I need to tell you something."

"About?"

"About your father. He's really working too hard, and…"

"Madam, please stick to the job you're being paid for. Don't interfere in our family matters," he snapped. She felt a sting as though he had slapped her face.

A week later Gunaseelan visited the office during lunch. Her heartbeat quickened. But he passed by as though she didn't even exist.

Tears welled up in her eyes. Did he really hate her so much? Just because she hadn't been able to believe his lies? Or—was it possible that there was some truth in what he had said?

Her thoughts were racing so fast she worried she was losing track of reality. She was deeply hurt with Gunaseelan's attitude. But the next day changed everything.

Devanathan arrived at work that morning looking very unwell. Aruna mustered up some courage and asked him, "Do you have a headache? Can I make you some tea?"

He started to shake his head, but then admitted, "Sure—I'm not feeling too great, actually."

As she was making the tea, the intercom buzzer sounded—and didn't stop. Something made her switch off the stove and rush into Devanathan's office, where she found him collapsed in his chair with his hand on the intercom.

She ran up to him and placed her hand on his chest. His breathing was labored and irregular.

She began acting at lightning speed. She laid him flat on his back, loosened his clothes, splashed water on his face, and called his physician on his mobile.

The doctor arrived almost at once and took over the treatment. She called for an ambulance, and then phoned the construction site to inform Gunaseelan. She also called Devanathan's house, but learned that his wife and daughter were away at their native village. She decided to let Gunaseelan worry about informing his mother, and went back to help the doctor. The ambulance arrived, and the doctor got in with Devanathan, telling her: "When Gunaseelan comes, ask him to meet us at Apollo Hospital. I'm admitting Devanathan there."

Gunaseelan must have been breaking all the speed limits, for he was at the office within an hour. He left immediately for the hospital, leaving Aruna in charge of the office.

All day, she couldn't get Gunaseelan's worried face out of her mind.

Around four in the evening, Gunaseelan called the office. "How is he?" she asked.

"They say it will take a day before they can tell me anything."

"Don't worry sir, your father will be all right soon. Let's hope that by this time tomorrow, he'll be sitting up again."

He thanked her, and gave her the telephone number of the post office in his mother's village. She called, and got in touch with the mother, who promised to leave for the city at once.

Next, Aruna informed her own family that she was going to be delayed. She made a thermos full of coffee and some idlis for Gunaseelan, and left for the hospital. When she saw Gunaseelan alone in the hospital corridor, her heart went out to him. She served him the idlis in a clean tiffin box. When he finished it she gave him the coffee.

"What about you?" he asked.

"There's more," she assured him. They had their coffee. She went to clean the thermos and the dishes and then returned to sit quietly next to him. She couldn't bear his obvious tension, his clenched hands. She started to caress them softly, when he quickly grabbed hold of her hand and gasped, "Aruna, can you stay here with me a little longer? I'll make sure you get home safe."

"Of course," she said without hesitation.

They sat holding hands for a long time, until Dr. Prakash Rao came out. "Not to worry anymore, Gunaseelan. Your father is conscious. I've given him a tranquilizer so he can rest for the night. Be back here at around seven tomorrow, and I'll advise you on his further care." Then he turned to Aruna. "Are you the secretary? Smart woman! Without your timely action, it's hard to say what state Devanathan would be in now." And with that, he left for the day.

As if suddenly realizing that her hand was still in his, Gunaseelan slowly raised it to his wet eyes. "Thank you, Aruna—thank you very much," he whispered.

Aruna offered to ask her father to come pick her up, but he insisted on calling a cab to take her back. Once home, she told her parents what had happened, and then fell into her bed and crashed into a deep slumber.

The next morning she wondered if she should go to the hospital before she went to the office, but decided against it; she didn't want to impose.

Gunaseelan was in his father's office even before she got there. He called her in and told her that his father was already on the road to recovery. He had asked Gunaseelan to take over the meeting with the Minister of Industries.

If the chairman had been able to make arrangements like that, he must be feeling better. So, why was Gunaseelan still so tense? She gathered the papers he would need for the meeting. Devanathan had already prepared notes. She also gave him some background information about the minister.

The meeting was a success. He briefed her on what had happened, and asked her to prepare a report to take to his father. When she had finished the report and brought it back into the office, Gunaseelan was sitting with his head buried in his folded arms.

He looked up, and she ran to him, embracing him with a whispered, "Guna!"

⚯ 8 ⚯

Gunaseelan, as if he had been waiting for her, melted into her arms. She realized that her midriff was becoming damp with his tears, and his body was shaking with sobs. Slowly she ruffled his hair. "Guna, it will all be okay. Stop worrying now."

He calmed himself and raised his head up again. She rushed to fetch him a glass of cold water. "What happened?" she asked.

"The doctor called this morning and told me that Appa had a heart attack. And do you know why? Because he was overworked. And it's all my fault!" He sank back into his chair and clenched his eyes shut. "I suffered one defeat and ran away like a coward, dumping all my responsibility on him. If I'd come back when you told me your concerns about his health, he wouldn't have had to go through all this. I can't believe how selfish I've been," he said in a strained voice.

"I was too harsh with you," she confessed softly. "I'm sorry."

"Whether you were right or wrong, you took a firm stand. That was no reason for me to put this burden on Appa. I should have considered his age at least. I knew full well that his health wasn't good…"

He was beating himself up with feelings of guilt. She felt guilty too, for completely different reasons. She regretted having been so harsh with him, but she still didn't think she was wrong to have refused him. She was not ready to feast on a used plate.

The next morning, on her way to work, she worried about how Gunaseelan would act. Would he be embarrassed? Or abrasive?

But happily, he was back to the way he had acted before the marriage proposal. Just once, he teased her: "Do I have to weep and sob to get you to call me 'Guna' again?" But he didn't force the point. So the matter ended there.

There were moments when she wished that there was no Aarthi in his life. But she never let herself ponder on such things for too long.

On the whole, things were back to normal. The chairman's family had returned immediately to Chennai, and now Devanathan was back home, recovering. He called to thank her, as did his wife, Kalavathi. "You have given my life back to me. I have to compensate that gesture. I had dreamed of something else, but that was not to be. Still, I want to give you a gift of gratitude. You must accept it, please don't refuse." She sent Kanmani over with a parrot green silk sari with a dark red border. Kanmani stayed for an hour of pleasant conversation, but when she left, Aruna felt despondent. What a wonderful family, and what a pity she had to refuse to become a part of it!

Since Devanathan was on doctor's orders to rest for the next two months, Gunaseelan took over the responsibilities of the office. His first move was to give Aruna more power so that the entire burden of the daily office work would not depend on him.

If her increasing authority and the fact that she spent more time with the young boss irritated anyone in that office, it was Sundari. It got worse when she approached Aruna with an application for leave, and was turned down.

It was during this time that Aruna's uncle visited her home. He was also in the construction business. "There is a call for a tender to build flyovers in the city," he told her. "There's a good margin in it too. If your company can complete the job on time, it will mean even better assignments in the future."

"Periyappa, why are you giving this information to a competitive agency? Wouldn't your MD sack you for this?" asked Aruna.

"Part of me wishes he would," sighed her uncle. "My company is the most corrupt in the business. Where the proportion of cement to sand should be one-is-to-four, my company does the same job with a one-is-to-ten ratio. In a small assignment, this practice wouldn't be too dangerous. But when building something like a flyover, it could cause a major disaster. I'm hoping my company doesn't get the contract. That's why I suggested it to you."

The next day when she told Gunaseelan about it, he became enthusiastic. They found the government advertisement in the paper. "Let's do this, Aruna. The profit margin quoted here is huge. We can use the same laborers who are involved with the Chengalpet project. But we have to keep the details confidential until we get the contract. Our competitors could undercut our quote by a mere hundred or so, and take over the tender. So the entire matter should stay between the two of us. Not even the other office staff should know."

And so the two of them put together the quotation for the flyover. The whole office knew there were discussions going on about a very big assignment, but the details remained a secret. Almost every day, Aruna came in early and went back home very late.

She gathered the necessary information, helped Gunaseelan recheck the budget, fed it into the computer, printed it, got his signature, put it in a cover with the quote reference number, gave it to the dispatch clerk to be posted, and only then had a chance to breathe.

But the relief didn't last long. The Public Works Department turned down their quote. Gunaseelan inquired further and discovered that Aruna's uncle's company had secured the contract with a quote that was just a thousand rupees less than theirs. A project worth over fifteen crores was lost due to a difference on paper of a mere thousand! There was no way the competitors could have come up with such a tiny difference without inside information regarding Guna Construction's quote. So who was the informer?

He must be exposed—if there was a spy in their midst, it could affect all their future projects!

The chairman, having returned to the office after his month-long rest, presided over the investigation. The entire office staff was called in and Gunaseelan explained the situation. He spoke about the magnitude of the assignment, the profit that could have been made and the bonus that the employees would have received if they had won the contract. "The only possible explanation for losing the contract is that the information was leaked from here to the competitors. Who is the culprit? Do any of you have any suspicions? Be brave, speak up. Even if you think it's me, don't be afraid to say so. This organization respects the truth."

For a moment everyone remained silent.

"Come on, tell me. Whom do you suspect? Ayah, you go first," he said, indicating the maid who did the daily cleaning.

The maid just scratched her head. "I don't have a clue what you're talking about. Why should I suspect anyone? It's not good to be suspicious of people, it will only ruin one's life. You yourself should stop suspecting people." The staff burst out laughing.

"Oh, is it wrong to suspect people? That's good advice!" said Gunaseelan, throwing Aruna a meaningful look. "Ayah, you may go."

Aruna answered him with a look that said, *I didn't just suspect you. I saw!*

The interrogation continued when Sundari piped up confidently, "I suspect Aruna."

"Me? *Me?* Why would I do such a terrible thing?" stammered Aruna, shocked.

"For money, of course," replied Sundari.

"Why do you accuse Aruna?" asked Gunaseelan.

"I've got several reasons. First, the other employees have been with this company much longer than her. Aruna is the most recent addition to the staff. Secondly, she was the only one who knew about the contract. It would have been easy for her to make another copy of the quote. There were many days when she stayed behind at the office after we had all left. Also, her uncle works for Bina Builders, the company that got the contract. She could have sold the information through him. The typing pool never got any information to be typed—she was the one who handled the entire matter. Therefore, she's the only one who could be the culprit," said Sundari, and sat back.

Aruna thought she might faint. She had done no wrong, yet all the evidence was against her. The entire staff was looking at her with suspicion. She was fast losing hope of proving her innocence.

⋈ 9 ⋈

Sundari saw the chairman and the managing director exchange a look. Her heart sang out in victory. This was the moment she'd been dreaming of; dealing Aruna an insult so severe that she would be driven out in tears.

Gunaseelan rose to speak, "Well argued, Sundari, but I have a few doubts. If you can clarify them, then we can come to a decision."

"What are your doubts?" asked Sundari.

"How did you know Aruna's uncle worked for Bina Builders?"

She hesitated a moment before saying, "Aruna told me so, some time back."

"That's a lie! I've never discussed my family with you," roared Aruna. Gunaseelan silenced her with a sharp look.

"But how did you come to know that the contract went to Bina Builders at all? I don't think I mentioned that."

This shut Sundari up. She sat with her head bent.

"So it was you, wasn't it?" asked Devanathan. "I know that you came to this job with a reference letter from the assistant manager of Bina Builders. Now tell us how you accomplished this." Sundari looked away, furious.

Now the dispatch clerk, Somasundaram, rose. "Sir, that day, Aruna Madam gave me a thick envelope to post. Just after she left, Sundari came over to my desk. She was standing—how should I say it?—in a kind of sexy pose. She said she'd forgotten to bring lunch. She asked me to go down to the Chinese restaurant three streets away and get two orders of Chinese fried rice. She gave me a hundred rupee note, and said we could eat together. She winked at me, sir. I was so charmed by her pose, and the way she invited me for a free lunch with her, that I didn't suspect anything was amiss. But when I returned, I realized that the cover Aruna Madam had given me was still on my table. I am sorry, sir. I didn't expect anything like this to happen."

"It's alright. In the future, please lock everything away in a safe before you leave your desk," said Devanathan.

Next, Pavai got up to speak. "I'm not sure if this is important," she said, "but a few days ago, when I came back from lunch, I saw Sundari xeroxing a stack of papers. She complained that Aruna was making her work even during her lunch break. I don't know anything more than that, sir."

"So! I think you may all leave now. Guna, give Sundari a month's severance pay and dismiss her," said Devanathan, rising to go.

Sundari sprang up as if stung by a snake. "I have not been proved guilty! Why shouldn't I have lunch with Somasundaram and get to know him better? Why shouldn't I do the jobs Aruna assigns me in Pavai's presence? You haven't proved that Aruna is innocent, either, you know."

Aruna was speechless. How could she prove that she was innocent? Would they ever be able to fully trust her again?

"We are decided," said Gunaseelan firmly. "We have complete faith in Aruna. So you may leave. It will be better if you resign, otherwise we'll have to sack you."

Sundari, defeated, walked stiffly out of the office.

Aruna never took her eyes off Gunaseelan. He had complete trust in her? Since when?

Devanathan threw a look at Aruna and then said, "Guna, I'm leaving. You drop Aruna off and then come home." With that, he and the rest of the staff left.

Now they were alone.

He gazed at her for moment. Then he snapped his fingers in front of her face and whispered, "Hello!"

She gave a long sigh, and said softly, "How did you trust me so implicitly? All the evidence was against me. Why did you still think I was innocent?"

He looked into her eyes. "Yes, everything was against you. But I know you. I know how you work. And therefore, I believed in you."

Aruna felt as though he had charred her with a red hot iron. She knew him, too. And she knew how he worked. And yet she had not trusted him.

He had asked how she could have recognized him in the semi-darkness of the theatre. Perhaps he was telling the truth after all! Why had she still doubted him?

She had felt the urge to trust him before, but she had killed it, thinking it to be the imagination of her pining heart.

Why had this awakening come to her only now? It was too late. Trying to salvage the relationship at this point would be like trying to build a dam after the town had already been destroyed by a flood. If she had lost her chance, then she deserved to have lost it!

Tears streamed down her cheeks. She looked yearningly at his face.

"Do you still love me?" she whispered.

His eyes grew kinder. "Come here," he beckoned.

Even before she took a step, he closed the distance with two steps. "Do you really think I could ever change my mind? Aruna, you know Appa has a private line. Why would I call your desk to speak to him? Didn't you guess that it was just to hear your voice?"

"Then why did you sound so harsh?" she asked.

"What else could I do? You had already turned me down."

"Oh!" she responded, joyously.

"Yes, 'Oh' indeed! Finally I've gotten through that thick skull of yours. Look up at me. Now do you trust me?" he asked.

"Now and forever. I trust you completely," she replied in a firm voice.

"Good thing you decided before I could show you this," Gunaseelan said, removing a fax from his pocket. "This arrived this morning… from Manohar."

Aruna read the fax: "'As per your advice, Aarthi and I got married here at the Indian Embassy. We will return to India as husband and wife.'"

"Yes, it is a good thing you waited to show me this. Otherwise you would never have known that I already trust you, from the bottom of my heart," she said, smiling.

"Good thing indeed! Now only more good things can follow! But we should fix a date for the wedding quickly, I can't last much longer," he said, rolling his eyes. She started to smile, but a thought struck her, and she stopped.

"What, my dear?" he asked.

"On account of Sundari's jealousy, you lost a good contract!" she said.

"No, we didn't, actually," he responded playfully.

She looked at him uncomprehendingly.

"A bridge collapsed today—one that had been constructed by Bina Builders. It's a huge black mark on their name, and the Secretariat has ordered that they should not be given any more government contracts. So we, as the next highest bidders, have got the contract instead! Appa took the call when we were gathering here for the interrogation. So now we're back on the winning track!" said Gunaseelan, laughing.

Aruna looked at him lovingly, and stood up on the tips of her toes to plant a kiss on his cheek. And then they held each other so tightly that not even a breeze could steal between them!

Cover of a Pattukkottai Prabakar novel in *Ullaasa Oonjal*, titled *Panam Kanne, Panam!* ("Money, Baby, Money!")

PATTUKKOTTAI PRABAKAR

Pattukkottai Prabakar started writing detective fiction in the 1980s. Famous in his neighborhood for writing non-stop, nearly twelve hours a day, taking only two breaks in the morning and afternoon for a cigarette and a cup of filter coffee, he has produced hundreds of short novels featuring his detective couple Bharat and Susheela. He also writes dialogues for Tamil films and many hit television programs, such as *Paramapadham*, the first Tamil "mega-serial" to be shown on Doordarshan.

He lives in Adyar, Chennai, with his family.

SWEETHEART, PLEASE DIE!
இனியவளே இறந்து போ! (1990)

ONCE UPON A TIME, Lady Moon went to Inspector Sky with a complaint. "Those rowdy stars keep cat-calling me and giving me dirty looks," she said. Inspector Sky sent Constable Rain Cloud to arrest them. But the stars vanished quickly...

No, no—that's a far too *ordinary* way to begin a short novel. Don't you find it a bit boring, Dear Reader? Well, I do. I'd like to start off a bit differently. With your permission, of course.

But there's one small catch. For me to begin the way I would like to, you'll have to agree to be an accomplice to a minor... transgression, shall we say.

Have you ever eavesdropped on a neighbor's conversation? Ever regretted that the bus you were traveling in did not stop long enough for you to take a longer peek at a beautiful girl bathing in a roadside stream? Ever seen a friend reading a letter that is clearly marked "Personal", and yet still tried to get a peek at the name of the sender? Ever tried to encourage your neighbor's child to discuss the fight his parents had the night before? When the local gossip rag writes: "Fresh from her scandalous bare-almost-everything performance in last season's hit film, the starlet has been seen around town romancing the actor best known for his devilish wink," do you start to drool just a bit as you read through the article?

If you replied "yes" to even one of the above questions, then, Dear Reader, I judge you eager enough! I think you'll be happy to join me in my little transgression—reading someone else's personal diary.

Whose, you ask? It belongs to a young girl named Madhumitha. Born *Panguni* 17th, 1967. A Taurus.

It's a very elegant diary. Smooth and pink, just like her... and begging to be read.

Here it is. Go on! Flip the pages!

What happened to the short novel, you ask? Oh, that can wait. We'll come to it in time.

Personal Information

Name: *Ms. Madhumitha Sundaresan*

Office Address: _____

Residential Address: *37, Burkit Road, T. Nagar,*
Chennai 600017,
India, The World.

Tel.: Office_____ **Resi:** *841526 (frequently out of order)*

S.B. A/C No.: *Haven't started saving yet.*

Height: *Tall enough.* **Weight:** *Light enough to be carried.*

Car/Motorcycle/Scooter No.: *I take a different bus every day; which number should I write?*

Insurance No.: *I don't plan to die anytime soon.*

In Case of Emergency Please Inform:

_____

Dear Madhumitha,

It's a good habit to keep a diary. But have you ever been able to stick to it for a full year? You'll make entries for all 31 days of January. In February you'll start skipping every other day. By March you'll be down to once a week, and from April onwards, the pages will remain virginal. Please, this '87, promise to write something down every single day. Okay, then, if not every day, at least write down all the important events. This is your personal diary; you should be completely honest with it, Madhumitha! Hugs and kisses for the New Year!

With love,
Madhumitha

January 1
Thursday

I was waiting at the bus stop, on my way to class. Manohar approached hesitantly, his arms wrapped around a gift box. His lips were wet. "Happy New Year. A small gift from me," he said. Why did I take it? I didn't even bother to thank him. But then, he didn't stand there waiting for a thank you, either. He jumped back on his motorbike and left, just like that. I waited until I got to college, and then I opened the gift under a tree on campus. It was this diary, which I'm writing in now. He'd scribbled on the first page: "Madhumitha: New Year's greetings for my sweetheart, from Yours Truly!" Not terribly exciting, really. I can't feel anything but pity for him. Should I tell him that tomorrow? I don't think I will. I don't love him, that's for sure. Still, it's a bit of a kick to have someone in love with me, even if that someone is Manohar. So I guess I'll play cat-and-mouse for a while longer. Let's see how far I can take it...

January Monday 12

Today I looked out the classroom window and there was Sridhar, standing under a tree and smoking, his white Fiat parked nearby. Just seeing him there set me off. The excitement welled up in me immediately, that craving for another taste of heaven!

I stood up and said to the Professor, "Sir, I have a terrible headache." "Fine, get lost then!" he said. So I left.

"Hey Sridhar, do you have the goods?"

He took out a cigarette packet and flipped it open. "All stuffed and ready. Get in! How many do you want?"

"Please! I've been waiting for it," I begged him, almost hypnotized, as I got into the car. He put his arm around my shoulder as soon as the car left the college campus. I didn't protest. He gave me one of the special cigarettes, which I hid in my handbag.

At night, after I was sure everyone was asleep, I shut my door, lay on my bed and lit the cigarette. "Paradise, here I come!"

February Wednesday 4

Manohar gave me a letter at the bus stop. I accepted it with a smile. Then, as usual, I tore it to bits as soon as I reached college.

Prof. Devendran lives near the campus. We often visit his house when we have questions about the course material. Today, I went there with Bhuvani. After giving us some tuition, he told Bhuvani she could leave. "Madhumitha, you stay here for a bit—I want to talk to you."

Once we were alone, he told me: "I know I shouldn't be interfering in your personal matters. But Sridhar is the most notorious student at this college. I see you hanging around with him a lot. Is there a love affair going on?"

I wanted to tell him that my love is not for Sridhar, but for what

Sridhar gives me. Try it once! You'll fall in love too! But of course I couldn't say that. So I simply said, "No sir, I'm not in love with him. If you think it's best, I'll stop speaking to him." Ha ha, fat chance!

March
Tuesday 31

Today's my birthday! Amma and Appa got me a new dress. I left to college with a box of chocolates. At college, there was a registered parcel waiting for me. There was a foreign sari and a letter that said: "Happy birthday to you, my sweetheart! I'm hoping that maybe you'll break your silence today. Yours truly..." Manohar, of course. I finally decided I shouldn't make the poor man suffer unnecessarily. I returned the sari to him at the bus stop in the evening. "Please, Manohar, forget about me. I'm not in love with you. Don't imagine stuff," I told him gently.

"But Madhumitha, you are my life..."

"Don't waste your words. Spend your love on a different woman. If I had a lover, he would be nothing like you. He'd be a real man. Here, take a chocolate."

He launched into some heavy dialogue: "Today is the day my love has died..."

I ran away quickly, before he could get too far into it.

April
Monday 13

Today was the last exam. I don't think I did too well. All I could think about was the new drug Sridhar had promised to let me try this evening. It's really expensive, I guess. Even a single drag is enough to give a big kick.

Sridhar was waiting for me in his car. "Didn't you take the exam?" I asked.

He just grinned. I asked him where we were going, and he said we'd go to his bungalow in Adyar.

There was no one home—it was just us. He shut the door, and offered me a cigarette. "Go on, take a puff!" I took it eagerly. Almost immediately, I felt like I was floating through the air. A tickling sensation played through my nerves. Colorful sparklers were sending thrills up and down my body, and laughter kept bubbling up through my lips. When Sridhar started stripping my clothes off, it felt like it was just happening in a dream. Then he laid me down on his bed...

This is a new, secret kind of heaven. How could I refuse?

May Thursday 7

Apparently, I'm not supposed to waste my holidays being idle. So Appa has signed me up for typing lessons. Thank you Daddy! Appa drops me off every day at the typing institute on his scooter. I have never once set foot inside the institute. I just wait for him to leave, and then I walk over to the Fiat that's waiting across the street.

And then we head straight for the Adyar bungalow.

Sridhar has some wild logic to defend what we're doing. "Look, we're not bothering anyone. We're not stealing anyone else's property. We're just sharing pleasure. What's the point of chastity anyway? We can stop all this once your marriage is arranged. Please, don't get any storybook ideas about us getting married—I don't believe in marriage. Why shouldn't I be able to enjoy any woman I want? Just as you don't wear the same outfit every day, but go for variety in your fashion—I believe in having the same variety in women. Like the kings, in the old days, with their harems."

Maybe it was just because I was high, but I thought he made sense.

I asked Bhuvani once what she thought of "variety".

"Yuck!" she said. "I can't believe what's happening to you."

June 20
Saturday

I was walking out of the institute when a familiar voice beckoned me. There was Manohar, sporting a thick beard.

"Congratulations," he said. "I was happy to see that you enrolled for a Master's degree."

"Oh, Manohar—please, stop pestering me. And why this bushy beard all of a sudden, ex-lover?" I teased him.

"Madhumitha, don't make fun of me. I worship you. I need to talk to you. My house is close by; please, will you come over?" he asked.

"I'm sorry, but why should I come to your house?"

"I know you don't love me. But I still have feelings for you. You encouraged those feelings. Please... I need you," he begged.

"Don't beg for love, Manohar. It has to come naturally. Don't squander your pride," I said.

"Would love come naturally for you if I owned a white Fiat?" he jabbed.

"Don't be stupid. That's not love, either. But I doubt you could ever understand the difference," I said, and walked off. Poor boy!

July 1
Wednesday

I had a strange experience today. As I was walking from the bus stop to college, I noticed a thin man with dark glasses following me. When I turned around, he bent down to adjust his shoe. In the evening, when I walked to the bus stop, he was there following me again. He stood near me at the bus stop.

"Hey mister, what do you want? Why have you been following me since this morning?" I asked him.

"I'm sorry. Is your name Kalyani?"

"No. Madhumitha. Why?"

"I saw an advertisement in *Dhinamalar* yesterday, about a girl of your age who has gone missing. She looked just like you. You're really not her?"

"Don't be stupid!"

"Sorry. I thought I could get the reward, that's why…"

When I told Sridhar about this later, he found it very funny.

"Stop laughing," I said. "I'm five days late for my period. Give me some of those pills you gave me last month."

July Saturday 18

Amma and Appa left for a wedding in Saidapet, and the minute they were out the door, I called Sridhar.

"Sridhar, I need a fix, bad. Can you bring me something? My parents are not here. They won't be back until late." When I asked it was only ten.

Sridhar was there in half an hour.

"Did you bring it?"

"Wait," he said, handing me a letter. "First, tell me if you recognize this handwriting. It came in the mail this morning."

It read: *Hey Sridhar: if you want your head to stay on your shoulders, stop speaking to Madhumitha!*

"Are you scared, Sridhar?"

"Who? Me?" He just laughed. "Shall I shut the door? Let's do it in your bedroom today."

I refused at first. After two puffs, I wanted it too.

As he was leaving, he asked about the letter again. "Who do you think it could be?"

It wasn't difficult to guess that the letter was from Manohar. He must be wild with jealousy.

July 29
Wednesday

I'm in a horrible mood. I just got to know that Amma and Appa have arranged my marriage. The boy's name is Paulraj, and his family will be coming next week to fix the alliance. There goes my life of pleasure and fun! It's all a plot to throw me out of this house. My nerves are already weak. Sridhar hasn't been coming to college for the past few days. The day before, his car passed me on the road. In the front seat was another woman, and he had his arm around her shoulder. I know Sridhar doesn't believe in fidelity—and how can I insist on it? It's not like he's my husband. Still, I couldn't help feeling sad.

I cut college that afternoon and took an auto to Adyar. He was there at home.

"Sridhar, my marriage is being arranged."

"Congratulations!"

"But I don't want to get married. I just want you, and my smokes," I wept.

"Oh come on! Give it up now. Stop coming to see me anymore," he ordered.

All right, quit flipping the pages. The diary is empty from here on.

✗ 1 ✗

Chalukya Apartments, Burkit Road—very posh. A five-storey building with two lifts, underground parking, lawn and garden, public telephone, security guard. And monthly rent to match all this, of course.

A signboard next to the manager's room listed the names of the twenty occupants. S. SUNDARESAN, DEPUTY MANAGER, SUGAR DIVISION, PARRY & CO., was listed as the owner of Flat 12 on the third floor. The same Sundaresan now drove into the garage, parked his scooter, and walked through the dimly lit corridor to the lift, carrying his helmet and briefcase. He rode up to the third floor and rang the doorbell of his flat. His wife, Radhika, pressed an eye to the peephole and then opened the door. He handed her his briefcase, removed his shoes and socks, and loosened his tie. "Madhu's not home yet?" he asked.

"No," said Radhika, placing the briefcase on the centre table and helping him get his coat off. She was a heavyset woman, almost eighty kilos.

Sundaresan took off his shirt to reveal a hairy torso, and changed into a *lungi*. He had a close haircut, thin moustache, the wrinkled brow of a man nearing his fifties, and the slightly puffy eyes of a beer drinker.

He washed up and then sat in front of the TV to watch the news. Radhika was busy in the kitchen. Soon she came out with a cup of tea and bowl of potato chips. "There was a call from Chidambaram," she said.

"What's the news?"

"They say they can't come on the ninth. They wanted to come on the tenth instead."

"What did you say?"

"How could I say anything, without consulting you? I told them you would call when you got home."

"I have no problem with either date."

"Madhu has a problem with it."

"What, has she got PMS or something?"

"No. She just doesn't want to get married."

"No girl agrees at once. She'll get used to the idea."

"She wants to complete her Master's degree first," Radhika answered, looking out the window.

"I came to know of this alliance through a friend. He's a very good man. That's why I want to hurry. She can continue her studies after her marriage, I'm sure they won't object."

"I told her that, but she says she won't be able to concentrate once she's married."

"What is she planning to do with her degree once she gets it? Is she going to look for a job? They just want a homemaker. This is a good family—it's not smart to delay, Radhika."

"I understand. But Madhumitha…"

"We need to help her understand. Let me talk to her. It's a quarter past seven—why is she so late today?"

"Maybe the bus is late. If you'd bought her that moped she's been asking for…"

"You don't get it. Do you have any idea how bad the traffic is these days? It's a struggle even for me, on the scooter."

"Oh, please! As if there aren't plenty of other women driving mopeds around town."

"Those 'other women' are not our Madhumitha, our only daughter." He picked up his coffee mug.

The TV serial took a break for advertisements. On top of the set was a toy dog bobbing its head. On the wall was a family photograph of Sundaresan and Radhika with Madhumitha in the middle, and another of a young Madhu sitting on a scooter. The last photo was a more recent one, and worth a more careful description.

In this photo, she stood in front of a scenic forest, in black jeans and a full-sleeved red shirt knotted around her belly. Her head was tilted slightly, so that her luxurious, shining black hair swung forward to cover half her front. She was flashing a smile that must have made the photographer's heart skip. Beneath her sculpted eyebrows, the eyes were rimmed with thick black eyeliner, and mascara separated every lash. Her wet, shiny lips were parted in a sexy pout. Whatever the creator had planted there beneath her neckline had yielded a ripe, bountiful harvest.

The doorbell rang. Radhika jumped up, hoping it was her daughter. But the woman who stood smiling in the doorway with a notebook in her hand was not Madhu, but her classmate Stella.

"Good evening, Aunty. Is Madhu in?"

"She hasn't come home yet. Did you leave college early?"

"She's not back from college yet?" Stella sounded surprised.

"She must have missed the bus. You drive a scooter, right? So you wouldn't have known. Come in and sit down, I'm sure she'll be here soon."

"No Aunty, we had a half-day at college today—our vice principal died, and they shut down classes after the first period. So I can't understand why she's not home yet."

Radhika flashed Sundaresan a worried look. He got up suddenly. "Oh! I forgot. She gave me a call at work and told me she was going to visit her aunt in Adyar. Maybe she decided to spend the night there."

Radhika saw Stella out, and shut the door behind her. "You have a strange memory," she said to Sundaresan. "How could you have forgotten that call the whole time you were sitting here worrying about her with me?"

"It just slipped my mind. I only remembered when Stella mentioned the college leave."

"I was scared to death, for a second there."

"Silly. What do you have to be scared of?"

"College has been closed since this morning, and here it is getting late and she's still not back—what kind of mother wouldn't be worried?"

"She's not so young. She's twenty years old."

"Is that supposed to be a joke?"

"What's for dinner tonight? Gosh, look at the time! It's eight already!"

"So what?"

"I have to meet a friend at Mambalam station at quarter past. I forgot that, too," he said, hurrying to the bedroom to change.

"What's going on with you today? How can you be so forgetful? Will you be home for dinner?"

"No. You go ahead and eat. I'll get something outside. Don't wait up for me, I'll be late," he replied, picking up his helmet and keys as he went out.

Sundaresan jumped on his scooter and within ten minutes arrived at the house of his friend, Ganesa Pandian.

"Hello!" Ganesa Pandian welcomed him. "I didn't know you were coming or I would have left some of your favorite soup."

"I didn't come for soup. Listen, I have to tell somebody... apparently there was a half-day at Madhu's college today. But she hasn't come home yet. I'm worried."

"Have a seat and stop stressing. She's an intelligent young woman. She must have just gone to see a film or something."

"No. She would have told us."

"Maybe she's visiting a friend?"

"That's why I came here, to make some calls. I couldn't risk giving Radhika a scare—you know what her heart condition's like. I told her a lie to keep her calm, and ran here with a list of Madhu's friends' numbers."

"Go ahead, use my phone. I'm here alone today, the rest of the family has all gone for a wedding," he said, handing him the phone.

"Hello? Can I speak to Bargavi please? I'm the father of a friend of hers... Hi, Bargavi? This is Madhumitha's father. Is she with you?"

"No, Uncle. She hasn't come here."

"When did you see her last?"

"She was in class this morning. Once they announced the holiday, I came home. Is there anything you want me to tell her if she comes by?"

"No, thank you... it's, uh, personal. Did she say if she was going anywhere?"

"No, Uncle..."

Sundaresan put down the receiver and dialed a different number.

"No Uncle, she's not here. I don't know where she went," said Bhuvani.

"Madhu and I had a fight about a month ago, Uncle. I haven't been speaking to her since then," said Aruna.

"I don't know," said Kalpana.

Sundaresan sat back, frustrated.

"What happened, Sundaresan? Did you and your daughter have a fight or something?" asked Ganesa Pandian.

"No. Have you ever seen us fight?"

"Then why are you so worried? She'll be back. It's only eight o'clock. She must have a good reason—I don't think she's a wayward sort of child. She might even have come home already. Why don't you call and see?"

"No. It might give Radhika a scare. I told the security at the gate to watch out for her though—let me call the manager.

"Hello? Chalukya Apartments Manager? This is Sundaresan. Could you please check with security to see if my daughter has come in? My phone's not working."

A pause. Then: "Security says she hasn't come yet."

By the time Sundaresan disconnected the call, Ganesa Pandian was dressed and ready to go out. "Let's go ask the friends who don't have phones. Come on."

Two hours later, Ganesa Pandian dropped Sundaresan off at his flat. "Don't worry too much. There's a good chance it will all turn out okay. Tomorrow you can decide if you want to inform the police."

Sundaresan came back home tired. Radhika asked him if he'd eaten. "Yeah, I ate," he said. "You get some sleep. I have a little office work to do." But he sat up doing nothing but worrying, watching the hands of the clock spin slowly around.

⚹ 2 ⚹

Bharat parked his motorbike at the Nelson Building and walked over to the lift. "REPAIR," announced a piece of cardboard stuck in the grill. He took a pen from his pocket and added the words "WHEN WILL YOU" above the word and a question mark below, and walked up the stairs to his office on the fourth floor. He paused to dust the Moonlight Agencies nameplate with his handkerchief before walking in.

There was a strange woman sitting at the front desk, feeding a sheet of paper into the typewriter.

"Hey, what's this nonsense? Who the hell are you?"

"Why are you raising your voice, sir? Who are *you*?"

"Who am *I*? This is *my office*! Why should I answer to you? Get up, woman! What are trying to do, steal our typewriter?"

"Hello, please mind your language, mister! I work here."

He looked her up and down, and mentally gave her a failing grade.

"What's your name, woman?"

"Marikkozhunthu."

"I don't care if it is. I've never seen you before. You must be in the wrong office."

"No, sir! I think *you* must be in the wrong office. This is Moonlight Agencies. Which office are you looking for?"

"Take a close look at me. Have you ever met me before?"

"No, sir."

"Then how can you claim I gave you a job?"

"When did I ever claim such a thing?"

"Hey Ravi!" Bharat shouted to the back of the office. "Where the hell are you?"

Ravi came running from inside. "What is it, sir?"

"Who is this woman?"

"Susi Madam appointed her."

"Repeat that once more."

"Susi Madam appointed her."

Bharat grabbed Ravi's ear and twisted it hard. "Sir! *Aiyyo...*," he cried, "Please! It hurts..."

"'Susi Madam' is it? How dare you call her by her name!"

"You wouldn't have understood if I'd just said Madam, that's why..."

Bharat glared at the new woman. *Susheela's going to pay for this*, he thought to himself as he walked into the inner office. Susheela was sitting inside, carefully clipping an article from a newspaper. "Good morning, Bharat," she greeted him.

"Skip the pleasantries. *Who* is that stick figure of a woman out there?"

"Oh, our new clerk?"

"Did you appoint her?"

"Yes I did. She was the best among the applicants."

"What do you mean, best! That woman doesn't even need a bra. But she stands there constantly adjusting her sari anyway…"

"Typical, Bharat, you didn't even bother to look at her face, just at her …"

"Her face is just as bad. Hardly any flesh on it! If I'd stared a little harder I think I might have been able to see her skull. What could you have possibly found attractive about her?"

"We can give her a modern name, if you'd prefer."

"You've decided on this woman, then? That's it?"

"I think you're going to have to learn to treat your staff with a little more respect."

"Susi please, not this woman…"

"Bharat, you seem to have forgotten our agreement."

"Which agreement is that?"

"We planned to hire four staff members for the office: an office boy and three assistants. Right?"

"Yes."

"Ok, Ravi's our office boy. Of the assistants, we agreed to have two women and one man. And, we agreed that I would get to select two of them, and you would get to select the other two."

"Fine. Ravi was your first selection—and I guess this one is your second."

"Yes."

"Okay then, now watch my selection. I'll bring in one male brute and one super-sexy babe."

"Hello, wait a bit. Our agreement had another clause to it."

"No it didn't."

"Yes, it did too. Of the two female assistants, one would be a married woman. You agreed to that."

"Marikkozhunthu's not married?"

"No."

"Ouch. So I have to select a married woman?"

"That was the deal."

"Would a divorcée count?"

"No way."

"Why not? To be a divorcée, a woman has to get married first, right? The deal was it had to be a woman that was married, not necessarily one that stayed married."

"Sorry. I won't accept it."

Bharat sat on his chair and sulked. Susheela handed him the telephone receiver and began dialing. "It's still early in the morning, can't you start being more serious? Here, Ramkumar called three times already."

Bharat reluctantly took the phone. "Hello, Ramkumar? Bharat here. Good morning. I had to go the bank before coming to the office. I finished that job for you. That fellow crashed the lorry deliberately to collect on the insurance. I have two witnesses who saw him do it. And their written statements, with their signatures. How should I send it across— post or courier? Alright, thanks.

"Did you make that library visit, Susi?" he asked Susheela after the call.

"I'm going today."

"Why the delay? We need to clear that point up before we can proceed further. It may be difficult to get a 1962 issue of *The Hindu* in the library. Actually, go straight to the newspaper office and get it. On your way, you can drop in at the lawyer's office and pick up a copy of that will from Gopalakrishnan."

"What will, is this a new case?"

"Yeah. A baby brother's suing an older brother for forgery. He claims the will the older brother produced, and the father's signature on it, are fakes. He's provided five original signatures. I have to send them to the lab for a UV test and then give them to the police."

Ravi knocked, opened the door and said, "Sir, there's a Mr. Sundaresan to see you."

◢ 3 ◣

Sundaresan was standing with his arms crossed, looking a bit like an over-aged school boy. His eyes were red and seemed not to be focusing properly. Susheela was waiting with her notepad. Ravi brought in coffee and placed it on a coaster. Bharat stubbed out his cigarette. "So when did you see your daughter last? Please, have some coffee."

"On the first, before I left to work, I offered to drop her off at the bus stand. She said she needed some more time to get ready. So I left without her. That was the last time I saw or spoke to her."

Bharat checked the date on his watch. It was Wednesday the fifth.

"Which college does she go to?"

"King Solomon College."

"Co-ed, right?"

"Yes, sir."

"Who are the other members of your household?"

"Just me, my wife and my daughter. She's my only child. But right now it's only me at home."

"Where's your wife?"

"She's in Tirupur, her native town. Originally, we'd both planned to go there on the second, for my sister-in-law's wedding. When Madhumitha went missing I changed the plan and sent my wife alone. The very next day I began my search."

"Something doesn't sound right. Your daughter mysteriously disappears, and her mother runs off to a wedding?"

"Sorry, I left out an important point. My wife doesn't know yet that Madhumitha is missing."

"How come?"

"She's a heart patient. There is chance of a hole forming in her heart. We've made a booking for an open-heart surgery at CMC. The doctor there is Vigneswaran, a very good cardiologist. In the meantime, she's not supposed to get any sudden exciting or worrying news. She's even been advised not to laugh or speak too loud. We've recently made arrangements for Madhumitha's wedding. If I were to tell my wife what's happened, I'm sure she wouldn't be able to bear the news. So I had to hide it from her."

239

"Has Madhumitha's wedding been finalized?"

"The groom's family was supposed to come on the tenth. I've asked them to postpone the visit by a week."

"Is your daughter happy about the wedding?"

"She didn't object too much. Listen, I told my wife that Madhumitha is away on a college tour. I have to find her in four days, before my wife returns. I need your help! Please!"

"Try to keep yourself under control, Mr. Sundaresan. Tell me what efforts you've taken in these past three days."

"I spoke to every one of Madhumitha's friends, checked with every relative outside town over the phone, and I visited all the ones that live in the city personally. I couldn't find a single clue."

"Well, it wasn't a smart move to wait four days before approaching us. You should have gone to the police the next day. We'll register a complaint at the station. Don't worry, we can keep it out of the press."

"I came to you to avoid the police; I don't want the publicity."

"I'll take your case. But we'll let the police help too. It will be useful to us. Tell me about Madhumitha."

"She's a social girl, lots of friends. And she's a daddy's girl—we're very close. She prefers to wear modern clothes."

"Any boyfriends?"

"Of course not!"

"No romances at all?"

"Chee... no!"

"Have you had to discipline her for anything, recently?"

"No."

"Does she have her own room at home?"

"Yes."

"Did you search it?"

"Yes. I searched all through her cupboard and her desk, looking for some clue as to where she could have gone. But I didn't find anything." Sundaresan's replies came quickly.

"You've taken leave from work?"

"Yes."

"I'll need your address, the names and telephone numbers of her friends, and of your close relatives. I'll inform the station inspector over the phone. Then I'll come to your house after lunch and we'll write out a statement. We'll search her room again and then go meet the inspector. Then we'll decide on our next step," said Bharat.

"Yes, sir," replied Sundaresan, and supplied him with the names, telephone numbers, and addresses. "I want you to understand, money is not an issue here. I need to have Madhumitha back before my wife returns."

"She's coming back on the ninth? We have four days then. We'll do the best we can."

"What do you think, Bharat?" Susheela asked after Sundaresan had left. "He's already wasted four days. Why did you say we'd meet him at lunch, couldn't we have started right away?"

"I had my reasons. Before we go to his house we should get a few basic facts cleared up."

He grabbed a notepad and starting jotting a few things down:

1. *Confirm the death of the vice principal of King Solomon College on the 1st.*
2. *Check in the commissioner's office if any young woman has died or been hurt on the 1st in any traffic accident or otherwise.*
3. *Get an appointment with cardiologist Vigneswaran.*

"What's the point of all that?" asked Susheela, peering over his shoulder.

"This is a list of stuff for you to do. I've got some other work," he replied. He leaned back in his chair, turning away from Susheela, and held up Madhumitha's photograph, the one with the forest scenery in the background. "Little darling! Sweetie-pie! Where did you go?"

Susheela came round the desk to check.

"Quite a face she's got!" Bharat said.

241

"Yeah. But your fingers are wandering away from her face. What are you trying to do, feel up her photo? Watch it!" ordered Susheela, snatching the photo away.

"It's a nice shirt she's got on, that's all. How come you never wear anything like that, Susi? It'd look good on you. Hey!" he suddenly exclaimed. "I didn't notice before—there's no slogan on your T-shirt today! Just a plain color! Why the break from tradition?"

"Remember the day we had the inauguration ceremony for the new office? And I got hassled about my shirt? I decided, from then on, not to wear T-shirts with slogans on Wednesdays."

"Why Wednesdays?"

"Because the inauguration was on a Wednesday." She laughed, and spun around so her back was facing him.

"You wretch! You've got the slogan on the back!"

The words PLEASE SEARCH ON THE OTHER SIDE were printed on the back of the T-shirt.

"That doesn't quite make sense, my dear."

"Oh?"

"This T-shirt wasn't meant for someone of your build. There's no need to search for something as obvious as lorry headlights."

Ducking to avoid a whizzing paperweight, he continued: "What I mean to say is, it would be more appropriate for Marikkozhunthu." Then he doubled over, reeling from a hard punch to his stomach.

"Ten days of karate class! How you like it?" smiled Susheela, and did a demo kick in the air.

↗ 4 ↖

"This is Madhumitha's room," said Sundaresan. He was wearing a simple casual shirt and lungi.

Bharat stood with his arms folded as Susheela got the recorder ready.

On the wooden cupboard was a poster of Boris Becker, captured mid-stroke, wearing Adidas shoes. Next to him was Maradona in a sweat-soaked shirt hoisting a trophy, and after that was Srikkanth holding up his cricket bat to shade his eyes.

"She's a big sports fan," explained Sundaresan. "She watches all the matches."

"Does she play any games herself?"

"She plays chess with me sometimes."

The bedspread was unwashed, with pillows spilling out of the covers. There were skirts strewn over the chair at the desk, two pairs of jeans hanging on a hook, an overflowing laundry basket, and a black bra on the bed.

"My Madhu can never keep her room clean."

"Are any of her clothes missing?"

"What do you mean by asking that?"

"It would help us figure out whether her disappearance was her own plan, or not."

"Are you implying that she might have run away? Never! She's not like that. Madhumitha is just a child."

"Sorry if I offended you, but we can't let any possibilities go unchecked."

The wardrobe was filled with very modern outfits, along with one small pile of saris. Rows of colored bangles lined the drawers along with sticker bindis, lipsticks, mascara, earrings, and necklaces.

"She loves dressing up. I never interfere with it. She has total freedom."

"Looks like she's bit of a show-off."

"I suppose she is, yes."

"Do you remember what she was wearing on the first?"

"Of course. She was in a sky blue *churidhar* set. Everything from her slippers to her bindi was the same shade of blue. That was the set I gave for her birthday. Come to think of it, I have a photo of her wearing it."

Sundaresan rushed out of the room to get the photo. As soon as he was out of earshot, Susheela said softly, "The police said there are no reports of accidents or murders. I'm sure she's run away. She looks like the sort of girl that might fall in love easily."

"Don't come to hasty conclusions, Susi. It'll limit what you search for in your investigation. First, let's gather as much information as possible. Let's go over what we know about her so far."

"She's a sports lover."

"Especially if the sport is played by members of the opposite sex."

"Why do you say that?"

"Why doesn't she have a single poster of a female sports star? Why no Navratilovas or P. T. Ushas? Look who she's got on the bathroom door—Kamal Hasan showing off his bare chest!"

Sundaresan returned with the family album. He opened it and began to flip through the pages, showing each photo. "This is during our wedding... This was when we first moved into this flat... This is when Madhu was a baby..."

They watched Madhu grow up over the course of the following pages, smiling in different poses. The last snap in the album showed her blowing out birthday candles, wearing the blue churidhar.

"Let me hang on to this last photo," said Bharat. "Do you mind if we poke around? This is her reading desk, eh?"

The desktop was covered with a plastic sheet, which they removed. Underneath were books, notepads, sketch pens and ballpoint pens in a penholder. There were three drawers full of college stuff. One of the notebooks had been covered with a glossy magazine page.

"Who's this actress, Susi?"

"That's no actress, that's the female sports star you were looking for. One of India's best. Don't you recognize her? It's Shiny Abraham."

"Of course! I didn't recognize her in casual clothes. Excuse me, Mr. Sundaresan, does your daughter keep a diary by any chance?"

"Hmm..." Sundaresan had to think about it.

"No hurry. I doubt it, anyway; if she did, it would be on her desk, right?"

They checked the attached bathroom, with its tiled walls, washbasin, shower, soap stand, and towel rack. The floor was dry.

"Anybody else use this?"

244

"No one except Madhu. We have a separate one in our bedroom, and there's a small guest toilet too."

"Fine. Let's move to the living room."

"Mind if I smoke?" said Bharat, lighting a cigarette. "Let's be frank and honest, now. You've told me everything?"

"Why would I hold anything back?"

"I just need to be sure. What is Madhu's normal routine? Tell me exactly what she does from the moment she wakes up."

Sundaresan began listing the details of Madhu's daily schedule. Susheela took notes. When they were finished, Bharat rose from his chair. "Go get dressed. We'll leave for the police station."

As Sundaresan left to change, Bharat turned to Susheela. "Susi, this Madhumitha is no innocent chick. She has two faces, one for her home and one for the rest of the world."

"What makes you say that?"

"What I saw in the bathroom."

"What did you see?"

"There was a cigarette butt in the toilet. That's Madhumitha's private bathroom. She's been sneaking *dhum* in secret! You were in there for an hour, too. Did you find anything?"

"I've got something here in my hand—a very important something!"

"What is it?"

Just at that moment Sundaresan walked back in, dressed in pants. "Shall we go?"

Susheela signaled that the explanation could wait.

✗ 5 ✗

Having handed over a written statement and a black and white photo to Inspector Suresh Menon, and having accepted his promise to do his best, they came back out of the police station.

"We'll meet again tomorrow," Bharat told Sundaresan, and rode off on his bike with Susheela at the back.

"Stop at that hotel, please," said Susheela after they'd gone a short distance.

"Why, you're hungry? We just had coffee and snacks at the station."

"If you'll just do what I tell you, and take me up to the A/C dining room, I *might* share the clue I found in Madhumitha's room with you."

It was half past three. The dining room was practically empty. The waiter came with glasses of water. Bharat ordered two plates of hot bajjis and two glasses of rose milk.

As the waiter walked off, Bharat asked, "So, what is it, Susi?"

"I looked under Madhumitha's bed to see if I could find any dirty books or anything..."

"Okay, cut the prologue please, show me!"

"A 1987 personal diary," she said.

"Wow! Where is it?"

Susheela got up, sat down next to Bharat and lifted her T-shirt. The diary lay flat against her stomach, tucked into her waistband. Bharat snatched it quickly. Their order arrived, but they ignored it, excitedly examining the diary in the dim light of the dining hall.

"Excellent. Just as I had thought. Didn't I say this girl Madhumitha had two faces? Here we see the second face," he said, tapping the diary.

"Can drug addiction turn a good person into a demon, Bharat?"

"Of course it can—and obviously has. It can make a person think that sex is as casual as shaking hands. This is a very bold girl we're searching for, Susi."

"How could she have completely hidden all this from her family?"

"It looks like she smokes before she goes to bed, wakes up in the morning, cleans the room, and flushes all the evidence down the toilet. Well, this diary gives a new angle to her disappearance, that's for sure."

"Drink your rose milk."

He drank, deep in thought, oblivious to his surroundings or the piped music. After some time a triangular plastic plate arrived with the bill tucked under a teaspoon. The waiter flashed them a hopeful grin.

Bharat took a ballpoint pen from his pocket. "Take down some notes for me," he said, handing the pen to Susheela. Susheela removed the notepad from her bag.

"Who is this Manohar? What's his address? Who is Sridhar? Who was the guy who was following Madhumitha around for a whole day, and what was he up to? Who wrote the threatening note to Sridhar? We need quick answers to all these questions, Susi."

"Okay, where are we supposed to get them? Shall I place an order at Spencer's shopping mall?"

"I'm serious, don't joke around. We have to hurry. Let's go meet her friends."

"Bharat, shouldn't we tell Sundaresan about the diary?"

"Definitely not. Don't mention it to him."

"Why? We could ask *him* about Manohar and Sridhar."

"Two reasons why we shouldn't. First, he has a very high opinion of his daughter. We shouldn't spoil that unless it proves absolutely neces-sary. Second, we can't be sure he's being completely honest with us." He took out the list of Madhumitha's friends. "Let's go visit Bhuvani first."

Susheela checked her watch. "She'll still be in college, Bharat."

"Then let's go to the college. You pretend you're Bhuvani's neighbor. Go to the head office and tell them her mother is unwell."

At the college, Bhuvani walked outside to the tree to meet them, dressed in a sari, hugging her books to her chest. She seemed completely untroubled.

"Madam, please forgive us," said Bharat. "That bit about your mother being sick was just a story. We had to say something to call you outside." Her reaction confused him. "Why are you laughing?"

"My mother died when I was five years old. My friends thought it was pretty weird when the peon came in to say she was unwell. What is this about, anyway?"

"Do you have to go back to class in a hurry?"

"Oh, no. I have to thank you, actually—I had a pounding headache, and couldn't wait for the class to finish."

"Can we take a walk to that park over there? We can leave my bike here. I need to talk to you about Madhumitha. Susi, watch my bike," said Bharat, and then quickly changed his mind when he saw the look on Susi's face. "On second thought, why don't you come with us."

Even the birds in the park were napping in the afternoon heat. The trees stood at attention. Not even a leaf dared to sway. The park bench was rusted, and the concrete had long since fallen away from the steel frame. Susheela took a fan from her bag and began fanning herself.

"Were you and Madhumitha close friends?"

"I'm not sure she *has* any close friends. She'll talk with us when she feels like it, and ignore us when she doesn't. Are you from the police?"

"No, we're with a private agency. You're aware that Madhumitha's been missing since the first of the month?"

"Yes."

"How did you find out?"

"Her father called me on the phone to ask if I'd seen her. She's been absent from class for the past four days. So I guessed."

"Any idea where she could have gone?"

"I don't know. She didn't tell me anything."

"What's Madhumitha like? Her character?"

"She used to be a sweet girl. But she's changed, recently."

"How do you mean, changed?"

"She began talking differently. She'd start spouting some vague philosophy: 'Life is fleeting, so we should seek pleasure every minute. We should pursue whatever gives us happiness. If we can disregard the constraints of morality and discipline, the world becomes an ocean of gratification. Fidelity rations contentment. The joy is in seeking variety.' Because of this new attitude of hers I stopped talking to her."

"I see. Do you know a boy named Sridhar?"

"Yes, he's a student at this college—a total rogue. I heard that some-one saw Madhumitha riding with him in his car once."

"What does Sridhar study?"

"M.A. History, second year."

"Do you know his address?"

"You can get it from the college office. But he hasn't attended classes for at least a week. He comes when it pleases him. Actually, he only comes to catch his daily ration of women. Rowdy rascal!"

"Is he from a rich family?"

"Yes. He's the son of a well-known real estate developer. You must excuse me; I'm allergic to cigarette smoke."

Bharat put his cigarette back in his case. "Sorry. Did Madhumitha have a boyfriend?"

"Not that I know of," she replied, shaking her head so her hoop earrings swung.

"Did she ever mention a Manohar?"

"Manohar? Yes. She told me there was some idiotic guy named Manohar in love with her. She even showed me a letter, which she said was the fourth one she'd gotten from him. Then she tore it into bits."

"Do you know anything else about him?"

"I know he writes poetry. That's all."

"Miss Bhuvani—what a beautiful name that is. You'd never believe what my new secretary goes around calling herself! Never mind, that's off the topic. So anyway—your vice principal died on the first?"

"Yes, that's right."

"Did Madhumitha speak to you on that day?"

"We just discussed our lessons."

"Was she cheerful?"

"Of course."

"Did you both go to the bus stop together?"

"No, I have a moped. I didn't notice where she went after class."

"Can you do me a favor?"

"What?"

"You must ask your classmates a question for me. Can you check with them and find out if anyone saw where Madhumitha went, once the holiday was announced? That information would be very helpful to us."

"I'll do it first thing tomorrow morning."

"Here, take my card. If you learn anything, please give me a call."

They returned to the campus. Bharat watched Bhuvani walk away to the parking lot. "She's got a nice rhythm to her walk!" he murmured.

Susheela took hold of his chin and forcefully turned it away. "That will do," she said.

"Susi, I need you to go to the college office, flash your smile and charm two addresses out of them."

"One is Sridhar. Who's the second?"

"Professor Devendran. We have to check everyone who knew Madhumitha, from the tailor who made her blouses, to the manager of the typewriting institute, to the vendor next to the bus stop. Now hurry up and come back before I finish this cigarette," said Bharat, lighting one.

◢ 6 ◣

The young man stood motionless, with his arms crossed. There was a thick beard on his face; his pants and shirt were creased and dirty. His gaze was fixed on the rotating ceiling fan. The doctor sat in front of him on a swiveling chair. Next to him sat a worried old man, bald-headed, with wet eyes.

"It's like this all the time now, doctor. He just stares vacantly into space. If I ask him to come and eat, he breaks into sobs. If I scold him, he laughs. Lately he has stopped talking altogether."

"How long as this been going on?"

"For about a month, doctor, he's been very quiet. He'll come to the table, eat his food, scribble something on a piece of paper, and leave— just going through the motions, mechanically. He has even stopped talking to his mother. People said he was possessed, so we took him to an exorcist. They said he was under the influence of a curse. We spent a lot of money to have the curse removed, but it was no use. Some said if we could just manage to get him married, he would snap out of it. So, we found a girl among our extended family to get him married to. We started making the arrangements. But in this past week, he has become even worse. He keeps laughing and crying for no reason."

"Some mental disturbance. Don't worry. I can straighten him out," said the doctor, taking his pen out. "What is the patient's name?"

"Manohar."

"Manohar, please look at me."

Manohar's eyes slowly turned down to give him a long, blank stare, and then went back up to the ceiling fan.

"Do you know me? Who am I? Answer me, please. Shall I switch off the fan?" He signaled to the nurse, who was standing a discreet distance away. She switched off the fan, and Manohar looked away.

"Can you hear me?"

He nodded.

"Tell me your name."

"Manohar," he replied, and the doctor sighed in relief.

"Thank God, he's still conscious of his self. So he has not yet reached an extreme stage," he told the father. Turning back to Manohar, he asked, "Would you like some coffee?"

Manohar nodded, and the doctor sent for some. Next he checked his pulse, blood pressure, and listened to his chest. Then he asked several more questions. Manohar's reply to each was either a simple "Yes" or "No." Not once did he say more than a single word at a time.

The doctor turned back to Manohar's father.

"What did your son study in college?"

"B.A."

"What does he do?"

"Nothing much. He used to help me with my accounts sometimes, or go to collect my installment payments."

"What do you do?"

"I own a pawnshop."

"Did your son have a big disappointment recently, or did some tragedy take place at home?"

"Nothing like that, doctor. We have one daughter and one son. My daughter is married and now lives in the States. We may not be rich, but we can afford to give him what he wants. He asked for a motorbike; I got him one. Not once have his mother and I ever said no to him. He used to write poems. Some were even published. We have never stood in the way of his happiness."

"I would like to see some of his poems."

"I'll bring them tomorrow. He's filled two full notebooks."

"Come see me at six in the morning tomorrow—but not here. Can you bring him to my house? I managed to get a few words out of him just now—maybe in a more comfortable setting I can get him to speak more freely. I need to understand what's going on in his mind. Only then can I begin my treatment. For now, I shall prescribe a few medicines that will calm him down and help him sleep."

The father got up and said, "Fine. We'll see you tomorrow. Come Mano, get up. Let's go."

Manohar was staring at the doctor's pen. It took three shouts and a shake of his shoulders to make him get up.

⚔ 7 ⚔

They left King Solomon College with the addresses in hand.

"I'm going straight to the office," said Bharat, dropping Susheela off at the *The Hindu* building. "I'll call Sridhar and then start my meeting. Then I'll go see the professor. You finish your work here, then go see the lawyer and pick up the copy of that will, and come back to the office."

Back at the Nelson Building, Ravi opened the office door, and Bharat went into his room. "Ravi, ask that woman to come here."

Marikkozhunthu entered hesitantly. "Sir, I'm sorry about yesterday. I didn't know who you were, and I was impolite. Please forgive me."

"I'll forgive you, on one condition."

"What is it, sir?"

"From this moment onwards, your name is Madhavi. Go down to the government gazette tomorrow and get it changed. And, don't you ever wear modern clothes?"

"I'd love to, sir. But they're very expensive."

"Is that it? Then I'll give you an advance on your salary. You must dress only in modern clothes from now on. Understand?"

"Yes, sir."

"And then this long plait, with the ribbon at the end—that's a no-no. Go to a beauty parlor and get yourself a better hairstyle. The agency will bear the expense."

"Thank you very much, sir."

"Have you ever heard this proverb? 'If you can't get all the things you like, learn to like all the things you have.' I'm going to transform your look completely. Here: take this cassette, rewind it to the beginning and transcribe the whole thing. Don't miss a word."

When Marikkozhunthu—or rather, Madhavi—had left, Bharat dialed Sridhar's number. While the phone was ringing, he called Ravi over, handed him a ten-rupee note, and pointed to his empty packet of smokes.

"Hello, can I speak to Mr. Sridhar?"

"Who's this?"

"This is Padmanaban, a friend of his," said Bharat.

"Sridhar isn't coming home until the tenth."

"Where is he now?"

"He's on a package tour to Singapore and Malaysia. You didn't know?"

"Who are you, sir?"

"His father."

"Which company has arranged the tour?"

"Golden Travels, have you heard of them?"

"When did he leave?"

"On the thirtieth. Is there anything important?"

"No, sir, nothing that can't wait till he's back. Thanks." He looked through the directory, found Golden Travels, and dialed. "Hello," said a smooth, silky voice and the other end.

"Ma'am, I'm calling from Moonlight Detective Agency—I need a few facts. When did your package tour to Malaysia and Singapore leave?"

"On the thirtieth."

"Do you have a Sridhar in your passenger list?"

"One moment, sir..."

Bharat picked his teeth with a paper clip.

"Yes, sir. We do have a Sridhar."

"When is this group scheduled to return?"

"On the evening of the tenth."

"Thank you."

When Susheela returned, he put the copy of the will in the safe and said, "From what's written in the diary, Sridhar is the strongest suspect—but he also has a strong alibi. He left to Singapore on the thirtieth and won't be back until the tenth. Madhumitha disappeared on the first."

Susheela sat in the chair opposite to him. "On to the next name on the list, then. Manohar. Bhuvani didn't tell us anything useful about him."

"I disagree. We know this Manohar is a poet—that's a clue."

"So what's our next step?"

"I made an appointment to meet Dr. Vigneswaran at 5:30 this evening. I'll see him, and then go see Sundaresan's friend Ganesa Pandian, plus one more of Madhumitha's friends, and then head home. You take an auto, go meet Professor Devendran and the rest of the girls on the list, and come to my house. I'll drop you off later at the hostel."

He went into the attached bathroom, washed up, combed his hair and powdered his face. As he was leaving, he stopped in the doorway, and said to Susheela, "Susi, do me one more favor. Call up the local magazines that publish poetry, and ask if they know of a poet named Manohar. Check with Higginbotham's, see if they stock a collection of poems by Manohar. Call every poet from the *Who's Who* directory and ask them if they know of a Manohar. You must be able to get some information from at least one of those sources. Oh yeah, by the way—I've changed Marikkozhunthu's name. She's Madhavi from now on. Give her a week, and you're in for a surprise. She was a real clay pot before, right? But just watch, it's an empty field that later bears fruit!"

Fearing she might launch another missile at him, Bharat quickly ducked out and shut the door.

The doctor had grey hair and dark lips, and wore a tie and thick glasses. "How can you expect me to disclose confidential information about my patient?"

Bharat replied, "This is just a request, I'm not compelling you. Your answers may help us understand this girl's actions. In fact, we're not sure if this Madhumitha I mentioned is alive at the moment. We're not able to make a break in the case."

"What's the connection between the missing daughter and the mother's health?"

"I wanted to confirm that everything the father said about the mother's health condition was true."

"What would you like to know?"

"What is the exact condition of Radhika's heart?"

"In a word, it's critical. I sent them over to CMC because she needs open heart surgery."

"You told her husband to avoid giving her any shocking news…"

"Yes, that could easily affect her heart. There is a weak spot—she shouldn't be allowed to take too much of a shock. I advised them that she shouldn't run, or exercise, or carry heavy weights, or laugh too vigorously, or worry too much."

"A daughter might confide in her mother more than in her father. That's why I thought it would be good to make inquiries of your patient. However, from what you say, I would be putting her life in danger. So Sundaresan was being honest with us—thank you, doctor."

Bharat went outside, and brought his bike to life with a swift kick.

Ganesa Pandian was outside watering his garden when his young son told him that someone had come to see him. He removed the towel he had tied around his head and came in to greet Bharat.

"Sundaresan is half dead with worry, sir," said Ganesa Pandian. "Now he has two problems. He has to find Madhumitha, and he has to keep his wife in the dark. She…"

"We know about her heart condition. Does Madhumitha come here often?"

"Not very often. When she does, she helps my wife in the kitchen, and sometimes she plays carom with me. She used to tear off all the foreign stamps from the letters I received. Sundaresan never buys any popular magazines, fearing that they'll spoil her studies. But in my house, we love reading. She used to say the only reason she came over was to browse through our magazines. She could never resist a glossy picture—she'd tear them out and take them home."

Bharat remembered the posters and magazine covers in Madhumitha's room. "Who else lives in this house?"

"Myself, my wife and our three kids. Vidhya's in seventh standard, Ramesh is in fifth, and Narayanan is in fourth."

"Did Madhumitha ever discuss anything personal with you?"

"Never. We would just talk generally, about music or films."

"When did you see her last?"

"Maybe a month back."

"Were you here on the first?"

"I was here. I haven't taken a day off work for the past two months. On the first, my family wasn't here. They were out of town at a wedding."

"What's your best guess about Madhumitha's disappearance?"

"I can't understand it. I don't believe she would have run away from home. Something terrible must have happened. All I want is my friend Sundaresan to be happy. I am praying for that every day. Vidhya, fix our guest a cup of tea, would you …"

9

Susheela stepped down onto the street as the auto-rickshaw came to a stop. "Come on, Ravi, get down."

He followed her, saying, "*Akka*, I'm feeling shy."

"Why?" said Susheela, tugging her T-shirt down.

"If I'd I known you were going to take me out, I would have worn full pants to the office this morning."

"Is that all? Anyway, you look better in shorts. Come on," she said, ruffling his hair, and checking the house number printed on the visiting card.

The double door stood ajar.

"Sir?"

From a room next to the hall, a man with a half-shaved cheek peered out.

"We're here to meet Professor Devendran."

"I'm Devendran. Please come in and have a seat. I'll join you in two minutes."

Susheela sat on the plastic wicker sofa. "Sit down Ravi. We have a few minutes—why don't you ask you me any questions you have about detective work. Or any questions at all," she said, pulling out a few magazines arranged on the centre table in front of her. Ravi pointed at her T-shirt, which today bore the slogan Swellingly Yours, and asked, "Okay. What does that mean, Akka, written on your shirt?"

"Oh dear—I guess I was too hasty. On second thoughts, Ravi, when you have questions, keep them to yourself." Just then, the professor came in, wiping his face with a thick towel. Susheela rose up to greet him.

"Sir, I'm from Moonlight Detective Agency. Your student, Madhumitha, has been missing for the past four days. We've been assigned the job of finding her. We'd be grateful for your cooperation. But before that, can you ask someone to get me a glass of water?"

The professor gave a sad sigh. "My family is in Karaikudi," he said, and went to bring a glass of water himself.

Susheela began her questions, all of which he answered. Half an hour passed. When they rose to leave, the professor said, "I strongly suspect that Sridhar is behind this."

They waited for an auto, caught one, and Susheela ordered, "Mylapore." Turning to Ravi, she asked him, "Why do you look so glum?"

"You said you would clear my doubts. But then when I did have a question, you refused to answer it."

"You should only ask questions appropriate to your age."

In Mylapore, Madhumitha's friend Barghavi was playing shuttlecock with her brother. She, too, answered their questions.

⁄ 10 ⁄

Bharat had returned home, removed his shirt and pants, hung them up, and changed into a lungi when Susheela entered with a "Good evening."

"Are you done already? I came in just five minutes ago. Hey, I thought you'd decided not to wear T-shirts with slogans on the front on Wednesdays."

"That rule's only for the office."

"Whatever! Did you use any salve for the swelling?"

She punched him in the back and said, "In the professor's house, Ravi asked me what my T-shirt meant."

"Ravi? Why did you take him along?"

"How else am I supposed to train him for detective work?"

"He doesn't need any training. His job is to fetch coffee and tea and dust the tables. I've seen the way you look at him, and I don't trust your motives. That's why I asked him not to wear long pants to the office."

"Come on, he's a kid. Don't corrupt his young mind."

"What, *I'm* the one corrupting him? Who gave him money to buy *Debonair*, was that you or I? He went and flipped through all those pictures, and then came complaining to me that you read dirty books."

Susheela put her handbag on the sofa and stretched her arms.

"Please, don't do these stretches in front of Ravi. You can't trust that kid. I happen to know that he watches a lot of Malayalam flicks. He might get some ideas and make a grab at you."

"Go on. Tell me what happened."

"Vigneshwaran confirmed everything Sundaresan said. We won't be able to talk to his wife. She shouldn't find out that Madhumitha is missing."

"And then?"

"A month back, she tore the centrefolds out of the magazines in Ganesa Pandian's house and put them up in her room."

"Maybe that's her hobby. The covers from the professor's magazines were also missing. He said Madhumitha took them with his permission."

"That's not important. Did you find any new leads?"

"No. Everything in the diary seems clear. The professor told me that he had reprimanded her about hanging out with Sridhar. She apparently stopped going to his house after that, even to clear doubts about the class. On the first of the month, she was participating enthusiastically in class, and everything seemed normal. He thinks Sridhar must be behind it."

"Who did you see next?"

"Barghavi and Pritha. Did you go to meet that other friend?"

"Yes, Aruna—a rich girl. She's even got a swimming pool in her house. She didn't seem to care whether Madhumitha was found or not. But I got a tip from her, anyway."

"What?" she asked eagerly.

"Boil some water, let it cool a bit, and soak in it for five minutes while it is still warm… truly a simple method."

"What do you mean?"

"Apparently that firms up one's structure."

Susheela took him by his collar and barked, "You are supposed to be investigating Madhumitha's case, not getting beauty tips. That's it—no more individual investigation. From now on, we'll stick together. I won't ever leave your side."

"You're very welcome, Susheela. According to Tamil literary tradition, that means you're ready to share my bed. I'll be waiting!"

"When will we get to move this to the next level? I don't think we're ever going to find Madhumitha. What use is all this questioning?"

"No Susi. We're being as thorough as we can. So there are no straightforward clues—when we find the right switch, the curtain will open, and there will be Madhumitha. Hey, did you find our poet?"

"I made twenty-four phone calls in all, Bharat. But no one seems to have heard of a poet by the name of Manohar."

Bharat stayed silent for a few minutes and then said, "Susi, when a young girl goes missing, what are the usual reasons?"

"One, she could have been in love, and eloped. Two, she could have been kidnapped and sold to a red-light area in Bombay. Three, she could have been murdered by some enemy. Four, she could have had an accident and died. Five, somebody could be keeping her hidden somewhere."

"Which one of those do you think is the most likely?"

"Close your eyes and think hard," Susheela said. "Let me borrow your bike to get back to my hostel. Hopefully we'll make some headway tomorrow."

Once Susheela left, Bharat took out Madhumitha's diary once again, and read it over and over. Sridhar would be back only on the tenth. Manohar was yet to be located. They had no useful clues from anybody. They desperately needed a break in the case.

✗ 11 ✗

The break came the next morning at eight, while Bharat was shaving, in the form of a call from Inspector Suresh Menon.

"What?" he exclaimed. "I'll be there right away." He dialed Susheela at once. "Susi, the police have found Madhumitha—sorry to say, they found her dead. She's in the General Hospital mortuary. The inspector just called me."

"How sad! Where did they find her?"

"We'll find out when we meet them. I'll go check it out."

Bharat finished shaving and bathing and took an auto to the general hospital, where he found Sundaresan weeping. He put a comforting arm around him.

"Have you identified the body?" Bharat asked Inspector Suresh Menon.

"I'm not sure you can call it a body anymore," he said. "Have you ever seen a corpse that's been soaking in a sewer for four days, Bharat? She's badly decomposed. The nails and teeth have fallen off, stomach bloated, face swollen… Horrible, just horrible! I only identified her with what remained of her face and her clothes."

"Have you done an autopsy?"

"That will come later."

"Can I see the body?"

"Come along. Her body's all folded up. You can forget about eating lunch."

They walked into the mortuary. Compared to the rest of the hospital, it was almost peaceful.

"Lift the sheet a little—show him."

The attendee obeyed.

Bharat's stomach churned. Was this the beauty he had seen in the photograph, her head tilted at a forty-five-degree angle, smiling into the camera? Was this the angel blowing out the birthday candles, with her dimples flashing?

As they walked back he asked, "Where did you find her?"

"Not too far from her house—on the same street where Sundaresan lives. There was a public complaint that a manhole on Burkit road was not shut properly. The corporation workers had come to repair it, and found a stench worse than any sewer. It was a human body. I was called there immediately. By the time we could get her out… oh, it was hellish!"

"So, was it murder?"

"I'm sure of it. Someone killed her and dumped her there. If the sewer had been flowing freely, the body would have decomposed completely. Because it was relatively dry, the corpse was still there."

"But because of the delay, won't it be difficult to find out if there are any injuries?"

"The skull is cracked on the bottom, and the skin is split there too. She could have been hit with a club. But the post-mortem report won't be of any use in finding the murderer. We'll have to begin from Sundaresan's house."

"We already started our investigation there, and have come halfway. I'll meet you at the station in an hour and give you those details."

"Thanks. I should go meet the coroner," said Suresh Menon, and left.

Bharat went back to Sundaresan, who was standing under a tree.

"Sir, did you see her? Did you see my Madhumitha? What crime did she commit to deserve this?" His already-wet handkerchief became soaked even further.

"The body's not in a condition to be taken back home. Sign it over to them so they can dispose of it. And your wife..."

"How am I ever going to tell her? Oh God! I don't understand anything anymore."

"Please don't worry. We can't bring back a life that's already been lost. However, we can try our best to save a life that's still here. Make a request to the police that neither your name, nor Madhumitha's, is released to the media. Hide everything from your wife. Tell her Madhumitha is on a college tour for a month. Then you can wait until after her surgery to break the news to her. Have you collected all of your daughter's belongings from the station?"

"Yes, they gave me a list," he said, taking a slip of paper from his pocket. "But her books, tiffin box and slippers are missing."

When Bharat entered the office, he had no time to notice that Madhavi was wearing pants. He waited impatiently for Susheela to finish her phone call.

"Who was that, Susi?"

"I called all the big magazines yesterday. Today I called the smaller, literary magazines. I am yet to get hold of Manohar. Tell me, how was Madhumitha?"

"Manohar's address is in the diary. I didn't notice it in the beginning. Let's go. Bring the bike keys."

On the bike, Susheela whispered into Bharat's ears, "I don't remember seeing Manohar's address in the diary!"

"It's not written there directly. However, there are a few clues. It says he gave her the letter and then left on a bike. Then it mentions that his house is near her typewriting institute. That institute was Vinayaga Institute in Kodambakkam. Therefore, he must live in that area."

Bharat stopped his bike at a repair shop in Kodambakkam. The moment he mentioned Manohar, he was told that he was the pawnbroker's son. The shopowner even pointed out the house.

The board said Si. Tha. Azhagappan Bankers. He called out, "Sir?" and a woman wearing about two kilos of gold on her neck and ears peered out at them.

"Who is it?" she asked.

"We need to see Manohar."

"He's just taken his pills and gone to sleep. Who are you? What do you want? His father's at the shop."

"What's wrong with Manohar? Is he unwell? I'm a friend of his."

"Please come in."

Manohar was asleep on a cot in the hall. Bottles of pills were arranged on a stool near the head of the bed. A thick notebook lay next to the bed with a pencil in it. A week's worth of dirt clung to his shirt and dhoti.

"What's wrong?" asked Bharat.

"He's been mentally disturbed for over a month now. He talks strangely, bursts into sudden laughter. We've been giving treatment. Apparently, they are going to give him shock therapy. Please sit down. Were you his college mates?"

"Yes," said Susheela, sitting down on the chair. "What is this notebook? Can I take a look?"

"Those are his poems, I believe. He writes them throughout the day. The doctor also wanted to see them. He said my son was in love with a girl, but it all went *phut!* He thinks maybe that disappointment has sent him over the edge. We never would have objected to his choice… Let me make some tea for you."

As she left, Bharat looked at Susheela. "Look what a state Madhumitha's games have brought him to!"

Susheela flipped through the poetry notebook.

Skies, butterflies, breeze, angels, flowers…. The poems were simple and immature.

Then she found one on the subject of love.

> The air that touches your skin now touches mine,
> and thrills me
> Your discarded scraps are my sacred food
> At least, can you let your shadow embrace mine?
> Why not? Has your heart been sculpted from stone?

This went on for pages.

Susheela pointed out another one. "Bharat, look at this!"

> *Sweetheart, Please Die!*
>
> Do you want to know
> the depth of my Love?
> Sweetheart, please die!
> I shall die too
> and come as a ghost
> to continue
> loving your spirit!

"Imagine—she rejects someone who loves her so deeply, and instead becomes close to Sridhar. Now look at this fellow! Totally shattered…"

Bharat's voice woke Manohar. The mother, re-emerging with the tea said, "Son, they've come to see you."

"Are you well, Manohar?"

Manohar stared at them vacantly for a moment before snatching the book from Bharat. He made a strange noise, and then turned all his attention to the ceiling fan.

"God knows what he sees there, in the fan. He keeps staring at it all day. Ask him a hundred questions, his eyes will just stay glued there on the fan."

Bharat removed the prescription from the pile of medicines and noted down the doctor's name and address.

"When did he go to the doctor?"

"He took a turn for the worse last week. On the first, my husband and I left him alone at home and went to Melmaruvathur Temple. The day after that, he started this really bizarre behavior. We took him to see the doctor at once."

"Think hard before you answer this: When did you leave him alone at home?"

"On the first. It was our turn to serve the temple in our association."

"Thank you. We'll go now."

"Susi," said Bharat as they came outside, "we need to meet the psychiatrist who treated Manohar right away. I've got an idea he may be faking this 'mental disturbance'."

⚡ 12 ⚡

Ramasubbu, the psychiatrist, twirled his spectacles by the frame. "Impossible!" he said with conviction. "It might be easy to fool a lay person by feigning insanity, but not a psychiatrist. Manohar is afflicted with a distress and anxiety disorder resulting from severe depression. He is not normal."

"Are you sure?" asked Bharat.

"One hundred percent!"

"Can you give me a written affidavit to this effect?"

"Of course."

"I don't actually need it. I just wanted to make sure you were certain. Thank you."

"What do you think's going on?" asked Susheela as they left.

"Madhumitha goes missing on the first. Manohar becomes mentally disturbed on the first, also. She dumps him, he gets furious with her. Maybe he finishes her off, dumps her into the manhole, and the next day, he starts pretending he's lost his mind..."

"But the doctor is certain he's not acting."

"Susi, we promised to give the inspector the information we gathered. We still haven't met Sridhar because he's out of the country. Therefore, we have no way of knowing who wrote the threatening letter. And there is one question left unanswered."

"What's that?"

"Who was that guy who followed Madhumitha around for a whole day?"

"You really think that's important?"

"What, you don't?"

"When Madhumitha asked him, that guy said he was looking for a missing girl of her age. Why not assume he was telling the truth?"

Bharat took out Madhumitha's diary from the bike's side box, and flipped to the July 1st entry. "'I'm sorry, is your name Kalyani?' he said. 'No, Madhumitha. Why?' 'I saw an advertisement in *Dhinamalar* yesterday, about a girl of your age who has gone missing...'"

"Yesterday here means June thirtieth," said Susheela.

"So our next stop is..."

"The *Dhinamalar* office to check if his claim was true or false."

At the newspaper office, they introduced themselves. "Mani," called out the clerk, "bring in the issue from the thirtieth... be quick."

Flipping through the issue, they found no such advertisement.

"So he was lying," Bharat said, outside the office. "Then why was he following her?"

"Maybe just a girl chaser."

"No Susi, such a person wouldn't have been able to come up such a good lie so quickly."

"Maybe a policeman, then?"

"But she wasn't a criminal."

"Maybe a detective, like ourselves?"

"There you go, that sounds better! The man could have been from another agency, appointed to follow her. Okay, now I need a hello."

"Hello!"

"I meant, I need a telephone."

"There—that provision shop's not too crowded. Come along."

While Susheela was asking about the price of sugar and which incense sticks had the best fragrance, Bharat used the shop's phone to call every private detective agency in the city.

"Hello, this is Bharat from Moonlight Agency. Did you take up the job of following a King Solomon College student named Madhumitha?"

He asked the same question several times, before Silver Night Agency said "Wait... yes... you're right."

"Thank God! Who gave you that assignment?'

"You must be joking, sir! You know we can't reveal our customers' names. Would you give out *your* customers' names?"

"No, I wouldn't. But this is a very critical situation."

"Sorry, sir. There's absolutely no way we can release that information. I wouldn't even have told you that we were the ones following her, except for the respect we have for you as fellow detectives."

✗ 13 ✗

Inspector Suresh Menon removed his cap and placed it on top of a huge pile of faded, taped files, dog-eared forms, and ink-stained rulers. Two dim tube lights lit the room. The walls were lined with charts listing the crime records for the area, mug-shots, and a register with the names of those who had spent time in the station's lock-up.

Suresh Menon was flipping through Madhumitha's diary. Susheela was checking the film listings in a Tamil newspaper. Bharat was standing in the doorway, watching Suresh's reaction to the diary entries.

When Suresh shut the diary, Bharat stubbed out his cigarette and approached the desk.

"So what do you think?" said Suresh Menon.

"Your murderer is named in that diary."

"Who is it?"

"Answering that question is your job. Susi, give it to him."

"What's this?" he asked, taking the stack of papers that Susheela handed him.

"Our report—all fourteen pages of it. Everything's in there, from Sundaresan's first visit to us yesterday down to our last investigation."

"Very kind of you, Bharat."

"My pleasure. You can read through it thoroughly later. For now, I'll tell you my guesses."

"Please."

Bharat unbuttoned the top button of his shirt and pushed back the collar. "I've got three suspects. The first is Sridhar. He wanted to totally cut off his relationship with Madhumitha, and he could have been worried she would make trouble. He planned his ten-day tour to Singapore, and hired a mercenary to bump her off as soon as he was gone. That's theory number one."

"Logical. And suspect number two?"

"Manohar, who has an excellent motive. He was deeply in love with Madhumitha, and was rejected by her. On the first, he's home alone when Madhumitha shows up for some reason. He finishes her off, and then pretends to have gone insane. Or maybe the murder itself actually sent him over the brink. That's theory number two."

"I don't exactly get the picture. But I'm sure your report will help me get a clearer idea."

"My third suspect," said Bharat, taking his time, "is Sundaresan."

"What? Sundaresan? Her father?"

"Why not? See if you can find a hole in this theory. Sundaresan is well-respected, upper-middle-class, a monthly wage earner, and a disciplined man. Suppose he's grown suspicious that his only daughter has a secret vice. He hires a private detective to watch her activities. Naturally, he would have found out about the drugs and about her dalliances with Sridhar. He even finds out that Sridhar's been having it off with his daughter right in his own house. He's shocked and saddened. It's too much for a father to take. He is furious and disgusted with his daughter. He decides that this wayward girl should not be allowed to live. On the first, when a sudden holiday is announced, she calls him to tell him she's going to her aunt's house in Adyar. He asks her to come and meet him first. He kills her, dumps her in the sewer, and then pretends to be searching for her, with his friend Ganesa Pandian as a witness. To make his act more believable he hires our agency. So what do you think, could it be Sundaresan?"

"You have a very fertile imagination. Yes, I suppose it could be him. But how to prove any of this?" asked Suresh Menon, scratching his head.

"That's what you get paid for. Call me if you need any help," grinned Bharat as he shook the inspector's hand.

Outside, Susheela said, "So Bharat, looks like the case is over, as far as we're concerned."

"Yes. In fact, it was over when the body was found. Now it's a job for the police. I don't think Sundaresan is in any mood to pay our fee, so why should I show any more interest in the case? After all, Madhumitha wasn't my wife or my lover... right?"

"Let me drive the bike. You sit at the back," said Susheela.

"No, I've got a terrible backache. It'll be more comfortable if you sit at the back."

"Why? I don't understand."

"If I'm driving, then you can cushion me at every bump."

"You never give up, do you? Come, if you're going to keep up with this kind of talk, then let's stop at some temple on the way home."

"Why?"

"So we can get married," she said, with a shy smile.

"Oh, wow! It's been a long time since you acted all traditional around me. Give me that innocent look one more time," pleaded Bharat.

✗ 14 ✗

Friday the 7th: Madhavi arrived at the office with her hair cut short. "Not bad," commented Bharat.

Saturday the 8th: Ravi had managed a thin line of moustache. "Looks like you've drawn it on with a pencil," said Susheela.

Sunday the 9th: Bharat woke up at ten. When Susheela arrived, they played a game of chess for an exciting new stake. But when Bharat won, she welshed on the bet.

Monday the 10th: Around four in the evening, Bharat called Suresh Menon.

"Hello, this Bharat speaking."

"Hello, how are you?"

"Fine. I just wanted to know if there were any developments in the Madhumitha case. Today's the tenth; Sridhar should be back. I couldn't help being curious."

"I tried getting dramatic with Sridhar. But it didn't work."

"What happened?"

"I called him pretending to be the hired killer, asking for more money. But he called my bluff. I went myself and spoke to him. I told him about her diary, and that he was the prime suspect. But he just reacted coolly. 'Yeah, I had sex with her—several times. But I told her right at beginning I wasn't ever going to marry her. I never had any argument with her. What reason would I have had to kill her? I wasn't even in the country when the murder took place. That's all I'm willing to say, without a lawyer next to me.'"

"Who wrote him that threatening letter?"

"He showed me the letter. It was Manohar's handwriting—it matched the writing in that poetry notebook you gave me."

"I thought so."

"We searched Manohar's house completely. We even took our search dogs. We had him checked out by a government doctor. He's truly nuts—no way he could be faking it."

"And Sundaresan...?"

"We searched his house twice. We moved the inspector general's office to find out who assigned Silver Night Agency to follow Madhumitha."

"Who was it?"

"Not Sundaresan. It was one Paulraj, from Chidambaram."

"Who's this Paulraj?"

"He was the man who was supposed to marry Madhumitha. He wanted to find out more about her. She was followed around for three days; apparently, she was behaving herself during that time, so he was satisfied with her character."

"Did Sundaresan's wife come back?"

"Yes. He's given her the story that Madhumitha is off on a tour."

"And Madhumitha's diary?"

"We don't want the family to know about it."

"Good. What's your next step?" asked Bharat.

"I've appointed men to keep an eye on Manohar, Sridhar and Sundaresan. But I'm beginning to think we should follow Ganesa Pandian, as well."

"Go ahead, tell me your theory."

"Madhumitha was a very beautiful girl. She frequently visited his house. On the first, his whole family had gone out of town for a wedding. Suppose she came to his house after the holiday was announced, to have a game of carom. Suppose he tried to force himself on her. In the struggle, she died."

"Very imaginative. Get your proof. All the best."

"What happened?" asked Susheela, when he disconnected the phone.

"The police have not progressed an inch. But did you notice Madhavi? Miles of progress there!"

"You're getting worse," she said, and pinched his cheek, so hard that he yelled with pain. At the sound, Ravi came running into the room with a English magazine in his hand.

"Hey, Ravi, when did you start reading English magazines?"

"I was just looking at the pictures, sir. Madhavi Madam brought this in," he said, handing it over to Bharat. The words NATARAJAN CIRCULATING LIBRARY were stamped on the cover.

"Susheela, tell me again who this woman is. Isn't this the same cover we saw in Madhumitha's room?"

"Let me take a look—Shiny Abraham. Yes, she had covered her notebook with the same picture. Wait a minute! This magazine is dated July 15, 1987!"

"So?"

"This is the same magazine I saw, without the cover, in the professor's house."

"So? What are you so excited about?"

"He told me that after the day when he advised her not to get too friendly with Sridhar, she stopped coming to his house. According to the diary, that was back in February. Then how did she get a July magazine cover from his house?"

"Hey, wow! You're right, it's a new lead!" exclaimed Bharat. Just then the phone rang.

"Sir, this is Bhuvani, Madhumitha's classmate. You questioned me in the park."

"Yes. Tell me."

"Sorry I took so long to call—I went to Kutralam with my family. I was only able to make inquiries today."

"About what?"

"Have you forgotten? You wanted to know who in our class was the last person to see her."

"Oh, right. Did you find out?"

"Yes. It was Ranganayaki. She was waiting at the bus stop, and saw Madhumitha walk down Venkataramana Street."

"And?"

"That's all she knew, sir."

"Thank you, Bhuvani. Would you like to join my agency sometime?" But before Bharat could finish the question, Susheela had disconnected the call.

He picked up the bike keys and said, "Come along."

"Where?"

"To see the inspector. You know what's on Venkatramana Street, don't you?"

"What, did a new restaurant open?"

"Typical. No, silly—that's where the professor's house is."

∕ 15 ∕

"Let's not waste any more time with formal inquiries," said Bharat. "Get your search warrant and the dogs ready. We'll land there in style."

And they did—to Professor Devendran's great surprise.

The police officers' search revealed two large packets of heroin. The dogs sniffed out a spot in the garden, where they dug up Madhumitha's slippers, tiffin box and books.

"Do you want to give your statement here or wait until we get you to the police station?" asked the inspector.

"I'll confess everything. It wasn't a murder—it was an accident. I'm a drug user; recently Madhumitha had found that out about me. When the holiday was announced, Madhumitha came here looking for drugs. She told me, 'Sir, I'm begging you shamelessly: Can I have a stuffed cigarette please? I'm an addict... usually I get it from Sridhar. I'm craving for one badly. If you refuse, I'll commit suicide.' So I said okay, and I gave her one. She lit it right here. Then she started behaving very strangely. She told me, 'Variety is important in life; there is nothing wrong with it; come along.' She hugged me and started taking off her clothes. I lost control; the beast inside me took over. We went to the bedroom upstairs and had our fun. Afterwards, she went down to make tea—but she was too high to walk steadily. She slipped and fell down the stairs. I ran to help her, but she had cracked her skull open. She was dead.

"I panicked. I waited until that night. I own an auto-rickshaw that I rent out. In the night, I put her body in the auto, drove to the sewer opening, and dumped her there. Then I cleaned up the house and the auto, and buried her stuff in the garden."

"At this point, can I give you a bit of free advice, Professor?" Bharat lectured. "In the unlikely event that you escape execution—in case you ever have to dispose of any more corpses, please don't bury them with all their belongings. Just burn them. Much safer."

"I swear I didn't kill her."

"You know, I believe you. I think the inspector believes you. Now you have to try and make the court believe you."

"Good show, Bharat!" complimented the inspector.

"Bah, what did I get out of it? If Madhumitha was looking for 'variety', I was free on the first, too. I would have given her a dozen cigarettes."

"Bharat," said Susheela, "shut up!"

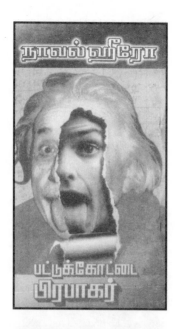

Covers of Pattukkottai Prabakar novels, published in (clockwise from top left)
Great Novel, Novel Hero, Oonjal, and its previous incarnation *Ullaasa Oonjal.*
Bottom left art by Jayaraj, other artists unknown.

PUSHPA THANGADORAI

Pushpa Thangadorai is the alter ego of Srivenugopal, who began his career in the 1960s writing religious travel guides to Hindu temples and pilgrimage sites. In the early 1970s, under the pen name Pushpa Thangadorai, he started publishing grisly true crime stories on the side. *My Name is Kamala*, probably his best-known work, was based on extensive interviews with prostitutes working in the red-light districts of Delhi and Bombay. *Kamala* was serialized in forty-three weekly installments appearing from 1974-75 in the magazine *Dhinamani Kadhir* along with illustrations by Chennai artist Jayaraj, some of which are reproduced here. The novel was so hugely successful that the author was compelled by readers to extend the story for several months past the initially planned last installment.

What follows is excerpted and abridged from chapters 24-33. The narrator, Kamala, is a Tamil girl who has been abducted and sold to a brothel in Delhi, where she is kept under lock and key by the wicked Madam Sindhu and the even more sadistic Madam Nirmala. Though she has been there nearly a year, she still dreams of escape.

MY NAME IS KAMALA

என் பெயர் கமலா (1974-75)

Remember I told you about the two girls who were kept locked in the room downstairs? Well, after three months, they disappeared. I have no idea what happened to them. Now there were two new girls in that room. Both were high school students, one from a convent. I heard they had been kidnapped and brought here to Delhi, and that they had been refusing to eat since the day they arrived. Sindhu Madam had bought them for 1500 rupees each.

We could hear their screams as they were beaten throughout the day. It made us feel awful; no one, till then, had received such a harsh punishment. We wanted to go down and have look at them, but we couldn't. After a week one of them was finally taken up to the top floor. She must have relented, unable to bear the punishment any longer. The other girl was beaten for two more days, but on the third day, the ground floor was silent. I was eager to know what was happening.

On the fourth day, Sindhu asked me to put on a *churidhar* and *kameez*. I got ready. At nine that night I was taken out to one of the waiting auto-rickshaws. Sindhu and I rode together in auto with a load of harmoniums and tablas. As we got on our way I paid careful attention to the route we were taking, hoping to figure out how I could get to G.B. Road in the event that I managed to escape.

I had been kept indoors for so long that now, out in the open, the people on the road seemed like characters from a dream.

We arrived at a big house, the same one I'd been taken to for my initiation. I understood that one of the new girls was going to be presented to the owner of the house. We entered and I sat in the hall. The new girl was taken to a nearby room to have her make-up done. After a while I peeked in, and Sindhu saw me, and called me inside.

"Kamala, this kid is still acting stubborn. See if you can talk to her in your language. I think she's from somewhere in the South," she said.

I saw the girl for the first time. I was shocked. She was really very young, just fifteen or so. She hadn't even lost her baby fat. Her face was swollen from prolonged crying. Whiplash scars were visible on her neck and hands. She looked completely terrified. I stood there gaping at her. The make-up people had left. The music started, and Sindhu left as well, telling me to bring the girl out soon.

I slowly lifted the girl's face. Even her eyes seemed to tremble in fear. "What's your name?" I asked in Kannada.

She grabbed at my hand and wept, "Are you from Karnataka too?"

"I'm from the South, yes." I replied.

"I beg you, please. I can't understand a word of what they say. They've brought me here by force. What is this place?" she implored me, through tears.

"Please don't cry. Tell me your name," I asked.

"Indrani."

"Indrani, I was also brought here by force. Listen to me. Just obey, do whatever they tell you to. Don't bother trying to rebel. It's no use. You'll only be beaten more," I advised her.

She looked at me doubtfully.

"Please don't think I'm one of them," I pleaded. "I'm your friend. I want to escape from all this someday too. Believe me."

Outside, the music was picking up speed. Sindhu called out, "Kamala, come on now, bring Indrani out here."

"Get up," I told her.

She started crying again.

"Stop crying!" I said, wiping her face. "Your tears are of no use. Just follow their orders. Someday, someone will save us from this." I redid her make-up, told her to smile, and took her out.

What happened then was similar to my own experience, except for one crucial difference. After a period of beatings, I had acquiesced. But Indrani stood firm in her refusal. Finally, they had to give her a tranquilizer. In the end, it was under the influence of the tranquilizer that her body was sullied for the first time.

She was brought back to the establishment in the morning. She was bleeding and in severe pain. She was kept in the room downstairs and a doctor was called to attend on her.

I didn't get to see Indrani again for the next two weeks. In the third week, she was taken up to the second floor. That was the training school for all the adamant girls. On the fifth day I saw her coming down the stairway on my way to the toilet. She wouldn't even smile at me. She had lost weight and there was a bandage on her left cheek near the ear.

"Indrani, don't be scared. Remember me? I'm your friend," I said softly.

"Chee! Are you a woman? Sinner! You say you're a Kannada girl, yet you do nothing to help a fellow woman from your state. You've betrayed your own sister. Just because you've been spoiled, don't encourage me to become that way too," she burst out.

I was speechless. She was accusing me of the all the same things I had accused Daya of, when she had tried to reassure me. Indrani left abruptly. I hoped that she would come to understand my empathy in time.

It had been a full year since I had come into this establishment. It was in December that I was brought in, and now it was December again. We had no calendars. The only way we would know when a new month had begun was from the crowd in the first week. Some men came on specific dates, some on specific days of the week. Our customers were our calendars.

In that time, my Hindi had improved a lot. That was a good thing—I wasn't as scared of everything as I had been when I couldn't understand the language. Also, being able to speak to other girls there was some comfort.

Two months later, Indrani was moved to our floor. Her attitude had changed completely. She came right up to me and clasped my hands. "Kamala, please, forgive me," she said. "I had thought very wrongly of you. I've become one among you now. Let's plan our escape!"

I asked her how she had been captured, how she had come to be here.

She was from a middle-class family, had been a student in a convent school in Karnataka. She had been sitting outside her house studying one afternoon when a black Ambassador car stopped in front of the house. The back door opened. In the car was another girl, wearing the uniform of Indrani's school, who called out to her. Approaching the car, Indrani saw that there were three men inside; the driver, one in the passenger seat, and another sitting next to the girl. "The teacher wants you," said the girl. "Get in."

Doubtfully, Indrani asked, "Which teacher?"

But by then, the man in the front seat had gotten out and come behind her. He pushed her into the car, and the other man held her hands tightly. The door was slammed shut and the car sped away. She was gagged, and her hands bound. She vaguely remembered being brought on the train to Delhi in first class, forced to lie down throughout the journey.

"Guess who the girl in the uniform was," Indrani asked me as she completed her story.

"Who?"

"It was that fat girl, the one upstairs!"

I couldn't believe it. "*She* did this?" I asked angrily.

"Don't get wild, Kamala. I'm sure she didn't do it willingly. She was forced to do it."

"Didn't anyone notice you going to the car?"

"Maybe. But no one realized I was being kidnapped," she replied.

* * *

I already told you something about Balbir, the Punjabi man who was my regular customer. It was only then, after I had gained some fluency with Hindi, that I came to understand his deep attachment to me. It was really amazing: whenever he came, he would treat me with the same respect and dignity as he would his own wife. He would never hurt me; he always tried to satisfy my every wish.

The only tenderness I found in that place was with Balbir. He told me a lot about his family, especially his wife, Rupalekha. In the beginning, I didn't pay much attention, but later I started listening more carefully. Rupalekha would actually send me her wishes. I found this bizarre. I couldn't believe that a wife would send her wishes to her husband's prostitute friend. But from what Balbir told me, I came to realize that she was genuinely a good person. Now there was a strange sort of friendship between us two women, though we had never met. She sent me a photograph of hers, and on festival days she would send me sweets. Having heard about my troubles, she would send kind messages. One day, she asked for a photo of mine. I didn't have one, so Balbir asked Sindhu's permission to bring a photographer. But Sindhu refused.

Now, though, it had been a whole month since Balbir had come, and I was truly hurt. I imagined that maybe the two madams, Sindhu and Nirmala, had banned him from the establishment.

One Saturday evening, I was running a slight fever—but we couldn't make a fuss about such things. It must have been about six o'clock. I had had my face done, and was sitting in the hall. Suddenly I heard a voice.

"Kamala!"

I turned around and there was Balbir. He had a smile on his face, but he looked broken.

When we went inside the room, he started sobbing. He didn't stop for a long time. He chest heaved inside his jibha.. I had never seen a man cry like this.

Finally he whispered, "Rupalekha is dead."

I was shocked, and I began to cry, too, as though I had lost a close relation. "How did she die?" I asked.

"She was carrying a pot of water, and she just collapsed. She was in bed for two days; then on the third day she lost consciousness, and the next day she died," he said. "The doctor said she may have been suffering from a heart disease that she didn't tell anyone about."

He spent the entire night with me. It must have cost him a hundred fifty rupees. We stayed awake through the night, consoling each other.

A Hindi girl came down with a fever and was sent to the room downstairs. Kirthi was told to take care of her. We didn't like that—the Hindi girl was not a member of our clique. She had come into this profession willingly. Such girls enjoyed a lot of privileges here. They could come and go as they pleased. They were even allowed to go out to the movies. We always thought of such girls as madam's pets. Some of them were as fierce as the madams. They would not hesitate to threaten or slap us. It was another one of our duties to do whatever chores such women asked of us.

When Kirthi returned after four days, we demanded to know why she had agreed to help one of those women.

"I was looking for a way to escape," she replied.

"What, Kirthi? How?" I asked.

"A few weeks back they sent me downstairs to help Indrani. I noticed something then. I think I'll be able to remove the screws of the bolt from the inside after they shut me in at night. I haven't been able to do it yet, since I didn't have a screwdriver."

"So have you found one?"

"No. But I think I can do it with a ladle handle. So this time when I was downstairs, I managed to steal a ladle, and hide it in that room. Next time I will escape!" she said. "I already oiled the screws so it will be easier to loosen them."

I was thrilled. "Kirthi," I exclaimed, "if even one of us can escape from here, she will be able to set the rest of us free!"

Not long after that, Kirthi got her opportunity. A girl from Bihar fell sick—she was a very quiet girl, who never acted boisterous with anyone. Kirthi was given the responsibility of nursing her.

Kirthi was thrilled. She said goodbye to all of us, and before she went downstairs, she whispered into my ear: "Kamala! When I escape, I promise to go to the police and set all of you free. Don't worry!"

We prayed every night that she would succeed.

The first night nothing happened. The next night, as well, all was quiet. It wasn't until later that I found out what happened on the third night, but I'll tell you now.

The first two nights downstairs, Kirthi had been all nerves. She was determined to escape this time. She resisted sleep, staying awake until three in the morning. She tried to loosen the screws with the ladle she had hidden there, but she was not able to. The screws were stuck fast. The first night the door was bolted and padlocked from the outside, so all she could do was oil them. The next night, it was padlocked from the inside, but she made too much noise trying to loosen the screws; she thought she heard someone moving outside, and stopped. The third night she finally managed to loosen the bolt.

Carefully, she removed it from the door frame and placed it on the floor. When she looked up she heard a sound. Her heart stopped for a moment. There was someone next to her. It was the sick girl, Nisha. She was silent. Kirthi was in tears. "Nisha, please don't give me away. I can't take any more torture. I was wrong to do this. I won't do it again, I promise," she cried.

Nisha took her to the bed, made her sit on it and said, "Why are you so scared? I won't give you away. You can go!"

Kirthi was shocked.

"Where can I go, Nisha?"

"Wherever you want!"

"No Nisha," Kirthi said, still wary. "I don't want to go anymore. I'll stay here."

"No Kirthi. You must go. Don't be scared! I've been in this business for ages, it's what I'm used to. But I know that you and many others have been forcefully brought here. I don't like that. I won't stop you from escaping. Go now! I am very grateful to you for caring for me since I've been sick." Saying this, Nisha gave her a ten rupee note and bade her farewell.

Kirthi asked Nisha to share the secret of her escape with either me or Daya. Then she thanked her again and quietly snuck out of the room. Nisha followed her, watched her disappear through the main entrance, then bolted the main door, shut the room door, and went back to bed.

In the morning around eight, Nisha informed the madam that the lock was open and Kirthi was missing. After that was a huge hullabaloo. Both the madams ran around screaming at everyone. Dolly, Sindhu Madam's right hand, made the servants search the house high and low.

The bathroom on the top floor did not have a roof. They checked to see if she might have climbed over it, but it wouldn't have been possible to jump down from such a height. Sindhu sent a servant out to fetch her goons, the ones she paid a monthly salary to keep her informed—the *paanwala*, the cycle shop owner, the tea shop owner, the bum. They promised to bring Kirthi back by that night. That was how we first learned of the vast network of spies that the madams had set up to prevent us from escaping, to report anyone suspicious lurking around the house, and to look out for the police.

It was two days before we learned what had transpired downstairs between Nisha and Kirtha. The first time Nisha met us and tried to explain, we thought she was spying for the madam, and didn't trust her. We avoided her for some time. It was only after Kirthi had been gone for a few days that we began to believe her.

When it became clear that Kirthi had really gotten away, we were elated. We were sure that liberty was not far away.

A week passed. Sindhu was very strict with us. She imagined that we had been accomplices to Kirthi's escape. She found fault with everything we did. She was also furious with Nisha for sleeping through Kirthi's getaway.

Every morning, we waited for the police to arrive. We would get excited at any unusual sound. And every day that the police didn't come, we found new excuses with which to console ourselves. But gradually, our hope began to wane.

No help came.

Kirthi was a good friend to all of us. She had yearned for freedom even more we did, if that was possible. She would not have let us down on purpose. She must have been unable to reach the authorities for some reason. Perhaps she was caught by some other gang and sold to a different establishment. Or maybe she escaped to Mysore, because Delhi was not safe for her.

Or maybe it was something else entirely. Once a woman comes into an establishment like this, the terror she experiences cannot be put into words. Very soon, she becomes mentally weak and depressed. She begins to fear just about everything and everybody. Even if she does manage to escape, she may no longer possess the self-confidence to raise her voice and demand anything. Even if she gets an opportunity, she will fail to take advantage of it.

* * *

One day Balbir returned. He began talking about taking me out again. "Balbir, I'm ready to come; but you have to make all the arrangements," I told him.

"Fine. I shall speak to Sindhu tomorrow," he said.

"What will you tell her?"

"Wait and see," he said.

The next day, around four in the evening, Sindhu came to the hall to take a head-count. Balbir caught up with her as she was going downstairs and said, "I need to ask you something."

"What?" asked Sindhu.

"About Kamala."

"What about Kamala?"

"I would like to take her out."

"Take her out and?"

"I want to keep her by my side… perhaps marry her, if she will accept," said Balbir.

"Ha! What, *Sardar*, have you gone mad?" asked Sindhu.

"No, I'm not mad. I want to take her, with your blessings. I am prepared to pay something," insisted Balbir.

"How much is something?"

"How about one thousand? That's what you paid for her."

Sindhu roared with laughter. "Sardar! You're a smart man. I didn't buy her just to sell her to you. I'm running a business here."

"So take the money I give you and buy another woman! I'm ready to give you two thousand. You'll be able to buy two women with that."

"Sardar, you can offer me lakhs of rupees, and I'll still refuse to sell

Kamala. The girl is a gold mine. Since she came here, my business has been thriving," Sindhu said.

Balbir went on with his appeals, raised his rate to three thousand, even begged her. But Sindu would not budge.

Balbir came back into my room, disappointed. Our hopes that money could buy my freedom from Sindhu were dashed.

The next day, Sindhu came looking for me. "Kamala! Has that Sardar got you hypnotized?"

"You think I would let myself be fooled, *Didi*?" I said, feigning laughter.

"Don't be a sucker. These men are all cheats. He probably wants to buy you so he can turn around and sell you to an agent in Dubai. Don't trust him. Just be nice and get him to spend his money. Don't expect him to make you his wife. That'll never happen. His caste would never permit such a marriage. It's all lies!"

I was hurt when she said this, but when I thought about it that night, I had to admit that Sindhu might be right. It was because I trusted a man's word that I ended up in this hell. Suppose I trusted a man again just to be shipped overseas to an even worse fate?

* * *

I often saw Indrani near the toilet. Every time, she would beg tearfully, "Kamala, when are we going to get out of this hell? I cannot bear to stay here any longer!"

Since she was new in the establishment and very beautiful, she had many customers. She didn't get enough rest, and was always exhausted. "I want to die, Kamala," she told me once. "But in this place, they won't even allow me that."

Since Kirthi's escape, I had gained more trust in Nisha. She was a quiet girl—usually engrossed in a Hindi magazine—but she was very self-confident.

Because she had come into this profession by choice, she was not watched over strictly. She had permission to go up to the top floor and look down on the streets. Only women who came here by choice had this privilege; it was the way the establishment advertised itself. Also, Nisha was allowed to go out into the street to buy fruit. We were very jealous of these freedoms of hers. In the evenings, whenever a customer chose one of us, we would have to move immediately to his side. But Nisha might just wave him off, until a customer she was interested in came by. We never understood how it was that the Madam allowed her so much liberty. Her only friends were Hindi-speaking girls.

Naturally, we had assumed from all this that Nisha was proud and selfish. But then it was she who had helped Kirthi. I started to think that if I got to know her well enough, she might help me escape, as well. But it was nearly impossible even to see her. When she was there, she was usually surrounded by her friends.

One day, Nisha spotted a bangle vendor on the street and went out to buy some. It was around three in the afternoon. I took a break from putting on my make-up and went down to the hall. When she came in with the bangles, I said, "Hi!" She replied with a smile and showed me the bangles.

"Very lovely," I said.

We chatted for a while. Then I told her, "I'm sorry, Nisha—I was wrong about you. Most of the Hindi girls are not friendly with us, but you are an exception. I'd like to spend some time with you."

"Me too, Kamala. Wait here for me, I'll go put these bangles away," she said, and ran up the stairs.

Even before she could return, Dolly appeared out of nowhere. "Kamala, what are gossiping about with Nisha?"

"I didn't start the conversation," I lied. "She was just showing me her new bangles."

Perhaps Nisha heard, for she came down the stairs just then, saying angrily, "Dolly! What are you threatening her for?"

"She was talking to you. It's my job to be strict with her."

"She didn't speak to me. I spoke to her," said Nisha.

"She's not allowed to talk to anyone. Sindhu Madam's orders!"

"Come on, she's allowed to talk to whoever she wants. Listen, Dolly, I know how you came here. I know all the pressure you were under and how you suffered after you got pregnant. So please don't go bossing everyone else around, or I'll report you to Sindhu," said Nisha.

It made me very happy to see Dolly put in her place like this.

Turning her back on her, Nisha took my hand and led me into the next room. "I have to talk to you, Kamala."

I was eager to hear what Nisha had to tell me. We went into an empty room. It was only three in the afternoon, and the place wasn't open for customers yet. Nisha sat down on the bed, but it had a foul smell, so instead we sat on the floor.

"Kamala, it seems like you girls from the South all hate me. I tried to get to know you, but most of you avoid even looking at my face. Even after I helped Kirthi, nobody trusts me."

"Of course it's not like that, Nisha," I protested. "I wanted to get to know you too. But we're scared of the Hindi girls. And anyway, Dolly doesn't allow us to talk to you. We are very grateful for your help to Kirthi, and we promise to keep it a secret."

"I don't like it when a girl is forced into this profession," said Nisha. "It troubles me deeply when they abuse girls here. I shut my ears tight. When they were beating you, I had to leave this place for a while. There are some here who take pleasure when someone is hurt. Thank God, you're under Sindhu's charge. If you had Nirmala as your madam, you would have been even worse off. Both she and her husband are sadists! They love to watch girls get beaten black and blue. And the madam on the top floor is the worst. She even pushes her own man around. To get girls to comply with her demands, she'll starve them for three days, then feed them for three days, then starve them for three days again. That's her usual pattern of punishment. After two rounds of that, the girls usually give in."

While she was talking, I was agonizing: Should I ask Nisha to help me, or not? Finally, I decided to do it.

"Nisha, will you do me a favor?"

I was a little scared. I was waiting fervently for her reply.

"Do you want to escape?" she asked casually.

"Yes!"

"How do you expect to survive?"

"I'll return to my family."

"Ok. How are you going to do it? Do you need my help?"

I was embarrassed. I had no clue how to escape. I was hoping she would come up with something.

"I don't know. Can you tell me a way?"

Nisha thought for a moment. Then she said, "Kamala, did you know that since Kirthi escaped they've put a big lock on the main door?"

"No, I didn't know that."

"These days, the maid gets up at five in the morning, along with Sindhu. They watch every customer who leaves the building. So it won't be easy."

"That's why I need your help."

"I told you how I helped Kirthi escape. But I'm worried. If Madam comes to know about it, she'll kill me. And then there's Dolly, who already hates me; she's constantly watching, waiting for me to make a mistake. She'll get suspicious if she sees us together, too. So I won't be able to help you openly. Kamala, I need this place. I need it to survive. So I have to be careful. Please don't think I'm reluctant to help you. If you come up with a plan, I'll do my best to help," she said.

"Okay, Nisha. Can you post a letter for me when you go out?"

"Who will you write to?"

"My family."

"You're going to ask your family to come here and take you back, right?"

"Yes."

"But if you do, and your family lands up here with the police or something, it will affect everyone, including myself. Most of the girls in this building are here because this is the only way they can make an income. You will ruin all of that. And if Madam finds out that your family is coming to look for you, she'll hide you. They'll drop you by rope into the neighbor's house behind, and then have you moved to a secret place. No; the only way is for you to escape alone, like Kirthi did," she said.

She was right, of course. But I couldn't accept her argument about the establishment getting affected and the other women's source of income being wiped out. It's only because establishments like this one exist in the first place that hapless women like me are abducted and pushed into this trade. How many families have been destroyed by places like this?

292

How much suffering has been caused? But we could not speak openly about our hell. So I just nodded as though I accepted Nisha's argument.

* * *

There were a few other incidents around this time. Among us women who were thirsting for liberty, there was Yasho, who was mute, but also extremely beautiful. She was always smiling, but somehow sad-looking as well. She would communicate with us in sign language. She was from Maharashtra, but could understand Kannada.

One day she fell to the floor, clutching her stomach and groaning awfully. Madam Nirmala shut the windows so she wouldn't be heard. Yasho was writhing on the floor like a hurt animal. Her eyes were dilated, her face clenched in pain, and there was dark spittle on her lips.

"What happened, Yasho?" demanded Nirmala.

Yasho was not signing anything. Nirmala lost her patience and told the maid to hold Yasho still while she slapped her face again and again. Yasho only groaned louder. Finally the doctor was brought in. He checked her and said that she had taken poison, and gave her an antidote. The antidote made Yasho puke endlessly. I don't know what she had taken, but she was in agony for hours.

It was four in the evening. We were doing our make-up. Customers were streaming in. Along with the regulars that evening came a lot of young men, with heavy moustaches and sideburns. Some of them were constantly smiling. I learned later that it was because they were on drugs. Most of us women avoided these youths. Only the Bhutanese, Nepalese and Punjabi women would take them as their customers. But the men, of course, preferred South Indian women. They would beg the madam for us. But Sindhu would always tell the students, "Only if the girls want to!"

One day one of the students gave some white powder to a Nepali girl. There was music playing in the main hall. Suddenly the Nepali girl got up and started to dance. We were surprised—it wasn't any traditional style of dancing; she was just doing some strange, free movements. We had to bring her down by force. After that she slept for two days. We found out later that the student had given her LSD.

* * *

I finally met Indrani again, after a long time. She was puking in the washbasin next to the toilet.

"Indrani, what happened?" I asked, shocked.

"Don't get upset. I couldn't digest the korma, that's all," she said.

"Thank God! I was worried."

She washed herself and turned to me. She seemed to have lost weight. "Kamala, when will we get free? Are we stuck here forever? Can't you make some plan?" she asked, as usual. I tried to comfort her with a few words that I didn't believe in myself. Indrani was really having a hard time there. Her tiny frame, slim body and well-shaped figure put her in great demand with the customers; they were willing to wait in queue for her. She could never get any rest in the nights. Sometimes she even missed her meals. The call rang our constantly: "Indu, there is someone here for you…" Even in the morning hours, our only time to sleep, people would come for her. Once I saw Indrani woken up from sleep at ten in the morning. It saddened me greatly to see that.

One night at nine o'clock, having just finished with a customer, she came out into the hall only to find two more men waiting there. She tried refusing, but Dolly would not let her off. Indrani started towards the room, but after two steps, she collapsed. Immediately they dowsed her with water, gave her a cup of hot tea and pushed her into the room. It was no surprise that someone forced to live like a sex automaton kept losing weight.

We suggested that she try not to be so submissive, so that the customers would stop demanding her services. She tried following our advice, but because of her age, it was easy for the men to compel her.

"Don't worry," I said, trying to comfort her. "We'll be free soon."

She buried her head in my chest. "Kamala, they don't even give me time to digest my food. My body is falling to pieces. Will there be no end to this?"

I didn't know what to say. Tears welled up in my eyes. Just then another call came: "Indu, customer for you."

She was in Nirmala's group. If she were with us under Sindhu, she would not be under so much pressure. Sindhu was the kindest among the three madams in this establishment—maybe not *kind*, but she was better than the other two. We could say no to a customer if he was difficult. She gave us that much liberty, as least. If someone came during my rest hours, she'd say, "Sir, Kamala is fast asleep. Why don't you come later?" But Nirmala Madam was crazy for money.

One night Sindhu was throwing us a small party. Sindhu's husband, who was sitting next to me, slapped me on the back and said, "I'm going to marry Kamala. Kamala is the didi of this house from now. Not

Sindhu." Everyone, including Sindhu, laughed at that. Dolly did not come for this party.

After dinner, I went to leave my plate in the backyard. The full moon was visible in the tiny bit of sky there. Ah, how long it had been since I had seen the moon! I'd forgotten it even existed. Had that bright white face always glowed down on us? I stared and stared, happy and sad at the same time.

I've told you before about Balbir. I also told you that he wanted to take me away from here. Even after his attempt to buy me for three thousand rupees failed, he did not give up. We mulled over several different plans, but none seemed workable. Finally, I came up with the idea of throwing a binge that would cause enough distraction for me to get away.

"How much would a party like that cost?" he asked.

"At least five hundred."

He agreed. We planned for Balbir to come with three friends. Each of them would choose a woman and start drinking. Then we would invite Sindhu to drink with us as well. As soon as she got drunk and started dancing, I would slip out of the building. Once I was outside, I was to wait at the third lamppost down the street, where one of Balbir's friends would pick me up.

The plan was full of holes, but still, we decided to go ahead.

I think it was a Wednesday. I didn't know that Balbir was going to put our plan into action on that day; it had been almost two months since we had talked about it. Although he had visited during that time, he hadn't mentioned anything about escape.

Balbir and his three friends were sitting in the room next to the hall. The boy from the cycle shop brought up six big bottles of beer, glasses, and chickpeas. The friends came into hall and selected their girls. That was where they made the first mistake.

Everyone in the building knew that Balbir liked me. So there was no problem with me going to him, without even being asked. But one of the other friends had been told to choose Daya. Apparently she was in her room with a different customer—we hadn't known when Balbir and his friends would come—so the friend chose the wrong girl, one who looked a little bit like Daya. He had whispered in her ears to confirm, "Are you Daya?"—and for some reason she had nodded. Her full name was Sukanya, but we called her Suya for short, so maybe she heard it as Suya.

Anyway, when the women came into the room, I was shocked to see that Daya was not with them. Neither Balbir nor I knew what to do. We couldn't send this woman back and ask for Daya without arousing suspicion. So the party got off to a bad start.

But this was *my* escape bid, *my* chance to get free. If Daya missed her chance, that was just her hard luck.

We sat down together, and the party went into full swing. Balbir and his friends were laughing loudly; one of them started to sing; beer bottles were broken.

Balbir's friends had never been to a place like this before. Though he had warned them not too, they soon became smitten by the women. One of the friends was actually being seduced into following his girl into her room. Balbir got angry and raised his voice. "Sathya Singh, what are you doing? We only came here for a drink and some fun," he said, and glared at his other friends too.

It was past eight. I was expecting Sindhu to arrive any time. She could smell beer from miles away.

Two hours passed. Sindhu had still not arrived. Only if she came could we put our plan into action. We were counting on her to force us to buy more liquor, so the party would start to spread across the building and everyone would get drunk. I was worried that an excellent opportunity—and a lot of money—was about to be wasted.

It was half past ten when Sindhu finally came up the stairway. She was already drunk. Balbir invited her to join the party and offered her a beer, but she refused. "I've already had four drinks tonight!"

"Sindhu, I've brought the beer especially for you. How can you refuse? Is that really your capacity, just four drinks? Come on, take the glass." Everyone was trying to get Sindhu to drink, and before long, she did.

The noise level rose. More beer was bought in. The cycle shop boy was running up and down the stairway getting more liquor. The other girls on the floor all dropped in for a drink, and slowly, the whole building joined the party. Now they were switching over to whiskey. A glass was pushed into everyone's hand, whether they wanted a drink or not; everyone got tipsy. Sindhu's loud laughter crackled above the noise. We began to sing and dance. Balbir and his friends were determined to get all the girls drunk. As time went on, they even started mixing the beer and the whiskey. There was a steady supply of snacks, as well. The room was half full of empty beer bottles. There was no place left to dance, so we moved to the hall. A few of the women could barely even stand up.

Sindhu insisted that I share a drink with her. "Didi," I said, pushing it back at her, "Balbir has over a thousand rupees in his pocket. We can keep drinking till dawn!"

"You're a real pro, Kamala!" laughed Sindhu. "You really know how to milk the money out of a man! Yes, keep my glass full, and I'll keep drinking till his purse is cleaned out."

Balbir kept the booze flowing, sparing no expense. Sindhu was quite drunk, but she still wouldn't take her arm off my shoulder. I wanted to move away, but she wouldn't let me. Every time I squirmed she'd ask, "Kamala, where are you off to?" and hug me tighter.

Balbir had gone downstairs. The servants there were waiting for their share of the liquor. He made them wait at the landing, mixed a round of stiff drinks, and sent it down for them. After half an hour, he signaled to me that they were all sloshed. I was getting excited.

Then I remembered Nisha telling me the front door would be locked. If that was right, I needed to find the key; where could it be? Cautiously, I felt at Sindhu's waist for the keychain. On the right side, there was a bulge under her sari. Was that the key? I had to tell Balbir. But three new customers had come in with a bottle of rum, wanting to join the party. Balbir was busy fixing their drinks. He didn't notice my excitement.

Sindhu was drunk, yes, but not completely out. By now her legs were on my lap, her sari in disarray, and she was ordering the girls around: "Don't stop till you've milked them for their last coin." The men who had just come in were staring at her and laughing amongst themselves.

I saw Renu sitting in a corner with a glass of beer, giggling to herself. She had her own style of drinking. Dolly was there too, getting drunk. Her baby was whimpering beside her.

There were two men in the hall who were not partaking. They were Indrani's customers, who had both come hoping to spend the whole night with her. Balbir kept inviting them for a drink, but they refused. He was still too busy serving drinks to the others to talk to me.

Finally, Indrani emerged from her room to see off her customer. (Everyone follows that ritual here. Some girls even go to the front door to give a parting kiss.) The two men waiting for her jumped up, and each one grabbed one of her hands. She was already exhausted, and this made her wild. She knew very little Hindi, so she took off in English. Hearing the raised voices, Sindhu looked up. This was my moment to escape her grip. I rushed to Indu and said to the men in Hindi, "What are you, animals? Can't you give her a minute?"

Then I told Indrani, in Kannada, "Hurry up and choose one. There's more than enough liquor here—get him drunk, and then you can sleep peacefully."

I went to Balbir and told him to look out for the key. By then Sindhu was calling me back. "Kamala, come here. I want to sleep on your lap."

I couldn't refuse. I went back to her and Sindhu curled herself around me. Then I caught a glimpse of the key peeking out from her right hip. Aha! I looked up at Balbir. He had seen it too. But how would we get it away from her?

Indrani's customers had launched into a verbal war. She had selected one, but the other insisted that he had come first, and started a fight. Balbir and Sindhu got up to try and sort it out. Indrani sat down next to

me. "Indu," I said, "I'm going to try to get away tonight. If I make it, I'll get the rest of you out as well. Tell me, where is Daya?"

"She has a customer for the whole night."

"Will you tell her that I'm going?"

"Of course I will."

By then Sindhu had managed to end the argument by throwing both of the men out of the building. They went off grumbling, "There's no justice in the world!"

"Have some beer," I told Indrani. "Not much, just have a glass. Your body needs it." Renu always told us that we should have a glass of beer between customers to keep ourselves fit for the trade. Initially Sindhu had to force me to take a drink, but by now I would do it myself. I still couldn't stand the smell, though.

Balbir was already dancing in the hall with the others. Everyone was smashed, and the dance was wild. He tried to get Sindhu to join, but she protested. "Leave me alone, I'm tired," she said. He dragged her to the dance floor anyway.

Everyone started to clap, and she danced around them like a demon. Finally she staggered back to me and again flopped onto my lap. She had passed out. I took advantage of the moment to slip the key out from her sari and hide it under my leg. I looked around nervously, wondering if someone had seen me do it.

Balbir had. He came over to me on the pretext of giving me a drink and stealthily took the key. Ten minutes later, he signaled that he had hidden it near the door.

The song and dance continued until everyone dropped from exhaustion. They ate what they could and started looking for a place to crash. Dolly was already asleep. One Hindi girl switched off all the lights and put the night bulb on. Slowly, I held Sindhu's head up and tried to slide my leg out from under it. But she stirred. "Kamala, will you let me sleep?" she grumbled.

I couldn't believe she was still sober enough to talk. I sat back. Time was flying. Balbir was sitting against the wall looking at me. "Go on," he mouthed. I tried again, but Sindhu growled at me, "Kamala, sit still!"

I waited, and then tried once more. This time she just opened her eyes wide and glared at me. Silently, I sank back.

Everything was ruined. Now I had no escape.

TAMILVANAN

Tamilvanan (1921-1976) was the founding editor of the hugely influ-
ential magazine *Kalkandu* (the name means "sugar crystals"), which
published fiction, articles about state politics and the world of cinema,
and pages of factoids. His wildly popular, globetrotting sleuth Shankarlal became an icon in 1960's and 70's Tamil Nadu; the character
inspired several films and television serials, and his trademark black hat
and black sunglasses sparked a fashion craze. Tamilvanan was closely
associated with the Dravidian socio-political movement of his times,
and despite the foreign settings of the Shankarlal stories and the sometimes obvious influence of the James Bond films, his language is pure
Tamil, eschewing even the most common English loan words in favor
of their sometimes obscure Tamil equivalents.

TOKYO ROSE

டோகியோ ரோஜா (1967)

Tokyo, capital of Japan! The cars seemed to outnumber the people.
A few pedestrians, having parked their cars on the side of the road,
went about their shopping like pretty butterflies. The roads were jammed
full of automobiles of many different makes and models.

One of them was driven by Shankarlal, king of detectives, with his
beautiful wife, Indra, seated beside him. Indra was eyeing the shop windows as the car crept slowly forward. Shankarlal, irritated, loosened his
tie. The traffic jam was so bad it had taken over half an hour to move
just a furlong. The car in front of him stopped completely, and he cut
the engine.

The shop owners were just beginning to open their shops, displaying
their wares lined up in the windows.

"Indra," said Shankarlal. She turned towards him, smiling. "Looks like we might be spending the whole day here! It seems that every fourth person in Japan owns a car now," he continued.

"What's this road called?" Indra asked.

"The names of these Japanese streets are very difficult to remember—let alone the names of Japanese people! But at the last crossing we passed a signboard that said Mitsubishi Avenue. Didn't you see it?"

"I did see it, but I forgot it already," replied Indra.

The car ahead of them moved an inch. Shankarlal followed it.

"It's nine o'clock—people are in a hurry to get to work. The traffic will be backed up for another couple of hours," said Shankarlal.

"So let them be in a hurry. Why do we have to join the battle?" asked Indra. "We came here for a holiday."

Shankarlal had a good idea of what was coming next. He asked her anyway. "What do you want to do, Indra?"

"Let's just park the car here, and go into one of these shops and browse around for a while. The traffic will ease up by that time," said Indra.

Shankarlal laughed. "I've heard that there's nothing you can't find here on Mitsubishi Avenue. It's hard to resist. You're right, it'll be better than sitting stuck in this traffic."

He parked along the white line, and they got out. The car had been their first purchase upon arriving in Tokyo. Indra looked at it with pride. "*Athaan*, we must take this car back to India with us when we return," she said.

"I'm going to need to hire a separate cargo ship to take back all your purchases," he teased. He locked the car and they headed toward the shops.

The stores were stocked with everything from the latest car models to the newest games, and catered to tourists from all over the world. The salespersons were Japanese, well trained in Western etiquette.

Indra entered a toy shop. There were four beautiful saleswomen. One of them walked up to them, and gave a silent gesture of welcome. Shankarlal and Indra walked through the aisles eyeing the toys.

Another saleswoman was wiping away some invisible dust from a countertop with a wet rag. Suddenly, the rag turned blue! The woman's clothes turned blue too. Yelling, she rushed to a sink at the back of the store to wash. Blue water gushed from the tap.

Pandemonium broke out. Indra looked around fearfully, but Shankarlal remained calm. Another saleswoman had touched the countertop, and found her hands turning blue as well.

"What's going on? Why is everything turning blue?" wondered Indra.

"Be patient. Take care not to touch anything, or lean on the shelves," replied Shankarlal, and went to take a closer look.

Just then, loud screams were heard from the road outside. He rushed out. At the hotel next door there was a crowd of Japanese talking excitedly amongst themselves. Shankarlal went up to them. He could not understand exactly what was being said, but their panic was obvious. He peered into the hotel. On the tables were teacups with blue tea in them.

"What happened?" he asked.

"I don't know!" the agitated manager replied. "The tables have all been suddenly stained blue. The tea's turned blue too. The customers think I'm trying to poison them."

Shankarlal came back out and joined Indra.

"I'm scared to even stand here," said Indra. "The saleswomen have fled the shop! One girl was saying that this is all because of the nuclear experiments that America and Russia are carrying out; she said invisible particles of the atom bomb are floating in the air and turning everything blue. Could it be true?" she asked.

Shankarlal looked back at the road. A thick crowd had gathered. Terrified that another nuclear holocaust had hit, the people ran around in circles, gripped by abject fear. A man came rushing out of a barbershop, his face covered with foam. "The soap in the salon has turned blue!" he shouted. "It must be the atom bomb! No one who's touched the blue stuff will survive!" He took to his heels, not even pausing to wipe the foam off his face.

In the following few minutes, the cars lining the road disappeared. A police squad arrived and began making inquiries in the shops. Not knowing how to respond to the widespread terror, the police called on the fire squad for help. Fire trucks drew up, clanging their bells, but when they began to hose down the shops the water that gushed out from the tanks was blue. The policemen and firemen stood with their mouths hanging open, scared to move.

"Athaan, please! Let's get away from here! I'm frightened," said Indra.

Silent and determined, Shankarlal walked back to the car. The police commissioner had arrived; they ducked quickly into his vehicle to avoid being spotted.

Shankarlal sped away from the scene, never taking his eyes off the road.

"It's bizarre. Why did everything turn blue? Do you think it really could have been caused by an atom bomb?" asked Indra.

Shankarlal did not reply; he just concentrated on his driving. He turned the car down a side street.

"Where are you going? This isn't the way to our house," said Indra. The car turned again, down a narrow lane, and came to halt in front of an apartment building.

Shankarlal got out, and Indra followed. "Who are we visiting?"

"Just follow me. I'll explain later."

They climbed the steps. Shankarlal's leather-soled shoes made no noise. They walked up to the fourth floor, where he began checking the nameplates on each door. He stopped at a door which had a bicycle propped against the wall next to it. The nameplate read HIROSHI WAKIYAMA.

Shankarlal knocked. A thick Japanese voice replied from within, and the door opened. A man looked out at them curiously. Shankarlal shoved his way past him into the room. He seemed to be searching for something.

"What do you want? What are you looking for?" asked Wakiyama, in English.

Shankarlal did not reply; he walked straight into an adjoining room. On the floor was a blue sack, open at the mouth. Dark blue powder had spilled from the sack onto the floor.

Smiling, Shankarlal turned back to Wakiyama. "Did you come home just now, with this sack on the back of your cycle?"

"Yes," replied Wakiyama. "Why do you ask?"

"Because you have sent the entire city of Tokyo into a panic!"

"What kind of powder is that?" asked Indra.

"Indra, be patient. Mr. Wakiyama, am I correct in surmising that while you were riding down Mitsubishi Avenue, this sack fell off your cycle?" asked Shankarlal.

"Yes," replied Wakiyama, still not understanding what this was all about.

"And there was a heavy gust of breeze?" asked Shankarlal.

"Yes, you're right. The sack broke open and a lot of the powder spilled out. So what?"

"You should go have a look down Mitsubishi Avenue. You've nearly caused a riot. Everything there has turned blue! The fire squad has started washing the avenue down. The people are scared that it's nuclear fallout. When the powder fell on the road, it wasn't visible to the naked eye. But if even a tiny amount comes in contact with water, it turns the water blue."

Wakiyama laughed out loud. Indra still looked worried and confused.

Only Shankarlal stayed calm. "See? My hand has turned blue now, because of the sweat."

Wakiyama said with a smile, "You still don't get what it is?"

"Yes, I think I know."

"Tell me, then."

"Ink powder, correct?"

"Absolutely! I invented this stuff. The ink is bright and clear when mixed with water; the letters glow and can even be read in the dark. I had taken it over to a pen company, to try to sell it to them. But they rejected my invention. I was on my way back, disappointed, when it all happened as you said."

"I followed your cycle tracks. That was how I found you. Please contact the police immediately and tell them what happened. They might never guess this."

"I will, at once. Please tell me who you are. You both look very familiar, but I don't seem to recall your names. Do you visit Tokyo frequently?" asked Wakiyama.

Shankarlal replied with a smile, "I've been here a few times, but I don't think I've had the pleasure of meeting you before. I am Shankarlal, and this is my wife, Indra."

Wakiyama was taken aback. "Shankarlal? Really? The famous detective? Yes, I've often seen your photos in the newspaper! Now that I think of it, I did read that you were visiting Tokyo. Please, have a seat! I've heard you're fond of tea. We Japanese make the best tea in the world."

Excitedly, he rushed to kitchen to make tea. He lit the stove and then came back to make a telephone call. He spoke to the police commissioner for over five minutes, explaining what had happened.

He returned with three cups of hot tea. But just as Shankarlal was going to take a sip, the tea turned blue. He set his cup aside with a laugh.

"What's wrong?" asked Wakiyama anxiously.

"It's okay, Wakiyama. Just the effects of your new invention. I suppose this will last for a few more days—but not to worry. We should be going."

Shankarlal and Indra had rented a bungalow in the quiet suburbs of Tokyo. That evening, the police commissioner dropped by to thank Shankarlal for his help in solving that morning's mystery. Madhu, Shankarlal's elderly butler, served them tea. On seeing him, the commissioner asked, "So, you've brought Madhu along too? How about Kathrikai and Manickam, what have you done with them?"

"If we had brought them, we would have had to bring their wives along as well. Then we would never have been able to get any rest," said Indra.

After the commissioner had left, the telephone rang. Madhu answered the phone, but quickly put the receiver down and walked back to Shankarlal. "I don't think I'm of any use to you here in Japan. I can't understand a word of what the person at the other end of the line is saying! It's a woman's voice, but I don't know what she wants."

Indra took the call instead. The woman spoke rapidly in Japanese.

"What do you want? Please speak in English. Do you know English?"

"I do, I do. I'm sorry; I didn't even realize I was speaking in Japanese. Is this Indra? Shankarlal's wife?" the woman said in English.

"Yes, this is she. What do you want?"

"I need your help. You are the only ones who can help me now. I'm in very great danger. Please save me!"

"How did you get this number?"

"I'll explain that later. Please, promise that you will help me! I need to give you some important information."

"What kind of danger are you in?"

"There's no time to give you details. Please, will you please come to my house immediately?"

"Right now?"

"Yes, now! This very moment! You can save a woman's life. Please bring Shankarlal along."

"Why don't you go to the police?"

"That wouldn't be any use. Besides, I can't go to them…"

Even as the woman was speaking, there was the loud *rat-a-tat-a-tat* of a machine gun, the sound of shattering glass, and then a dull thud.

"Hello? Hello?" called Indra. But there was no reply, only the sound of a car speeding away.

"Athaan!" she shouted.

Shankarlal was by her side at once.

"Indra, what happened?"

"There was a woman at the other end who said she was in danger and wanted to see us at once. Then I heard gunfire. Now the line is silent," she replied fearfully.

"Don't disconnect the call. I will try to find out where the call was made from, using the other telephone in the bedroom."

Within a few moments, he learned from the telephone operator that the call was made from a public booth, at an intersection a mile away from their bungalow.

They ran out to the car. He tried asking Indra to stay behind, but to no avail. "I have to know who this woman is, and if she is safe. I'll drive, you tell me the way," she insisted.

Indra drove, and she drove fast. The bright street lamps bathed the city in light.

There was a crowd gathered at the shattered phone booth. Police vans were already at the scene.

"Is she dead?" Indra gasped.

"You stay in the car. I'll go and find out," Shankarlal told her, and hurried to the scene.

The police investigator recognized him. "Welcome, Mr. Shankarlal. I'm glad you're here in Tokyo, to help us with this murder case."

He looked inside the booth. A Japanese woman lay dead on the ground. Her back and the walls of the phone booth were riddled with bullet holes.

"Who is this woman?" he asked the policeman.

"We don't know that yet."

"Who are you waiting for?"

"For the commissioner. We've been told not to remove the body until he can inspect the scene of the crime. He should be here soon."

"Will you let me know as soon as you get some details about this woman? I am very interested in this case."

He rushed back to the car. The crowd had recognized him by now, and ran forward to shake his hand and get his autograph. He jumped into the passenger seat and told Indra to drive away fast.

"Why don't we wait for the commissioner?" asked Indra.

"We're just here as visitors in Tokyo. I don't want to step on any toes."

"How did the murder happen?"

"That's not difficult to guess. She was shot while she was speaking to you on the phone."

When they returned to their bungalow, Madhu asked, "*Thambi*, this is such a beautiful city, with such lovely people. How could such a horrible crime happen here?"

Shankarlal replied with a wry smile. "Madhu, you have not yet understood Tokyo. We must accept the fact that there are as many evil people here as there are good ones."

At that moment, the telephone rang. Madhu answered it apprehensively. He heard a male voice, speaking in Tamil, say he was coming to meet Shankarlal at once.

"Did he give his name?" asked Shankarlal.

"No, he didn't. But he sounded frightened," replied Madhu.

It was already ten, well past Indra's bedtime. Shankarlal often went to bed much later, staying up with a book. But tonight he was not interested in reading, and Indra was too rattled to sleep.

"I thought we came to Tokyo to rest and have a holiday," grumbled Indra, disgustedly.

Madhu intervened with a laugh. "I used to have the same complaint before Thambi got married. Now it's your turn. I seriously think that to get any real rest and relaxation, the two of you will need to travel to a deserted island somewhere. Even then the police may track you down for help."

"Madhu, people look to us when they are in danger. It is our duty to help them. People come running to me when they know I am the only one who can save them. But look what happened to this poor woman, this evening! She died before I could even find out her name. How can I rest until I find the killer?" asked Shankarlal.

"That woman is dead. She cannot be brought back to life. I have no doubt you will find the murderer. But I can't understand who this Tamil man could be, demanding to see you at this late hour," said Indra.

"Be patient," advised Shankarlal. "We'll find out soon enough." He was now expecting two visitors: the police commissioner and the stranger.

He stayed silent throughout his dinner. Shankarlal was used to crime scene investigations and dead bodies. He could drive the most horrible scenes out of his mind and casually sit down for a meal. But Indra was not so indifferent; had she laid eyes on the murdered woman, she would not have been able to eat.

Just as they finished their dinner, the doorbell rang. Madhu opened the door to reveal a man of about thirty—tall, with strong features, dressed in expensive clothes and shoes.

"I have come to meet Shankarlal. I called earlier."

Madhu let him in. When the stranger saw Shankarlal, he looked apologetic. "I am sorry to disturb you at this hour," he said.

Shankarlal could tell the man was greatly disturbed; he was sweating profusely.

"Can I get you some water?"

The man nodded. Madhu brought a glass of water, which the man drank in one gulp.

"You look as if you've had a good scare."

"It's true."

"What's your name?" asked Shankarlal.

"My name is Mudikondan. You've probably never heard of me in Tamil Nadu. But you would have heard of my wife. We came to Tokyo very recently," said the man.

"Who is your wife?"

He took a moment before responding. "Neelavalli, the film actress."

Indra sat up in surprise. "Neelavalli? I haven't missed a single one of her films! But when did she get married? I never read anything about that!" she exclaimed.

Mudikondan replied with a smile, "We got married three months back. But we kept it under wraps. We had planned to make an announcement after we returned from our honeymoon."

"But why would you keep your marriage a secret?" asked Shankarlal.

"Because that was what Neelavalli wanted to do."

"But why?"

"She was a little superstitious about it. She had an idea that her popularity would wane if the marriage was publicized. There are four of her films to be released over the next three months. She wanted the marriage to remain a secret until then," said Mudikondan.

"How funny! I thought secret relationships like that only happened in Hollywood. To think that our film stars are the same!" said Indra.

"But I can't keep it a secret any longer. I have come to beg for Shankarlal's help. I believe that my wife is in great danger."

"What's the trouble?" asked Shankarlal calmly.

"This morning we went shopping on Mitsubishi Avenue. There was a panic there about things turning blue. I asked her to remain in the car while I went to find out what was happening. When I returned, she had disappeared."

"And then?" asked Shankarlal.

"I thought that perhaps she had become frightened waiting there in the car alone, and had returned home. I got a cab and went back to my place. But she wasn't there."

"When did she come back?" asked Indra.

"She still hasn't. I don't know where she is! I contacted all the hospitals to find out if she had an accident or something, but it was no use. I read that you were here so I came to you for help."

"How did you know where to find us?"

"I bribed a newspaper reporter. Three hundred yen."

"Where do you think your wife is?"

"I think she's been abducted," said Mudikondan.

"Was she wearing a lot of gold?" asked Indra.

"She only wears a lot of gold on screen. She left all her costly jewels back in India."

"Was she carrying money?"

"A little change, perhaps. She wouldn't have been abducted for that. I am sure I'm going to be contacted soon by the kidnappers."

"So how did you come to the conclusion that she's been kidnapped for ransom?"

"This is my reason. A week ago, she appeared on television here and was interviewed about the Indian film world. That interview was telecast all over Japan. She had many visitors after that, especially Japanese women. She struck up a friendship with one of them—an insurance agent. Neelavalli found her charming."

"Did she ask Neelavalli to insure herself?"

"Neelavalli has already been insured for a huge amount in India. But this woman told her about a new scheme."

"What scheme?" asked Shankarlal.

"Everybody knows that Neelavalli is extremely wealthy. Because of that, there's always a risk of her being kidnapped. This woman offered a scheme whereby in such a case, the insurance company would pay the kidnappers to release her."

"How strange! How could the police allow such a scheme?"

"Without receiving a ransom, a kidnapper would not let the person escape alive. The police allow the scheme in order to save lives. Then, they set traps to catch the perpetrators after the ransom has been paid."

"What if the person is still murdered, even after the ransom is paid?" asked Indra.

"It could happen, after all," said Shankarlal. "They might kill her, fearing that she would be able to identify them."

Mudikondan was visibly shaken.

"That's why I need you. You have to help me get her back alive," he begged.

"Who knows that she has taken this insurance policy?"

"No one but me. The Japanese insurance saleswoman assured us that it would be kept confidential."

"How much has she been insured for?"

"70,00,00,000 yen. The policy is valid for the duration of her stay in Japan."

"You are convinced that she's been kidnapped. Well then, there's not much we can do until you are contacted," said Shankarlal.

Just then the telephone rang. Shankarlal answered it.

"Is this Shankarlal?" asked a Japanese woman at the other end.

"Yes."

"Listen carefully. Neelavalli is safe. Get the 70,00,00,000 yen ready within two days. I'll call again and tell you the drop spot; you'll come there alone and hand over the money. This is the only way you can help Mudikondan. Understand?"

"Yes," replied Shankarlal.

"The money should be brought in 100 yen notes."

"Yes. Can I ask your name?"

"My name?" she laughed. "My name is Tokyo Rose." Then the line went dead.

Shankarlal turned to Mudikondan. "They must have known you were here. They want 70 crore yen as ransom."

"What are we going to do?" asked Indra.

"I'm going to collect the money from the insurance company, and take it myself," said Shankarlal.

He took Mudikondan by the arm, and rushed with him to the car.

They drove to the Government Medical Hospital. There were a pair of police vans waiting outside. The policeman escorted Mudikondan alone into the hospital, while Shankarlal waited in the car. When Mudikondan returned, his face had gone pale.

"What is it?" asked Shankarlal.

"I had a look at the body. It's her—the Japanese woman, the insurance agent. They have riddled her beautiful body with bullets. How sad!" replied Mudikondan.

They drove away. After some time, Mudikondan broke the silence.

"Who could have killed that woman?"

"There's no way of knowing for sure yet," replied Shankarlal. "But I have a guess."

"Can you tell me?"

"She must have been killed by the same kidnappers who took your wife."

"I don't get it."

"I don't think it stayed a secret that Neelavalli had taken out this huge insurance policy."

"But we haven't told anyone!"

"I'm not saying you did. It could have been the Japanese woman herself who spilled the information. Maybe that was why she was killed, and your wife kidnapped. She must have called me earlier in an attempt to save herself."

On hearing this theory, a tremor ran through Mudikondan's body. "What do you plan to do next?" he asked.

"The kidnappers asked me to get 70 crore yen ready. You get in touch with the insurance company."

"You'll drop off the money yourself?"

"Any other option?"

"I am very grateful for your help and for your courage. I have faith that you will bring my wife back alive."

"Man survives because of faith. Come and meet me tomorrow."

"I certainly will. There is one thing I can't understand though. How could they have known that I had contacted you?"

"You'll understand very soon. Please note down your address for me," said Shankarlal.

When he returned home, Indra and Madhu were waiting eagerly.

"What happened? What did you find out?"

"Quite a few things! Mudikondan identified the dead Japanese woman as the insurance agent."

"What was the name of the other woman who spoke to you on the phone?" asked Indra.

"She said her name was Tokyo Rose. That's a well-known code name. During World War II there was a female radio announcer who went by that name—no one ever knew her real one."

"How strange! How can there be a connection between her and this case?' asked Indra.

"There is a connection. At the beginning of that war, Japan was victorious in many battles. That was because they had been preparing for war for a long time. They had spies all over the world, so Japan was informed in advance about the movements of the American and British troops. In Tokyo Rose's radio broadcasts, she talked openly about all the secrets the Japanese had discovered. It was Japan's way of thumbing their noses at the enemy; the Japanese thought it was a big joke. But America and Britain did not find it funny. This woman is teasing us with that pseudonym," explained Shankarlal.

A little while later, the police commissioner arrived.

"I've been expecting you. If you hadn't turned up soon, I would have called you myself," said Shankarlal.

"I heard that you went to the morgue," said the commissioner.

"I brought another person along with me: Mudikondan, an Indian, husband of the actress Neelavalli. She disappeared this morning. He suspected that she had been kidnapped. While he was here, the kidnapper contacted me with the ransom demand," Shankarlal informed him.

"It's amazing how many people in Tokyo seem to know your phone number," laughed the commissioner. "We've verified that the dead woman was in fact an insurance agent. Her name was Tohiko Isawa."

"Was she married?" asked Shankarlal.

"Yes. Her husband seems to have been very much in love with her. He was devastated at the hospital. They were married only a few months ago."

"What is her husband's name?"

"Sutomu Takaya."

"What does he do?"

"Presently, he's unemployed."

"Why?" asked Shankarlal.

"The wife was earning good money. So he felt he didn't need to."

"Maybe he decided not to work because he wanted to do the cooking at home," Indra suggested.

"Nothing like that. I think he's just an idle sort of chap," said the commissioner.

"We should keep an eye on him," said Shankarlal. "There is every chance that Isawa told him about Neelavalli's insurance policy."

"True," agreed the commissioner.

"Do you suspect that *he* is behind the kidnapping?" Indra asked her husband.

"It could be! Isawa called us for help. He could well have knocked her off," said Shankarlal.

"Then why don't you arrest him?" Indra asked.

"Not until Neelavalli has been found," replied Shankarlal.

"Is there any proof that she actually has been kidnapped?" asked Indra.

"I'm still guessing. We have to find out what happened to her car," said Shankarlal.

"I'll make inquiries about abandoned vehicles, and let you know if anything comes up," said the commissioner.

When the commissioner left, Shankarlal called the number Mudikondan had given.

"Mudikondan, I need some facts."

"Please ask," said Mudikondan.

"What kind of car was your wife in?"

"A Datsun—a Japanese car. We bought it here."

"What's the license number?"

Mudikondan told him.

Half an hour later, the telephone rang, and Shankarlal answered it. It was the police commissioner. "We found the Datsun abandoned at the foothills north of Tokyo, thirty miles from here."

Shankarlal thanked him.

"We're going to give you control of this case. Tell me the next step."

"Come over tomorrow evening, and I'll tell you my plan," replied Shankarlal.

"So what are you going to do?" Indra asked him the next morning.

"I'm going to wait until Tokyo Rose gets in touch. Anyway, the insurance company will need a day to get the cash ready."

Shankarlal's patience was legendary. He never broke a sweat. As he got up, his cowlick flopped forward into his eyes.

Indra laughed. "You may be able to handle an army of criminals, but not your own hair."

"I'm going to check Neelavalli's house and Isawa's house. I'll be back soon," he said as he left.

Mudikondan was not expecting such an early visit from Shankarlal. Neelavalli's bungalow was huge and luxurious. There were many Japanese servants and maids buzzing around. Shankarlal guessed that the rent must be astronomical. But then, Neelavalli was a film star. It was not really surprising that she would require such luxury.

"I came to see Neelavalli's room," said Shankarlal.

The room was beautiful, befitting a princess. Such a lavish room for such a short stay! Shankarlal noticed the costly upholstering of the furniture, and the jasmine perfume on the dressing table.

When he came out he saw a Japanese servant sweeping up cigarette butts from the floor. Shankarlal laughed. "So, you didn't get much sleep, I take it?" he asked Mudikondan.

"How could I? I don't think I will sleep until Neelavalli is back safe. I smoke cigarettes the way you drink tea."

"Why is it that you have so many servants?"

"My wife had too many visitors; we needed all these servants to take care of all the guests. But I don't need them anymore. I'll send them off today," replied Mudikondan.

"I've made arrangements with the insurance company, to collect the cash. Then we'll wait for the next call."

"I hope you don't run into any danger," said Mudikondan.

"My car will be wired by the police. They will follow a mile behind me."

"I'm happy with the plan. But, you must make sure that this brings no further danger to Neelavalli," Mudikondan requested.

"I will take full responsibility for that," Shankarlal reassured him.

Next, he went to check on Isawa's house. It was a tiny one, surrounded by a neatly kept lawn. There were two constables outside. He took their permission before entering the house.

Inside, Takaya was reading at the table. Rising, he asked, "Are you Shankarlal?"

"Yes."

"Please, you must help me. I have lost my wife—but the police are keeping me here under house arrest. Please tell me who killed my wife. I will avenge her death myself!" he sobbed.

"I'll do my best. Can I see Isawa's room please?" asked Shankarlal.

It was a simple room, but modern and comfortable. Shankarlal noticed a lingering scent of jasmine. He saw a handkerchief under the bed. He picked it up and sniffed it. Jasmine! But here, on the dressing table, there was only one bottle of perfume—rose. Neelavalli must have been here, recently. But why?

He returned home without a word to anyone.

The promised telephone call came that night—it was Tokyo Rose on the line. "I hope the cash is ready. You can start now. Come alone. Take the highway west out of Tokyo for forty miles. You will find a big rock outcropping on your left. There will be a note left for you there which will instruct you how to proceed."

"I'll start now. What about Neelavalli?" asked Shankarlal.

"We'll return her to you by tomorrow morning. But you must ensure the cash is there in full. And no one should accompany you. Understand?"

"Yes."

Shankarlal put the bag of money in the back seat of his car. He switched on his wireless set, and informed the police of his plan.

Behind him, three unmarked police cars followed at a distance.

Forty miles further on, Shankarlal got out of the car to search around the rock. Eventually he found the note, written in English. "Drive north. Stop when you have driven twenty miles. But tell the policemen following you that they must go south, or you'll all be in great danger."

Back in the car he told the police over the wireless, "I'm supposed to head south. Meet me twenty miles from here."

But he turned to the north instead. Twenty miles ahead he slowed down; the car was traveling up a rocky incline. Suddenly he heard a sound from the back seat of the car, but before he could turn around, he felt a pistol pressed against his neck. He did not look around at the person in the back seat.

"Who are you?" he asked. He got no reply. He brought the car to a halt. Silently, his right hand moved to the door handle; with a sudden move, the door flew open and Shankarlal rolled out of the car to the ground. The pistol went off. Shankarlal jumped to safety behind the rocks. The person who had been hidden behind him clambered into the front seat and drove off at a great speed.

The police cars that had been sent in the opposite direction had realized by now that Shankarlal was missing. Coming back up the road, they met the detective walking down the hill.

"What happened? Why are you walking?" asked the commissioner.

"The kidnappers got the money. I rolled out of the car to avoid being shot," said Shankarlal.

"Are you hurt?"

"No. Let's go."

"What? Don't you want to chase down the kidnapper?"

"No. I know who it is. Tomorrow Neelavalli will be back, safe."

"How do you figure?"

"Wait and see. Let's meet tomorrow, early morning. You'll have a few surprises waiting for you."

The following morning, Neelavalli's house was buzzing with excitement. Neelavalli was home and safe, and her husband welcomed the police commissioner and Shankarlal with a smile. "Thank you so much for bringing my wife back!" Mudikondan exclaimed.

"And I must thank you for saving my life," said the actress. "When the kidnappers took me from Mitsubishi Avenue, they forced me to drive the car at gunpoint. I got a look at the man holding the gun, but after that, they kept me blindfolded—I didn't see anyone else. But Shankarlal, why didn't you bring Indra along?"

Shankarlal replied with a smirk. "Initially Indra did want to meet you. But this morning, she decided she could wait, and meet you later—in prison."

"What? Prison?" squawked Neelavalli.

"That's right."

"Why would we go to the prison?" Mudikondan demanded.

"You know very well why. But the commissioner still doesn't, so I'll explain. You've been living a very lavish life here in Japan. The Indian government does not allow endless foreign exchange to be taken out by Indian tourists. Even I was only allowed a limited amount. That's why I brought Madhu with me, rather than hire Japanese servants."

The commissioner interrupted him. "But you are our guests here! We would have been happy to give any assistance you needed."

"I know, but it wouldn't be fair for me to accept. Anyway, Neelavalli was in a cash crunch here. It was around this time that Isawa sold her the insurance policy. Takaya came to know about it; his wife was unaware of his criminal connections. He contacted the Indian couple and together they came up with a scheme to make an easy 70 crore yen. He thought his wife Isawa would cooperate with the plot, but she turned out to be an honest woman. When Neelavalli was being kept hidden in her house, Isawa threatened to go to the police. Then she reconsidered; if she went to the police, her husband would go to jail. So she called me instead. That was when Takaya, her own husband, shot her down in cold blood.

"Then he shifted Neelavalli to a new location. They abandoned the Datsun and moved her in with Takaya's gang. Now Mudikondan made his move; he contacted me and gave me this tale about his wife being kidnapped. He prearranged the Tokyo Rose call. I didn't figure it out until I saw a handkerchief, scented with jasmine, in Takaya's bedroom. If he had forcibly kidnapped her, then there's no way he would have taken her to his own house."

"So where's the money, then?" asked the commissioner.

"Not to worry. Takaya was under house arrest, so it must have been Mudikondan who snuck into my car while I got out to find the note. Therefore, the cash must be in his possession," said Shankarlal.. "I'm sure it's right here in this bungalow! Arrest these two, please. They're now your responsibility," smiled the king of detectives.

He strode away, ignoring Neelavalli's screams: "Please don't arrest us. We'll return the money!"

PRAJANAND V. K.

The three monthly publications *Great Novel, Best Novel,* and *Everest Novel,* which nearly always carry stories by Rajesh Kumar (and occasionally Indra Soundar Rajan), have a fixed length of 144 pages. If the Rajesh Kumar story is not quite long enough to fill those pages, the publisher looks for short stories to pad the book. Some of these come from Prajanand V.K., an ardent Rajesh Kumar fan and writer who submits his writing in envelopes with no return address. At the time of the first printing of this anthology, his identity was unknown; we are happy to announce that he has since come forward, revealing himself to be an 18-year-old college student from Coimbatore.

His disarmingly simple crime fiction stars Sasivaran and Sabapathy, two police detectives with a sense of logic and morality all their own.

A MURDER AND A FEW MYSTERIES

ஒரு கொலை சில மர்மங்கள் (2005)

IT WAS MORNING. The telephone rang softly, and Inspector Sasivaran pressed the receiver to his ear.

"Yes, hello... police station?"

"Yes."

"Sir, this is Dr. Hemanth Kumar speaking." The voice sounded strained.

"Tell me, is there a problem?"

"Sir, my wife Uma has been murdered in her room."

"What?" Sasivaran shot up. "I'll be there at once." He banged the receiver down and walked out. Sub-Inspector Sabapathy, who had been browsing through a file, got up from his desk and followed him.

The bungalow was huge, surrounded by tall trees, and must have been designed by a gifted architect. But there was no time to appreciate that now; this was the bungalow in which Uma was lying dead. Nallamuthu, the watchman, opened the gates, and Sasivaran's jeep came to a smooth halt in the portico. The story is warming up now!

Sasivaran and Sabapathy got out of the jeep and entered the bungalow.

Hemanth Kumar was seated on a sofa in the living room, drenched in sweat. His eyes were wet.

"Where is the body? Which room?" inquired Sasivaran.

"Please come this way." Hemanth led them into a room on the left. Uma was on the cot, a nylon rope tied tightly around her neck. The telephone receiver near the cot was hanging off the hook.

"Sir, I was away in Delhi for two days, attending a conference on heart surgery. Uma was alone here. The murderer must have used that opportunity," said Hemanth, with labored breath.

"And your watchman?"

"He was here, sir."

"So if we question him, we can find out all the visitors who have come to the house over the last two days. I'll do that right now." Sasivaran moved to the gate.

Nallamuthu threw away the beedi he was smoking when he saw Sasivaran.

"Hello, sir!"

"Ahem. Did anyone come to visit Uma in the last two days?"

"Yes sir. Madam was visited by her brother Ganesh and her friend Malathi."

"Just the two of them?"

"Yes, sir."

"Would you suspect either of them?"

"Oh, no, sir! Both are lovely people. They would never dream of doing such a thing."

326

"We're not looking for character certificates from you," snapped Sasivaran. "That's what *we* are here for, to find out if they are good people are not," he said, and returned to the bungalow.

"Sabapathy, have you finished the formal enquiry with Hemanth?"

"Yes, sir."

"Have you informed the press?"

"Yes, sir."

"Have you searched Uma's room thoroughly? Did you find anything out of the ordinary?"

"Except for the telephone receiver hanging off the hook, everything seemed undisturbed, sir."

"Fine. Let's go." Sasivaran walked towards the jeep.

At the police station, he took out the post-mortem report, gave it a glance, and then looked over at Sabapathy.

"This report is completely useless," he said.

"Why?" asked Sabapathy.

"It says she was strangled by a nylon rope. But there are no fingerprints on the rope or her body."

"Shit!" sighed Sabapathy. "So where do we go from here?"

"Two people came to visit Uma. One was her friend Malathi and the other her brother Ganesh. Let's begin the investigation with the brother," said Sasivaran.

Ganesh's eyes were red and fiery with two days of continuous crying. Sasivaran and Sabapathy were seated in front of him.

"Tell me, Ganesh. Who, in your opinion, could have murdered your sister?"

"I swear, I have no idea. My sister was a wonderful woman. If I ever catch the murderer, I'll chop him to pieces with my bare hands!"

"Ganesh, I think you are a talented actor."

"What? What do you mean? Am I acting?"

"Yes, I think you are! Before coming here I met your family's lawyer.

It just so happens that according to your father's will, if Uma dies before you do, you stand to inherit everything. Am I right?"

"Yes… and so what?"

"So, we think you could be the murderer. On that premise we are going to arrest you. Please come with us."

"Sir, I swear, I did not murder Uma! Please believe me! Please don't arrest me, please!" Ganesh sobbed.

"Now look here, Ganesh, we're only arresting you on suspicion. But if you refuse to cooperate then we'll have to get tough."

Hearing this, Ganesh changed his attitude immediately, and walked along with the policemen to the jeep.

"Sir, I don't think Ganesh could have been the murderer," declared Sabapathy.

"Why not?"

"Everyone I've questioned describes him as a very kind and generous man. He's been doing a good job of running his late father's business—they have a huge turnover and a healthy bank balance. Above all, he loved Uma very much. For her wedding, he gave her a new Maruti car. How can you be sure that such a man would have murdered his own sister?"

"I realize all that, Sabapathy. It is not as if I found any strong evidence against Ganesh, either. So there is an 'X' involved in this murder."

"And we have to apprehend that 'X'."

"Ahem. Yes. There are many mysteries hidden behind this murder of Uma. We will have to solve them first."

"Sir…. Whom shall we question next?"

"Uma's best friend, Malathi…."

Malathi began to weep the moment Sasivaran told her about Uma.

"Please control yourself, Ms. Malathi."

"Sir, Uma and I were classmates in college. She was a beautiful person. She had a lot of friends. How could anyone have murdered her?" she dabbed her eyes with her handkerchief.

"Ms. Malathi, we have a few official questions to ask you. But we can't do it here. Can you come to the police station?"

"Sir, I am supposed to get married next week. It won't look good if I have to go to a police station a week before my wedding."

"Fine. I just have one important question. Why did you go to see her?"

"To invite her for my wedding."

"Fine. We'll take our leave, then." Sasivaran and Sabapathy got back into their jeep.

"Sir, does that mean we do not have to worry about Malathi anymore?"

"No. Make sure Constable 502 is watching her movements."

"Yes, sir!"

A week went by. Ganesh swore that he had visited Uma only to present her with a diamond ring for her birthday. The police later found the ring still in Uma's room, which seemed to confirm his story—much to his relief.

Next, Malathi. An invitation to her wedding was found on the living room table. There being no incriminating evidence against her, she was also dropped from the list of suspects.

Sasivaran felt like his head was about to burst.

"Sabapathy, I had asked Uma's body to be photographed from every angle. Have you collected those photographs?"

"Yes sir, I have." He handed a plastic folder over to Sasivaran.

Sasivaran carefully looked at each photo. When he came to the third photo, a bulb finally switched on in his brain.

He stared and stared at a tiny object under the bed on which Uma was lying, spread out on her back.

"Sabapathy, you missed an important clue while you were searching Uma's room."

"Is that right? I was very meticulous, I thought."

"Yes, you searched carefully. But the clue was small and well hidden, so you missed it. Anyway, I've found it now. And it has revealed the real murderer."

"What do you mean, sir? You know who committed the murder? Who, sir?"

"You'll get your answer soon. First bring the jeep around. We have to catch him before he absconds!" Saying this, he ran to the jeep. The jeep sped away like Arjun's arrow.

Nallamuthu, the watchman, was sobbing in the lock-up. His eyes were red and swollen.

Inspector Sasivaran lifted his chin with the end of his *lathi*. "Look here, Nallamuthu; we know that you are the murderer. You'll want to know how we cracked the case, of course. Well, when Sabapathy first searched the room, he missed the clue. Hemanth Kumar, Uma's husband, was out of town then. We questioned her brother, Ganesh, and her friend, Malathi. We found them innocent. It was only when we looked at the photos of the crime scene that I found the clue—even though it was well-hidden under the bed. It was the butt of a beedi!

"Uma's husband is a heart surgeon. He couldn't possibly be a smoker, as he is aware of the evil effects. Even if he occasionally did smoke, he would certainly smoke high-class cigarettes, not beedis. Uma's brother Ganesh doesn't smoke. That leaves Malathi. She is a woman, an *Indian* woman! An Indian woman will not touch a cigarette—why, she will never even venture into a smoking zone! The only person who smokes in that house is you, and you smoke only beedis. Now tell me, why did you murder Uma?"

When Nallamuthu remained silent, Sasivaran gave Sabapathy a look. Sabapathy understood, and rapped Nallamuthu's kneecap once with his lathi. He screamed, "Sir, don't hit me—please! I'll tell you everything."

Sasivaran lit a cigarette and sat back to listen to him.

"Sir, I have worked like a dog for Uma Madam for four years. One day my mother had a chest pain. The doctor said she needed surgery, and that it would cost fifty thousand rupees. He insisted that she must have the operation within a week, or else she would die. I didn't know what to do! I begged Uma Madam to lend me that fifty thousand, and asked her to take it from my salary in installments. She refused. My mother died after a few days.

"I was furious. If she had helped me in my moment of distress, I could have saved my mother. But she didn't. I resolved that the person who had caused my mother's death should not remain alive. I read plenty of crime novels. I took the idea of using gloves from them. When her husband went out of town, I had my chance. I went into her room with a nylon rope. When she saw me, she knew what I intended to do. She tried to call the police. I knocked the receiver out of her hand, pinned her on the bed and strangled her with the rope till she died. I always smoke a beedi when I'm tense. I even entered Uma's room with a beedi hanging on my lips. It must have fallen there while I was strangling her," sobbed Nallamauthu.

"That's it," said Sasivaran gleefully.

"Not bad, sir. Even a beedi is useful in solving a mystery," congratulated Sabapathy.

A press reporter had a question for Sasivaran, "Sir! I'm Kannan, from *Minnal Oli* magazine. I had asked you last week if you would write a serial on your investigations for our journal. Do you remember?"

"Yes… of course, I can oblige."

"Which case do you want to begin with?"

"My latest investigation, of the murder of Dr. Hemanth Kumar's wife, Uma."

"What will you title the report?"

"*A Murder and a Few Mysteries!*"

REVENGE

ரிவெஞ்ச் (2007)

by PRAJANAND V.K.

THE OPEN GROUND was bordered by huge cardboard poster cutouts of Minister Jagatratshagan, shown smiling with his palms folded together. Over five hundred of his party cadres were gathered there, all wearing the party uniform. Jagatratshagan roared into the microphone.

"The opposition accuses me of having no respect for my cadres. I have just one thing to say. Listen to me; I have signed over my life to this party. I am the property of my cadre!" The air thundered with applause.

From the top of a building across the ground, a pair of eyes watched the drama unfold. The watcher held a state-of-the-art rifle in his hands.

"The opposition also says that I view women as mere sexual objects," Jagatratshagan continued. "How can they fling such accusations at me? I am a man who accords all the women of Tamil Nadu with the same respect as I do my own mother." The crowd clapped once again.

Anger raged in the heart of the man watching him in the crosshairs. *If you respect every woman as you would your mother, then what did it mean when you raped my Nirmala?* He chewed his nails furiously, and aimed the rifle at Jagatratshagan's heart.

"Every single woman of Tamil Nadu is as my mother, my Goddess!" cried Jagatratshagan passionately.

No! You cannot be permitted to go on with these lies. I, Nirmala's brother, will not allow you to deceive the people any longer! He made the decision— and pulled the trigger. The bullet rocketed straight into Jagatratshagan's heart. Jagatratshagan collapsed in a pool of blood, as his security guards and the crowd watched stunned.

All around Jagatratshagan's body, forensic officers were searching with their magnifying glasses for clues. Press photographers clicked their cameras from every angle of the scene. Commissioner Dhanapal turned to Sasivaran and Sabapathy, who saluted him. "You have exactly a week to catch whoever did this. Any longer and the case will be moved to Delhi. That will mean big trouble for us." With that, he walked away.

Sasivaran approached one of the forensics officers. "Have you found anything?" he asked.

"Sir, the murderer aimed straight for the heart. The bullet has not penetrated very deep, but it has caused a great loss of blood. We can't see the back of the bullet yet, but once we retrieve it, I'm sure it will turn out to be from a foreign gun. Beyond this, we just have to wait for the post-mortem report."

"Ok," shrugged Sasivaran, letting his eyes roam over the ground. He did not think that the murderer had been standing among the cadres; shooting a minister down from the middle of a crowd of five hundred and escaping unhurt would have been impossible. He gazed at the one tall building that stood near the ground like a lonely orphan. A bulb switched on in his brain. "Sabapathy, let's go over to that building," he said, walking towards it. Sabapathy followed him, puzzled.

On the terrace of the building, Sasivaran asked, "Sabapathy, you can see the platform on which Jagatratshagan was speaking clearly from here, can't you?"

Sabapathy took a good look before he replied, "Yes, sir."

"My guess is that the killer aimed from here."

"Looks like it, sir."

"Let's search this place thoroughly. We might find some clues."

They explored for over an hour, but found nothing useful, and returned disappointed.

Sasivaran sat in front of Jagaratshagan's personal assistant.

"Your name?"

"V. Arumugam."

"Mr. Arumugam, do you know if the minister had any enemies?"

"Every member of the opposition is his enemy!"

"Leave the political parties out of it. Does he have any personal enemies?"

Arumugam thought for a while. "Not that I'm aware of."

"Ok. How long have you been his P.A.?"

"Just for the past two months."

"What happened to the previous P.A.?"

"She was a woman—her name was Nirmala. She died—I mean, she was murdered."

"What? Who murdered her?"

"Her brother stabbed her to death because she refused to give him money for liquor. The print media carried the story on the front page, sir…"

"Fine. I'll go now—but please let us know if you learn about any personal enemies the minister may have had."

He met Sabapathy outside.

"What does the minister's post-mortem report say, Sabapathy?"

"Nothing that will help our investigation much, sir. Because the bullet was lodged in the centre of his heart, he died on the spot. He lost over two litres of blood."

"Ok, Sabapathy, you may go. I need to go home to freshen up a bit."

He headed home. As he got off his bike, he noticed a piece of paper stuck to the compound wall of his house. He read it with growing alarm.

Dear Sasivaran,

You are trying to impede my goal. Please do not pursue this case; it won't turn out well for you if you do. If you don't give up your pursuit, then you will meet the same fate as the minister.

Sincerely Yours,
Jagatratshagan's Yaman

Two days passed with no fresh clue. Unable to sleep, Sasivaran turned restlessly in his bed. It was past one o' clock. *Who had the courage to come up to my compound and paste that poster on my wall? What did he have against Jagatratshagan? Why did he resort to murder?* The sound of a motorcycle broke into his restless thoughts. *Who could it be at this hour?* Taking his torch from the bedside table, he walked to the living room window and quietly pushed aside the curtain. A man wearing a helmet stood next to the wall with a sheet of paper in his hand. His bike was parked nearby. The man removed a bottle of glue from his pocket and calmly spread it on the poster.

Sasivaran's blood boiled. *He has come to warn me again. What cheek, to come right into the lion's cave!* Sasivaran moved to the back door.

The man was now pressing the poster onto the wall. He proofread the poster with his pen-torch again.

Dear Sasivaran,

I know that your wife and child have been sent out of town. I warned you two days ago, but you are still on this case. I know you are alone in the house. Either you let go of this case, or you will let go of your life, and leave behind a widowed wife and an orphaned child.

Sincerely Yours,
Yaman, hungry for a few more Jagaratshagans

Satisfied, the man turned with the pen-torch and was stunned to see Sasivaran standing there with a calm smile on his face.

The man attacked him, but Sasivaran soon overpowered him and knocked him unconscious. Sasivaran carried him into the house, laid him on the bed, and tied him up to the bedposts. He was still unconscious. Sasivaran brought a glass of water and poured some on his face. He slowly opened his eyes.

"Sir... sir... where am I?"

"It's not a police station, I promise you that. I never arrest anyone without proper investigation."

"I... my name is Vinod."

"Fine. Now tell me, why did you kill Jagatratshagan? You've claimed that you will kill many more Jagatratshagans; why?"

"Have you heard of Nirmala?"

"The minister's personal assistant? I heard that she was murdered by her brother."

"I am that brother, sir."

"What? You? Then you have committed two murders."

"No, no... I have killed only Jagatratshagan. I did not kill my Nirmala!"

"Can you explain, please?"

"Can you untie me?"

Sasivaran trusted the look in his eyes, and loosened the knots. The man leaned on the bedposts and began his story.

"Sir, my name is Vinod. Nirmala was my only sister. We lost our parents as young children. I worked in the mill, and put her through school myself. After her graduation, she joined Jagatratshagan as his P.A. I was already aware that he was a philanderer. I begged her not to take up the job, but she would not listen to me; the pay was too good. One day, the thing I feared most happened. She went to his room to get his signature for a file, and that monster molested her. Afterwards he pressed a few rupees into her hand and told her to keep it quiet. She came home heartbroken. I had just returned from work and was having my dinner.

In front of me, she burned the money Jagatratshagan had given her, and then she ran into her room with a knife in her hand, and locked herself in. I couldn't do anything but stand at the window sobbing, 'No, no, please don't...'

"My sister, through tears, told me what had happened. Screaming that she did not want to live any more, she stabbed herself to death, even as I stood there watching.

"Finally I broke open the door. Nirmala, the sister I had brought up with so much love, was now lying on my lap, gasping her last breath. She begged me not ruin my life by taking revenge on Jagatratshagan, but to go to the police and lodge a formal complaint.

"I wanted to fulfill her last wish. So I left her body at home and rushed to the station, wrote out a complaint and asked them to arrest that ogre. But by my bad luck, the inspector was one of Jagatratshagan's allies. He jailed me—me, an innocent man—on the charge of murder. He accused me of being an alcoholic and killing my own sister in a dispute over liquor money. I had tried to remove the knife from her stomach, and my fingerprints on the weapon worked against me.

"I was sentenced to life in prison. It was then that I determined that Jagatratshagan, who had destroyed my sister's life and my own, should live no more. I escaped from prison, procured a rifle from a friend who lives abroad, and shot him dead.

"But my vengeance is not complete. I have a list of politicians who have ruined the lives of many women to satisfy their sexual lust. I must annihilate each one of them to save women like my sister. This is my only goal. When I heard that you were investigating this case, I wanted to scare you off, so I put up the poster. You would not give up. So I tried putting up another poster, but you caught me. Come sir, let's go..."

"Where?" asked Sasivaran, with tears in his eyes.

"To the police station, sir," said Vinod.

"No, man! I cannot arrest you. You are free to go."

"Sir? But why?"

Sasivaran sighed. "Look Vinod... I, also, had a sister once. Her name was Tharangini. She died very young, of blood cancer. I remember how

337

hard it was to watch my sister dying from that horrible illness—I could not take it. But for you… your sister was molested and committed suicide right in front of your eyes! How could you possibly bear the pain?

"I believe what you have done was just. If no one had come after him, Jagatratshagan would still be preying upon countless other women. You have eradicated a poisonous weed. I don't think that what you have done is wrong.

"What would happen if I arrested you? I would be acting to protect all the politicians who disrespect and abuse women. How would that be in the nation's best interests?

"No—I believe you are a divine incarnation, born to rid this world of such pestilence. I do not want to impede your goal. But you must leave this place immediately. You never came to my house, I never saw you. Now go—and hurry!"

Vinod grabbed Sasivaran's hands. "Sir—Thank you," he cried. He put on his helmet, kickstarted his bike and fled.

The sun was up. Sasivaran looked at the clock. It was already seven. He had his bath and was dressing for duty when his cell phone rang.

"Hello, Sasivaran. Any progress in the case?" barked Dhanapal at the other end.

"No sir, no progress. I don't think I can crack this one. Please relieve me from the case."

"I don't believe I'm hearing this from you!"

"I'm sorry, sir," said Sasivaran. Not waiting to listen to the commissioner's response, he cut the call and dropped the mobile into his pocket.

Joke, from the inside back cover of *Best Novel.*

CUSTOMER IN A VEGETARIAN HOTEL:
   "Is Chicken 65 available?"

SMART-MOUTHED SERVER:
   "No, but Chikungunya is available.
   Shall I get you two plates?"

RESAKEE

R. M. Kumaravel, the publisher of *Great Novel, Best Novel,* and *Everest Novel,* is an unassuming man of wonderfully dry humor who runs his business out of a tiny one-room office up a narrow lane from Chepauk Stadium in Chennai. He sometimes needs to hunt for short stories to fill out the fixed number of pages of each of his monthly publications. If he's unable to find anything suitable, the publisher himself steps up to the need of the hour and pens a story of his own, using the name Resakee (formed from the first syllables of the names of his three daughters). The following is one such story.

GLORY BE TO THE LOVE THAT KILLS!
சாக வைக்கும் காதலுக்கு ஜே...! (2006)

✔ 1 ✔

CHENNAI. MYLAPORE DISTRICT. Sai Baba Temple. 10:00 A.M.
It was a Sunday, so the crowd was huge.

Sasi and Raghu waited patiently and piously for their turn in the queue.

Sasi was 24 years old, and beautiful. When she smiled, you wanted to spend the whole day just looking at her. She looked like an angel in her purple sari.

Raghu was 28 and very handsome, with curly hair, a wheatish complexion, and a heart of gold. He was completely smitten with his angel.

Both worked in the same office and—of course—were deeply in love with one another. They had come to the temple to pray that they would be able to unite soon in marriage without opposition from their families. They followed the queue into the main hall, prayed silently, and came out again.

"Raghu, when are you coming to meet my father?" Sasi asked hesitantly.

"Right now, if you're ready. Shall we go?"

"No, not yet, Raghu. I'll break the news of our relationship slowly. Then I'll let you know when you can approach him…."

"I don't understand you, Sasi. You've asked me a question and then answered it yourself! Listen, my mother is very old—she'll be no trouble to convince. The only possible trouble will come from your father."

"You don't have to worry about that. I'll get us past whatever trouble comes."

"Super! I appreciate your courage. Let's go for a coffee," he said, and started his bike. Sasi's mobile rang. She answered; it was her father.

"Sasi, where are you?"

"Appa, I'm at Baba Temple. Is there a problem?"

"No problem! I've arranged for a boy to come and see you at six this evening, after *Rahu kalam*. So don't go visiting your friends, get back home right away. Okay?"

Sasi put her mobile in the handbag and looked at Raghu.

"What's wrong, Sasi?"

"I don't know how to tell you this. Our troubles have just begun."

"I don't get it."

"A potential groom is coming to check me out this evening."

"Phoo! Let them come. You can always say you don't like the man."

"No Raghu, it's not that simple. If my dad takes a liking to him, then our affair is dead."

"So, what do you want me to do?"

"There's no other option now, Raghu. Let's go to my house and tell Appa about our affair."

"Okay! If you've finally found the courage, how can I chicken out? Come on, let's go and face your father."

Mandevalli. Sasi's house. 11:20.

They cautiously entered the house. Sivanandham, Sasi's father, was in the living room watching a talk show on Sun TV. He looked at them puzzled.

"Appa, this is Raghu. He works with me."

"Sit down, please," said Sivanandham, pointing to the sofa. Raghu sat down hesitantly. Sasi's mother, and her sister, Jyothi, came in from the kitchen. Sasi began to talk anxiously. "Appa, Raghu and I ..."

"Yes?"

"We're in love. We would like to get married."

Sivanandham sprang out of his chair. "What? Are you telling me you love *this* guy?"

"Appa, please be respectful."

"People only deserve respect if they know how to behave."

"Appa, this is about my life."

"There's a groom coming to see you this evening!"

"Please, ask him to stay away. I don't want to marry him. Say yes to this alliance, please!"

"Never! You think you can just drag any loafer in here, ask me to get you married to him, and expect me to agree? Do you think I'm an idiot?"

"I really don't care whether you agree or not, Appa. I want to marry him."

"It will never happen. Forget about it!"

"I'll never marry any other man."

"Then you won't see me alive!"

"Oh, stop threatening me, Appa! I've told you my wishes."

"What, you think this is an empty threat? If you can be so adamant, just imagine the adamancy of your father!" Saying this, he ran to the writing desk, opened the drawer, took out a medicine bottle, and poured the contents into his mouth.

At once, a big scene broke out amongst the members of the house. Sasi's mother beat her stomach and began wailing. Jyothi started to sob. Sasi ran to her father and begged him, "Appa, why did you do this?"

Raghu, realizing there was an emergency, rushed away on his bike and returned shortly with an auto rickshaw.

He and the auto driver put Sivanandham, by now unconscious, into the auto and hurried to a hospital close by.

◢ 2 ◣

Kariappa Hospital, Room 105.

Sivanandham sat on the bed, next to his wife, his daughters, and Raghu. The doctor entered the room.

"What is this, Mr. Sivanandam? You should be more sensible. You could have lost your life! You're lucky your family brought you here in time. Even ten minutes later, and you'd be dead. Please think carefully before you act in future, and take the medicines I prescribe." Turning to Sivanandham's wife, he continued, "You have nothing to worry about, Madam. You can take him home in the evening."

Sivanandham waited for the doctor to leave. As soon as he was out of earshot, he said, "Listen, woman: if your daughter agrees to marry the man I choose, then I will come home. If not—I know of plenty of surer methods of suicide. You'll never be able to save me."

Sasi's mother addressed her daughter. "Now, at least, you must change your decision. I'm not willing to lose him!" She turned to Raghu. "He is a stubborn man. Please, for his sake, forget my daughter, I beg you!"

"Please Madam, don't! I won't pursue your daughter any further. The survival of our love should not cost the life of another," said Raghu.

"Appa, tell me this," Sasi asked her father dejectedly. "Suppose, after my marriage to a man of your choosing, he comes to know of my love for Raghu. Did you stop to think about that?"

"I don't care!" Sivanandham shot back adamantly. "I don't care if he does find out and sends you back to my house. I don't even care if he dies soon after your wedding and you come back as a widow. You have to marry the man I say you should marry, and that's it!"

Sasi was shocked. She turned to Raghu. "I'm so sorry, Raghu. From this moment onwards, we are no longer lovers; we are simply colleagues at work..."

Even before she could finish the sentence, Raghu stormed out of the room.

The word *widow* kept ringing in Sasi's ears. "Fine, Appa. I shall marry the man you choose," she told him. To herself, she thought, *and I will make sure to return to your house as a widow, as soon as I possibly can.*

⚔ 3 ⚔

Chennai. Marina Beach. 6 P.M.

Sasi was sitting on the sand, waiting for Raghu, worried because he was late. When he finally arrived, he sat down at some distance away from her.

Sasi was hurt, but tried not to show it. "Raghu, I have something important to ask you."

"What, Sasi?"

She asked with tears in her eyes, "Have you truly forgotten our love?"

"How can I ever forget, Sasi? Still, I have no other option but to stay away."

"Maybe you can stay away, but I can't."

"What do you mean?"

"Raghu, I want you."

"Don't be silly. Your wedding is ten days away."

"Raghu, I'm serious. Are you ready to do anything for me?"

"Of course! Ask away."

"You must not go back on this promise."

"I won't. Tell me."

"You have to commit a murder!"

"Murder! Who?"

"The person who was the reason our love could not materialize. The man I'm going to marry."

"Satya?"

"Yes."

"Don't be an idiot, Sasi. You can't play around with your life like that."

"If you won't do it, then I'll follow my father's example, and kill myself."

"Sasi, this is too much. I can't think straight. It's just not possible."

"It has to be possible. I need you, Raghu. I refuse to live with that man."

On the beach, some distance away from the couple, stood two young women. One of them was named Rosie. She was a colleague of Satya, and she was capturing the whole scene on her camera phone.

"Hey!" her friend asked, surprised. "What are you doing?"

"Do you know who that woman is? She's the one who is going to wed our friend Satya. I'll forward this scene to his mobile after the marriage."

"What do you stand to gain from that?"

"It will cause problems in their married life, and they'll soon be separated. Then Satya, who until now has spurned my love, will begin to like me. Then we will get married."

"You're a smart woman, indeed!" laughed the friend.

∢ 4 ∢

Raghu sat among his gang of friends.

"What's the matter, Raghu? You said it was important."

"I hardly know where to start. You know Sasi and I are in love."

"Of course. And we also know she's getting married next week to somebody else. So?"

"She's not willing to forget me."

"Then why did she agree to the wedding?"

"Her father forced her. Now she wants me to commit murder!"

"Murder? Who? Her father?"

"No, her future husband."

"What?"

"She's serious!"

"And after you kill him?"

"She says we'll wait for a while, and then marry."

"Listen Raghu, don't do anything silly. It's easy to kill, but very difficult to get away with it. You have to be very clever to succeed."

"So what should I do?"

"Kill!"

"What? I thought you would come up with a way for me to get out of this. Instead you're also talking just like her."

"What is this, Raghu? That woman has more guts than you have! She wants her future husband killed, and you're being chicken. Come on, be a man!"

"I'm scared of the police."

"So it's only the police you're worried about. Otherwise, you would go ahead and kill him, right?"

"Yes..."

"But Raghu, don't do the killing yourself. We'll hire someone, and invent a motive for the murder, too."

"You think we can manage it?"

"Of course!"

"How?"

"You have to be patient. We can't bump him off before the wedding, or else suspicion will fall on you, because of your love affair. Let the wedding take place. By then, we'll have found the right person to hire to finish off your lover's husband. Okay?"

"Fine..."

"We have to be aware of every move they make after the wedding, so we can plan."

"You can trust Sasi to keep us informed about that."

"Good. Now this calls for a celebration!" Cheerfully, they opened their liquor bottle, unaware that fate was about to upset their plans...

∦ 5 ∦

It had been a grand wedding.

Sasi had already moved into Satya's home. But still, three days after the wedding, nothing had yet happened between them. Sasi had wisely postponed all "interesting activities" until the honeymoon.

Satya was on the phone. "Yes. We leave by the Nilgiri Express tonight. So, send your cab to Metupalayam station, early tomorrow morning."

"How many days do you need the car for?"

"Three days."

"Fine, sir. The cab will be waiting for you."

He put down the phone. "Sasi?" he called.

"I'm here," said Sasi, approaching him with a smile.

"You finish the packing. I have to go to the office for a few hours. I'll be back soon. Is my food ready?"

"Yes."

"Set the table. I'll go for my bath," he said, walking towards the toilet.

The moment she heard the shower go on, Sasi jumped into action. She dialed quickly. "Hello, Raghu? Satya will leave for work at half past nine in a white Maruti. Take down the car number," she said softly, and then quickly put down the phone.

8:10. Raghu called up his friend Jagan, gave him the details about Satya's car, and asked to be informed once the deed was done.

Jagan told his henchman, "As soon as the car passes Palavalkam, make them stop. Grab the driver, and start screaming at Satya for robbing your business contract before you stab him. The driver will give the same story to the police. No one will suspect us..."

"You're a criminal mastermind, Jagan. Yes, we shouldn't let the car into the city, there would be too many people around. We'll return in evening, you keep our cash ready," said the henchman.

9:20. The telephone rang.

"Hello, Satya here."

"Satya, this is Ranganathan. Have you gone through the two files I sent over?"

"Yes, sir. I'll bring them with me now."

"Aren't you leaving on your honeymoon tonight?"

"Yes, sir."

"Go ahead and leave on your honeymoon. Just send the files with your driver. You can report next week."

"Thank you, sir!" Satya disconnected the line, and asked Sasi to call for the driver.

"Take these files to the manager," Satya told Babu, the driver, when he came in. "You can leave the car at the office. I'll collect it when I return."

The driver put the files in the back seat and started the car.

Ten minutes later, he was stopped at an intersection, when the windowpanes were suddenly smashed in. A man poked his head through the rear window and shouted, "Hello, our mark's not here!" Turning to the driver, he demanded, "Where the hell is Satya?"

The driver's voice trembled with fear. "He's at home!"

Within a few seconds, the gang had disappeared. The driver rang Satya on his mobile and explained what had happened. "It's alright," said Satya. "Leave the car for repairs and take an auto to my office, and inform my manager."

Satya put down the phone and sat puzzling over the recent developments.

⚡ 6 ⚡

"Sasi, Sasi!"

"What happened?"

"I don't know what's going on. Someone out there wants me dead. Our car has been attacked. When they saw I wasn't in the car, they fled the scene..."

"Is the driver alright?"

"He's fine. They were looking for me."

"But why?" asked Sasi innocently.

"I don't know. I don't get it. Maybe they were after someone different. I'm confused," replied Satya. "Don't be scared, Sasi. Get the packing done. I have to go down to the car and find out how bad the damage is. But please, be careful," he warned her as he left.

The phone rang.

"Hello?"

"Can I speak to Mr. Satya?"

"He is not here. This is his wife speaking."

"Oh. Madam, he'd asked for a cab to be waiting early tomorrow morning in Metupalayam. Will you please take down the car number?"

"Yes, tell me."

Sasi noted down the number and immediately called Raghu. "I'm sorry your plan bombed. However, tomorrow a cab is coming to meet us at Metupalayam. Take down the car number." She read the number, and went on, "This time, make a tight plan. Don't goof up."

"Don't worry, Sasi. This time we'll hit him for sure," Raghu assured her. "Enjoy your trip."

Next, Raghu called Jagan. "Send your men immediately to Ooty. I'll take the Inter-City Express bus, and be there in time to support Sasi once her husband is dead."

In turn, Jagan told his men, "Stand on the road to Kunoor, pretending to repair your car. Thumb down Satya's car for a lift. When they slow down, get to work. Take the woman's jewels so it looks like a robbery. Empty Satya's pockets, too."

⚡ 7 ⚡

As he and Sasi disembarked from the Nilgiri Express, Satya caught his first glimpse of the tiny narrow gauge train that takes passengers between Metupalayam and Ooty. He was awed.

So, when a cab driver came up and told him their car was waiting outside, Satya's only response was, "I'm sorry, I've changed my mind. I don't want to go cab to Ooty anymore; I want to take this train ride."

"But sir, I can get you to Ooty in two hours. This train takes six!"

"I'm not here on official business. I'm on my honeymoon. I don't have to report in Ooty at any particular time. Do me a favor. Take this money and get us two train tickets to Ooty. After that, you can drive up and wait for us at the Metro International Hotel."

He hugged Sasi close to his chest as he walked to the train.

Sasi, not expecting this sudden change of mind, was dying to get to a phone so she could speak to Raghu, but could do nothing but grin and endure his embrace.

The mountain train slowly crept up the slopes like a worm. Young men kept getting on and off while the train was in motion. Satya was lost in the scenic beauty.

8:45. Raghu's men were waiting for Satya's cab on the road to Kunoor. When the vehicle with the license number they were expecting came around the bend, they stuck their thumbs out. But the cab just sped past them. They had to get back in their car and chase it for some distance before they finally caught up with it. One of them went up and peered inside cab. Finding only the driver inside, he went wild with frustration, and socked the driver's jaw.

"Hey man! Why didn't you stop the car?"

"This cab has already been hired. I can't take extra passengers without prior approval. I'm sorry," said the driver, wiping his bloodied face.

"So where are they?"

"Who...?"

"The people who hired you!"

"They took the mountain train. I was told to wait for them at the hotel in Ooty."

"Which hotel?"

"Metro International."

They let the driver go, called Raghu on the phone, and informed him of the latest developments. Raghu asked them to wait for further instructions and sat back expecting Sasi's call.

Metro International Hotel.

When the driver reported the incident to Satya, he could no longer doubt that someone out there wanted him dead. *Who is it? Why would they want to kill me? Who stands to gain anything from my death?* he thought to himself.

Sasi grabbed his arm. "Why are you so lost in thought? We're here on our honeymoon. Let's go out for a walk."

A few tourists were out boating on Ooty Lake.

Satya hired a pedal-boat at the counter, and they got in. Together, they pedaled the boat away from the shore. "Do you know how to swim?" asked Sasi.

"Nope, I don't," replied Satya with a grin.

An idea flashed in Sasi's brain. *Raghu, watch and learn. I'm going to succeed where you keep goofing up,* she thought to herself.

Then, suddenly, she got up. Her idea was that the moment she stood, Satya would also stand and help her sit down, and then she could topple him over. She would, of course, yell for help; but by the time it came, Satya would have drowned.

But Satya didn't stand. "What do you think you are doing, Sasi?" cried Satya, tugging at her hand. The boat began to rock, and it was Sasi who fell into the water. Not knowing what to do, Satya began screaming.

"Help! Help! Please, someone, come save my wife…"

Hearing his screams, the lifeguards plunged into the water and started to search for the submerged Sasi. They rescued her quickly, brought her to the shore, and pumped out the water that she had swallowed. An ambulance arrived and she was taken to the hospital.

Raghu, completely unaware of all this, sat waiting for her call…

⚡ 8 ⚡

At the hospital, Satya sat next to Sasi's bed. A nurse came in with a prescription and said, "Please get these tablets." He left for the pharmacy.

Immediately Sasi became active. She took her mobile from her bag and called Raghu.

"What's going on, Sasi? Why haven't you called?"

"I'm sorry. Things got out of control. Satya is always by my side. I tried to push him into the lake yesterday; instead, I fell in, and now I'm in the hospital."

"*Aiyyo!* Are you alright?"

"I'm okay. Satya called for help and had me rescued."

"Where is he now?"

"He's gone to get my medicine."

"When will you return to the hotel?"

"In a little while."

"Fine. This evening, after six, bring Satya along for a walk. We'll follow you and finish him off. Is that alright with you?"

She heard footsteps. "We'll talk later," she whispered, and cut the call.

It was the nurse. "Have you got the medicines?"

"He's gone to get them."

"You're very lucky to have a man like him for a husband."

"Why?"

"He's been at your side from the moment you were admitted. We told him to go back to the hotel, promising that you would be cared for. But he refused. He stayed awake and watched over you. He hasn't even eaten since last night."

Sasi was shaken. A strange uneasiness came over her. Satya returned with the medicines. The nurse explained the course of medication and finally said, "This pill is to help you to sleep in the night. Take just one."

They returned to the hotel.

⨟ 9 ⨟

Sasi couldn't stop thinking about what the nurse had said. *Was Satya really such a special man? Is it possible that he might even forgive me, if I told him about Raghu? Was I being hasty in deciding to kill him?* Her thoughts raced.

Around five o' clock that evening, Satya said, "Sasi, I'll go check with the reception about interesting tourist spots."

As soon as he left the room Sasi called Raghu again. "Raghu, come to my room at once. Bring a thick rope to tie Satya up."

"Why? Aren't you going for your walk?"

"No. Come right away." Even as she finished saying this, Satya entered the room.

"Who is that secret love of yours?" he demanded.

"What secret love? What are you talking about?"

"Goddamn it! I know everything. I even know who your lover is. Do you want to see?" he shouted, and thrust his mobile in front of her face. On it was a picture of her and Raghu.

"This is…" Satya cut her off with a stinging slap on the cheek. She stumbled backwards. Just at the moment, Raghu walked in, and caught her before she fell to the floor.

"So you've come in search of your love, have you?" Satya barked. "Of course! Now I understand. You two engineered all those attempts on my life, didn't you? I'm going to the police at once!"

Raghu glanced at Sasi, who at once tripped Satya into a chair. Raghu tied him up with the rope while she stuffed a cloth into his mouth. Then she gave the doctor's prescription to Raghu, and whispered in his ear.

"Are you sure? But they won't allow more than two at a time, Sasi," said Raghu.

"We need plenty of pills. You'll need to take the prescription to several medical shops," she ordered.

Raghu left. She shut the door and turned to Satya, who was staring at her helplessly.

⚘ 10 ⚘

Sasi slowly walked up to the glaring Satya. "If you promise to stay quiet and listen, Satya, I will free your mouth."

Hearing her call him by his name, instead of the respectful address, made him even angrier. It was the first time in the five days since their wedding that she had failed to be polite.

He nodded and she pulled out the gag.

"What the hell is happening here?" he demanded.

"Shhh...! I'll talk and you'll listen. Raghu and I are deeply in love with each other. But my father would not accept our love. He even attempted suicide to stop us. We couldn't bear to anger him any further. That was why I agreed to marry you."

"Why couldn't you have told me this before the wedding?" Satya asked in a soft voice. "I would have helped you two. At the very least, I would have refused to marry you."

"That's all water under the bridge. Anyway, after the wedding, we planned to kill you, then wait for a while before getting married..."

"So those goons were sent by you?" asked Satya.

"Didn't I tell you to shut up? You escaped that morning when you were supposed to go to your office, and again on the way to Kunoor. I tried to push you into the lake myself, but even that backfired. We had a plan to finish you off this evening. Now that you've learned everything about Raghu and me from your damned cell phone, I've changed the plan."

"Can I have a few words now?"

"What do you want say?"

"It's still not too late to release me. Go ahead and get married to Raghu. Even now, I have no objections."

"You might have no objection. But society will never approve."

"Why are you worried about society? I'll just be happy if the two of you can have a life together."

"No, Satya. That won't be possible. I have a different plan now."

"What is that?"

"Two lives are going to end here tonight!"

"What?" Satya yelped in fright.

"Who's going to die now?" asked Satya hesitantly.

"Raghu, and myself."

"No Sasi, please don't do anything stupid. I will never interfere in your life, I swear it."

"No Satya. You are truly a good person—unbearably good. Maybe that was why all our attempts failed. Your true heart saved you."

"You can sing my praises later. Now please untie me."

"I won't. You must sit and enjoy what is going to happen to me now. We should never have thought of killing you. You did nothing wrong. You shouldn't have to lose your life just because you tied the thali around my neck. It was wrong of me to have fallen in love. It was wrong of my father to have forbidden that love. And it was very, very wrong for Raghu and I to have behaved as we did after the wedding. All the mistakes are ours.

"In these five days, you have never once tried to force yourself on me. You've treated me with total respect and dignity. You sat awake and cared for me in the hospital. My heart is now reformed."

"Please listen to me, then. Change your mind about this stupid decision."

"No! Don't try to stop me. But I do need one favor from you, Satya."

"What do you want?"

"After I die, I want you to marry my younger sister, Jyothi."

Satya gaped at her.

"Please," she continued, "promise that you will. I gave you none of the pleasure that was your rightful due as my husband. Please forgive me for being so selfish."

"Okay. I promise to marry Jyothi. But that still doesn't mean you have to die!"

"No, Satya. There's no other way."

With that, she took a paper and pen from the table, and sat down to write a letter.

To:
Police Inspector, Ooty

Dear Sir,

The love between Raghu and me was deep and strong. My father, however, wrenched off its wings. We must prevail; our love must prevail. So, we have decided to die together. Please don't question my husband, the man I've been married to for five days. He has done no wrong.

The fault is entirely my father's.

It was *he* who objected to our love.

It was *he* who threatened us with suicide.

It was *he* who forced me into this marriage.

It was *he* who has now left us no option but to die together.

And so, please, take legal action against him.

Sincerely,
Sasi
Satya's wife of five days; Raghu's love, for eternity

Slowly, she folded the letter twice, and placed it under a paperweight on the table.

Raghu entered with a paper bag full of sleeping pills.

Sasi dialed the Ooty police. "I'm calling from Metro International Hotel, room number 213. Two lives are going to end here soon. Please have the bodies collected." Immediately, she cut the call.

Raghu sat down next to her and handed over the pills. There were twenty in all. She gave him ten.

Satya began screaming. "Please! Please don't! Sasi, stop!"

Sasi gave Raghu a look. He got up, stuffed the gag back into Satya's mouth, and returned to sit next to Sasi. She brought a jug full of water.

Holding hands, they shouted together, "Glory be to the love that kills!"

They threw the pills into their mouths and drank the water.

Satya struggled helplessly in chair, watching them slowly die. In a few minutes both of them grew still. Just as they breathed their last, the police broke down the door.

The inspector walked over to the table and picked up the letter.

✎ 12 ✎

High Court.

Sivanandham stood in front of the judge, in the stand for the accused.

"So, Sivanandham. Have you read your daughter's letter?"

"Yes."

"And what do you have to say?"

"She was an immoral girl who made a bad decision."

"So you claim to be innocent, do you?"

"Yes."

"You are the reason that those two are dead now!"

"No, I am not. I do not regret any of my actions."

"Why didn't you to accept your daughter's relationship?"

"I did not like Raghu."

"Did you inquire about him, and find anything objectionable about his character?"

"No."

"Why not? You might have found out that he was truly worthy of your daughter. Was it right to reject him so thoughtlessly?"

"Yes."

"You rejected him because your ego would not allow you to accept your daughter's choice. Am I right? You even threatened them with your life. You were determined to keep them apart. Because of your stubbornness, you put Satya's life in danger as well. You alone are responsible for the deaths of Sasi and Raghu. It is a great wrong for parents to threaten to kill themselves in order to keep lovers apart.

"Actively killing someone is not the only way to commit a murder. It is also a crime to be the reason behind the loss of another's life. It was wrong, too, for the lovers to try to murder a spouse who entered the marriage with no knowledge of their affair.

"It is the aim of this court to prevent such tragedies in the future. Therefore, the court finds Sivanandham guilty of being the prime agent of this terrible misfortunate, and sentences him to six months imprisonment. The court is now adjourned," declared the judge.

Sivanandham stood between two police officers.

His wife stuffed the pallu of her sari into her mouth to keep from crying aloud.

Satya gently guided her and Jyothi to the car. His heart whispered: *Glory be to the love that kills!*

The End

Dear Readers,

May I have a few moments, please?

Glory Be to the Love That Kills! is loosely based on a true story. A few months back, in Kunoor, a woman and her lover killed her husband just sixteen days after the wedding.

In my story, I have attempted to emphasize that it is a sin for the wife to kill her husband. I am confident that you will agree with me on this point.

I am interested to know what you think of this story. Feel free to mail me at the Best Novel office with your thoughts.

Yours truly,

Resakee

TAMIL FAMILY NAMES

Amma	Mother
Appa	Father
Anna	Elder brother (or any older man)
Thambi	Younger brother (or any younger man)
Akka	Elder sister
Thangachi	Younger sister
Athaan	Literally, male cross-cousin: a paternal aunt's or maternal uncle's son. This family member is considered an ideal husband for a girl in many Tamil communities, and so Athaan has come to be used as a general reference to the husband.

NOTES

HURRICANE VAIJ

rudraksh	berry of an evergreen tree from North India used as a prayer bead.
Dhinathanthi	daily Tamil newspaper.
Moonlight Agency… Susheela's T-shirts	this is reference to the recurring characters in Pattukkottai Prabakar's detective fiction (also in this collection). Susheela is known for wearing T-shirts bearing slogans that make bawdy reference to her ample chest.
Mukarundhasami	literally, "broken-nose god."
kumkum	sacred red powder given in temples.

paati	grandmother, or any old woman.
sanyasi	Hindu ascetic
dhool	Super!
Jai Jawan, Jai Kissan!	Hindi: "Hail to the soldier, hail to the farmer!"—a nationalist political slogan Arthreyan has presumably picked up from his video indoctrination.

IDHAYA 2020

| kolam | decorative design drawn by female members of a family in front of the home using rice powder. |
| veena | a Carnatic stringed instrument. |

MATCHSTICK NUMBER ONE

benami	when someone amasses wealth illegally or seeks to evade tax, and hides the property in the name of another person, this person is called his benami.
Nasik coupons	currency notes; the city of Nasik, in Maharashtra, is the site of the Indian mint.
Nakeeran	a biweekly Tamil news magazine.
Junior Vikatan	a monthly Tamil news magazine.
photo… to be garlanded	in Hindu households, flower garlands are hung over large portraits of deceased relatives.
Kali Yuga	the last (and current) Vedic era before the collapse of the universe; a time of injustice.
marukaal marukai	a medieval punishment in which the right hand and left leg are chopped off.

THE RAINBOW

fortune-telling parrot
: in this type of divination, a trained parrot picks cards bearing images of various gods from a stack

mandap
: temple courtyard with a ceiling, held up by columns, but without walls.

crorepati
: millionaire; literally, someone with at least one crore (1,00,00,000) rupees.

Q & A WITH RAJESH KUMAR

"socials"
: genre of Tamil novel concerned with contemporary themes, as opposed to "historicals".

Gnanapeet and Sahitya Academy Awards
: the two most presitigious Indian literary awards.

ME

thali
: a gold chain or turmeric-smeared cord, tied around the woman's neck by the groom in the wedding ceremony.

RIPPLES

Ahalya
: in the *Ramanayam*, Ahalya is the wife of Gautama Maharishi; Indran looks at her covetously, for which Gautama curses her to be turned to stone.

THE REBIRTH OF JEEVA

Raghav... your cousin	the son of a maternal uncle or paternal aunt is considered a good match for a girl in most Tamil communities.
anthakshari	a game played by two teams of singers, where each team has to sing the first lines of a song beginning with the last syllable of the previous song.
Thayee, Devi, Amman	all names for the Mother Goddess.
Aiya	Sir, as to a rural feudal lord.
thali	a gold chain or turmeric-smeared cord; the tying of this cord around the woman's neck by the groom signifies the moment of marriage.
conniving uncle	the word used is *Sakuni*, the maternal uncle of the Kauravas in the *Mahabharatham*, who helps them defeat the Pandavas in a dice game.
forefathers	the Tamil is *gothram*, one of the seven clans/lineages traced back to the rishis of the Vedas.
Dr. Wilson	a figment of the author's imagination.
mandap	temple courtyard with a ceiling, held up by columns, but without walls.
diya	small oil lamp made with brass or clay.
Vitalacharya	director of several of the above-mentioned Telugu mythological films.
pottu	religious mark on the forehead.
paati	grandmother, or any old woman.
Gajamuka Vinayakar	elephant-faced Ganesh.
Kali Yuga	the last (and current) Vedic era before the collapse of the universe; a time of injustice.
Ambulimama	a popular monthly journal for children.
Thalaiva	headman, or "big man".

THE RICH WOMAN

ragalai   a mother-in-law vs. daughter-in-law fight.

DIM LIGHTS, BLAZING HEARTS

isthrikaaran   a man with a cart for pressing clothes.

yaar   casual address among friends.

kuja   a brass pot for carrying drinking water

NRI   Non-Resident Indian; an Indian national
                            settled or working abroad.

SWEETHEART, PLEASE DIE!

Panguni   the third month of the Tamil calendar,
                            March–April. The Hindu zodiac has the same
                            sun signs as the Western system but they are
                            offset by about a month.

Dhinamalar   daily Tamil newspaper.

Marikkozhunthu   an old-fashioned name, meaning a fragrant
                            herb used in temple festivals.

dhum   cigarette

Madhavi   a courtesan character in the Tamil epic
                            Silapathikkaram.

Debonair   a popular Indian semi-pornographic magazine.

Malayalam flicks   the state of Kerala, whose main language is
                            Malayalam, has a thriving soft-core porn film
                            industry. Very few pornographic films are
                            made in Tamil Nadu.

MY NAME IS KAMALA

paanwala	one who sells paan, a digestive made with betel pepper leaves.
Sardar	a male follower of the Sikh faith.
Didi	literally, elder sister; or any woman older than the speaker (Hindi).

TOKYO ROSE

Kathrikai and Manickam	Kathrikai and Manickam are Shankarlal's driver and gardener, respectively, back home in Chennai. The nickname Kathrikai, which means "eggplant," derives from the fact that he is rather portly and has a tuft of hair which sticks up from his head.

A MURDER AND A FEW MYSTERIES

lathi	police baton

REVENGE

Yaman	Hindu god of death

GLORY BE TO THE LOVE THAT KILLS!

Rahu kalam	Rahu is the deity of the solar eclipse; there is a period of ninety minutes each day where he rules the astrological charts, and this is considered an inauspicious time.

Pritham K. Chakravarthy is a theatre artist, storyteller, activist, freelance scholar, and translator based in Chennai. Her academic interests include media, performance art, gender, and nationality; she has been a research associate for UC Berkeley, the London School of Ecnomics, and the University of Toronto. Her research projects have ranged from studies of Aravanis (the transgendered community of Tamil Nadu) to biohazardous waste disposal in India. Her recent translation projects include *Zero Degree* by Charu Nivedita, also available from Blaft Publications.

Rakesh Khanna was born in Berkeley, California. He studied music and mathematics at UC Santa Cruz and IIT Madras. Since 1998, he has lived in Chennai, where he works as editor-in-chief for an e-learning website.